Eileen Thornton lives with her husband Phil and their cat Toby, in the pretty town of Kelso in the Scottish Borders.

She has been a freelance writer for seven years and during that time her illustrated articles and short stories have appeared in several national magazines. She has also contributed a story to an International Anthology and another to an Allergy Charity.

The Trojan Project is her first novel.

A selection of Eileen's published work can be found on her website.
www.eileenthornton.co.uk

THE TROJAN PROJECT

Eileen Thornton

THE TROJAN PROJECT

AUSTIN MACAULEY

A CIP catalogue record for this title is
available from the British Library.

ISBN 978 1 905609 09 3

www.austinmacauley.com

First Published (2008)
Austin & Macauley Publishers Ltd.
25 Canada Square
Canary Wharf
London
E14 5L
Printed & Bound in Great Britain

DEDICATION

For Phil, my husband and best friend.

With much love and gratitude.

ACKNOWLEDGEMENTS

A big thank you to John Lamont MSP, Euan Robson former MSP, William Leslie and Malcolm Bogaert, for their help with technical details. I would also like to thank the staff at Austin & Macauley, most especially Annette Longman, Chief Editor, for having faith in my novel and Ross Malik, for his help and guidance during the process of production. I would also like to give a mention to Moira & Jack Hughes and Gina & Terry Brandom, who painstakingly pointed out the errors in my manuscript during the early stages of development. Thanks also to Lorna Read and Barbara Mellor, for their appraisal of the opening chapters. Finally I would like to mention Valerie, simply because she is my one and only sister.

PROLOGUE

"Oh my God! What on earth...?" Sarah screamed out, as a huge ball of light rose from behind the distant hills. Frozen with fear, she could only watch in horror as it slowly turned a sinister shade of green, while continuing to climb into the night sky. It grew larger and more vivid with every passing second before finally coming to rest high above the hills.

The glare was blinding and Sarah cupped her hands around her eyes to shield them from the brilliant rays beaming down onto the cottages in the valley below. Yet strangely, the farmhouse and fields on the hill where she stood were still in complete darkness. She wondered how it was possible.

Terrifying screams coming from the valley below interrupted her thoughts and, turning back to look down the hillside, she saw men and women fleeing from their homes. The people below were her friends. She wanted to go to them, to comfort them. But the light was too intense, making it impossible to see properly.

Then it was gone. It was almost as though an unseen hand had flicked off a switch. The whole episode had lasted little more than a few seconds, yet to Sarah it seemed like an hour.

Trembling with fear, Sarah thought of her children. They were still sleeping in the farmhouse at the top of the long winding drive. She tried to move, but her legs felt like two lead blocks and she slumped to the ground – her heart beating wildly. Then a horrifying thought occurred to her. A massive explosion might follow such a bright ball of light.

She heaved herself from the ground and began to make her way back to the farmhouse, forcing her stricken legs to move faster. She stumbled in the darkness and crashed to the ground, gashing her arms and legs on the sharp gravel. Scrambling to her feet again, she moved forward, unaware of the pain or of the warm sticky blood oozing from her wounds.

"Come on, Betts! Come on quickly!" she screamed out to the old sheepdog to follow her. She had to get back to the house – to her children. Their safety was the only thing on her mind. She must reach them before the explosion: they would be frightened – even worse, they might be killed.

Killed! That one dreadful thought gave her the extra strength she needed. With a sudden burst of energy, she bounded forward. She had to get her two children away from the house at all costs. Sarah's mind was racing as she drew nearer to the farmhouse. Where would they go? Perhaps if she took them over the hill, behind the farm, they might be sheltered from the blast. There they may have a slim chance of survival. But on reaching the door she stopped and turned back to face the valley. Something was missing. What was it?

Looking out into the darkness, she realised the screams in the valley had stopped. Now thinking back, she recalled how even before the light had disappeared, the screaming had ended.

Listening hard, she realised there were no sounds at all. She glanced around nervously. Even at this time of night, it was never this quiet. There was always the reassuring hoot of a distant owl or the gentle rustling of nocturnal animals foraging for food in the undergrowth. Where were they tonight?

Tears rolled down Sarah's cheeks as she stood alone by the door. Burying her face in her hands, she desperately wished Pete would come home.

CHAPTER ONE

Sarah had worried about her husband all evening. After putting the children to bed, she paced up and down the kitchen floor, growing more concerned with each passing minute.

Glancing at the clock for the umpteenth time, she wondered where he could be. What was keeping him so late? Pete always made a point of being home in time to read a bedtime story to their two young daughters. Four-year-old Josie and little Becky, half her age, looked forward to it and nothing short of an emergency could keep him away.

But this evening Sarah had even more reason for concern, as Pete believed she was spending the night with her friend in Alnwick after a trip to the theatre. He should have collected the children from Laura, the wife of Dave, one of his farmhands, several hours ago.

As it turned out, Josie had awoken that morning with a sore throat. Though a dose of throat syrup seemed to cure it, Sarah cancelled her arrangements for fear of it recurring. But Pete wasn't aware of the change of plan. When she had tried to reach him on his mobile, she couldn't get through.

At first she hadn't been too worried: the Cheviot Hills were probably blocking the signal. Besides, Laura would explain what had happened when he arrived to pick up the children. But Pete had never turned up. Nor had he rung Laura to tell her why he was late.

Sarah telephoned Laura several times during the early evening, desperately hoping she might have news of why Pete had been delayed, but the answer was always the same.

"I'm sorry, Sarah, but I promise to call you the moment I hear anything."

Something had happened. Sarah was sure of it. She knew Pete wouldn't simply leave his children with Laura without calling her first. Feeling helpless, she sat by the phone almost willing it to ring – yet it remained silent. Finally, unable to stand it any longer, she rang Laura again. Dave should be home by now; it was possible he might know where Pete was. However Laura had no words of comfort; in fact quite the opposite.

"Sarah, now I'm worried. Dave hasn't come home either. I understood he was working around the lower fields today. Could there have been a change of plan?"

Assuring her she didn't know of any changes to her husband's arrangements, Sarah hung up; deciding not to ring again. Laura obviously had problems of her own. She switched on the television and sat down, only to stand up a few minutes later. She paced the floor again, pausing only for a moment to straighten a picture on the wall. Glancing at the clock, she checked the time against her watch. It was no good, she couldn't simply wait here; she had to do something.

Turning off the television, she looked in on the children. They were still sleeping soundly. They wouldn't wake: they always slept right through the night. It would be quite safe to leave them for a few minutes while she walked down the drive to the farm gates. From there she would see the headlights of Pete's truck when he swung into the lane.

Outside, the air felt warm against her face. The long hot summer, reluctant to make way for autumn's golden colours, was lingering on. Overhead, the night sky was clear and the stars glittered in the heavens like large diamonds. It was a perfect evening. The kind of evening she and Pete enjoyed spending together on the porch.

Tonight though, Sarah was too worried about her husband to notice. Pete was never this late unless one of the animals was in distress. Desperate to find an explanation, she wondered if that might be the reason why he was late tonight. But then she dismissed it; he would have called Laura to tell her.

Sarah knew Pete had gone to check the sheep on Top Meadow, a lovely green pasture high up on one of the hills on the far side of the valley. Taking his two working dogs, he had set out early that morning, intending to pick up a couple of farmhands on the way. She tapped her foot nervously on the gravel. They should have been back hours ago. Why wasn't he here?

Standing there by the farm gate in the darkness, she suddenly became aware that the animals were restless. They were stamping their feet and making strange sounds; something was troubling them.

She listened hard. Was it a beast – a fox, perhaps? Only recently a neighbouring farm had lost several sheep to a fox. Though she couldn't hear anything, the thought of something out there disturbed her, and despite the warmth of the night she shivered and pulled her jacket tightly around her. If only Pete were there he would know what to do.

Looking down into the valley, she felt reassured by the warm glow of light coming from the farm's cottages. Everything seemed normal down there. Surely if there was something wrong the farmhands would know about it? Many came from a long line of farming families, and knew instinctively when trouble was lurking.

She looked down at the old collie by her side. "I'm imagining things, Betts," she murmured.

But when the dog began to growl softly, Sarah's fears returned. Bending down to place a restraining hand on Betts's collar, she was further alarmed to find the hairs on the dog's neck were bristled.

"What is it, old girl? What's out there?"

She strained her eyes against the darkness, but was unable to see anything. For one brief moment she toyed with the idea of going back to the house for Pete's gun. A shot into the air might drive away whatever was worrying the animals. But that was all she could do. She might be a farmer's wife, but she had never been a farmer's daughter. Having been brought up in one of the most exclusive areas in London, she didn't have the stomach to kill anything. She knew even Pete was loath to shoot any animal unless he believed it was absolutely necessary.

She scanned the lane again, desperately trying to pick out the headlights of her husband's truck. But only blackness stretched before her. Surely he wouldn't be much longer?

Feeling very alone, she allowed her mind to drift back to the time before her marriage. Her parents had warned her she would be left on her own most of the day.

"Farming is a hard life, especially for a girl brought up in the City with all the luxuries it has to offer," they had told her. "There will always be the crops or some sick animal to see to. That's not for you, Sarah. A farmer's wife needs to be born into that kind of life."

Her father, Sir Charles Hammond, being an eminent government scientist, had been in a position to send his only child to the very best of schools. As she was fluent in three languages, her parents had encouraged her to become a diplomat.

Ronald Woods, her mother's brother, was Secretary of State for Foreign Affairs. Occasionally, while on various assignments around the world, she had accompanied him as his interpreter. But though she enjoyed working with her uncle, she had never considered taking on such a role permanently. Continually flitting from one boring meeting to another didn't appeal to her.

A few years ago her parents, especially her mother, Irene, had been keen for her to marry Rick Armstrong, a young colleague of her father's. His excellent prospects made him a more suitable son-in-law.

"He has a brilliant mind," her father had said on more than one occasion. "Though a little impetuous at times, he'll go a long way. He has a great deal to offer a wife."

To please them, she had accompanied Rick to several functions. But though she found him witty and charming, she could never envisage spending the rest of her life with him. Then quite out of the blue, while attending a charity dance with Rick, she had met Pete Maine.

Her eyes had been drawn to the tall, young man standing alone in the far corner of the ballroom. Constantly straightening his tie and flicking non-existent fluff from his jacket, he looked rather shy and ill at ease, almost as though he would rather be somewhere else. Her eyes had lingered on him for a few minutes, trying to remember whether she might have seen him at another recent gathering. But no, she wouldn't have forgotten such a striking young man.

Later that evening, as she and Rick passed by him, Pete gave her a boyish grin. His brown eyes, almost the colour of his hair, were warm and friendly. Though she smiled back, neither said a word. However when Rick disappeared to the bar to order drinks, he had sought her out.

While they danced, Pete told her he was a farmer, having inherited Hillsdown Farm in Northumberland from his grandfather. "I don't like the City. I'm only here at my brother's insistence." He laughed. "He thinks I need a break."

His enthusiasm for the farm fascinated her. He wasn't just a farmer at all – he was a man of ideals and principles, who felt responsible for the men who worked for him and the animals he reared.

When the dance ended, he began to escort her back to where Rick was waiting. But on the spur of the moment, he changed direction and led her into the garden. "Sarah, I know that you and I together could make the farm work."

She had been rather taken aback. How could he make such a judgement having only just met her? "You don't know anything about me and I know nothing of farming," she had uttered.

It was true. Until a few moments ago, she had never given a thought to where food came from or how it was produced. As far as she was concerned, it was delivered to the house on a regular basis from Harrods.

But taking her hands in his, Pete had spoken earnestly, assuring her he knew everything he needed to know. "As soon as I saw you, I wanted you to be my wife."

Strangely enough, she found herself attracted to him and agreed to meet him the following day. After several dates, all within the space of a week, she couldn't imagine life without him and they were married after a whirlwind romance. It had seemed like a fairy tale. Things like that didn't happen in the real world.

At first her parents had been quite alarmed, but Pete quickly charmed them with his sense of humour and kindness. However, Rick's attitude had been quite different. She knew he loved her, he had never made a secret of it, yet she had never given him any reason to assume she felt the same about him. There had always been something about him...

Her thoughts were suddenly interrupted, when she believed she saw the lights of a car in the distance and for a few brief moments her spirits lifted. But the light was too small. It was probably someone with a torch checking out the animals in the valley. She sighed as she bent down and stroked Betts's head. "No, it's not him yet, old girl."

She turned her thoughts back to Rick. His reaction to her engagement had been alarming. He told her she was foolishly throwing her life away.

"What has he to offer a girl like you?" he had roared. "With me you could have everything. Parties, holidays, clothes – a wonderful life could be yours for the taking. Instead you're marrying some farmer and going to live in the middle of nowhere. Why, for God's sake? I don't understand! Explain it to me."

Taking her hands in his, he had squeezed them so tightly her fingers turned white. "Don't you see? You'll be tied to the kitchen sink – these hands are made for diamond rings, not farm work."

Laughing nervously, she had pulled away from him. "It won't be like that at all, Rick. I love Pete and want to be with him."

19

"Then so be it" he yelled, before striding down the hall. "Don't say I didn't warn you."

Still gazing down the lane, Sarah rubbed her fingers. Even now, over five years later, she could feel Rick's hands crushing her own.

It was on her wedding day when she had next seen him. Calling at the house, he had grasped her arms and shaken her so violently, she almost called out for her father.

"Why, Sarah?" he asked, harshly. "You'll be an old woman before your time. You're not the sort to be a farmer's wife. You'll miss the bright lights of city life. You were born to be with me. This should be our wedding day." Then suddenly he let her go. "Mark my words you'll regret it." And he was gone.

But Rick couldn't have been more wrong; she had never regretted a moment. She loved Pete and enjoyed her life up here in the north of England. The farmhouse was set high up on one of a range of hills that surrounded the lush green valley below. She delighted in the magnificent views from the windows and the fresh, sweet smell of clean air that greeted her every morning. It was a far cry from the noisy, traffic-congested streets of London.

She still saw Rick when she visited her parents in the City. He usually called at the house when she was there. Then four months ago, quite unexpectedly, Rick had called at the farm. He explained he was in the area on business. She recalled thinking it strange he should have work so far away from London. Had it simply been an excuse to see her?

Since then she had seen him about a month ago, when she and the children were staying in London. He had called to discuss something with her father and Irene invited him to stay for dinner. After exchanging a few pleasantries with Sarah, he disappeared into Charles's study.

Shortly afterwards, both she and Irene had been most concerned when they heard raised voices.

Though they couldn't make out what was being said, it was clear that the two men were arguing fiercely about something. Emerging from the study red-faced and very angry, Rick left the house without a word to Sarah or her mother.

Afterwards, Charles made several telephone calls before joining them for dinner. He wouldn't be drawn on Rick's rapid departure, even though her mother mentioned it casually in conversation a couple of times.

Nevertheless, Sarah hadn't failed to notice her father's agitation during the evening and had often wondered about it.

Sarah's thoughts were interrupted again when Betts's growl grew louder. Still holding the dog's collar, she opened the gate and stepped out into the lane. Betts began to bark loudly and tugged to be free. Feeling even more afraid, she tightened her hold on the dog's collar and started to make her way back to the farmhouse. Then, seeing a glimmer of light in the distance, she hesitated.

Could this be Pete? Betts pulled to be free and she loosened her grip. Watching the dog run down the lane, Sarah almost cried with relief. It must be Pete's truck; it had to be. At last her husband was home. But as Betts returned whimpering, her doubts flooded back.

Looking closer, she saw that the light had changed to a sickly green colour and wasn't in the lane at all. It was rising from beyond the hills and appeared to be growing larger and brighter by the second. She had never seen anything like it before. Slowly it began to climb into the night sky. "Oh my God! What on earth is that?" she screamed

****

Bewildered, Sarah couldn't recall how long she had stood by the farmhouse door. Since the light had disappeared, a heavy silence had fallen over the valley. It was too quiet, even a slight sound would have helped to reassure her. She was about to enter the house when she saw a movement in the sky.

"Please – not again," she murmured to herself.

Peering through the darkness, she wondered whether the light was returning, but then she saw a strange cloud – a sort of mist. It was the same bright green colour as the ball of light. A cold shiver ran down her back as she watched the cloud unfold over the valley rather like a thick blanket. Within a few minutes, not one of the cottages could be seen through the dense fog. Yet surprisingly, the sky above the farmhouse and the surrounding fields was still quite clear.

Sarah could take no more: her legs began to give way beneath her and she gripped the doorframe for support. Glancing across the farmyard towards the fields nearest to the house, she was able to pick out the familiar shapes of the cows. But there was something wrong. What was it?

Then she realised there was no movement. Though they were all on their feet, not one cow was moving. She swallowed hard. Why the hell weren't they moving?

Breathing deeply to stop herself from fainting, she called Betts and staggered into the farmhouse. Slamming the door shut, she pushed home the bolts. Safely inside the house, she slumped into one of the chairs. Tears rolled down her cheeks. What was going on? Where was Pete? What was the green light in the sky? Then there was that thick cloud – and the animals. What was wrong with the animals? Questions raced through her mind, but she had no answers.

Wiping her eyes, she climbed the stairs and crept into the children's bedroom. Mercifully they were still sleeping, blissfully unaware of what had happened. Noticing Josie's teddy bear had fallen to the floor, she lifted the covers and placed it in the bed next to her daughter. It was Josie's favourite toy. She would be upset if it wasn't in her bed when she awoke.

For one brief moment, she thought of waking the children and going in search of Pete, but then thought better of it. No! That was a stupid idea. It would only alarm them. It would be best to wait until morning.

Besides, Pete could arrive home any minute now. Seeing the strange light in the sky, he would abandon whatever it was he was doing and go to Laura and Dave's for his children. Dave – was he home yet? Moving over to the window, she stared out across the fields to where she had first seen the glow of light. But the light had gone and there was nothing there now – nothing except the strange cloud still enveloping the valley and the distant hills.

Looking closer, she noticed it had now turned a brighter green. What was the cloud? And where had the light come from? There was nothing beyond the hills except a reservoir and the dam. Further on, there were only more farms and a couple of small villages and somewhere in-between was an old power station. But nothing went on there any more. It had been closed down when the new one was opened over a year ago. Now the grounds were patrolled by security staff as there was still some equipment awaiting removal. Once that was cleared, the old building would be boarded up and sold off.

Just as she moved away from the window, some lights in the distance caught her eye. Could this be Pete's truck? For a moment, she felt a weight was being lifted from her. But her hopes were dashed when she realised the lights were too small to be car headlights. It was probably still the farmhands using torches as they checked out the livestock. When more lights appeared, she felt a little reassured. So many people carrying torches must mean everyone in the valley was safe.

But the cloud cast a sinister glow over the valley and Sarah swept the curtains tightly together to block it out. A feeling of utter despair fell upon her and she began to tremble as fear welled up inside her stomach. The events of the evening had caught up with her. If only Pete were to come home, everything would be alright again.

Shaking violently, she stumbled across to the small sofa in the corner of the children's bedroom. She decided to spend the night on there. The large empty bed she shared with Pete seemed cold and uninviting. She pulled her knees up to her chin, curling herself into a tight ball in a futile effort to shut out her fears.

Pete's disappearance stirred up long-forgotten memories of a similar occasion. She was a little girl again, excitedly waiting for her father to return from work. She wanted to show him something she had made at school. But he was late, just as Pete was now. Laughing, her mother told her 'that Daddy was busy at work and he would see it the next morning.'

But during the night, she had woken to hear her mother talking on the telephone. "I'm worried; he's never this late. For goodness sake, do something. I want to know what's happened to my husband."

Sarah recalled how she had lain in bed trembling with fear as she listened to her mother's voice. Believing something awful had happened to her father, she had curled herself into a tight ball, just as she was doing now.

Of course her father was at breakfast the next morning. Absorbed in his work at the laboratory, he had simply lost all track of time. Yet Sarah had never forgotten and tonight history seemed to be repeating itself. Josie had been waiting anxiously to show Pete a picture she had drawn with her new crayons and Sarah had told her that 'Daddy would be home soon.'

Back in London, all those years ago, Sarah's mother had been able to telephone the laboratory to find out what had happened to her husband. If they hadn't found him, she would have called Scotland Yard and insisted the whole of the Metropolitan Police force should begin a search.

Out here it was different. There was no one to call. The nearest police station was some miles away in Wooler, and even then it was only an annexe of Sergeant Gilmore's house. With Mrs. Gilmore frowning on anyone who called her husband in the middle of the night for anything less than a murder, Sarah's only real option was to lie awake and listen for Pete's truck turning into the lane. But though she tried hard to stay awake, tiredness soon overcame her.

She fell into a troubled sleep, dreaming Pete was in danger of falling into a deep black hole. Clinging onto the sides, he screamed frantically to her for help as he was sucked downwards.

Still dreaming, Sarah saw herself reaching out for him. But though she hung over the edge of the hole and stretched out her arms, she couldn't quite reach him.

"Please help us!" she cried out to a strangely familiar figure in the shadows. But the figure merely turned away.

CHAPTER TWO

Sarah awoke early; she hadn't slept well. For a moment she wondered why she was squeezed onto the small sofa in the children's bedroom. But as the events of the previous night flooded her memory she sat up quickly, wincing when a sharp pain ran down her cramped legs. Stumbling to her feet, she hurried downstairs looking for a sign that Pete might have come home. But there was nothing: everything was as she had left it.

Of course he hadn't been home! He wouldn't have slipped in and out of the house like a shadow. He would have sought her out to tell her he was home and all was well.

She swallowed hard. Pete would never have stayed out all night unless something serious had happened. Was he lying hurt somewhere on the hill? She recalled the dream she'd had during the night and her stomach turned over.

Taking a deep breath, she decided that once the children were dressed, she would leave them with Laura and drive up to Top Meadow to search for her husband.

"Where's Daddy?" Josie's voice came from the top of the stairs.

"Wait there for me, darling." Sarah called out. "I'm coming."

"He still hasn't seen my picture." Josie held up her drawing.

"I'm afraid Daddy had to leave early this morning." Sarah climbed the stairs and hugged her daughter. "He didn't have time to wait for you and Becky to wake up. But he's looking forward to seeing your picture later, when he comes back from the fields." Despite her fears, Sarah smiled, trying to put on a brave face. "I've got a good idea. Once we've all had breakfast, we'll go to see Laura. I'm sure she would love to see your picture. You could take your drawing pad and crayons. She might ask you to draw something for her."

Downstairs Sarah slowly drew back the curtains. She hadn't dared do it earlier, fearing what she might see outside. But thankfully everything was back to normal. The strange green cloud that had smothered the valley the night before had dispersed. Now the sun was beginning to peep from behind the distant hills and the cows in the fields nearest to the farmhouse were tugging at the grass. She heaved a sigh of relief. Could she have simply imagined the whole thing?

She was about to move away from the window when she caught sight of the animals in the lower fields, near the farm cottages. They all appeared to be lying down. Looking more closely, she saw they were very still. Not one of them was moving.

Why was no one seeing to them? Come to think of it, she couldn't see anyone at all. Normally by this time of the morning the farm was buzzing with activity. Perhaps she should call one of the herdsmen and find out what was going on.

Picking up the telephone she dialled a number. There was no reply so she tried another. But again there was no reply. The same thing happened on her third call. By now she was beginning to panic. Someone should have answered the phone. Most of the men had wives at home; where were they? It was only then that she thought about calling Tom.

Tom had joined the farm as a young man when Pete's grandfather had first acquired the land many years ago. Though he was now retired, Pete had allowed him and his wife Martha to stay on in their cottage. But then Pete had done the same for so many of the men who had helped his grandfather build the farm from this fertile land.

"They were all good men, Sarah," Pete had told her. "Grandfather relied on them in the early years, especially Tom. I know he would have wanted them all to remain in their homes on the farm."

Sarah's hand hovered over the phone. Should she disturb Tom? After all, he was getting on a bit now. Perhaps after years of getting up early to milk the herd he was at last enjoying the opportunity to lie late in the mornings. But she knew that wasn't the real reason for her hesitation. What really bothered her was how Tom would gloat at her having to call on him.

Tom had never approved of Pete marrying a 'townie', always maintaining he should have chosen a woman more used to farming. A woman who was strong, a woman capable of helping out on the farm whenever necessary – in other words a woman like Alice; his own daughter.

If only she could have reached one of the other men. Mick, Josh, even old Ned, any one of them would have been more sympathetic. Staring down at the phone, Sarah grabbed the receiver before she changed her mind.

"Hello." Martha's voice came down the line.

"Hello, its Sarah here." There was a hissing sound on the line so she raised her voice. "I was wondering if Tom could come over to milk the herd this morning. I know he's retired and all, but I've tried ringing a few of the hands and there's no reply. It's so unusual, I can't understand it." Not wanting the children to overhear, she lowered her voice. "Pete didn't come back from Top Meadow last night. I'm worried, Martha. Have you any idea who went up there with him? They may know what's happened."

"No I'm afraid I don't, Sarah, but I'll ask Tom to come over right away. Have a word with him when he gets there, he might know who went with Pete." Martha hesitated. "It's strange, but now you come to mention it, I haven't seen anyone about this morning either." She laughed. "Though I must admit, we overslept a little so we could have missed them."

Sarah shivered. It was getting worse. Despite Martha's reassuring comments, they wouldn't really have slept late. Old habits died hard. After years of rising with the sun every morning neither of them could stay in bed, even if they wanted to. "The last time I saw the farmhands, was when they all ran from their homes to see the ball of light in the night sky," she said at last. "By the way, what did you and Tom make of it? I found it very frightening." As she spoke, the hissing sound on the line grew louder.

"What did you say, Sarah? Sorry but the line's bad."

"Last night. What did you make of the light in the sky?" Sarah repeated.

"What light?" Martha raised her voice, trying to make herself heard. "Tom and I were in Wooler until very late last night. Everything seemed quiet enough when we got home."

"Never mind, Martha," Sarah yelled into the phone. "I'll speak to you later, please ask Tom to come as quickly as he can."

Once Sarah had hung up, she washed and dressed the children. She was strapping Becky into the child's seat in the car, when she saw Tom herding some cows towards the milking shed.

"Morning, Sarah. Lovely morning." He glanced fleetingly at the sky. "Quiet though. Not much happening. I haven't seen a soul this morning – must all be too busy." He jerked his head towards the herd. "I'll get this lot sorted and then I'll go down for the others in the lower fields." He paused. "Mind you, I'd have thought you could do this for yourself by now, lass. Good thing for you I'm still around. Now my Alice could have milked this lot with her eyes shut."

"Good for her," muttered Sarah. She was annoyed at the way Tom spoke to her. She had put up with it these past five years, but today she was in no mood for his stupid remarks. Lifting Josie into the car, she told her to wait with Becky. "I'll only be a minute, sweetheart. I'm going to have a quick word with Tom."

Moving across to Tom, she took his arm and steered him a little way from the car. "I'm sick and tired of your ridiculous comments. For God's sake man, didn't Martha tell you why I asked you to come up here? Pete didn't come back last night. He believed I was in Alnwick and that the children were waiting for him at Laura's, yet he didn't turn up to collect them, nor did he call her to explain why. Now you and I both know he would never simply go off and leave the children waiting. Do you understand what I'm saying?" She paused for breath. "Are you simply being more stupid today or still trying to prove a point? If you know who went up to Top Meadow with him, then tell me."

Tom rubbed his chin. He was unused to being spoken to like that, especially by some chit of a girl. "I don't know for certain, I didn't see them go off, but I reckon it would be Josh and Ned. They're the two he normally takes up there."

He grinned. "Fancy you not knowing that, you being the farmer's wife and all. I'd have thought Pete would have discussed it with you the night before he went up there."

But Sarah was unimpressed at his sarcasm. "Tom, don't you ever give up?" she retorted. "Yes, I am the farmer's wife. Not your daughter Alice as you'd hoped, but me, Sarah, 'a townie'." She made quotation marks in the air with her fingers. "I had thought you'd be used to it by now. But whether you like it or not, I'm here to stay. I have enough to worry about this morning without you twittering on about how your Alice could run the farm with both arms tied behind her back."

"I..." Tom began.

But Sarah hadn't done with him yet. Five years she had listened to his spiteful remarks, and now at last she was going to have her say. "Shut up! I haven't finished. It may come as a surprise to you, Tom Marsh, but during the long evenings in the farmhouse, the farmer and his wife have far more pleasurable things to do than discuss whom he may or may not take up to Top Meadow!"

Tom blushed. He was surprised at her outburst. "I'm sorry. I don't really mean anything; I'd always hoped that..."

' ,

"Yes, I know exactly what you hoped," she interrupted. "Over the last five years you've made it perfectly clear that you wanted Alice to be the farmer's wife. But Pete chose me, not Alice."

She sighed. This wasn't the time for arguments, but she was so worried about what had happened to Pete that she needed to lash out at someone. Still, she hadn't meant to sound so harsh and besides, she quite liked Alice.

"Your daughter married a good man. Luke loves her and will do anything for her. They're expecting a baby soon aren't they?" Sarah hesitated, "Your first grandchild."

"Yes," whispered Tom, tears forming in his eyes. "The baby's due next week." He looked away. Sarah was right: Alice had found herself a good man in Luke.

When Pete had chosen Sarah, it should have been an end to the matter. But instead he had tried to make her feel out of place from the first moment she set foot on the farm. What had he hoped to achieve? Had he really believed that Sarah would move out to make way for his daughter Alice?

He had been a fool to even think it. It was obvious to everyone that Pete and Sarah were besotted with each other. And Sarah was right, Pete would never leave his children and go off somewhere without a word to anyone. Even he knew how Pete doted on his kids.

Another thought suddenly struck him. Sarah couldn't have told her husband of his bitterness towards her. If she had, there was no doubt Pete would have spoken to him. Perhaps he and Martha would have been asked to leave the farm. Where would they have gone? How would they have lived?

Reaching out, he touched her arm. "It won't happen again," he muttered gruffly.

She nodded. "Thank you, Tom. We won't mention it again." It wasn't much of an apology, but she could guess how much it had cost him. Tom was not the sort to use the word, 'sorry'. "Now I must go and find Pete."

"I'm sure there's no need to worry, Sarah. It's probably taken them longer than expected to round up the sheep. Up there on Top Meadow there're no fences to keep them in, so the stupid animals run all over the place. Even with the dogs, they're difficult to round up. My guess is the men spent the night in the old shepherd's hut to save going all the way up again today. There's always some tinned food up there, soup and the like. And as for not ringing anyone, perhaps Pete couldn't get a signal up there in·the hills." He shrugged. "He probably realised Laura wouldn't mind looking after the children 'til morning."

"I expect you're right, but I'd still like to see for myself." Despite Tom's words of comfort, Sarah was unconvinced. Pete would never have stayed away all night, without calling Laura first. He would have made darned sure he found a spot where the signal was good.

"I'm going to drop Josie and Becky off at Laura's, then I'll drive up to Top Meadow. Would you keep an eye on things here? I know I couldn't leave the herd in better hands. I shouldn't be too long. I'll take Betts with me. If the men are up there she'll find them." Then she had another thought. "How did you find the herd this morning?"

"These here are from the fields around the farm, they were a bit slow to move at first, but they seem alright now. I'll go and get the others shortly. Why do you ask?"

"When I looked out of the window, the animals in the lower fields appeared to be lying down. If you think they need the vet Tom, go ahead and call him. Pete's very proud of his stock, he wouldn't want them to get sick." She smiled. "But I know we can rely on your judgement."

Driving down the lane, Sarah glanced at the children through the rear view mirror. She was relieved they hadn't been affected by her argument with Tom. They weren't used to her losing her temper. However Becky was happily peering out of the window, while Josie seemed to be drawing another picture. Sarah smiled to herself. No doubt this one was a present for Laura.

Rounding a bend in the road, she was forced to pull up sharply when she saw something lying up ahead. At first sight, it seemed like a large bundle of partly burned rags. But no! Looking closer, she was able to make out the form of a man.

Thinking he had been in an accident, she turned off the engine and jumped out of the car. Now, with the engine silenced, she could hear him crying out in pain. "Wait with Becky," Sarah called out to Josie, as she began to run towards the man. "Stay in the car!"

"I'll help you," she called out as she came closer to the figure in the road. "I'll take you to a doctor."

At the sound of her voice, the man made an effort to raise his head. Until he heard her speak, he hadn't realised anyone was there. At last someone had come. He had no idea how long he had lain there. But he mustn't let her touch him. By God! She mustn't touch a single part of him.

"No! Go back... go back." His voice was slurred. Sarah could hardly make out what he was saying.

"Don't... come... near... me." He spoke slowly, finding it difficult make his mouth move properly.

"No!" she shrieked, as he turned towards her. His face and hands were so horribly burned – yet at the same time they were shining. No, shining wasn't the right word, they were glowing. Even in the bright sunlight, there was a positive glow radiating from them.

Repelled by his terrible disfigurement, Sarah took a step backwards. "My God! What happened here?" She peered down the lane, expecting to see his vehicle. Had there been an accident? Was his car burnt out? But the road ahead was clear. "What happened to you?" she repeated.

Recognising her voice, the figure strained to lift his head further off the ground. "Sarah! Sarah!"

Taking a closer look, she caught her breath. Though barely recognisable through the charred flesh, she was able to make out the features of Dave. This was Laura's husband.

"No! No! It can't be!" She cried. "Have you been in a fire?" Fumbling in her pocket, she pulled out her mobile and tried to press 999. "I'll call an ambulance."

As she waited for a response, a thought struck her. "Was Pete with you, Dave? Did you see him?" Now hysterical, she fired questions at him. "Where is he? Tell me! Where's Pete?" Inching forward, she noticed Dave's clothes weren't only burnt and ragged there was something else. They were wet – they looked sticky.

"No! No! Stay... away!" Though faint and slurred, his speech was desperate. "For God's sake, Sarah, don't... touch me. Back there a bird touched me and... Get away... quickly!"

She could hardly understand him, but the urgency of his tone caused her to stop in her tracks. At the same time she also noticed something running down his face and hands. Sweat perhaps?

There was still no answer from the emergency services and she shook the phone violently. "What's the matter with this damn thing?" She stabbed her fingers on the buttons again. This time there was a hissing sound;

similar to the one she had heard on the telephone in the farmhouse. But after a few seconds the line went dead.

"What's happening? Why can't I get through to anyone?" Feeling helpless, Sarah looked down the lane. Why wasn't there anyone around? Where was everybody? Normally this lane was buzzing with farmhands moving livestock from one field to another.

"Go... back." Dave struggled to form the words.

"But I must get you to a doctor." Sarah's voice trembled as she fought back the tears. "And then I have to find Pete. He didn't come back from Top Meadow. I was on my way up there when..." She looked up at the hills ahead. "I was going to take the children to Laura's before going to find him."

"No!" Dave's voice was becoming more slurred "Laura's... dead. Pete's... dead." He croaked.

"They can't be!" she screamed out at him. "What are you talking about? I don't believe you. Pete isn't dead. He can't be dead. Not dead." Sobbing hysterically, she repeated the words over and over. "Not dead! Not dead!"

"I'm so sorry, Sarah." Dave's voice was but a whisper.

"No! You're mistaken, Dave. My lovely Pete isn't dead. He's up there, on Top Meadow. He's checking the sheep. I'll find him. He's up there!"

Pointing towards the hills, she screamed out Pete's name. "Pete! Pete! Answer me!"

But there was no answer. There was no sound at all, except for the eerie echoes of her voice as Pete's name rang around the valley.

"No, you... must... go..." Dave was finding it difficult to form the words. His mouth would no longer move properly; he couldn't hold on much longer.

Sarah's head was reeling. Her legs felt like they were about to give way beneath her. She took a few deep breaths, hoping the sudden gulp of fresh air in her lungs would help her recover. But was the air fresh? Perhaps it was contaminated with whatever had caused Dave's demise.

Slowly, she looked around, not really knowing what she expected to see. What did contaminated air look like? Well, she had been standing here for several minutes and she was still alive. Or was she? Of course she was! She was still thinking, breathing. Even Dave was still alive – only just, but he was still alive. Whatever it was that had inflicted this terrible thing upon him wasn't in the air – well, not anymore.

"At least let me help you back to the farm," she said, turning back to Dave. "Tom's there; he'll call the doctor. Then I'll come back for Pete."

Moving closer, she realised the liquid moving down his face was too thick to be sweat. It was more like treacle. What was it? She watched as this thick substance continued on its course and hung threadlike from his chin before finally dripping onto the road. The same thing was happening to his hands.

"Oh my God!" she yelled, as she realised what was happening.

She quickly turned her head away. It was all too horrible. The treacle-like substance was Dave's flesh! His flesh was melting! But surely it wasn't possible. Yet it was. Already she could make out his white bones as they pushed their way through what was once his skin. Sarah felt a sickness rising in her throat.

Never had she seen anything so gruesome, so horrific. Dave's flesh was melting and forming pools of thick slime in the road. She wanted to run back to the car and drive away. It would be so easy – no one would blame her. But she couldn't simply go off and leave him. That wasn't her way. Dave was Pete's friend and Laura's husband. No! It was impossible she would turn and walk away. Nevertheless, she placed her hand over her mouth as she turned back to face him.

His flesh was beginning to melt more quickly. She could see his white skull breaking through his forehead. How could this man still be alive when his flesh was dripping from him? Oh my God! What pain was he bearing to stay alert and speak to her?

Desperately trying not to show her revulsion, she kept her voice low. "Dave, for God's sake, please tell me what I can do to help you."

"There's nothing... you can do..." Dave's voice grew fainter. "Take the children away... Pete is gone. I know; I went to Top Meadow with him. Ned... was... sick... I took... his place." He pointed towards the car. "Pete would want you to save... his children. We heard the sound... saw the light – the mist... we should have... Tell them, Sarah... tell them all..." he broke off.

"What sound? What sound?" Sarah screamed out. Again her voice echoed around the valley. "And what about all the others down there in the valley? Shouldn't I warn them? They have children..."

Tears streamed down her face. This wasn't real. It couldn't be happening to her. Dave lying here... He said Pete was dead... But no, it wasn't possible.

"It's too late... all dead. Go before it's..." Dave could say no more. At last he was slipping away. Mercifully for him it was over. He had fought the agonising pain to stay alive long enough to tell someone of the horror in the valley: to warn them against touching anything – now that was done, he could let go.

Covering her face with her hands, Sarah could stay on her feet no more and she sank into a crumpled heap on the road. What should she do? She wanted to find Pete, but Dave said he was dead. Peeping through her fingers, she looked again at the remains of Dave's body.

Even now his flesh was still melting. So were his clothes. Soon there would be nothing to identify him. Only his bones would be left lying in a pool of slime that was once the flesh of a vibrant young man. Or would his bones melt too? What could have caused anything so horrible? In a state of shock, she was unable to move. Still feeling sick, she covered her eyes in a futile effort to block out the ugliness of the scene.

After a few minutes, she heard the sound of a bird fluttering above. Come to think of it, it was the first bird she had seen or heard all morning. Peering through her fingers, she saw a crow land on Dave's head. It began to pull at a fragment of melted flesh still attached to his skull.

Revolted, she heaved herself to her feet and ran across to the ditch by the side of the road. Unable to hold back any longer, she was violently sick. She couldn't recall ever feeling so ill. Her head still spinning, she clung desperately to the trunk of a tree to stop herself from falling over. Was Pete really lying dead somewhere up there on Top Meadow? Had his flesh melted away as Dave's had done? She didn't want to believe it.

"No!" she yelled. But there was no one to hear her.

Her mind was racing. Dave had been with Pete at Top Meadow, so how had he managed to get this far and why wasn't Pete with him? Pete would have tried to reach the children. Why was Dave alone? Though she knew he was dead and could tell her no more, she still looked towards his body for answers.

The bird was still tugging mindlessly at the flesh on Dave's skull. But then, it squawked and fell onto the road, writhing in agony. A few minutes later, it was dead; its feathers growing wet as the skin beneath began to melt.

That could have been her. She held her stomach as the thought brought back the nausea. If Dave hadn't stopped her from touching him, she would be lying there alongside him, just like the poor bird. Turning back to the ditch, she sank down in the grass and retched over and over again, even though there was nothing left in her stomach.

"Mummy! Mummy!"

Sarah sharply swung her head and looked towards where she had left the car. In her terror, she had forgotten about the children. But now Josie had stepped down onto the road.

Clutching her picture, the child was walking towards Dave's remains. Dutifully, Betts was by her side. "Would you like to see my pictures?"

Sarah was thankful she had parked some distance from Dave's body. At least the children couldn't possibly have seen what she herself had witnessed.

Scrambling to her feet, Sarah wiped the back of her hand across her mouth and ran towards her daughter. Scooping Josie up into her arms, she hurried back to the car, yelling out for Betts to follow. Not even a dog deserved to die like that.

"No darling," she said, forcing her taut lips into a smile. "The man is too tired to look at your pictures today. We'll come back and show him another time." Still trembling, Sarah tried to speak calmly, not wanting her children upset. She helped her daughter back into the car and urged Betts to follow. "Wait there with Becky and Betts. I'll only be a moment."

Reaching into the glove compartment, she pulled out the binoculars and looked down the lane. Was Pete lying down there? But there was nothing. The lane was empty. Sweeping the glasses across the fields, she saw the cows lying in the grass. They were motionless; exactly as they had been when she saw them from the window. Focusing the glasses, she realised what she was seeing were skeletons – surrounded by a thick slime. Her stomach turned over as she pulled the binoculars away from her eyes.

She was in the middle of a nightmare. In a little while she would awaken to find it had all been a horrible dream. She pinched herself so hard she squealed. This wasn't a dream at all, this was really happening.

Taking a deep breath, she turned the binoculars back towards the animals and saw a strange glow coming from the slime. The same glow that had lingered around Dave's face and hands. It was only then she noticed the grass in the fields was brown, almost as though a fire had swept through the whole area. Even the trees were bare; the empty, scorched branches looked like skeletons – reminding her of Dave's body.

Quickly turning away, she swung the binoculars back and forth until the farm cottages came into view. At first she could only see the buildings, but looking closer she was able to make out some shapes lying on the ground. What were they?

She gasped. My God, they were people or they had been. But like the animals, their flesh had melted. It was as Dave had said. Lowering the glasses, she closed her eyes. Was Pete one of them? Had he met the same fate while trying to help his farmhands?

Slowly lifting the glasses to her eyes again, she continued to scan the area around the cottages. She could see a glow coming from the slime. Was this the glow she had seen last night? Back then she had believed it to be the farmhands using torches to check the animals. But now she wondered about that. Was it possible she had actually seen those poor people glowing in the dark? She swept the binoculars around the bodies, searching for Pete. Yet how would she know it was him?

On the other hand, she must remain positive. Hopefully he was still alive up there in the hills. She owed it to him to find out. She turned the glasses towards Top Meadow, but couldn't see anything moving. It was too far away and the binoculars weren't powerful enough.

"Pete! Pete!" She screamed. Lowering the binoculars she listened – desperately hoping to hear his voice calling to her. But there were only echoes.

Running forward a few steps, she cried out again. "Pete! Pete! If you can hear me, for God's sake answer, say something." But again, only the echoes responded.

"God in heaven if you can hear me," Sarah murmured, sinking to her knees. "Please don't let Pete be dead."

Feeling sick again, she struggled to her feet and placing her hand over her mouth, she looked towards the ditch. But thinking of her children waiting in the car, she stumbled back to them.

Glancing once more at Dave's body lying in the road, she shuddered. Something was running from his nose and mouth. She gasped, realising it could only be his brain. Yet, for some reason, his eyes, wide open and staring, were still whole and in their sockets. Her eyes fell on the bird lying alongside Dave's head. Once it had been a creature soaring high above the treetops, now it too was a mere skeleton.

She tried to start the car, but her hands were trembling and the key slipped through her fingers, onto the floor. Finally, after several attempts, it found its mark and the engine sprang to life. After a final glance at Dave, she headed back to the farm.

She brought the car to a screeching halt in the farmyard and screamed out for Tom. "Where are you?" She jumped from the car. "Tom, for God's sake, where are you?"

"Stay in the car with Betts," she told the children. She slammed the door shut and ran towards the milking shed.

"What is it?" Looking concerned, Tom ran out to meet her. "Have you had an accident? Are the girls alright?"

"The people in the valley, they're all dead!" Sarah paced back and forth, wringing her hands as she spoke. "Oh my God Tom, they're all dead!" She stopped walking and faced him. "Do you hear what I'm saying? Every last one of them – they're dead!"

She was crying so much, Tom could hardly make out what she was saying. He grabbed her arms and shook her hard.

"Calm down, Sarah! I don't understand you. Who's dead?"

"How can I calm down?" She tried to pull away from him, but he held her tight. "Everything – everybody, they're all dead! He told me every damn thing is dead! The people, the cattle, the sheep... and..." She paused and closed her eyes. "And Pete; my lovely Pete is dead."

"Who told you?" Tom shook her again. He needed to get some sense out of her. "For goodness sake, Sarah calm down and tell me – who told you?"

Still sobbing hysterically, she rambled on.

"I saw him with my own eyes... lying there... he was burnt; his clothes were burnt... But worse than that, his skin was melting... it was dripping onto the road and yet his face was glowing. How is that possible?" She buried her head in Tom's shoulder. "It was horrible... horrible. What's happened? For heaven's sake, Tom, what are we going to do?"

"What are you saying? You've made a mistake." He laughed. "All you saw was a pile of old rags, probably dropped by a passing tramp. You're letting your imagination run away with you."

"It's all true," she said, sharply. She grabbed his arms. "I'm not imagining it! Do you really think I could imagine anything like that?"

"Look, you stay here and keep an eye on the cows and I'll go down there and take a look for myself." Tom made as if to move away.

Suddenly regaining some self-control, she pulled him back. "No! Stay where you are! I'm not mad. I know what I saw."

She ran to the car and pulled open the door. "Here, take the binoculars and see for yourself."

Thrusting the glasses into his hands, she pointed down the lane. "The body lying there is Dave. Before he died he told me everyone in the valley was dead."

Sarah watched as Tom swung the glasses to and fro. Though they weren't particularly powerful, he could still see that the animals in the fields below were lying dead with a thick substance surrounding their corpses.

Tom pulled the binoculars away from his eyes for a moment and took a deep breath. "I would never have believed it if I hadn't seen it with my own eyes."

He lifted the glasses to his eyes again and took another look down the lane towards his nephew's remains. "You're sure that's Dave?" he muttered.

Sarah nodded. "I'm sorry, Tom." She took his hand. "Yes, it's Dave. He spoke to me. He warned me not to touch anything. He said I should go and tell someone what had happened."

"What'll we do, Sarah?" Tom sobbed. "What'll we do? How will I tell his mother? She's my sister; Dave was her only son."

But then something even more dreadful dawned upon him. "My Alice! She's down there. Tell me she's not dead!" He grabbed Sarah's arms. "My lovely Alice and Luke, they can't be dead. I've got to find them. Alice! Alice!" He screamed out her name.

Sarah understood the pain he was feeling. She too didn't want to leave the valley without first finding Pete. But she now knew that was impossible. Her first priority was to take the children to safety. If one of them was to touch a single drop of the melted flesh... she swallowed hard to shift the lump in her throat. Tom must be made to realise the danger. His grip on her arms had tightened and his nails dug into her flesh.

"Stop it! For God's sake stop and listen to me!" Pulling herself free, Sarah rubbed her arms. "We must move what's left of the herd back up to the high ground behind the farm. After that they'll have to fend for themselves. Then you and Martha must come with us and go into Wooler to raise the alarm."

But Tom wasn't listening. He was still mumbling over and over. "Not dead. I must find them. Not dead."

Sarah slapped him hard across the face. "Tom! Pull yourself together. Get Martha, we must all get away from here."

"Martha!" Tom yelled out, suddenly regaining his sanity. "Oh my God, I'd forgotten. Martha was going to see Alice this morning. I must go after her." He began to run towards his home. "Martha! Martha!"

Sarah chased after him. "Come back! You can't go down there – it's not safe."

Grabbing his arm, she managed to pull him to a halt. "I'm sorry, Tom, but if Martha's already down there, then it's too late. If you go after her, you could both die."

"No! I can't let her die." Sobbing, Tom yanked himself away from her. "She's my wife. What would I do without her? I can't..." He broke off.

"I know, Tom! Believe me I know how you feel. But..." Sarah paused. It was no good. How could she tell Tom what to do? If she didn't have the children to think of, she would have gone straight up to Top Meadow in search of Pete.

She nodded. "Alright, Tom, but if Martha's not in the house then you can't go after her. If she's touched anyone down there, then..." She softened her tone. "I know how much you want to find her. God only knows how much I want to find Pete." Sarah glanced towards the hills. "He's alive up there somewhere. He's got to be. Dave said he was dead. But I don't believe him. Yet..." Her voice trailed off as she relived the vision of Dave lying in the road. She shivered. How could Pete still be alive? How could he have survived that?

"I won't leave my Martha." Tom's voice was soft, but forceful. "I'm going after her. Hopefully I'll catch her before she gets down there. But if not..." He glanced across towards Sarah's car. "But you must go; you have the children to think of. I've known Pete since he was a boy. He would want you to save yourself and the children." He sighed. "With Alice and Luke both gone, I need to find Martha. Go, Sarah! Tell everyone what's happened here. Someone must know something."

Seeing he was determined, she laid her hand on his shoulder. "Go then, Tom, but don't touch any of the remains. Dave's last words were that I mustn't touch him and he was right."

She quickly told Tom about the bird. "If you find Martha and she's already dying don't..." Sarah looked away, unable to finish.

Tom nodded. Looking at her, he patted her arm before running off towards his cottage, screaming out Martha's name all the while.

Sarah hurried back to the car, not daring to think what might have happened to Martha. Or what would happen to Tom, should he find her dying and tried to help.

"Where's my daddy?" wailed Josie. "I want my daddy. He hasn't seen my pictures yet." She held out the picture she had drawn while in the car. "This one is for Laura. Why can't I show her? She likes to see my pictures."

"I know sweetheart." Sarah answered without looking at the picture. "But Laura isn't feeling well. I don't think she would want us to call on her today. We'll show her your lovely drawings when she feels better. Daddy can't come home yet; he's busy with the animals. I've told Tom we're going to Wooler so Daddy will meet us there."

She turned away to hide the tears in her eyes. She wanted to sit down somewhere and cry until there were no more tears left. But there was no time; she had to get the children away from here. "Wait in the car until I come back. I'm going into the barn to see to the cows and then we'll go into the town. I'll leave Betts with you."

Making sure the car doors were locked, Sarah ran into the barn and led the cows towards the fields behind the farmhouse and pulled the gate shut. Hopefully they would make their way to the top of the hill and over to the other side. At least, she had done her best for them.

Back at the house, Sarah threw a few clothes for her and the children into a bag. Her mind was racing. She knew some people in Wooler, who would care for the children while she went back to Top Meadow to search for Pete.

Grabbing a couple of the children's favourite toys, Sarah ran back to the car. After a final glance at Top Meadow she drove off, desperate to get her children to safety.

CHAPTER THREE

Pete kissed his wife tenderly. "Enjoy your evening at the theatre. Tell Laura, I'll collect the children at four-thirty sharp."

"Do you think they'll be alright?" Sarah was anxious. "I've never been away from them all night, what if they need me?"

Sarah had been looking forward to spending an evening at the theatre with her friend in Alnwick, but now the time had almost come, she wasn't quite so sure.

"They'll be fine," Pete reassured her. "I'll pick them up at half-past four and bring them home for tea. After that, we'll play a few games before bedtime. They'll love it." He laughed. "Hide and seek seems to be the game of the moment."

"I know." Still unconvinced, Sarah sighed. "But what if...?"

"Forget about the what ifs." Pete kissed the end of her nose. "Go with Jenny and enjoy yourself."

She smiled. "Yes, I'm being silly. I'll tell Laura to have the children ready by half-past-four." She paused. "Only, you will be careful, won't you?"

"Of course I will. I'm only going up to Top Meadow. What could possibly go wrong up there?"

Sarah laughed. "Not a thing. It's so peaceful up on the hill, I almost wish I was coming with you."

Pete clasped his arms around his wife. "Perhaps it's just as well you're not. With you there, I'd never be able to concentrate on the sheep." He kissed her again. "I'd better go. The men will be waiting for me."

He called out for Lad and Bob, his two collies. Ushering them into the truck, he set off down into the valley, pausing only for a moment to look back and wave to Sarah.

It was a fine morning, ideal for checking the sheep on Top Meadow. He was making an early start. Having such a large flock up there, it always took some time to round them up. And with Sarah spending the night in Alnwick, he needed to be back in time to pick up Josie and Becky. However, Josh and Ned knew the ropes, so they should be finished in good time.

Rounding the bend, he could see two men waiting for him at the bottom of the lane. Even from a distance there was no mistaking Josh, a tall, thickset, young man with broad shoulders and muscular arms. It was he who clambered into the truck first, his suntanned face breaking into a wide grin as it rocked gently under the weight of his bulky frame.

The other man standing there was Dave. He was the complete opposite of Josh: medium in height and rather thin.

"Where's Ned?" Pete asked, looking around.

"He isn't too well this morning." Dave climbed into the truck. "I offered to stand in for him. He'll work down here today – nearer home."

Pete grinned. "One too many last night?"

Dave laughed. "Yes, you've guessed it. But it's not everyday you become a grandfather."

"That's true." Pete reflected on both times he had become a father. They had been the most wonderful experiences of his life. Being a grandfather must come pretty close.

On the way up the hill, Pete reminded the men to look out for Daisy and Belle. "I like to know they're okay."

The two farmhands grinned. "Yes, we know all about your soft spot for those two sheep," said Dave. "They must be the luckiest sheep in the county."

Pete laughed. "I know what you all think of me, but having nursed them back from the dead, I wouldn't part with either of them."

He had always liked animals. Despite rearing them for food, he took a keen interest in their welfare and maintained that while he was responsible for them, he would see to it they were well cared for.

He remembered how the ewe had had a very difficult delivery, which had left both animals extremely weak. The vet had suggested it might be best to put them out of their misery. But Pete refused and had spent the next few days nursing them back to health. Once they were strong enough, he had taken them to Top Meadow and every year he marked them clearly, instructing his men to leave the two sheep in peace.

Pete pulled up sharply. Luke, another of his farmhands, was waving him down.

"I've checked out the animals down here and everything's fine, would you like me to come up to Top Meadow with you?" he asked.

"You're sure they're okay?" asked Pete.

"Yes I couldn't sleep, so I was out extra early this morning. I assure you there's no problem with the animals. I simply thought you might like an extra pair of hands."

Pete accepted the offer readily. "I need to get back early today, so you'll be a great help." Luke climbed into the back of the truck.

Up on Top Meadow, the men spent a few minutes taking in the view. On a clear day like today you could see for miles. Pete wished Sarah was here to enjoy it with him.

Dragging his attention back to the sheep, he noted that only a few of his flock were grazing nearby. Most of them were probably spread out across the other hills. The longest part of the job on Top Meadow was locating the sheep. How much easier it would be if the areas were fenced off. But like his grandfather, Pete believed fences and walls would spoil the hills. Even in the valley, he kept the fences to a minimum and used existing hedges where possible. He sighed. "Best get on with it," he murmured. Calling the dogs, he instructed them to round up the sheep.

The morning passed quickly and the men stopped for lunch. But anxious to finish the job in time to collect the children, Pete didn't allow them to linger, promising the men time off another day. Even so, it was almost four o'clock when they rounded up the last group of sheep.

Suddenly one of the dogs began to growl softly. Pete looked around, half expecting to see a stranger who had climbed the hill to admire the view. Yet there was no one. He shrugged. Perhaps a small animal was rustling in the grass. But when the other dog started to growl and the sheep became restless, he became more concerned.

"Lad, Bob; heel," he called out softly. Obediently the dogs ran to his side.

"What's up?" Josh ran towards Pete.

"I don't know." Pete gazed down the hillside. "The dogs and sheep seem to be sensing something. Can you hear anything?"

Listening hard, Josh shook his head. "No, I can't hear a thing, but if the animals are behaving strangely, there must be something out there."

By now the others had joined them, but the only sound they heard was the soft murmur of the breeze rustling through the grass. Cupping his hands around his ears, Pete suddenly picked out a low sound.

"Wait! I can hear something." He listened again. "It's a sort of whirring sound." He pointed towards the reservoir. "It seems to be coming from over there."

As the men followed Pete's gaze, the sound grew louder and suddenly the sheep began to run towards the cliff edge. Believing them to be in a blind panic, Pete instructed the dogs to round them up. But the sheep continued to run towards the edge of the cliff. Now fearing the animals would fall to their deaths, the four men split up and tore after them in a desperate attempt to make them circle and slow down.

However, it soon became obvious that nothing was going to stop them and the men closed their eyes in horror when the sheep disappeared over the edge. Pete sank to his knees. In his mind's eye, he could see several of his pedigree flock lying dead at the bottom of the cliff.

Some time lapsed before any of the four men could face taking a look over the side.

"Where have they gone? I don't see any of them." Josh was the first to reach the cliff edge.

"That's ridiculous. They can't have vanished into thin air," Pete uttered. He came alongside Josh and stared down into the valley. "They must be down there somewhere."

But, before anyone could reply, the two dogs followed the sheep down the hill and they too, disappeared from view.

"What the...? Where've they gone?" asked Dave, joining the others. "There must be a ledge or something."

One by one, the men carefully followed the dogs. Once over the side they found it wasn't quite as steep as they had first thought. From above, there appeared to be a sheer drop to the bottom, but on closer inspection the men found there was a narrow ledge. Nevertheless, there was still no sign of the sheep – or the dogs.

Carefully making their way along the ledge, the men came across a small opening, not visible from the top of the cliff. A muffled bark came from somewhere deep inside. Peering through the gap, they saw a long tunnel stretching out before them. Dave and Luke were the first to crawl through the opening. It was a tight squeeze, but somehow they pulled themselves along the narrow tunnel.

Josh eyed the small opening cautiously. Being a larger man, he knew it would be more difficult for him to get through. But apart from his size, there was something else. He was also afraid of confined spaces. Not wanting to show his fear, he closed his eyes and took a deep breath before pushing himself into the tunnel. Feeling the walls pressing against him he began to panic, and beat his fists against the floor.

"Josh!" Dave called out. "Take it easy. You'll be fine, simply take it more slowly. Push your arms out in front of you and heave yourself forward."

The sound of Dave's voice only a few feet away calmed Josh a little. Taking a few deep breaths, he dug his fingers in the side of the tunnel and pulled. Inch by inch, he moved forward. Thankfully the tunnel widened slightly and after a few more hard pulls, he fell into a large cave. He could only manage to nod his thanks to Dave before sinking onto a large rock.

Pete had been about to follow Josh, when he noticed the whirring sound had grown louder. Keen to know what it was, he hung back for a few minutes and listened hard. However, still unable to identify the sound or where it was coming from, he crawled through the tunnel.

By now Dave had struck a couple of matches and from the dim light the men could see the sheep grouped together in the far corner. It was obvious they had been here before.

"Well I'll be blowed!" Pete looked around in amazement. "In all the years I've lived on the farm, I've never seen or heard of this cave before. Even my grandfather can't have known about it. I'm sure he'd have mentioned it to me. The sheep must come in here for shelter. They're not as stupid as people think." He dusted himself down. "We might as well wait here for a while. I don't think we'll get them out until the noise has stopped."

Pete was still curious about where the sound was coming from. There wasn't anything over on the far side of the hill except the reservoir and dam and of course, the old, disused power station. But he didn't believe it was coming from any of those.

A more reasonable explanation was that someone on one of the neighbouring farms was using a power saw. Out here, on a quiet afternoon, such sounds carried a long way.

The light from Dave's matches allowed the men to find a few dry twigs to make a small fire. Now able to see better, they were surprised at how large the cave was. Interestingly, there appeared to be several openings leading off.

Dave suggested they should each take a tunnel and go off to see what was down there. But though Pete was keen to explore, he felt they should stick together. "Without proper lighting we could very easily lose each other. If we're going to do this, I think we should choose one cave and all go together."

Josh didn't relish going into the dark tunnels with only a few lighted twigs serving as a torch. But he was equally loath to being left alone in the cave. Swallowing hard, he followed the others down one of the tunnels only to find it came to a dead end a few hundred yards in. Trying the next one, the group found it more hopeful. It appeared to be taking them downhill.

"I think we should leave some sort of a trail. We could end up wandering around here for ever." Josh took a few deep breaths. They had walked quite a way and though he was trying to stay calm, tiny telltale beads of sweat were forming on his forehead. From his early childhood, his greatest fear was to be lost somewhere in the dark; this was a little too close for comfort.

"Yes Josh, you're probably right," Pete replied. "But we haven't anything we can use to mark a trail. Perhaps we shouldn't go too much further today. We'll come back another time when we have some proper torches." Carrying on for a few more yards, he found that the tunnel forked. "Which way?" He looked from one tunnel to the other in turn.

"Neither!" Josh wiped his brow. He was beginning to panic. "Not today anyway. I think we should go back."

"It's all quite exciting, though, isn't it?" Dave rubbed his hands together enthusiastically. "Those people who discovered the tombs in Egypt must have felt something like this."

Interested in Egyptian archaeology, he had read several books on the subject. Peering through the darkness, he felt very excited. This cave might be a far cry from the Valley of the Kings, nevertheless it was his first experience of being in some long forgotten place and he was relishing every moment of it.

"I wonder if we'll find anything at the end of this tunnel." Dave continued. "You know the kind of thing I mean? The body of some long lost soul, who found his way down here, but couldn't find his way out again."

"Shut up, Dave!" Josh could feel the blood draining from his face. Thankfully it was too dark for the others to notice. The idea of finding some long lost body didn't appeal to him at all. He was no Indiana Jones. To his mind, they had been in the caves too long already. He breathed a sigh of relief when he heard Pete agree with him.

"Yes, Dave, I understand what you mean. I'd be very interested to find out what lies ahead. However I think Josh is right. Without adequate lighting, it would be foolhardy to go on." Pete knew of Josh's phobia. Why let his friend suffer any longer? "I think we should go back to..." He paused. "Listen, can you hear anything?"

Luke was the first to speak. "It's that whirring sound again, the one we heard outside. It's very faint now, I'm surprised we can hear it at all."

"Earlier, when I reached the opening of the cave, it seemed to grow louder," said Pete. "I thought it might be someone using a power saw, but like you say, Luke, it's strange we can hear it all the way down here. It must be really loud now."

Josh turned and began to run back up the tunnel towards the main cave. "Come on!" he yelled. "We should get out of here." The thought of a long lost body was bad enough, but hearing strange noises came a close second.

The others followed him, though they tried to take more care. "Don't run, you idiot," called out Dave. "You're likely to stumble over something in the darkness and break your leg."

Josh slowed down and Dave was the first to catch up with him.

"That was stupid. You're a big bloke, Josh. How would we have carried you out of here?"

Back in the cave, Pete gathered up more small sticks and set them alight.

"I don't think we need to wait here any longer." Josh was anxious to get back outside. Never had the fresh air been more appealing.

He had seen all he wanted to see. Besides, he still had to face going back through the narrow tunnel at the entrance. "We've checked all the sheep and they're fine. There's nothing to stop us from leaving them in here. They seem to know their way around. They don't need us any more."

But Pete wasn't so sure. Desperate though he was to see his children, he felt he shouldn't leave the sheep until the noise had stopped. "They might do something stupid, like run out and fall over the cliff."

"I thought you said they weren't stupid." Josh argued.

As far as he was concerned, they had done the job they had come here to do. The sheep were okay. To be truthful, at this moment, they were probably in better nick than he was. If there had been a problem he would gladly have offered to help. But as it was, all he wanted to do was to get out of this wretched place.

"For heaven's sake, Pete, they must run in and out of here all the time. It just so happened that today, we were here to see them do it." Realising he was panicking again, Josh took a few deep breaths.

"He does have a point." Luke was starting to feel hungry and besides, he too was tiring of this cave. He looked at his watch. "Do you realise what time it is?" He peered along the tunnel. "It's dark out there, we've been in here for longer than we thought. Weren't you supposed to pick up the children at half past four? It's long past that."

"Yes." Pete looked at the sheep. It was true; he really should go. Josie and Becky would be waiting for him and he had promised he wouldn't be late. But at the same time, concern for his animals nagged at him. What if that noise didn't stop? Would they wander down the tunnels and be lost forever?

"You guys get off home," he said at last. "I'll wait up here for a little while longer. Take the truck. I'll come outside and ring Laura to let her know what's happened."

"Don't worry about phoning my wife. I'll explain when I get home." Turning to go, Dave looked back. "Are you really sure about this?"

"Yes. You go ahead. I won't be long. I'll give Josh a ring when I'm at the bottom of the hill and he can bring the truck to me there."

Luke and Dave scrambled through the tunnel.

Josh took it more slowly. Pleased to be outside again, he took a couple of deep breaths before joining the two men in Pete's truck.

They were almost at the bottom of the hill, when Dave caught sight of a bright light through the reversing mirror. It seemed to be rising from behind the hill. He stopped the car and turned around to take a better look. By now it had turned a sickly green colour.

"What is it?" Luke was impatient. This job had taken much longer than he had expected. His wife was expecting their first child and he hadn't intended to leave her so long.

Dave pointed to the green light. Now very curious, the three men stepped out of the truck to take a better look. They were amazed at how bright it had grown even in those few moments.

"What do you think it is?" asked Dave.

"I don't know." Josh felt uneasy. "Perhaps we should go back for Pete."

"It's probably nothing." Luke didn't feel like going all the way back up the hill. "Besides, he's in the cave. He won't have seen it from inside there and it'll probably be gone when he comes out."

"All the same, I think I should go back for him." Josh felt uneasy about leaving Pete up there alone. The light was getting brighter all the time. If the situation were reversed, Pete would have gone back for them. "Neither of you need come; you can easily run down to your homes from here. I'll take the truck and go back." Jumping into the vehicle, he turned and headed back up the hill.

"You're a fool," Dave yelled out after him. "You're a damn fool. You should go home." Glancing back at the light, he pulled at Luke's arm "Come on, leave him, he'll be okay. We still have some way to go. Strange thing is the noise has stopped."

Luke nodded, still looking up at the light. First the sound and now this green light; something was wrong. But turning around he saw Dave running towards the distant cottages and chased after him.

Reaching the top of the hill, Josh clambered out of the truck. Half running, half stumbling he found the entrance to the cave. Not wanting to go back inside, he began to call out to Pete. But the ball of light had grown to an enormous size and he could feel an intense heat coming from it. Alarmed, he threw himself into the narrow tunnel – suddenly seeing it as the lesser of two evils.

Pete leapt to his feet as Josh's head burst through the opening. "What the hell is it? Have you had an accident?"

"I came back for you," Josh gasped, desperately hurling his large frame through the opening. "There's some kind of strange green light in the sky. It's growing in size and getting brighter and hotter by the second."

As he spoke, he threw himself into the cave. However his foot dislodged a large rock at the edge of the tunnel, causing the smaller ones to fall.

Realising what was happening; Pete reached out and pulled Josh away as the rocks continued to avalanche. The two men could only look on helplessly, as the small tunnel leading into the cave disappeared behind a mass of boulders.

An eerie silence followed the rock-fall. It was only after the dust had settled that Josh spoke out.

"I'm sorry, Pete," he whispered. "I was desperate to get away from the light. But I should have been more careful. That tunnel can't have been used by people my size."

Pete didn't answer. Instead, he picked up a few twigs and held them against the flames of the small fire, before walking across to the pile of rocks. Pulling at one or two of the smaller stones, he found they came away easily, but some of the others were very large. It would take a great deal of time and effort to move them. Sitting down on one of the rocks, he pulled out his mobile phone; there was no signal. What else could he expect buried here deep in the hillside? "What were you talking about? A green light in the sky, what light?" he asked, at last.

Josh explained what he had seen. "I'm telling you, it was growing in size all the time it was climbing into the sky. By the time I reached the cave, it was huge. I just wanted to get away from it." Josh sighed and scraped the toe of his boot through the dust on the cave floor.

"Couldn't it have been fireworks or something?"

"No!" Josh said sharply. "I'm not so stupid that I wouldn't know a few fireworks. No, this was... big – enormous, bright green and very hot."

"Okay, Josh. It's just that..." Pete's voice trailed off as he nodded towards the rock-fall.

Wandering across to the cave entrance, Josh examined the blockage. Watching him, Pete's thoughts drifted to Sarah. He wondered whether she had enjoyed her afternoon with her friend. They would be preparing for the theatre now. Absentmindedly, he glanced down at his watch. No doubt Sarah would ring home to speak to the children before she left. She wouldn't want to...

Noting the lateness of the hour, he leapt to his feet; he had lost all track of time. The show would be half way through. If Sarah had rung home, there would have been no reply. She would be so worried... Surely she would have called Laura and learned how he had stayed with the sheep?

But then he sighed, realising it would have been too early. Dave wouldn't have been home when she rang. They would have still been in the cave.

Pete felt uneasy. He knew the number of her friend in Alnwick. Why hadn't he called Sarah himself? He could have told her what was going on. He always called her if he was going to be late, it was something he had promised when they were first married. Until today he had kept his word.

Frustrated, he kicked out at a stone on the ground. What a mess. He should have gone back with the others instead of waiting here. They had been right. The sheep would have been fine on their own. Now he, Josh, two dogs and a large number of sheep were stuck in this cave and he couldn't even ring anyone.

Sitting down, a picture of Sarah flashed through his mind. She had given up so much to marry him and move to the farm. He was aware her parents hadn't approved of him; well, not at first anyway. Nevertheless, she had married him. He smiled to himself. Sarah certainly was a headstrong girl.

He was also aware that Tom had wanted him to marry Alice; often pointing out his daughter's many qualities. It was true: Alice was a capable woman and he had always known she would make an ideal wife for someone. But not him. That special something had never clicked. In fact no one set his pulse racing the way Sarah did. Until he met her, he had often wondered whether he would ever find the right girl. But then fate, in the shape of his elder brother James, had taken a hand.

Never cut out to be a farmer, James had gone to work for a large company and was now an important figure in the organisation. It was he who should have been at the charity dance in London, but at the last minute an urgent matter had arisen in New York.

Telephoning Pete, he insisted he should take the ticket, saying it would be a great night out for him. "Make a weekend of it, or even a week or so," he had said. "You can use my flat. It'll do you good to get away from the farm for a while."

Pete had made all kinds of excuses, but his brother wasn't having any of it. "Take the ticket and go to the dance. You'll enjoy it," he had said. "Heaven knows you could do with a night out. You never leave the farm. It could give your life a whole new perspective."

And so it had, because it was at the charity dance that he first encountered Sarah. She seemed to be around his age: twenty-two or perhaps a little younger. He recalled being struck by her fair skin, large blue eyes and soft golden hair that fell gently around her shoulders. Watching her as she

51

danced, she seemed so full of life. Even from across the crowded ballroom, her sheer exuberance had swept over him like a breath of fresh air.

Now his thoughts turned to his children. They would be asleep. Laura would have read them a bedtime story before putting out the light. At home, he normally did that. It was his one special time with his daughters.

His lovely girls, there wasn't anything he wouldn't do for them. They would break a few hearts when they were older: they were so pretty. There was no doubt they took after their mother: same hair, same eyes and the same good nature. Their mother... Sarah... He sighed. He and Josh had to get out of here, even if they had to...

"Could there be another way out?" Josh's melancholy tone interrupted his thoughts. "We've got to do something. We can't merely sit around until Dave and Luke remember we're up here."

Pete looked around the cave. The fire was dying out. Unless they found more wood or bracken, they would be in total darkness. Dave had thought to leave the matches, but they wouldn't last long.

"First things first," Pete said briskly, jumping to his feet. He had noticed the concern in Josh's voice. "We've got to find something else to burn. We can't go fumbling around in the dark."

Picking up a burning twig, he held it aloft as he walked to the back of the cave. "Over here. There're some twigs lying here. They must have blown in over the years."

The two men gathered together a bundle of dry sticks.

"Put those on the fire Josh, we need more light. I'll see if there's something we can use as a torch and then we'll be able to have a good look around." Pete tried to sound optimistic; there was no point in alarming Josh further. "You never know, there could be another entrance."

Stumbling around the dimly lit cave, Pete tripped over something. Taking a closer look, he found it was a part of a branch from a tree. It felt very dry; it would burn perfectly. It must have lain in here for years. Someone must have dragged it in. It was too big to have been blown in by the wind. Had someone spent the night in here? He shivered and cautiously looked over his shoulder – were they still here?

"Look what I've found," he said, pulling himself together. He showed the wood to Josh. "Check to see if there are any more pieces like this."

As luck would have it, they found a few more large pieces of dry wood.

"Well, now that we have some better lighting, we can take a good look at the blocked entrance," said Pete. "Perhaps between us, we'll manage to move the rocks. If not, then we'll try the tunnels. But one way or another Josh, we're going to get out of here."

"I wish Dave hadn't talked about long lost souls of people trapped in caves," said Josh, glumly. "It kind of rings true right now, doesn't it?"

Pete tore recklessly at the rocks, the thought having already crossed his mind. "One way or another," he repeated, more to reassure himself than Josh. "We're going to get out of here."

CHAPTER FOUR

Early morning shoppers in the small market town of Wooler turned their heads in surprise, when Sarah brought her car to a screeching halt a few yards from the police station. They were unused to such scenes in the quiet town and a few people clucked their tongue at her rashness.

Sarah would have parked closer to the station if an enormous vehicle hadn't been blocking the way. As it was, she was forced to squeeze herself and the children between two large packing cases lodged on the pavement, before reaching the station entrance.

Inside, Andy Simmonds, the young constable on duty, stared at Sarah in disbelief as she poured out her story. Bright green lights in the night sky, glowing, melting bodies, obviously the woman was mad. Glancing down at the large book on the desk, he noted there had been no other reports of strange goings on the previous evening. Being such a stickler for detail, Sergeant Gilmore would most surely have recorded anything so unusual.

The constable recalled how over the last few weeks, Headquarters had sent several memos to outlying police stations, informing the officers how to deal with weirdoes. To be truthful, they hadn't used that word, but surely it was what they meant.

One memo in particular, had touched on the subject of people claiming to have seen strange lights and UFOs in the night sky. However, to his knowledge, this was the first one to walk into this police station. It would certainly be something to discuss with his colleague, Constable Manners, when he came back from the petrol station after filling the police car.

"So tell me again, what exactly did you see?" Simmonds poised his pen over the note pad.

He was following police procedure to the letter. The constable on duty must look interested and alert at all times, no matter what the public had to say. Though the police college had used true-to-life situations during the training of young cadets, he couldn't recall them coming up with this one.

"You must understand, it's not every day we get people in here saying they've seen lights in the sky and people lying in the road with their skin dripping all over the place." He paused. "You're the first, actually."

Laying down his pen he tried to recall what the last memo had said. 'Above all else, keep calm.' It had read. 'You could be dealing with an unstable character, who may have violent tendencies'. He studied the woman in front of the desk carefully. She seemed quite level-headed, but then how could he tell? She might lash out at him at any moment.

Leaning across the desk, he smiled broadly before adopting his most sympathetic tone. "Perhaps you'd like to take your children home and think about it? I'm sure in a few hours you'll see the whole thing in a completely different light." He winced at his unintended pun.

Sarah stared at him. Was he making fun of her? Did this wretched, brown-eyed, pompous young man believe she was making the whole thing up? Her husband could be lying dead somewhere and here he was, telling her to go home and think about it. Who did he think he was? Go home, indeed!

"No." She thumped her fist on the desk. "I know you think I'm crazy, but I'm telling you the truth." She raised her voice. "For heaven's sake, at least check it out."

Hearing the commotion, Sergeant Gilmore appeared in the doorway. He had been enjoying a nice cup of tea. With Mrs. Gilmore away visiting her mother at the other end of the country, he had thought he wouldn't be interrupted.

"What on earth is going on in here?" he asked, frowning at his constable.

Sarah retold her story, hoping the older man may be more helpful. "You must believe me," she wailed. "Despite what your constable thinks, I'm not making it up."

"Mummy, when can I show Daddy my pictures?" Josie was becoming impatient and tugged on her mother's jeans. She held up her two drawings. "I drew this one when we were in the car. I have two now."

"Hush, dear." Sitting Becky on the desk, Sarah bent down and hugged Josie. "We'll see Daddy soon. You keep the pictures until then."

She was about to stand up, when she caught a glimpse of the picture Josie had drawn while in the car.

"What's this Josie?" Sarah took the drawing from her daughter's hand. It showed some hills with a large green object rising above them.

"I don't know. I saw it last night when I was in bed." Josie pointed at the large round object in her picture. "It was big and round and very bright."

Sarah handed the drawing to the sergeant. "Josie must have seen the light in the sky. I thought they were both asleep. Now do you believe me? Will you do something?"

The sergeant thought it over. He had a couple of friends down there in the valley. It wouldn't hurt to give one of them a ring and find out if there was any truth in what this woman was saying. If not, then he would have to insist she leave the station. He couldn't base a police investigation on the drawing of a toddler.

He looked at his watch. Perhaps he would try old Wilf, he was getting on in years now and only did a few odd jobs around the farm to keep active. He was usually in his cottage at this time of day. The sergeant dialled the number and was a little concerned when there was no reply. At least his wife should have been there. She had been housebound for the last year or so.

He decided to call his other friend, Dave. If he wasn't in, his wife Laura would be. She occasionally looked after the farmhands children. But again, there was no reply.

Slowly, he replaced the receiver and looked across at Sarah. "Neither of my two friends are answering the phone; Wilfred Barnes and Dave..."

Sarah looked up sharply. "Dave!" she interrupted. "You mean Dave Howard?"

The sergeant nodded. "Do you know him?"

Sarah lowered her voice. "It was Dave I saw lying in the road."

The colour drained from the sergeant's face. "Are you sure about that?" he uttered.

"Yes, of course I am," Sarah snapped. "I know Dave well. He's married to Laura. She looks after my children sometimes."

Gilmore nodded. Though unsure he wanted to hear anymore, he urged her to continue.

"Yesterday, Dave went up to Top Meadow with my husband Pete. I later learned it should have been Ned, who..." Sarah shook her head, she was rambling. "But you don't want to know all that. There was another man with them – Josh. Before Dave died, he told me Luke had also joined them and that they were all dead."

Recalling Dave lying there in the road, she shuddered. "He said that everyone was dead. Poor Dave, he looked... awful. Suddenly she felt sick again and her head began to spin. The room was going around and she could feel herself falling. She would have dropped to the floor if the sergeant hadn't caught her.

"Simmonds! Quickly bring a chair for the lady. And a glass of water," he ordered.

The constable brought a chair from behind the desk, before rushing off to the small kitchen for some water.

"Mummy!" Josie began to cry. "What's the matter with my mummy?"

"I'll be alright darling," said Sarah, reaching down to comfort her daughter. With Sergeant Gilmore's help, she lowered herself into the chair. "Mummy just feels a little tired."

She looked back at the sergeant. "It's the not knowing where Pete is..." She broke off, she couldn't bear to think of him lying somewhere, burned and dying. The constable came back with the water and she took a sip.

She smiled her thanks. "Perhaps you'd better pass Becky down to me. I see she's found the pens on your desk."

Simmonds picked up the child. Unused to handling small children, he held her at arms length as he passed her down to Sarah.

"Pete? Are you talking about Pete Maine?" Gilmore asked, suddenly realising who she was. "You're Pete Maine's wife?"

The Maine farm was well known in these parts. On more than one occasion, Wilf had told him how Pete looked after him and all the others who had been around in his grandfather's day. "He could have thrown us out of our homes to make room for new farmhands. But Pete promised we could stay for as long as we wanted; he even went to the expense of having new cottages built. He's a good, honest man."

"Yes, I'm Sarah Maine. Please Sergeant Gilmore, do something."

"Constable, get Manners on the radio," said the sergeant briskly. "Tell him to go out to the Maine Farm as quickly as possible and have a look around."

But then he had another thought. Dave was one of his best friends. They had been best man at each other's weddings. If it was Dave lying out there, he owed it to him to see his remains were treated with respect.

"No! Wait! Tell him to come in here straight away and pick me up. I'll go with him."

"I want you to stay here with Mrs. Maine." Sergeant Gilmore continued, once Andy had relayed the message. "Should something develop, while I'm away, I'll rely on you to use your initiative."

Taking Simmonds's arm, he led him a few feet away from where Sarah was sitting before lowering his voice. "This could still be something of nothing so keep it under your hat until you hear from me. I'll radio in my instructions once I've fully assessed the situation."

Whilst the sergeant believed the young woman had seen something extraordinary in the valley, it may not turn out to be exactly as she described. Therefore he had no intention of informing HQ of melting bodies on his patch until he had seen them for himself. It wouldn't do to start a panic if the whole thing turned out to be a hoax – not with the prospect of a promotion looming. Mrs. Gilmore wouldn't be at all pleased if he was turned down for the post of inspector in the City of Newcastle, because he had caused a commotion on the word of a young woman who had suddenly taken leave of her senses.

"Shouldn't I come with you?" asked Sarah, making an attempt to get to her feet.

She didn't really want to see Dave's body again, but she was still hopeful Pete might be alive and had somehow made his way back to the farmhouse.

"No, Mrs. Maine. It would be best if you waited here with the constable. After all, you have the children to consider." Laying his hand on her shoulder, Sergeant Gilmore gently pushed her back into the chair. "Don't worry, we'll take a good look around, if there's anyone still alive, we'll find them."

It was then Sarah remembered Tom and Martha. They were still at the farm. "Tom insisted on going back to find his wife," she wailed to the sergeant. "I couldn't stop him."

Glancing towards the window, the sergeant saw Manners pull up outside. "We shouldn't be too long," he said, walking towards the door.

"Don't forget what I said about touching anything," called out Sarah. "Dave was most insistent about that."

"We'll be careful," Sergeant Gilmore promised. "We'll be very careful indeed."

Simmonds watched from the window, as the police car disappeared down the road "We should hear some news soon. It shouldn't take them long to get to the scene."

Sarah didn't reply, leaving an awkward silence.

The constable coughed nervously and tried to think of something else to say. If only he could have gone down into the valley with Manners and left the sergeant to deal with Mrs. Maine and the children. He could feel her eyes boring into him – accusing him of his earlier lack of sensitivity. Thinking back, perhaps he could have been more helpful instead of dismissing her as a lunatic. But her story had sounded so far-fetched.

"I'll make you a nice cup of tea," he said at last. Not waiting for a reply, he scuttled into the kitchen.

Sarah watched him disappear through the door. She didn't really want any tea; she was far too upset to drink anything. But the constable hadn't given her the chance to refuse. She looked up at the clock on the wall. It should only take half an hour for the sergeant and his driver to reach the spot where she had last seen Dave. By ten o'clock, they would know she had been telling the truth. The appropriate authorities would be called in and Pete would be found alive and well. She sat back in her chair and took a deep breath. That was all she wanted; to have Pete back with her and the children.

****

It didn't take long for Sergeant Gilmore and his constable to find Dave's body. Gilmore gasped at the sight. He hadn't wanted to believe Mrs. Maine when she told him of what she had seen. But standing there looking down at Dave, it was even worse than she had described.

Gilmore was a hardened policeman, having served with the police force in London. There, as a young constable, he had come up against crime that people around here only read about over their cornflakes. He had even toyed with the idea of joining a friend in MI5, before taking over at Wooler. Yet with all his experience, he had never seen anything like this.

By now there wasn't a trace of flesh anywhere on Dave's body, only a thick pool of dark coloured slime surrounding his skeleton. Even Dave's clothes had melted and mingled with his flesh. If Mrs. Maine hadn't told him who it was, he would never have identified the man lying there. His friend would have been logged as an unknown.

Heeding her warning, he kept his distance as he gazed down at the slime that had once been his friend. But then he noticed something he thought rather strange. Dave's eyeballs were still whole.

Taking care, he moved a little closer to make sure. Yes, it was true. For some reason, the eyeballs hadn't melted. Instead they lay on top of the thick slime surrounding Dave's skull.

Why was that? Why hadn't they melted like the rest of the body? Gilmore made a note of it in his notebook: it could be important. He would ponder over it when he got back to the station.

He looked back at his friend's remains. Cautiously, he crouched down and made the sign of the cross. "Rest in peace my friend," he murmured, wiping a tear from his eye. He rose to his feet and looked across the valley. What had happened out here? Someone must know. All these lives lost. Why?

Glancing back to Dave's body, he sighed. "I'm sorry, Dave. I'm so very sorry."

He took a deep breath and brushed away another tear. This was no time to get sentimental. He owed it to Dave and Laura to find out what had happened in the valley. Someone, somewhere was going to pay heavily for this. Looking around the fields, he saw it was exactly as Mrs. Maine had said: everything was burnt to a crisp.

Hearing a noise, he turned and saw his constable being violently sick over the ditch. He couldn't blame the young officer. No one could have been prepared for a sight like this.

"I'm sorry about that, sir." Constable Manners wiped his face as he returned to his sergeant's side. "I'm alright now. It won't happen again."

At least he hoped it wouldn't. But taking another look at the body, he wasn't so sure and hurriedly took a couple of deep breaths. On the way here, Sergeant Gilmore had filled him in on what they might find. Yet to be truthful, he had thought the woman was mad. All he expected to find was a dead animal, half eaten by crows. But this was unbelievable. Even the post mortems the police college had insisted he attend, hadn't been this gruesome. If this was real police work, then he wasn't sure he was cut out for it.

The sergeant didn't answer. Instead, he bent down to take a final look at Dave's body. What could have caused the skin to melt like that?

Mrs. Maine had mentioned a bright light, but as far as he was aware, there wasn't a furnace or anything like that in these parts. And then there were the burnt fields to consider. Could some huge fire have caused the devastation? In that case surely the body would only have burned – not melted. He didn't know of anything that would melt a body. He shook his head, not having any answers. It would be up to the boys in Alnwick to work it out.

Reaching into his pocket, Gilmore pulled out a clean white handkerchief and bent down to cover Dave's skull. However as he did so, the tip of one of his fingers accidentally touched a tiny drop of melted flesh. Whilst it didn't actually feel hot, his finger felt as though it had been burned.

"My finger feels strange!" he exclaimed to Manners. He rubbed his hand on his coat, trying to remove the slight trace of flesh. But in doing so, he brought the offending finger into contact with two others. Now they too began to have the same burning sensation. He recalled Mrs. Maine's warning about not touching anything.

"Radio in to Simmonds; tell him what we've seen here. My orders are for him to telephone Alnwick Police Station immediately and inform them of the situation. They'll know what to do."

Running across to the police car, Manners dispensed with the usual codes and yelled into the radio. "Hello, Simmonds. Are you there?" But there was no reply, only a hissing sound punctuated with an occasional beep. He tried again. "Simmonds! Where the hell are you? If you're there, for God's sake say something. This is not the time to fool around."

There were times when both officers were so bored they would joke around on the radio. Sometimes they would pretend not to hear reports, while on other occasions they made stupid remarks or sounds.

"Simmonds, come in," he screamed. "This is a bloody emergency. There's a whole lot of trouble down here."

He listened hard. But there was still no reply, only the continual hissing sound. Blast! There must be no signal. He looked up towards the hills. The damn hills were blocking it out. Throwing the radio receiver back into the car, he ran over to Gilmore.

"I can't get through!" he declared. "There's no signal, it must be the hills. We'll have..." He broke off when he saw the sergeant's outstretched hand. His fingers had turned fiery red and were beginning to blister. "What the... We've got to get back. You need to see a doctor quickly."

Gilmore nodded and the two men ran over to the car.

"Let me put something around that." Manners pulled a couple of tissues from a box on the back seat. "At least these should keep the air from it until the doc takes a look."

The sergeant wedged his notebook on the dashboard while Manners wound the tissues around his hand. The blisters were spreading fast and had now reached the palm of his hand. Once the wounds were covered, the constable turned the car around and set off for Wooler.

Manners rammed his foot down on the accelerator. This was the first important call he'd had since becoming a policeman. He needed to get back quickly to write up his report.

Gilmore tried the radio again. The hissing sound was still there, but he continued speaking, hoping Simmonds might be able to hear him. "Mrs. Maine was right. We've seen Dave's body and it's exactly as she described. Something terrible has happened out here. Keep her there at the station." He went on to instruct Simmonds to get onto Alnwick and inform them of the situation. "These damn hills," he muttered, throwing down the instrument. "I hope Simmonds got all that."

"It won't be long before we're clear of the hills, sir. Then you can try again." As Manners spoke, he felt a strange sensation in his fingers. Taking his eyes off the road, he looked down at his hands. His fingers were red and swollen. What was happening to him?

"Sergeant!" Manners screamed out in terror. Lifting his hands from the steering wheel, he thrust them towards Gilmore. "Oh my God, look at my hands! I must have touched your fingers!"

"Keep your eyes on the road man!" The sergeant yelled out to his constable as the car swung out of control. "Watch where you're going!"

By now the car had left the carriageway and was veering across the road. Suddenly realising the danger, Manners tried desperately to bring the car back under control. But it was too late: he was driving far too fast. The car swerved off the road and smashed into a tree.

CHAPTER FIVE

Constable Simmonds tapped his pen on the desk. He was becoming increasingly concerned about Gilmore and Manners. It was well over an hour since the two men had left the police station. Surely he should have heard something by now?

He felt Sarah's eyes boring into him. "Sorry." He laid the pen on the desk and smiled awkwardly. "It shouldn't be long now." He glanced at the clock. "Perhaps the traffic was bad."

"We should have heard from them ages ago and you know it!" Sarah retorted. She was sick of sitting in this chair drinking endless cups of tea. The constable had insisted on refilling her cup the moment it was empty.

It seemed the police college spent hours instructing recruits that cups of tea worked wonders with hysterical women who suddenly appeared in police stations with half-baked stories about bright lights and melting flesh. The constable was polite, well mannered and doing his best to keep her calm. But right now she didn't want calm – she wanted action.

"For heaven's sake, the farm's only a half-hour's drive from here. Far less if you happen to be in a police car with a flashing blue light!"

"Yes," Simmonds agreed, not knowing what else to say.

He was relieved when a noise came from the radio. "That'll be them now. I expect they've found your husband safe and well and hungry for his lunch." He laughed. "I knew there was nothing to worry about."

He picked up the receiver and gave the station code. "Constable Manners, are you there? Is Mr. Maine with you?" He paused and listened for the familiar voice of Manners, but there was nothing except a loud hissing sound, followed by a series of short beeps. "The hills are interfering with the signal," he said, turning towards Sarah. "I expect they'll try again shortly."

Another ten minutes passed before the radio began to hiss again. Simmonds sprang to his feet. If they couldn't get through this time he would go out and find them. He knew the sergeant wouldn't be very pleased if he left the station unmanned, but he couldn't sit there any longer. Not with Mrs. Maine and her two children staring at him. The youngest one was alright; she was too young to know what was going on. But the older girl kept looking at him as though it was his fault her daddy wasn't there to look at her pictures.

He gave the call code and for one brief moment, he believed he heard the sergeant's voice. "Sergeant Gilmore, is that you?" Glancing across at Sarah, he smiled nervously. "Bad connection."

Turning back to the radio, he yelled into the receiver. "What's that you say? I'm sorry, but I can't hear you. Can you please repeat it...? Hello, hello..." The hissing sound grew louder and then suddenly the radio went dead.

Simmonds gave Sarah a sheepish grin as he put down the receiver. "I'm sorry, but I couldn't quite catch what Sergeant Gilmore was saying. I'm sure it was his voice though, so they must be okay."

Feeling uncomfortable under Sarah's gaze, he ran a finger around his collar. "I'll wait a few more minutes and if I don't hear any more I'll try calling them. They should be away from the hills any minute now."

Sarah was fed up with all this nonsense. She was tired of sitting here waiting for news. She opened her mouth to give the constable a piece of her mind, but it was Josie who spoke first.

"Mummy, can I have a drink of water?"

"I think there's some orange juice in the fridge in the kitchen." Relieved at the interruption, Simmonds pointed the way. He had a feeling Mrs. Maine had been about to voice her annoyance. "Perhaps your little girl would prefer that. Help yourself. I'll wait here by the radio in case there's further news."

Once Sarah was out of earshot, he picked up the receiver and tried contacting Manners. He was beginning to feel uneasy. Something wasn't right. Yes the hills were a problem, but Manners had always been able to get messages through before. And there was another thing, what was the hissing noise? Loss of signal was usually accompanied by a crackling sound – not hissing. Then there were the beeps. He had never heard those before – at least not since being at the police college.

Back then the instructors had touched on the subject of radio jamming. They had even given the recruits a demonstration of what it might sound like. If he wasn't mistaken, it had sounded something like the hissing and the beeps. He wished he had taken more notice. But on that particular day there had been a rather attractive young trainee WPC sitting next to him and...

A noise outside caught his attention. The van delivering goods to the shop next door had moved away and now a military vehicle was pulling into the space. Two soldiers jumped out and ran into the station.

"Good afternoon, Constable," said one of them. "I'm Captain Saunders." He waved his hand in the direction of the man behind him. "This here is Sergeant Patterson. We'd like to speak with Mrs. Maine. Is she still here?"

The officer smiled, but Simmonds noted it wasn't warm and friendly. It was indifferent – the kind of smile that could be turned on and off like a tap.

Unsure, the constable eyed the soldiers up and down. He had no real reason to doubt them. They hadn't been rude – just rather indifferent. He was on the point of informing them that Mrs. Maine was in the kitchen, when he saw a large truck pull up behind the soldier's vehicle. The driver came to a sudden halt, causing the canvas at the back to swing open and reveal several army personnel.

Someone inside swiftly pulled the canvas back into place, but not before Simmonds caught a glimpse of the men inside. He saw that some were dressed in outfits resembling space suits. They also carried headgear complete with visors and gas masks. Others held what looked like rapid-fire guns.

"We're waiting Constable! Where is Mrs. Maine?" The captain spoke again, but this time his tone was harsh and the thin smile had disappeared.

Simmonds' mind was racing. Something wasn't quite right. Come to think of it, how could they know Mrs. Maine was here? Manners hadn't been able to relay anything because there was no signal. Or was there? Glancing towards the radio, he recalled the strange hissing sound and the regular beeps. Had someone been jamming the radio, while listening in to the calls?

Looking back out of the window, Simmonds saw there was no other car in view. Mrs. Maine must have parked further up the road. Out of the corner of his eye, he saw the captain take a step towards him. Obviously he was growing impatient.

Simmonds knew he couldn't stall any longer; he was going to have to say something. "She left about ten minutes ago," he said, glancing at the clock. He tried to sound calm, though he could hear his heart pounding in his chest.

"Did she say where she was going?"

"Back to the farm, I think. But she may have changed her mind and gone elsewhere." Simmonds laughed, still trying to sound matter of fact. "Women do that, don't they? Sergeant Gilmore often says that his wife..."

"I see," the captain interrupted, his tone was gruff. Clearly he was not interested in what Gilmore said. "Not really very helpful."

"No!" Simmonds gulped.

After a brief pause, the soldiers turned to leave and Simmonds breathed a sigh of relief. But at that moment, Sarah and the children burst into the office. Hearing voices, she thought the constable had finally managed to get through to his sergeant on the radio and was receiving some news. At the sound of the kitchen door opening, the soldiers swung around.

"Who's this?" Sergeant Patterson seemed to have found his tongue.

"This is my wife and our two daughters." Simmonds answered before Sarah could utter a word. He stared at Sarah, desperately hoping she wouldn't deny it.

"Mummy, when can I show Daddy my pictures?" Josie tugged at her mother. She held up her drawings.

"Come over here then, sweetheart and show them to me." Constable Simmonds slowly bent down and held out his hand. "Let me see what you've drawn today."

Josie held back and looked up at her mother, this man was not her daddy.

Simmonds glanced at the two men and smiled. "She's shy when there are strangers around, though she's quite a little madam when we're on our own." He hoped they wouldn't notice the tiny beads of sweat beginning to form on his forehead.

Sarah looked at the soldiers and then at Simmonds. Why had he said she was his wife? These were the military, for God's sake. They were here for the good of the nation; they could help her to find her husband. Yet the constable seemed very agitated. Was there a reason for this charade?

"Go ahead, Josie," she said at last, making a point of mentioning the child's name for Simmonds' benefit. She pushed her daughter towards the young constable. "Show him your pictures."

Taking the pictures from Josie, Simmonds carefully tucked the one showing the green light under the more innocent drawing of a cow in a field. "Good isn't it? I think she'll make a great artist one day."

Sarah smiled at the soldiers. "My husband is so proud of both his daughters. This here is Becky. Are you family men?"

"The army is our family!" The captain's tone was brusque. He turned to his companion. "Come on sergeant, we'll go down to the farm and catch up with Mrs. Maine there. Thank you, Constable."

Nodding to Sarah, the captain turned and left the room. After a final glance around the office, the sergeant followed.

"Will you explain to me why I gave up the chance of asking those two soldiers to find my husband?" Sarah demanded once the men were out of earshot.

"I wasn't happy with their attitude." Simmonds avoided her gaze.

Still carrying Becky, Sarah strode across to the young constable. "You weren't happy with their attitude. What's that supposed to mean?" Her voice was harsh and sarcastic. "They're in the army aren't they? Attitude is their middle name."

"I'm sorry, but..." Simmonds paused as he handed the pictures back to Josie. "No! I'll be damned if I'm sorry. For a start they walked in here and asked to speak to Mrs. Maine. They didn't ask me for directions to your farm, nor even if I knew who you were. They asked to speak to you by name. Somehow they knew you were here. My guess is they were listening in on our radio; they were probably jamming it so the sergeant couldn't get his message through."

"But why?" Sarah exclaimed. "Why would they want to do that? You're imagining things."

"I don't know why. But if you can give me another reasonable explanation, I'll buy it. Believe me, I don't want to be mixed up in all this."

Glancing out of the window, he saw the truck follow the captain's vehicle down the road. They were heading in the direction of the Maine's farm.

Sarah hesitated. "I don't know... but there must be something. Perhaps Sergeant Gilmore and Constable Manners met up with them and told them what I'd said. They may have wanted to verify my story and came here merely to talk to me." She folded her arms. "The sergeant probably told them I was waiting at the police station."

"Then why didn't they go with the sergeant and take a look in the valley? Together, they could have checked out your story and come back here to make their report to all concerned."

Simmonds waited for her reply. When she didn't answer he continued. "I saw men inside the truck. They were wearing some sort of protective gear; similar to the type astronauts wear. Can you honestly believe they were simply driving around the countryside on the off chance that they might see people with their skin melting and dripping onto the road? No! I don't think so. They came prepared. As I see it, they already know there's been some catastrophe out here and are listening to all calls in the area for fear of the news getting out."

"I can't believe it. Your imagination's running away with you." Sarah gazed at the constable.

She knew he hadn't been in the force very long. He probably hoped he would be solving crimes in the Met after finishing his training. Finding himself in the sleepy town of Wooler, where criminals were very thin on the ground, must have been most disappointing for a man with his ambitions.

"Look, I didn't want to tell you this," Simmonds had to make her understand his concerns. "But they also had guns. There's a lot more to these men being here right now, than you think."

"Are you out of your mind? Why on earth would they need guns?" Sarah couldn't believe this was happening. "All I want to do is find Pete. I'm no threat to anyone."

"Yes you are." The constable tried to explain it to her. "Don't you see? You know what happened out there, you saw it all. Last night there was some sort of bright green light in the sky followed by a cloud. This morning you go out and find someone lying around in the road with their skin melting. You don't need to be a rocket scientist to realise the two are connected. People in high places won't want you to spread it around."

"High places, you mean the government? I don't believe it."

"Why not?" asked Simmonds. "Who but the government could instruct the army to seek you out using any method at their disposal?"

"Do you think they want to kill me?" Sarah's face turned pale.

"No! Of course not." The constable was quick to reassure her, even though he still believed it was an option. What better way to silence her, than to kill her, and him for that matter, especially if they thought he and Sergeant Gilmore had believed her story?

He softened his tone. "But they might want to take you into custody and question you about what you know. That way they could stop you from passing on what you'd seen. Look here! I think we should get away from here while we still have the chance. It won't be long before those men reach your farm and find you aren't there after all. They're bound to come back here."

"But what about the sergeant and the constable – they may have found Pete. All three could be on their way back here right now." Sarah didn't want to go anywhere without knowing what had happened to her husband.

Simmonds was doubtful they would ever be back. He felt sure Pete was dead and as for Sergeant Gilmore and Manners, they'd had more than enough time to assess the situation and come back here. Something must have happened to them. They could already be in military custody or they might even be dead. However he decided not to mention any of that.

"Mrs. Maine, please listen. When they come back and find we've gone, they'll come looking for us. They know we'll spread the word."

Sarah didn't hear. Her whole world had suddenly been turned upside down. Yesterday, everything had been normal. Pete had gone out to work on the farm just as he always did. Now, a mere twenty-four hours later, she didn't know if he was alive or dead, while one of his best friends was lying in the road with his melted flesh in a pool around his skeleton. She shuddered, would she ever be able to rid herself of that awful sight?

And then there were the others. From what she had seen through the binoculars, the families in the valley looked to be in the same condition. Poor Tom. He had gone to find his wife Martha. Were they both lying somewhere in the valley? She thought of the people in the farms and villages on the other side of Top Meadow. They must all have been affected too. How far had the light travelled? Could it have crossed the border into Scotland? She buried her face in her hands, trying to block out such terrible thoughts.

"Mrs. Maine!" Simmonds raised his voice. "Think of your children; we've got to get them away from here! If I'm wrong, then Sergeant Gilmore and the others will come looking for us. But in the meantime I truly believe we should get away from here as quickly as possible."

"What about the people here in Wooler? Shouldn't we tell them to move away?" said Sarah, trying to take control of herself. "We can't simply leave without warning them of the dangers in the valley."

"We must!" He softened his tone. "As long as they don't know anything about it, they'll be okay. It's only people like us, who know what happened last night that need to escape."

As he spoke, Simmonds made his way through to the kitchen. Gathering some food from the small fridge, he began to stuff it into a bag.

"Besides," he called out. "The army won't let anyone go down into the valley. They'll make up some cock and bull story about how there's a gas leak or something similar and tell everyone they should stay away until the danger has passed. That'll buy them time to clear up the mess."

Sarah looked up sharply. "Might I remind you that my husband may be part of 'the mess'!"

"I'm sorry," Simmonds said, coming back into the office. "I don't mean to be cruel or without feeling for your husband, but right now we've got to think about what's best for us – especially the children."

Sarah hesitated. She still wasn't convinced. As she saw it, the constable was jumping to the wrong conclusions. The army didn't rush in and take people into custody like that, nor did the government try to cover things up. This was England. Such things didn't happen here in dear old England.

Simmonds placed his hand on her shoulder. "Your husband would want you to take his children to safety. I know, because that's what I'd want if I had a family."

Sarah didn't want to leave without Pete. Tears ran down her cheeks as she looked up at the young constable. Damn the man, he was right! If her husband could speak to her right now, he would tell her to do anything she could to save herself and their children.

Simmonds handed her his handkerchief.

"Can't I phone my father?" she whispered, drying her eyes. "He'd know what to do."

"No!" Simmonds answered quickly. "Haven't you listened to a word I've said? If they're listening in on the police radio then they'll have the phones tapped as well. Even mobile phones aren't safe to use. We need to get well away from here before we even think of contacting anyone."

This was the age of technology. The authorities could do anything. They might already have a satellite pinpointing the small police station in Wooler, watching for them to make a move. But he didn't think so – not yet anyway. They still had a little time. Nevertheless, they would have to move fast.

Sarah sank into a chair. She recalled the interference on the line earlier that morning when she had been talking to Martha. Had they been listening in to her conversation even then?

"You could stay here," she said at last. "You'd be alright on your own. The military would believe you if you said you had no idea where I had gone."

"No. They'd never really be sure I wasn't covering for you. Besides, I can't leave you and the children to fend for yourselves. I'll come with you." He laughed as another thought occurred to him. "Anyway, a few words with the locals and the captain would soon learn I'm not married."

"Perhaps we could try making our way to London. Once we think it's safe, we could take a chance and call my father, or even my Uncle Ronald. He's in the government. He could speak to someone and call off the military." Sarah was thinking quickly. If she could get her children to safety, she would then be in a position to return and search for Pete. She would never truly believe he was dead until she saw his body with her own eyes – but how would she ever recognise him?

Simmonds wasn't sure about using the phones anywhere. But he didn't want to dampen her spirits, not now she had agreed to move away from the area, albeit very reluctantly.

"I'll get a couple of blankets from Gilmore's house and anything else I think might be useful," he said. "Thank goodness Mrs. Gilmore's away."

"Perhaps there are a few things in the sergeant's food cupboard that might be of use. Tinned stuff, I mean," said Sarah, looking into the bag Simmonds had packed. "All this food from the fridge is perishable."

"Yes, good idea. I'll take a look," he replied. "But we must hurry; we need to get away quickly."

It wasn't long before Simmonds came back with blankets and extra food. "That's all we have time for," he said. "We must get away now before the soldiers come back. We've wasted enough time already. We'll take my car; it's an estate model, so there'll be more room. Fortunately I filled the tank on my way here this morning, so there's no need to stop at the petrol station."

They loaded up the car. Simmonds unbolted Becky's seat from Sarah's car and fastened it into his own.

"Right then, Mrs. Maine, you get the children settled in the back. If you'd prefer, you can sit there with them. I suppose we have to take the dog?"

Betts was still sitting patiently in Sarah's car.

"Of course we do! Betts is part of our family. The dog goes too!"

71

"I had a feeling you were going to say that." Simmonds grinned. "Okay, she can squeeze in beside the bags of food behind the back seats."

"Thank you, Constable Simmonds. As for myself, I'll sit up front with you. The children will probably fall asleep once we get going. This has been quite a morning for them – for us all."

She instructed Betts to jump into the constable's car.

"I think as we're going to be travelling together, you should call me Andy."

She smiled. "In that case, my name is Sarah."

It was the first time Andy had seen her smile and he noted she was a very attractive young woman.

"Well, Sarah, I think we should be on our way. Perhaps it would be best if we used the unclassified roads, heaven knows there're plenty of them around here. They're rather uneven, but the upside is, we might manage to get through without being stopped by the military." He looked down at his uniform. "I think I should make time to stop off at my home and get into something more casual. This uniform is a dead give away."

"Okay," she said, eyeing him up and down. "But just grab some clothes. You can change further down the road. We'll look conspicuous if you leave us sitting outside your house for too long. We haven't come this far to be stopped by some inquisitive neighbour who thinks I'm leaving my husband to run off with one of the town's young constables."

Believing Sarah had a point, he only took a couple of minutes to grab some clothes from his house before running back to the car.

"From my bedroom window, I could see army trucks approaching the town," he yelled, clambering into the car. "They're on their way back. We've got to move quickly. They can't have seen us yet, so we still have a chance to get to the forest road, before they reach the station."

Looking behind, Sarah couldn't see anything. For a moment she felt unsure. Was she doing the right thing? She only had Andy's word the army would take her into custody rather than help her find Pete.

"This is it, Sarah. Tighten your seat belt, we're on our way."

He put his foot down and the car sped towards the edge of the small town. "We should be alright once we get onto the forest road."

She knew the road to be narrow and winding, with tall trees on both sides. It would give excellent cover for several miles before they finally came to open fields.

"Yes," she said, quietly.

Andy glanced at her. "I'm right about this, Sarah. I'm absolutely certain we're doing the right thing. We have to let people know what's happened out here."

Sarah thought of her husband Pete and forced back the tears. She desperately hoped he hadn't suffered the same fate as Dave and was lying dead somewhere.

"Yes, we must alert someone," she said, at last. "But if you think everyone is against us, who do we trust?"

"We'll find someone," he promised. "But for now, we must concentrate on the road."

On reaching the forest road, Andy pulled up and looked behind. So far, they weren't being followed, but it wouldn't take long for the army to put two and two together once they found the police station was empty.

Turning back to face the road ahead, he slipped the car into first gear and began to make his way along the narrow, winding track.

CHAPTER SIX

Charles Hammond grunted. He had been in a deep slumber when the persistent ring of the telephone had awoken him. Groping around in the dark, he switched on his bedside light; wincing at the sudden glare. Shielding his eyes, he glanced at the clock. It was only 4am! Who on earth was calling at this hour? Didn't they know what time it was?

Still half asleep, he picked up the phone. "Hammond speaking," he mumbled, wondering whether the caller might be his junior assistant. Being keen, the young man often rang late in the evening with some new idea he had stumbled upon. But four o'clock in the morning – that was taking it too far. "For goodness sake, Alan, don't you know what time it is? You really need to get yourself a life son. Perhaps then I'll be able to get some sleep."

Closing his eyes, he flopped back onto the pillow. If he kept his eyes shut, he might fall asleep again quite easily. He had been having a pleasant dream. He and Irene were cruising in the Caribbean on a fabulous yacht and…

The voice on the other end of the phone yelled something down the line, causing Charles to sit bolt upright.

"Ronald! What's that you say? What emergency? What the hell are you talking about? When did it happen?" He fired questions at his brother-in-law.

Irene sat up in bed. "Is that my brother? Where is he? Doesn't he realise what time it is here in England?"

Charles put his hand over the phone. "Hush, Irene! He *is* in England. This is serious." He turned back to the phone. "Sorry, Ron, that was Irene. Carry on."

"I don't know the full details," Ronald felt uncomfortable. Why hadn't Charles been informed? It was his department for God's sake! "But I gather whatever it was, happened last night. I only know because someone from Number Ten has been on the phone to inform me that my breakfast appointment with the Prime Minister has been called off due to an emergency in your department. Obviously I tried to prise a few details from him, but I couldn't get anything further. I think he felt he had said too much already. That's why I rang your home. I was surprised when you answered. I honestly thought you'd be over at the lab. I suppose I was being nosey really, but I was going to ask Irene what..."

"Last night!" Charles broke in, yelling into the phone. "Why the hell wasn't I informed before now? And come to think of it, why am I hearing about an emergency in my department from the Foreign Secretary? Where's Rick? Does he know about it?"

Irene's stomach turned over as she watched the colour drain from her husband's face. "What's happened?" She tugged frantically at his arm. "Tell me, what's going on!"

"Please be quiet, Irene," Charles snapped. "I'll tell you in a minute." He turned back to the phone. "Go on Ronald."

"I really don't know anything." Ronald swallowed hard. "I only rang to ask Irene for an update. I had no idea you didn't know about it." He wished he hadn't called. All he wanted to do now was get off the phone. He gave a hollow laugh. "Maybe it's not as bad as I thought. I could be making a mountain out of a molehill."

"Don't be an idiot Ronald! Of course it's bad!" Charles boomed. "Why else would the Prime Minister have someone call you in the middle of the night simply to cancel a meeting? This is outrageous! I should have been notified immediately." He climbed out of bed. "I'll go to the laboratory right away."

Charles slammed down the phone and strode across to the wardrobe. "I don't believe it. Why didn't someone ring me last night?"

"What is it?" Irene wrung her hands. "What's happened? For goodness sake, tell me what's going on." She climbed out of bed and ran over to her husband.

Charles was pulling everything out of the wardrobe. "Where are my shirts? Why is it I can never find a damn thing in this house?" he bellowed. "Is it too much to ask to have my shirts in the same place for two days running?"

Irene moved Charles to one side. Reaching into the wardrobe, she pulled out a clean white shirt. "They're all here, exactly where they always are. Now for goodness sake, tell me what's happened."

Over the years, she had watched her husband's lovely brown hair turn grey prematurely and the twinkle in his eye disappear due to his work at the laboratory. But more recently she had noticed lines of worry developing around his eyes and the furrows in his brow digging more deeply with every passing day. Now his once handsome face drooped in a hangdog expression. He had also lost weight, too much by her reckoning. He seemed to be wasting away – a man growing old before his time. Yet she had never seen him looking so tired and worried as he did tonight. What could possibly cause such anguish?

"There's been an emergency at the laboratory," said Charles, at last.

"I gathered that much. What emergency? What did my brother say?"

"Ronald doesn't know much about it. He rang here expecting to speak to you. He thought I would be at the laboratory." Charles thumped his fist on the dressing table. "Why the hell wasn't I informed? And where's Rick? He was at the laboratory when I left. He said he wanted to finish writing up some notes before leaving."

"Does he know about this emergency?" asked Irene. "Surely if he knew he would have..."

"I have no idea, Irene!" Charles pulled on his shirt. "I don't know anything!" He thrust his hand towards the phone. "You try ringing him while I'm getting dressed. Try his direct line at the laboratory and if there's no answer, try my office. He may have gone in there to check something out."

Irene's hand trembled as she dialled the numbers. "There's no reply at either number," she said at last. "Surely if Rick wasn't there someone else would answer your phone."

"You're right! Someone should have answered. What the hell is going on down there? Try Rick's home." Charles paced the floor, desperately trying to button his shirt. "Damn this shirt! What's the matter with it?"

Irene rang Rick's home number, praying he would pick up the phone, but there was no reply there either. Even the answer phone didn't respond.

"What do you think has happened?" she asked, putting down the receiver.

"How the hell do I know? I haven't got time to speculate, but it must be something serious for..."

Just then the telephone rang. Startled, Irene looked towards her husband. Charles strode across the room and picked up the receiver. "Hello," he barked down the line. "Not now! I have to..."

"This is the Prime Minister's office." A voice interrupted. "The Prime Minister wants to see you at Number Ten right now."

"But I was about to go to the laboratory. Can't it wait until I find out...?"

"No, I'm afraid not. The Prime Minister is waiting."

The tone was cold. Charles felt like a small boy being summoned by the headmaster.

"Very well. Please inform him I'm on my way." Charles slammed down the phone and looked at Irene. "The Prime Minister wants to see me. Obviously the man is going to ask me for a report and I've absolutely no idea what's going on. He won't even wait until I've called into the laboratory." Pulling on his socks, he groped around the bottom of the wardrobe for his shoes.

Irene sank onto the bed. A dreadful feeling of foreboding fell over her. "This has got to be really serious if the Prime Minister wants to see you at this hour."

"Of course it's bloody serious, I don't need you to tell me that," Charles retorted. "I'd already figured it out for myself."

He sighed and shook his head, feeling guilty at his outburst. It wasn't Irene's fault and he shouldn't take it out on her. He sat down next to his wife. "I'm sorry," he said, softly. He took her hand. "But I'm working in the dark here. I simply don't know why someone didn't call me if there was a problem."

Irene kissed her husband. "I understand." She patted his hand. "You'd better be off. It won't do to keep the Prime Minister waiting."

"What would I do without you, Irene?" Charles smiled. "I couldn't have gone on all these years if I hadn't had you to come home to."

He put on his coat. "I'll give you a ring as soon as I know what's going on." He kissed his wife before going downstairs and out of the front door.

****

The silence in the Cabinet Room at Number Ten was broken only by the Prime Minister drumming his fingers on the table. Robert Turner, a well-built, dark haired man, was unaccustomed to being kept waiting. He twisted around in his chair and looked up at the clock on the mantelpiece, checking the time against his watch.

"It really is too bad. Where is the man?" he grumbled. "I think that..." He looked up sharply as the door was flung open.

A bleary-eyed man, looking most put out at being dragged from his bed at such an ungodly hour, ushered Charles forward. "Sir Charles Hammond."

"I'm sorry to have kept you waiting, Prime Minister. I came as quickly as I could." Charles looked around to thank the man who had escorted him to the Cabinet Room, but he had gone. Back to bed presumably, where any God fearing man should be at this time of the morning.

He turned back to the small group of men seated around the large boat shaped table. The Prime Minister was in his normal chair: his back to the fireplace. Brian Tate, Secretary of State for Defence, was on his right. A thin-faced man, with hollow cheeks, which always gave the impression he was sucking on a lemon. Charles nodded to him. He recalled having had dealings with this man before. A cunning piece of work if ever there was one.

Glancing around the table, he noted that a sprinkling of the Prime Minister's devoted ministers had been hauled in. Charles wasn't really surprised. Where would Robert be without his spin-doctors?

Alan Crisp, Tate's personal assistant, was also present. He was a short, stout man with a bloated face and small bead-like eyes. His face had the strange habit of turning bright red when he wasn't getting his own way. He was a slimy character: always ferreting around the laboratory, pretending to know more than he did. He was known as Tate's pet poodle. All these men looked as though they had dressed in a hurry, obviously they too, had been hauled from their beds.

However, at the far end of the table were two high ranking military officers. Charles had never met them before. In contrast to the others around the table, they looked alert and immaculately turned out. Despite the seriousness of the situation, Charles hid a smile. Didn't the military ever sleep?

"Yes! Well, now you're here, Charles, perhaps you would care to bring us up to speed on this emergency." The Prime Minister's tone was stinging. Stroking his beard, he sat back in his chair and waited for an explanation.

Charles felt uncomfortable as Robert Turner's eyes bore into him. "I'm afraid I don't know anything about it myself yet, sir. I had only heard of the problem a few moments before your office rang."

"Problem! Problem!" Robert Turner leaned forward in his chair. "Oh I think it is a little more serious than a mere problem Sir Charles! Unless of course, someone in the Cabinet has overreacted." He narrowed his eyes and peered around the table at his colleagues before looking back at Charles. "Nevertheless, I was awoken in the early hours of this morning to be told a major disaster had occurred. In fact, I was given to understand it was the most dangerous catastrophe this country has ever encountered. I was also informed the incident originated from a department of which you are the head and yet you calmly sit there and tell me you know nothing about it." He slammed his fist down onto the table. "Perhaps you would care to explain to us how this is possible."

Charles couldn't answer. He still had no idea what the disaster was.

"We're waiting, Mr. Hammond." Sitting back in his chair, the Prime Minister folded his arms. "I'm sure we'll all be fascinated by what you have to tell us."

"Prime Minister, it's exactly as I said. I was not informed of any disaster. When I left the laboratory last evening, everything was working normally. If there had been the slightest hint of trouble, then naturally I would never have left the building. I really can't imagine why my staff didn't call me at the first sign of trouble."

"I see," said the Prime Minister. "It strikes me you're not in full control of your staff." His tone held a note of sarcasm. "Then I suppose I'll have to tell you what we know. Though I'm afraid it's precious little."

He went on to reveal how there had been an incident at the plant in Northumberland. "It appears the main container imploded. My informants say it will have caused untold damage, but I'm sure you are far more aware of the consequences than I. Perhaps now that you know what has happened, you can give us the correct course of action. Naturally we'll have to work quickly, but more importantly, very quietly. We must inform as few people as possible. This is a strictly need to know policy."

He glanced around the table. "Gentlemen, I'm sure you don't need me to tell you that if this gets out there will be full-scale panic, not only in this country, but around the world." Looking back at Charles he continued. "Now, what we need to know from you is, what can we expect? What are the full implications of the experiments you and your team have been carrying out?"

For a moment Charles was speechless. His mind was racing. An implosion! Oh my God! That would have caused the container to rupture, allowing the contents to escape. The very thought filled him with utmost horror and he tried to quell the sickness rising in his throat. It was the worst thing that could possibly have happened.

His heart pounded. From what Ronald had said earlier, he knew the problem was serious, but he never guessed it would be something on this scale. This was his worst nightmare.

"But that's impossible," he said at last, his voice almost a whisper. "There are several safeguards in operation. I supervised their installation myself. It was I who insisted they should be fitted in the first place."

"What form do these safeguards take?" asked the Prime Minister.

"They're designed to detect a problem in the early stages and close down the whole programme." Charles spoke mechanically. In his mind, he was still trying to work out what could have gone wrong. "With the programme shut down, Trojan would come to a halt. The safeguards are foolproof. Nothing can go wrong. Once they are switched on they can't be switched off without the appropriate codes…"

It was then it struck him. Sarah! His lovely daughter and her family lived only a few miles from the plant in Northumberland. Until that moment, his mind had been focused on how such a thing could have happened, but now the full significance hit home.

"Oh my God, no!" he uttered, sinking his head into his hands. What had become of Sarah, Pete and their children?

"Pull yourself together, Hammond! This is not the time to go weak at the knees," said the Prime Minister, brusquely. "For God's sake man, Trojan was your project. Working in chemical warfare you must have been aware that despite your safeguards, there was always a chance of something like this happening. You must tell us what to expect. Even as we speak, the military are preparing to go up to Northumberland to clean up your mess. But they must be ready for all eventualities."

He gestured towards the two generals. "That's why they're here. They need to know what they're dealing with. Tell us exactly what will have happened up there."

Furious, Charles slowly lifted his head and glared at the Prime Minister.

"*My* mess!" he exclaimed. Rising to his feet, he slammed his fist down onto the table. "You dare to call this my mess! Damn you, damn you to hell Prime Minister; this is your mess, not mine. Yes, I was in charge of the

Project, but it was you and those around you, who asked for it in the first place."

"Aren't you forgetting yourself...?" Robert Turner began, icily.

But Charles wasn't finished. "You politicians are all the same. Never content with what we as a nation have already, you always want more. You stand up at your conferences and tell the world they should rid themselves of weapons. As I recall, you even signed a treaty to that effect. But the bottom line is, you had to have something above and beyond what other nations have." He gestured to the ministers around the table. "You all wanted something just that little bit more terrifying – more evil, more destructive. Well now, Prime Minister, you have it."

He paused and looked down towards the officers at the end of the table.

"You want to know what to expect? I'll damn well tell you! Last night, when the container imploded, a huge green ball of light will have escaped and risen high above the power station. It will have hung in the night sky, shining so brightly that anyone looking at it will have been forced to shield their eyes or else be blinded. The rays, reaching out for several miles, will have charred and burned the skin of all those caught up in them. People and animals alike will have writhed in agony."

Ignoring a gasp of horror from one of the ministers, Charles continued. "But that gentlemen, was only the beginning. The light will have disappeared after a few seconds, only to be replaced by a green cloud. A cloud filled with a gas so horrific, that all your soldiers will find are skeletons."

He sighed and shook his head. For a moment he felt unable to go on. "What they will find," he repeated. "Are skeletons of people who were once human beings. People like you, people who might have been related to you, people, but for the grace of God, could have been you. The skeletons will be lying in pools of slime: a dreadful, thick, pink and black slime. This slime will be the melted skin, flesh and organs of anyone, who had been exposed to this cloud. Because that is what this gas does. It melts flesh." He thumped his fist down on the table once more. "Generals I ask you, can you really prepare your men for something like that?"

He was about to sit down, but changed his mind. "There's something else you must tell your men. Under no circumstances should they touch the remains of the bodies or the slime without protective clothing. I cannot emphasize this strongly enough. If even the slightest drop of slime touches any part of their body, they'll find themselves in exactly the same condition as the victims already lying there. Also, at this stage we're not sure whether a gas will linger around the slime; therefore it'll be necessary to wear breathing apparatus until you're sure it's safe. I'm afraid there is no antidote."

He looked around the table. "Have I made myself perfectly clear or is there anything else I can tell you?"

As there was no reply, Charles sat down. He ran his fingers through his hair; he felt sick to his stomach. Was his family lying there alongside those other poor unfortunate souls?

The ministers looked at each other uneasily. None of them had expected this. While it was fine for something of this calibre to be unleashed on the enemies of the British Isles, it was a different matter when it dropped into their own backyard. In the planning stages, the Prime Minister and his Defence Secretary had made the whole project sound essential to the nation's defence. Agreeing something should be done to keep Britain at the top of the defence league they had all gone along with the idea, fully accepting the Prime Minister's assurances that nothing could go wrong. But now it had.

Very shortly there was to be a General Election. The public was already disenchanted with some of the government's latest policies, if this were to get out it would be the last straw. But there was more to it than that. As ministers who had endorsed such a weapon, it wasn't simply a matter of being voted out of office for four or five years. Their whole career in politics would be over. They would be scorned, humiliated... it had happened before – a different situation perhaps, but always the same reaction.

"Yes, I see," said the Prime Minister, at last. He shuffled uneasily in his chair. He looked at the ashen faces of his colleagues, he was well aware of their thoughts. However, there was a slim chance they could get away with it, but they would need to keep silent. This whole business must be hushed up at all costs.

"Tell me, is there a chance the army will find anyone alive?" Robert Turner stroked his neatly trimmed beard thoughtfully.

"Yes, it is possible," said Charles. "Though many may have seen the light, those outside of its range would not have been harmed. As for the cloud of gas." He shrugged and thought for a moment. "Theoretically it only stretches as far as the rays of light. But yes, I believe there might be a

few people still alive, providing they haven't touched any of the bodies."
He desperately hoped his own family would be among any who may have survived.

But this was bad news to the Prime Minister. He didn't want anyone to be in a position to tell the world of what had happened. He could already hear his colleagues mumbling to each other. He would have to do something drastic to get out of this one.

If luck was on his side, everyone who had seen anything last night, would be dead anyway. It was only natural anyone seeing such a bright light in the sky would have gone to investigate. Hopefully, in an effort to help the dying, they too would have been struck down. Nevertheless, he had this nagging fear some might have survived. Should that be the case they would need to be silenced. An idea began to form in his mind.

"Mr. Hammond?"

The voice came from one of the officers at the other end of the table. Until then, neither of the two generals had moved a muscle: their faces totally without expression.

Charles looked up. "Yes? You have something to say?"

"I'm General John Bainbridge. Mr. Hammond, if even touching this... slime, can melt the skin... flesh, whatever, won't it melt through the special suits our men will be wearing?"

"Yes, it will – eventually," said Charles. "It will have melted the clothing of the victims in Northumberland very quickly, as their garments would have been thin and given no protection to the bodies. Sadly we know very little about Trojan at the moment. However, wearing protective clothing such as the army uses, will buy your men a little time. I gather the suits are loosely fitted and made of a very strong, thick material, therefore should something come into contact with the slime, the man will have a few seconds to remove the offending piece of clothing before any real damage can be done."

"I see," said General Bainbridge, thoughtfully. "Perhaps you can also tell us how we are to dispose of the... remains. What are we supposed to do with them? I presume we can't just go ahead and bury them."

"No, you can't," answered Charles. "Not in the normal sense anyway. I'm afraid the best I can suggest is that you dig deep pits and line them with a thick layer of concrete. When every single skeleton, together with the slime, has been placed in the pits, they'll need to be topped with another layer of concrete. They must not under any circumstances, be disturbed for several centuries, unless we come up with some form of antidote in the meantime. I appreciate that collecting the remains will be difficult. Your men will need to be armed with the stoutest shovels you can find. The slime will stick to the roads, which means that all the affected roads will need to be resurfaced with a thick layer of concrete. As for those bodies found in the fields, the same applies. Though concreting over fields and grasslands will be even more difficult. I do not envy you the task."

"Can't the bodies and slime simply be burned where they lie?" asked the Prime Minister. "Surely that would be a more simple method?"

"Yes it would," answered Charles. "But burning the skeletons and slime will give off smoke. This smoke will no doubt be filled with the same gas that caused the trouble in the first place." He shrugged. "Need I say more?"

There was a long silence, broken only by the voice of the second general. "Can I ask a question? I'm General Ian Lewis."

Charles nodded. "Go ahead."

"What I want to know is, why on earth didn't you start working on an antidote once the production of Trojan was underway? Something we could have poured onto the bodies or should I say skeletons, to make them safe to handle. Why leave it until we're faced with a catastrophe such as this before thinking about something to halt the process?"

"A good question and if only it were that easy," said Charles. "We scientists are always asking for the time to do just that. Of course we should have been working on an antidote." He paused and looked towards the Prime Minister. "But when we try to warn our masters about the risks of something like this, they don't want to know about antidotes and they shut their ears. We're told to carry on because they want results. None of you really understand what you're dealing with when you seek these kinds of chemicals. All you see is a weapon – a weapon powerful enough to knock out a million people in one swoop. In the face of that, antidotes have to wait. Yet they are so important. Not only for the reasons laid out by General Lewis, but it could have allowed us to clean up the land for future generations."

"So is there nothing we can do if one of our men comes into contact with the – slime?" General Bainbridge asked.

"No." Charles paused. "Though you could try cutting off the offending limb," he added, thoughtfully.

"This is not the time for jokes!" The general was appalled.

"I wasn't joking," said Charles, calmly. He looked around the table. "Is there anything else you would like to know?"

The Prime Minister's allies shook their heads. They had been stunned into silence. Even the Defence Secretary had heard enough for one night.

Charles nodded, but then a thought occurred to him and he looked down the table towards the generals.

"It would be most helpful in our quest for an antidote if you were able to collect samples of the melted flesh." He paused. "I know it's a lot to ask and it won't be easy, but it could be very useful. You see until now we haven't actually seen Trojan in action, so this is a first. You can collect some glass phials at the laboratory."

"Glass?" General Bainbridge raised his eyebrows.

Sir Charles nodded. "One of the things we do know about Trojan is that glass is unaffected by the weapon. The only problem is, glass is very easily broken. Therefore once your men have collected the samples, the phials will need to be treated with the utmost care. I'll see to it that they're supplied in a suitably padded, secure metal case."

"Well, Sir Charles, as always you've been most helpful and I'm certain the generals will do everything possible to get the samples you've requested." The Prime Minister smiled warmly. "We're all very grateful to you for spelling it out to us so clearly. I think that just about sums it up." He turned to the others around the table. "I'm sure Sir Charles would like to get off to his laboratory now and check out exactly what has gone wrong."

Charles hadn't failed to notice the change in Robert Turner's tone. It made him suspicious. Earlier the Prime Minister had been curt and abrupt. Suddenly he seemed almost friendly. But it also occurred to him that the Prime Minister was anxious to be rid of him. However, he didn't dwell on it. Robert Turner was well known for turning on the charm when it suited him best. All Charles wanted to do now was get out of here and telephone his daughter. If there were no reply, he would speak to the generals. Perhaps their men could look out for Sarah and her family.

Charles found himself alone outside in the hall. The man, who had been on duty at the front door when he arrived, seemed to have disappeared for the moment. And the disagreeable flunky, who had shown him to the Cabinet Room, was probably sleeping soundly in his bed, totally oblivious to what had happened to all those people miles away in the North East. But even if he knew, would he really care?

Charles had almost reached the door, when he realised he had forgotten his briefcase. He recalled putting it down on the floor by his chair, somehow he must have kicked it under the table.

Normally he was very careful about leaving his documents lying around, they could so easily fall into the wrong hands. But tonight, all he could think about was what had happened up there in the north of England. How all those people had been killed – murdered, and how his only daughter and her family could very well be among them.

Silently, he turned and hurried back along the corridor. He opened the first of the soundproofed double doors of the Cabinet Office and was about reach for the handle of the second, when he found he had left it slightly ajar. The Prime Minister was speaking and out of politeness, Charles decided to wait until he had finished.

"You all realise how important it is to keep this disaster to ourselves." The Prime Minister's voice rang out, he was unaware anyone else was listening. But standing only a few feet away, Charles could hear every word.

"If there should be a leak, not only would we face a backlash from the electorate, but also from the world. Therefore it is imperative the disaster be kept quiet at all costs."

The Prime Minister paused. No doubt he was giving his Cabinet time to take onboard exactly what he had said.

Charles immediately recognised the voice of the Defence Secretary, who spoke next.

"Yes, I think we all understand the consequences if it were to become common knowledge, Prime Minister. But we can never really be certain that someone who saw anything won't spill the beans. Especially with the kind of money the newspapers would pay for a story like this." He laughed. "Why, I could even be tempted myself."

Charles understood what Brian was getting at. In today's society, money was everything. The Prime Minister must be living in cloud cuckoo land if he thought he could persuade people to keep quiet about something of this magnitude.

"Our political careers are at stake, Brian," Turner hissed. "If we don't keep our heads we'll lose everything. I'm sure you, like the rest of us gathered here, are enjoying the lifestyle being in government has afforded us."

"Yes, I'm sorry," said Brian. "I simply meant..."

"In that case," the Prime Minister, interrupted, coldly. "I think we're all agreed. In the interest of national security, no one who saw anything last night should be left in a position to pass on the information."

There was a brief pause, before the Prime Minister spoke again.

"General Bainbridge, General Lewis, I'm sure you both understand what I'm saying."

Charles, still listening at the door, could hardly believe his ears. He grabbed at the doorframe to steady himself as a wave of dizziness swept over him. The Prime Minister's message was clear. Anyone found alive was to be killed. Murdered! It was horrible. How could he be so...?

Charles recalled how Robert Turner had put himself forward as a man of the people. He had won the last election on the grounds his government would be honest and open: promising there would be no secrets, no cover-ups. How could the man be so false?

"I'm not sure I can agree with what you're proposing."

Charles perked up. He recognised the voice. It was Arthur Goodwin, one of Brian Turner's ministers. He was a man well known in Parliament for his integrity and for being unafraid to speak his mind.

"I really cannot bring myself to be a party to anything of this nature," he continued. "While I won't repeat anything I've heard in this room tonight, I want nothing further to do with it. Therefore, as I do not wish to hear any more, I will take my leave. Gentlemen, I bid you all goodnight – or perhaps I should say, good morning."

Good for you, thought Charles. He took out his handkerchief and mopped his brow. How could they all sit there and say nothing? How could anyone agree with what the Prime Minister had in mind? All those men in there, yet only Arthur Goodwin had the gumption to voice his feelings. He imagined the others nodding and agreeing with everything Turner said, all watching their own jobs. The sound of muffled footsteps approaching the door interrupted his thoughts and he panicked. There wasn't anywhere to hide. The best he could do was to take a few steps from the door and pretend he had only just returned to collect his briefcase.

The door opened and Arthur came out. He was surprised to see Charles, but quickly composing himself, he closed the door behind him.

Putting a finger to his lips, he took Charles by the arm and steered him a few steps from the door.

"How long have you been here?" he whispered.

"Long enough!" Charles couldn't lie. In any case, his face would give him away. Like Arthur, he was unaccustomed to lying. "I came back for my briefcase. I left it in there." He pointed towards the Cabinet Office. "I admit I heard most of what was being said and I'm appalled."

"If I were you," Arthur whispered. "I wouldn't let anyone know that you heard what was said." He glanced along the corridor. "Where's the Duty Officer? It wouldn't do for the two of us to be caught out here together."

Charles wasn't listening. He shook his head. "I simply can't understand how they can all go along with what the Prime Minister is saying. Anyone with the slightest doubt had the chance to speak up and walk out with you. Why didn't they?"

Arthur smiled. "Unlike me, they're all power hungry. That's what makes them willing to agree to whatever the Prime Minister says. They hope he'll never forget how they stood by him in a crisis." He paused and looked towards the door. "I don't crave power. I'm a politician because I want to make a difference. My constituents know I always do my best for them and never lie. In return I have their respect." He sighed. "I realise the Prime Minister only appointed me as a minister because my reputation for being an honest man made his government look good. However, after tonight he'll no doubt give some serious thought as to whether he can trust me to keep silent." He frowned. "This leads me to wonder why I was asked to attend tonight. My opinion wasn't sought when the Prime Minister first discussed Trojan."

"Will you?" asked Charles. "Stay silent, I mean."

Arthur glanced towards the door again.

"That's a tough one. If no one asks me outright about what went on, then yes I will. However if..." He shrugged. "But now we should go. If I were you, I would forget about the briefcase. The Prime Minister will have it sent on. I think you should go to your laboratory and find out what went on over there. It seems to me you have a few problems of your own. Firstly, why did no one call you? I think that's something you really need to check out."

Charles was puzzled. Did Arthur know something he didn't? "Are you trying to tell me something?"

Arthur shook his head. "My lips are sealed. I know nothing for certain. All I will say is, you should speak to Rick, but above all, watch your back."

There were footsteps further down the hall. The Duty Officer was returning to his post.

"You leave first. He still can't see me standing here. I'll wait until he's nearer before I follow you," whispered Arthur. He nodded towards the Cabinet Room. "They all know you left before me, someone may check up."

Charles nodded. He hadn't thought of that, but it made sense, they couldn't be too careful. "See you again sometime?" he whispered, as he began to move away. The intonation in his voice indicated it was a question rather than a statement.

"We'll work something out, but don't ring me." Arthur hesitated. "I often have lunch at Luigi's in Pall Mall. If you should need me, look for me there."

Outside Number Ten, Charles nodded to the policeman on duty. He had often thought how boring the constable's job must be. But on reflection, he wasn't so sure. At least the officer could go to bed with an easy conscience. He would never lie awake at night, counting the number of people who had died a horrible death because of one of his inventions.

Charles drove to his laboratory at high speed. Thankfully the London roads were not yet busy; it was still too early for commuter traffic. His mind was racing, turning over what Arthur had said. 'Watch your back' – what had he meant by that? Was someone out to get him?

And what else had he said? 'Speak to Rick'. That was it; 'speak to Rick'. He wondered about that. Was it possible Rick knew something he didn't? Charles was already aware Rick was a headstrong, impatient young man, but he didn't really believe he would do anything without consulting him first. Hadn't he always treated Rick like a son? He had even introduced him to his daughter, for God's sake.

In the past, he had hoped the two might marry. But that wasn't to be. Sarah had chosen Pete and become a farmer's wife up there in Northumberland – where this terrible thing had happened. Tears welled in his eyes blurring his vision, and he was forced to screech to a halt at a red light. A tramp was stumbling across the road. Charles hadn't seen the lights change until it was almost too late.

Clutching a wine bottle under his arm, the old man shook his fist as he passed the car. Breathing deeply, Charles wiped the tears from his eyes. He needed to keep his mind on the road; he could have killed that old man. But how could he concentrate when Sarah and her family might be lying dead somewhere at this very moment?

Even if they had survived the weapon, it was possible they might have seen what had happened and were already on their way to report it. If so, the soldiers would... No! He couldn't bear to think about it. He turned his attention back to the tramp. Having crossed the road, he was now sitting on the kerb pouring the contents of the bottle down his throat.

The traffic lights changed to green, reminding him of the light in the Northumberland sky and he shuddered, before slowly moving off. Again a picture of Sarah sprang into his mind. One way or another he must try to contact her and Pete. He would need to stress they should not, under any circumstances, tell anyone of what they had seen. Nor must they touch anyone lying dead.

But on the other hand, what if he was already too late? His daughter was such a caring person she could have gone down into the valley to help the others. Even as a child, she had worried about anyone or anything in pain, often bringing home all kinds of sick animals she found in the park.

Another red light loomed up ahead. Charles slowed down and looked around for any pedestrians. He wasn't going to be caught out twice. Allowing his mind to drift back to Sarah and Pete, he realised that even if they were alive, it wouldn't be easy to get in touch with them.

He wasn't naïve. After hearing the Prime Minister's conversation, he knew MI5 would be called in and telephone lines tapped. He recalled Arthur saying not to ring him. Even messages on mobile phones would be tampered with. Also his earlier idea of speaking with the generals was out of the question; that would be almost like signing Sarah's death warrant. He must warn Irene...

Oh my God, Irene! He had forgotten about his wife. She would be pacing the floor waiting to hear from him. He needed to telephone her, but he would have to be very careful what he said. The red light continued to glow down at him. Why didn't they switch these wretched things off during the night? Didn't they realise some folks were in a hurry? Eventually it relented and as the amber light began to flash, he pulled away.

At the laboratory, Charles was forced to clap his hands over his ears when he pushed open the doors. The noise was deafening. It seemed every available man had been ousted from his bed and they all screamed back and forth across the room, desperate to make themselves heard. Even the night porter, whose position it was to guard the main entrance, was yelling out figures to a man on a computer. Documents, usually safely fastened to clipboards or hidden in files bearing the words, 'For Your Eyes Only', were strewn around the floor. Now he knew why no one had answered the phone when Irene called earlier: they couldn't possibly have heard it.

Charles was bombarded with questions as he fought his way through the laboratory. Brushing everyone aside, he hurried to find John Shaw, the chief technician who was in charge that night. He found him examining the dials on the largest of the four machines, the very machine that controlled the plant in Northumberland. Several other scientists were by his side.

Relief spread across John's worried face when he saw Charles. "Thank God you're here. I've no idea what happened. I had only arrived on duty when this machine suddenly started to go crazy. It's been doing that ever since. Once the pressure began to rise, nothing we did would stop it. I tried to shut off the main feed, but that didn't work." He threw down his pad. "Nothing I damn well did would shut down the bloody thing. I put out a call for the guy who had been on duty before me, but even he couldn't help. He said everything was running smoothly when he left. He had no idea what was happening." He ran his fingers through his hair. "If only you had been here, you could have stopped it."

Charles frantically checked over the machine. Like John said, the dials were still going wild. "Then why the hell didn't you call me?" he yelled. "As soon as it began to go wrong, why didn't you phone me? And why didn't the safeguards kick in?"

"They were disconnected," John screamed back. "The safeguards were disconnected."

"What!" Charles roared. "Why! Who the hell disconnected them?"

"You did!" John answered. "You wrote it in the duty book and signed it."

Charles couldn't believe his ears. It was going from bad to worse. "What are you talking about?" he bellowed. "I would never turn off the guards, especially if I wasn't here to see what was going on. We're still in the early stages. For God's sake man, you know as well as I do that something like this could happen. You still haven't answered my question, why the hell didn't you phone me?"

"You left a message saying you had an important engagement and weren't to be disturbed," said John, quietly. He was starting to have doubts. Had he misread the note? But then he recalled showing it to a colleague; they couldn't both have been mistaken.

"Take a look for yourself." John's tone was more defiant now. "The note is still on your desk. You said you would be out all night and your mobile would be turned off. What was I to do? I was so desperate I called in all the staff. I hoped someone could stop the damn thing, but it went ahead and blew anyway."

"But that's crazy," said Charles. "How could you believe I'd do such a thing? Have you ever known me to leave a message like that? Even when I was at my daughter's wedding, I left instructions I was to be called should you need me and we weren't even working on anything half as dangerous as this. Didn't it occur to you I would never leave the building after turning off the safety guards, let alone write a brief note saying I didn't want to be disturbed?"

Suddenly finding his legs unable to support him, Charles sank into a chair. This must surely be the worst night of his life. The most dangerous project he had ever worked on had imploded, allowing a deadly gas to escape into the air. At this very moment countless people in the north of England and possibly southern Scotland, were lying dead beyond all recognition.

He winced when he thought again of how even his own family might be included in the count. He yearned to know whether they were alive. Yet he didn't dare use the telephone to find out, for fear his phone was tapped. He couldn't afford to take the slightest chance, not with the army standing by to pick up any survivors only to silence them forever. And if that wasn't bad enough, everyone in the building believed the entire disaster was his fault. Who would have signed his name in the book, who could possibly have left the note – and why? Why hadn't Rick...?

He looked up sharply. "Where's Rick, didn't you think to call him? He was working in his office when I left. He said he would be here for some time. Wasn't he still here when you arrived?"

John shook his head. He wished he hadn't seen the wretched note. If not, he would have telephoned Sir Charles and all this might have been averted.

"No sir. When I arrived at ten o'clock to begin my shift, his office was in darkness. When everything began to happen, I tried ringing both his home and his mobile, but there was no reply from either." He paused. "I even tried to override the system, yet nothing I did would turn the safety guards back on."

Charles leapt to his feet and rushed across to the levers operating the guards. A swift glance told him the codes had been changed. What John said was true, without a key no one could reverse the system. But who in their right mind would want to do such a thing?

He inserted his key into the lock at the side of the levers. Once the codes had reset to zero, Charles was able to switch on the safeguards. The dials slowed down and everything went back to normal. But it was all too late. The damage was done.

Then another thought struck him. Who had told the Prime Minister? Charles turned to John. "I was called to a meeting with the Prime Minister at four o'clock this morning. Purely as a matter of interest, was it you who informed him?"

"No." John sighed. "But I can guess who did. Just when everything started to go crazy, Alan Crisp stuck his nose in the door. I don't know what he came here for, especially at that time of night, but as soon as he saw what was happening he shot off. Even a bird-brain like him would understand the seriousness of the situation. He probably couldn't wait to report the incident to Brian Tate."

Charles dragged his feet as he crossed the laboratory to his office. The fight had gone out of him. Once this was over, he was going to retire to the little cottage in the country he and Irene had always promised themselves.

Irene! He slapped his forehead. She would still be by the phone waiting for his call. Thinking of her reminded him of Sarah: mother and daughter were so alike. Both were very beautiful women. A few years back, they could have been mistaken for sisters. Even now, Irene was still a very striking woman.

Charles picked up the phone and dialled his home. But what could he say? He would need to choose his words carefully for fear of someone listening in. As he guessed, Irene was close by the phone, as it only rang once.

"Hello, Irene," he said. "I can't talk long. I simply wanted to reassure you that the meeting with the Prime Minister went well." That would satisfy anyone listening in. "I'll get back to you later, but in the meantime don't worry."

He hoped she wouldn't mention her brother's phone call. There was no reason to drag Ronald's name to the attention of the invisible listener. "Why don't you go back to bed? Like I said I'll speak to you again soon."

Fortunately Irene didn't say anything about Ronald. Sounding relieved, she said she would do as he suggested and go back to bed for a couple of hours.

After Irene hung up, Charles held the phone to his ear for a few seconds more. There was a click. He was right, they hadn't wasted any time in tapping the laboratory phones.

He sat back in his chair. There was less noise in the laboratory now. Since the safety guards had been put back into operation, everyone had stopped chasing around. Instead they were puzzling over why the pressures had risen in the first place.

But Charles only had thoughts for his family. He refused to believe they were dead. If there was any way to get out of the valley, Sarah would find it. She might only be a young woman, but Charles knew her to be a fighter, she always had been. She would do her utmost to save her children. At all costs, he must believe she was alive. Keeping that one thought in mind might get him through this insane situation.

Closing his eyes, Charles sank his head into his hands. How was he going to tell Irene about what had happened? She knew very little of the Project. Knowing his work was top secret, she had never pressed him to talk about it. Would she ever forgive him when she learned how his creation had killed their daughter and her family? But no! He sat bolt upright. Hadn't he already decided Sarah wasn't dead? Somehow, he would have to convince Irene of that.

Fumbling around the papers on his desk, he found the note John had spoken of. It certainly looked like his writing, yet he knew he hadn't written it. Someone had gone to a lot of trouble to forge his handwriting. It was very cleverly done. It would be extremely difficult to convince the men in grey suits that he hadn't written it.

But would they want to believe it? If the Prime Minister's plan to keep the whole thing quiet backfired, wouldn't this help to get him and his Cabinet off the hook? Already he could see the headlines. 'Scientist Shuts Down Safeguards: Hundreds Of People Die In Agony.' The papers would go on to tell how, 'As People Lay Dying, Scientist Didn't Want to Be Disturbed.' Put like that, it sounded rather like Nero playing the fiddle, while Rome burned.

Leaning over his desk, tears spilled down Charles's cheeks. How could he forgive himself for devising such a terrible weapon? He prayed his family had escaped and promised his maker he would have nothing more to do with weaponry. Burying his head in his hands once more, he began to cry.

CHAPTER SEVEN

"There still doesn't seem to be anyone following us." Sarah breathed a sigh of relief as she turned back to face the front of the car. "The soldiers can't have seen you leaving your house."

"Good," Andy replied. "At least we have a few minutes head start before they discover we've gone. I'll drive on a little further into the forest before I change out of this uniform."

Sitting back in her seat, Sarah shuddered as she reflected on the morning's events. So many people dead – it was all too horrible. Yet she still refused to believe Pete was among them. He would never give up without a fight. He had so much to live for.

"Are you alright?" asked Andy, glancing across at her. "You've gone very quiet. I think I liked it better when you were arguing with me."

Sarah swung around to face him. "I was thinking about my husband. I intend to come back to find him once the children are safe."

"Your husband's a lucky man." Now Andy had got her talking, he didn't want her slipping back into a melancholy mood.

"I wouldn't consider lying dead somewhere with your flesh melting, being very lucky," she retorted.

She bit her lip. She hadn't meant to sound so harsh, nor admit Pete might be dead. But deep inside she was hurting and needed to take her vengeance out on someone. Andy just happened to be at hand.

"I'm sorry." He glanced at her. "I didn't mean... What I meant was he's a lucky man to have someone like you, to care about him."

She smiled. "I'm sorry too. I didn't mean to snap at you. But I feel so helpless. I want to know who's responsible for all this. He should be dragged up here to see what he's done!"

Andy pulled the car over to the side of the road. "I think we're safe enough for the moment. I'll take the opportunity to get out of this uniform." Reaching over to the back seat, he picked up a shirt and jeans. "Hopefully these will make me look more like a family man." He scrambled out of the car and ran over to the bushes. "Keep a look out. If you see anything suspicious, sound the horn."

Sarah looked at her children. They were both sleeping and Josie was still clutching her pictures. She reached across to the back seat and gently removed the drawings from her daughter's hand. The poor little mites had been rushed around all morning. It was good they were able to sleep now.

"I've hidden my uniform under a rock behind the bush. It wouldn't do for anyone to find it in the car."

Sarah jumped. Andy's sudden appearance at the window had startled her. She should have been paying more attention. Anyone could have crept up and she would never have known. She would need to be more careful.

"We'll be off now," he said, climbing back into the car.

"You look different out of uniform. I'd never have recognised you."

He laughed. "Better or worse?"

"Neither, just different." She cocked her head on one side. "Better, perhaps; more boyish."

It was true. The uniform had made him look stuffy – older than his years. She knew he was about her age. Both he and Constable Manners had been given a mention in the local paper when they were newly stationed at Wooler, having arrived fresh from the police training college. Now wearing jeans and a brightly coloured, loose fitting shirt, he looked so much younger. Even his brown hair seemed to have taken on a more curly appearance. Earlier in the police station it had been plastered to his head – regulations style no doubt.

Andy started the car and continued through the forest. "You're not from these parts, are you?" he asked. "Your accent gives you away. Somewhere down south, I'd say."

Sarah told him about how she had been born in London and why she had moved up north.

"You mean to tell me, you left a life of luxury in the City to come up here and marry a farmer?" Andy's eyes widened at the news. He couldn't believe it. "You must have found it quite different from what you were used to. All I can say is he must be quite a guy."

"Yes, he is." Sarah smiled. "But the City isn't everything it's cracked up to be. I agree it has its good points. Like for instance, you're never lost for something to do. If you have the money, that is. But on the other hand, it's all rush, rush, rush. No one has time to reflect on anything. It's a rat race. Everybody's too busy trying to outdo their neighbours. Up here it's not like that. People take time to make sure their friends are okay. Surely that's more important."

"I guess so," said Andy, slowly. "Though I still can't see how you could settle in a place like Wooler after all that hustle and bustle. I found it difficult myself and I didn't come from the big smoke, only from a largish town in Lancashire." He laughed. "I've always wanted to go to London. Streets paved with gold and all that. When I joined the force, I thought I'd be sent there if I did well. I saw myself in Special Branch, or some other elite squad so I worked hard for my exams, doing all the right things. Yet look what happened. I ended up even further north, just my luck. You can imagine my disappointment – or perhaps you can't?"

They were approaching the end of the forest road. Very shortly they would leave the cover of trees for a more open country road. But if luck was on their side, they wouldn't meet any other traffic for a while. The further they were away from Wooler without bumping into anyone, the better.

However, as they were leaving the forest, a man ran across the lane and flagged them down.

Andy groaned. "What shall I do? Should I drive on?"

"No! We must stop. It could be an emergency." Sarah was concerned. "Someone might be hurt."

Pulling up, Andy rolled down the window. "What is it?"

"Could you give me a lift to Alnwick?" The stranger peered into the car. "I see you have room in there for one more. I'm afraid I got chatting and missed the bus." He pointed to a road in the distance. "It's another hour before the next one. I was on my way back home, but then I caught a glimpse of your car through the trees and..." He gave a toothy grin. "Well what do you say?"

Andy glared at Sarah. This was the last thing they needed. He should have ignored her and driven on. Alnwick was a large town. If they agreed to help him it would mean going into the town centre, something he had hoped to avoid. Staying on the more quiet roads was a far better option. However he knew how these local people stuck together. If they turned him down, the stranger might spread the word that a family of tourists refused to give him a lift. Any soldiers following them could even get to hear of it and might put two and two together.

"Yes alright, hop in." Andy forced a smile. "We're going to Alnwick anyway." As far as he could see, there was no reason for the man to believe differently. If questioned, the stranger would think they were a family touring the area, even if it was a little late in the season. But then these country folk believed townies were eccentric anyway.

"Anna, perhaps you would like to move into the back with the girls and let the gentleman sit up front." Andy nodded towards the back seat.

Sarah stared at him. Anna? Then she realised he didn't want the man to know their real names.

"Yes, Bill. That would be best," she replied, at last. She smiled. "The girls are a little shy with strangers."

"Mummy, where are we?" said Josie sleepily, as Sarah lifted her onto her knee.

"Hush, dear." Sarah put a finger to her lips. "Don't waken Becky, she's still sleeping. We'll stop for something to eat soon."

"Are you folks touring the area? My name's Bob, by the way."

"Nice to meet you, I'm... Bill and this is Anna, my wife." Andy had to think for a moment. It wasn't going to be easy to keep up the pretence. "Yes, we thought we would take a look at the northern countryside."

"A bit late in the year for tourists," said Bob, thoughtfully "Folks usually prefer to come up north when the weather's more predictable. We don't often get people here once all the attractions shut down." He smiled. "Tell you what; I'll direct you through a couple of lovely little villages. You might have heard of them, Bamburgh and Seahouses?" Without waiting for a reply, he continued. "Now they're a sight to behold. In the summer months people come in their hundreds. Many take a boat ride across to the Farne Islands, where Grace Darling used to live. I suppose you've heard of the lovely, brave lass who saved several people from certain death?"

"Eh – yes, we've heard all about Grace Darling. Isn't that right – Anna?"

"Good! Good!" Bob spoke before Sarah could reply. "I'll point out some landmarks as we go through the villages. I know quite a few people in both, I might even get a chance to say hello. Pity you've missed the opportunity to see the Grace Darling Museum. The kiddies would have liked that. Why is it you're here so late in the season? I must say I was most surprised to see you coming down the forest road. It's not often we see folks on that road once the tourist season is over. We locals tend to use the more straightforward routes from Wooler, due to the weather. The forest road can be bad later in the year. But I suppose you have to take your holidays when your company says so?"

The intonation in the man's voice indicated it was a question, rather than a statement. Andy was still wondering how to answer, when Bob spoke again.

"Though I must say, you've been lucky with the weather this year."

Andy gave Sarah as fleeting glance through the reversing mirror. This wasn't going to be easy. Like all country folk, Bob was not only a talker; he was also inclined to be inquisitive.

"Yes as you say, we've been lucky with the weather." Andy began to turn into a road, which would head them away from the villages Bob had mentioned. He hoped the man wouldn't notice. But Bob was having none of it.

"No! No! You're going the wrong way for the coastal route. Just keep going for another mile or so, I'll tell you when to turn off." He paused. "Now what was I saying? Oh yes, why are you here so late in the season?"

Andy thought quickly. "You were right, Bob. I had to take my holidays late this year as I've recently changed my job. Last in gets last choice on the holiday rota."

Hopefully that would be an end to it, but Bob had other ideas.

"So what line of work are you in then, Bill? And where are you folks from?"

Andy hesitated, not sure what to say. It was more than likely this guy was going to quiz him whatever he said. "I'm in the insurance business," he said at last. "And we live in London."

He might be on safe ground here. His brother was a representative for a large insurance company and often spoke of his experiences as a door-to-door salesman. And surely Sarah, having been brought up in London, could talk her head off about the metropolis and all it had to offer.

"Insurance!" Bob spat out the word. "Now there's a thing! I had a policy with a company for years without putting in a single claim. I paid out regular as clockwork. Yet, when I tried to claim for a burnt rug, I was asked to fill in masses of forms. I'm sure they thought I would get fed up and go away. But they'd picked on the wrong man. I stuck my ground until the bitter end. Mind you, once they paid me my money I cancelled the policy. They weren't going to treat me like that. I could have filled my house with carpets ten times over, with all the money I'd paid into the firm over the years. So what have you got to say about that?"

Andy tried to explain how the companies had to be sure people weren't trying to pull a fast one. He told him how the money didn't belong to the firm, but to all the people who had entrusted their money with them for a rainy day, so to speak.

But Bob couldn't see it and spoke at great length about how insurance companies were the lowlife of the nation, only pausing occasionally to give some directions.

"I have friends who are farmers," he continued. "They're insured up to the hilt, yet if anything happens to their stock, the company always finds a loophole. Now when I was in business..."

"Have you ever been to London?" Sarah asked, interrupting him. "It's such a wonderful place."

So far she had stayed silent. But she could see tiny beads of sweat forming on Andy's forehead and felt it was time to get involved.

"Yes," he said, turning around to face her. "I stayed with my friend for a month. I enjoyed it, right enough, but I was glad to get home." He wrinkled his nose. "I found it very noisy."

Sarah laughed. "Yes it can be like that to strangers. But you get used to it after a while."

She tried to look interested as he described some of the places he had visited while he was there.

"Ah! Here we are. We're approaching Bamburgh." Bob pointed to the castle standing high above the village. "Now look at that. Isn't it magnificent?" He turned back to Sarah. "Built on a volcanic outcrop, they certainly knew what they were doing in those days. No need for insurance cover, it was built to last." He laughed.

Sarah glanced at Andy. He looked so furious she thought he was going to burst.

"Stop!" Bob yelled, crashing the palm of his hand down onto the dashboard.

Andy pulled up sharply, believing someone had run out into the road. "What is it?" His eyes darted back and forth in front of the car.

"I can see a couple of my friends over there. You don't mind if I say hello, do you?" Without waiting for a reply, Bob wound down the window. "Jack, Alf, hello there. How are you both?"

The two men crossed over the road to greet their friend.

"This is Bill and Anna." Bob gestured towards Andy and Sarah. "They're on holiday and kindly offered me a lift. I was on my way to visit my brother in Alnwick, but like a fool, I missed the bus."

The two men nodded to Andy and Sarah. "Bit late in the season, to be holidaying in these parts," one of them said.

"That's what I told them," Bob replied. "But Bill's just changed his job and had to take what he could get. He's in insurance."

"Is that so? Still, you've had good weather," said the other man. "Say would you like to join us for a game of snooker at the club."

Andy clenched his hands around the steering wheel and breathed deeply. He was fast losing his patience. He and Sarah were trying to pass through the county unnoticed, yet this character, having thrust himself upon them, was now introducing them to his friends.

"Well, that would have been nice," said Bob, "But I don't want to be too late arriving at my brother's, so I suppose I'll have to say no. Besides, I think these good people want to get on."

However, another three miles down the road, just as they were approaching Seahouses, Bob called out for Andy to stop the car again.

"How would you like to live out there, Missy?" Bob turned around to Josie and pointed towards the Farne Islands. "Pretty bleak, I'd say, but it must have been exciting to live in a lighthouse." He pointed towards a distant island. "See, there it is. Now why don't we get out and walk down to the harbour and..."

"Look, I'm sorry to interrupt, but I really think we should be getting on!" Sarah snapped.

All this stopping for chats and tourist attractions was beginning to grate on her nerves. What she really wanted to do was to tell the man to get out of the car and leave them alone, but catching a glimpse of Andy's expression, she calmed a little. "The children will want something to eat soon and..."

"Oh, that's no problem," interrupted Bob, cheerfully. "We can stop for a sandwich at my friend's café in the village. He's open all year round. A few of the locals meet up there to catch up on the gossip. I'd like to see him again; it's a while since I was last down here. The bus to Alnwick doesn't come this way. I need to change buses to get to Seahouses."

Sarah clenched her fists. That wasn't what she had meant at all and would have told him so, if she had been given the chance to get a word in.

"This will be my treat," Bob continued, blissfully unaware he was causing a problem. "I'm having such a lovely day. Besides, you'll like my friend, he's a nice guy. His son is the village constable." He glanced down at his watch. "You know, the constable might even be there at the moment. He calls in on his father at about this time every day."

Andy's stomach flipped. The last thing he wanted right now was to meet another policeman. What if they had met each other before? In the country, officers were often moved from one station to another to cover sickness or holidays.

"No!" He yelled out before he could stop himself. "It's very kind of you." He patted Bob's arm, trying to make amends. "But I think it would be best if we could move on." He looked across at Sarah for support.

"Yes," she agreed. "I would prefer to keep going for a while longer, if you don't mind. Naturally we're grateful for your generous offer, but we do need to keep moving."

She raised her eyebrows at Andy. Was it enough to put the man off? But what else could she say without being downright rude?

"Well if that's how you feel." Bob sounded slightly put out. "I was only trying to help." He paused and smiled. "But I don't suppose you'd mind if I popped in and said hello to my friend? I promise I'll only be a few minutes."

Sarah shrugged. She did mind, but to argue further would have only made him suspicious.

"Mummy," said Josie. "Can I sit on the seat?"

"Of course you can, darling."

Sliding her daughter onto the seat, Sarah carefully moved the child's drawings out of sight. Josie might suddenly mention she still hadn't shown them to her father; how would they explain that away?

Fortunately, for the moment, Becky was still sleeping, but when she awoke, she would be hungry. No doubt Bob would see it as another excuse to stop somewhere for a meal. Why on earth did Bob have to miss his bus – or more to the point, why did they have to come upon him just at that precise moment?

A few minutes later, they were in Seahouses and Bob directed Andy to his friend's café.

"Are you sure you won't come in?" Bob hoped they might have changed their minds.

Andy shook his head. "No thanks. Like my wife says we'd like to move on as quickly as possible now."

He spoke calmly, but once the old man was out of earshot he almost exploded. "For crying out loud, Sarah, why did I listen to you? I should have driven on and left him standing there."

"Don't you yell at me!" Sarah folded he arms defiantly and threw herself back against her seat. "How was I to know the wretched man had missed his bus? I thought he was in trouble."

"Well he wasn't! And now we're lumbered with him." Andy peered up and down the road. "I daren't sit here too long. The policeman could come along at any minute and recognise me."

"Why, have you met him before?" Sarah's tone was indifferent. She was still annoyed at the way Andy had shouted at her.

"I don't know. I've never been to the Seahouses station. But it doesn't mean to say someone from here hasn't been up to Wooler. If he recognises me, our cover will be blown. He's sure to go in there and mention that another policeman is sitting in a car outside. Bob will wonder why on earth I've told him I'm in insurance and most certainly tell..." Andy suddenly crouched down in his seat. "There's a policeman over there now," he whispered.

Forgetting their differences, Sarah looked to where Andy was pointing. "Do you recognise him?"

He lifted his head slightly. "Oh my God, yes I do! It's Hawkins. He stood in for Manners earlier this year. He drove our police car. I think he came from Morpeth at the time; he must have been transferred here since then.

Andy quickly leant down across the passenger seat. "He called into the station at least once every day, so he'll know me if he sees me. As I recall, he's very ambitious. He sees himself as chief constable one day. He'd nick his grandmother, if it would get him a promotion. Though having said that, I see he's still a constable, so he hasn't done it yet." He paused. "What's he doing now?"

Sarah glanced across the road. "He's coming this way." Oh my God! What're we going to do?"

Andy tried to move further down his seat, hoping he wouldn't be seen so easily. "Of course he's coming this way," he whispered. "Didn't Bob say he called in on his father every day at around this time?"

Sarah watched carefully as the policeman came closer. She heaved a sigh of relief when he walked past the car.

"It's okay, he's going straight into the café," she whispered.

But then he stopped and, turning around, he looked across the pavement towards her. Smiling, he began to walk over to the car.

Sarah's stomach turned over. "Blast! He's coming back!" she hissed.

"Sarah, you must do something. If he sees me, we're sunk." Andy tried to pull himself closer to the floor, but the gear lever was in the way. "I can't get down any further."

Her heart pounding, Sarah watched the policeman. In a few seconds he would be near enough to see Andy crouching awkwardly between the gear lever and the handbrake.

"For God's sake, do something – anything, but get him away from the car." Andy was almost hysterical.

Sarah's hands trembled as she took a phial of perfume from her bag and sprayed it around her neck and down her cleavage. Swallowing hard, she looked down at Josie. "Stay here. I want you to be as quiet as a mouse, like when you play hide and seek with Daddy." She put a finger to her lips. "Don't say a word."

Still trembling, she leapt out of the car and hurried across the pavement towards one of the shops. Purposefully, she avoided looking at the constable and kept her eyes fixed on the window. Hawkins turned and followed her, exactly as she hoped he would.

"Is everything alright?" he asked. "You look a little lost." Her perfume filled his nostrils and he ran his finger around the chinstrap of his helmet. "Perhaps I might be of some assistance?"

"No. Everything's fine. We're touring the area and my husband went for a short walk to stretch his legs." Giving him one of her most winning smiles, she glanced at the car. "I said I would stay with the children."

Following her gaze, he smiled. "I hope he isn't too long. I see you're parked on a double yellow line. I don't want you to receive a ticket." He leaned towards her. "Not that I would do such a thing, especially to someone as pretty as you. But the traffic wardens around here are not quite so... considerate."

"You're so kind," she drawled. "I'm afraid we didn't notice. I'm sure my husband won't be long. She swept her fingers through her long blonde hair. "It's so nice of you to look out for me. I know my husband will be very grateful. After all, you can't be too careful these days; there's so much crime around. Though I hasten to add we haven't encountered any problems up here in the north." She rested her hand gently on his arm. "But then I suppose that's down to the commitment of police officers like you."

"We do our best." The sweet smell of her perfume reached out to him again and he took her hand in his. "Is there anything I can help you with? Where are you staying, perhaps I could call on you... and of course your husband. I would be delighted to show you both around our lovely Northumberland." He took a deep breath. "I... We have so much to offer."

Andy heaved himself up a little – just enough to see through the window. It was open slightly and he had heard every word. It seemed Hawkins hadn't changed. He remembered how the constable had honed in on every pretty girl in Wooler.

"Smarmy git," he murmured. "Trust you to try to make a pass at an attractive young woman, even though she's told you her husband is close by."

Hawkins turned back to face the car and Andy was quickly forced to throw himself down towards the floor. He groaned as the gear lever jabbed into his ribs. Hearing Josie laugh, he raised his head slightly and found her peering down at him.

"You're funny, like Daddy," she said. "Are you playing hide and seek as well?"

Andy smiled. "Yes," he whispered. "We must be very quiet." He placed his forefinger over his lips. "Like a mouse."

Josie nodded and copying Andy, she placed her finger to her lips. "Sshh," she said.

In the street, Sarah gasped having suddenly caught sight of Andy's head through the car window. Had the constable seen him? She hoped not.

"Are you alright?" asked Hawkins.

"Yes." Sarah took the constable by the arm and led him over to the shop window. "I'd just noticed something wonderful in this shop. There! That hat, don't you think it would suit me?"

Her mind was racing. She had to get rid of this wretched man somehow. "When my husband returns, I'll tell him of your kind offer to show us the sights. But I'm afraid I've promised to take the children to visit an aged aunt tomorrow. She doesn't see them often, so I can't disappoint her. However, my husband won't be accompanying me and will be at rather a loose end. I'm sure he'd be more than delighted if you were to show him around."

She paused and pretended to look anxiously up the street. "I'm beginning to wonder where he's got to. He's a historian you see and likes to visit ancient sites. The trouble is he tends to lose all track of time and as he's quite a bit older than me, I worry when he's on his own." Looking back at the constable, she smiled. "However, if a young, strong man like you were by his side, I would have no cause for concern. There must be lots of really interesting places you could show him. You could both spend such a lovely day together, looking at all the old ruins in the area."

Sarah peered up the street again. "If you'd care to wait for a minute or two, you'll be able to speak to him yourself, he shouldn't be long. You could make your plans now. My husband will want an early start, perhaps six in the morning and I know he'll be keen to look at every ancient monument you can show him, even if it takes until well after dark."

She held her breath and waited for his reaction. Hopefully she was right in thinking the constable had no intentions of taking her husband anywhere – let alone to some ancient sites.

"Ah, tomorrow... Well... eh... I'm afraid tomorrow is out of the question," he stammered. "I... I have a busy day ahead of me. Police business you understand. What a pity, I'm sure your husband and I would have got on well together."

"I see," said Sarah, quietly. Though inwardly she was laughing, she tried to sound disappointed. "Never mind, perhaps another time. He'll be sorry to have missed you. We'll be sure to look you up when we come back to this area."

Constable Hawkins smiled at Sarah, before beating a hasty retreat up the street. He decided to give the café a miss today. If the young lady mentioned the incident to her husband, he may come in and try to persuade him to change his mind. There was no way he was going to be lumbered with some dusty old fossil. Now the wife, she was a different kettle of fish. He sighed. Such a lovely young woman: slim, attractive, just the way he liked them. He wouldn't have minded getting up at six in the morning for her. If only she had been on her own, he could have had such a wonderful time...

Sarah continued to look in the shop window until the constable had turned the corner at the top of the road.

"He's gone for the moment," she said, returning to the car.

"That was quite a performance you put on out there." Andy grinned as he heaved himself up from his crouched position. He felt stiff and rubbed his aching limbs. "David Hawkins sees himself as a ladies man, but I think you put him in his place."

"He's a creep. I've met his sort before." Sarah glanced towards the café. "I wish Bob would hurry up. Why on earth did we have to get lumbered with him?"

"If he doesn't come soon, I'm going to drive off without him," Andy said, crossly. "He has so many friends around here; surely one of them would drive him back home."

"The trouble is," Sarah said, thoughtfully. "If we drive away, he's going to tell his friend in the café about the awful tourists who left him stranded. Then if he in turn mentions it to his son, the policeman, he might recall me telling him all about my aged husband. If he puts two and two together, he'll be suspicious and tell his sergeant, especially if he's keen to get on. Who knows what'll happen then?" She shrugged. "If the soldiers heard of it…"

"There are a lot of 'ifs' there," interrupted Andy. "Besides, surely we'd be long gone. And, come to think of it, what would the soldiers learn from it? They probably already know we're travelling south. Anyone in Wooler who saw us leave will have been able to tell them the route we took."

Sarah shook her head. "Oh! I don't know." She sighed. "Perhaps no one saw us leave. Anyway, I'm simply trying to think of every possible…" She threw her hands in the air; frustrated at not knowing what to say.

"Mummy, can I speak now?" Josie asked.

"Yes of course you can, darling." Thankful for the interruption, Sarah reached across and hugged her daughter. "What is it you want to tell me?"

Josie pointed at Andy and laughed. "That man is funny. He was playing hide and seek with me."

Andy grinned. "Yes I was, but I'm not as good as you."

Suddenly Bob came out of the café.

"Sorry I took so long, I was hoping to meet my friend's son, but he didn't come in today. It's very strange: he always comes into the café at about this time. Did you see him?"

Glancing at Sarah, Andy smiled. "We saw a policeman hurrying up the road. Perhaps he'd been called away on an emergency?"

"Well never mind, I'll see him another time. Now what else can I show you?"

"Hadn't we better get to Alnwick? Won't your brother be waiting for you?" asked Sarah.

Bob looked down at his watch. "Yes I suppose so. Time is marching on. I may have to stay the night."

Once Bob was in the car, Andy started the engine and set off down the road. He turned the corner and headed towards Alnwick.

"I thought you told me you were strangers here," said Bob, sharply. "Yet you knew which way to turn."

"I saw a road sign back there," Andy replied quickly. "Besides, we looked at our map while you were in the café."

He took a deep breath. He was going to have to be careful. This old boy was quick.

Sarah heaved a sigh of relief when they finally reached the outskirts of Alnwick. Very soon, they would be waving farewell to Bob and not before time. Instead of slipping quietly through the shadows, this old man had seen to it that several of his friends would be able to describe them in every detail.

"Where would you like me to drop you off?" asked Andy. "The sign ahead pointed the way to the town centre, so it can't be much further."

"Anywhere near Market Square will do," he replied. "My brother always sits there if the weather's fine, as so many of his friends pass by. The trouble is, he talks too much. No one else can get a word in."

Andy almost choked as he pulled over and stopped the car. The old man could certainly do his share, when it came to talking.

Bob made as if to get out, but then changed his mind.

"You're stopping here for a while aren't you? Perhaps you would like to park somewhere and look around the town. I know a nice place where you could get an excellent meal at a very reasonable price. It's over there." Bob pointed towards one of the restaurants. "I know the owner, I could introduce you and..."

"No!" Andy broke in quickly. He smiled. "If it's all the same to you, I think we'll push on. We didn't really plan to spend so much time getting here. We may even make it to Morpeth before we stop for a meal. The girls are quiet, so we might as well make the most of it."

Bob shrugged as he opened the door. "Thank you for the lift, it's been a pleasure to meet you. But it's a pity you're unable to look around the town. It's a very historic place you know. Medieval fair in the summer, lovely castle a short walk away – it's been used for all sorts of films."

He grinned and climbed out of the car. "But never mind, perhaps another time. I can see you want to be on your way. However, if you come up here again be sure to look me up. I'll write down my address." He leant back into the car. "Have you got any paper there? I have a pen."

Sarah closed her eyes. Were they never to be rid of this man? She wanted to yell out at him. Surely he must know they were never going to get in touch with him again. Gripping the seat in front of her, she wondered why Andy was reaching around in the glove compartment for a notebook. Why didn't he drive away and leave this bumbling old fool standing there?

Bob took the pad and wrote down his full name and address. "Have a good trip," he said, handing it back to Andy.

"Thanks we will. Enjoy the day with your brother." Andy pulled the car door shut.

"Speak of the devil! Here's my brother now," yelled Bob. "Wouldn't you like to meet him?" He began to rap on the window. "Stop! Wait!"

"Just go! For God's sake just go!" Sarah called out.

Pretending he hadn't heard him, Andy quickly drove off.

Glancing behind, Sarah saw Bob still waving and pointing towards his brother, while calling out for them to stop. Thankfully, they were moving away from him. However, turning back towards the front, she caught a glimpse of an army Jeep travelling on the other side of the road. "Oh my God! The army's here and Bob is drawing attention to us."

Andy slowed down, not wanting to make themselves even more conspicuous. "Perhaps they'll think he's shouting at someone else."

Sarah was still watching the Jeep. By now it had passed them. "It's alright, it's stopped." She heaved a sigh of relief. But her ease was short lived. "No! It's turning around." Her heart almost stopped beating. "Andy, they're coming this way. They're nudging their way in, a couple of cars behind us." She leant forward and prodded Andy. "They're following us. For God's sake, can't you hear what I'm saying? What are you doing fooling around here! Get a move on! Do something!"

"What can I do?" He slammed his hands on the steering wheel. "Can't you see? I'm stuck in traffic. I can't move any faster until the road is clear."

Andy glanced at Sarah through the mirror. Her eyes looked wild with fear – she was beginning to panic. She turned to look out of the back window. "Turn away!" he called out. "Don't look at them! Sarah! Pull yourself together! Try to..."

As he spoke, the traffic ahead started to move faster and he was able to pull away. "Thank God, we're moving again! Talk to Josie; point out the monument on the left. Do anything, but for goodness sake, Sarah, look natural."

Taking a few deep breaths, Sarah began to speak to Josie. "Look up there. See, there's a lion with its tail straight out the back."

While pointing at the monument, she glanced behind and saw the Jeep was still there. She felt a pit in her stomach and she began to tremble. "They're still behind us, Andy. They're onto us. Any minute now they'll pull us over." She grasped her children close to her and held them firmly.

A few moments later, she saw the Jeep turn off down a side street.

"Mummy, you're hurting me!" Josie cried out.

Realising she was clutching her daughters tightly, Sarah released her grip. "Sorry sweetheart. Mummy didn't mean it." She kissed them both.

She sank back in her seat. That had been too close for comfort! It was all Bob's fault. If anyone else asked for a lift, they would drive on!

Neither she nor Andy uttered another word until he pulled up a little way out of the town centre.

"Are you alright?" he asked, anxiously. "Do you want to move back into the front seat?"

"I'm fine," she lied. "I'll move up with you when we get on the road again, but first I think we could all do with stretching our legs. I'm sure the children would like something to eat." She knew Andy wanted to keep going, but she really needed to get out of the car for a while.

Andy smiled at the two girls. "Shall we have a picnic?" he asked.

"Yes, please!" said Josie.

Becky wasn't so sure. To her, Andy was still a stranger. She stretched out her arms towards her mother.

"It's alright, sweetheart." Sarah swung the toddler across onto her lap. "We're all going to sit by the river and have something to eat and then play a game." She looked at Andy. "Drive to somewhere you think will be safe enough to stop for a while."

"Where's Daddy?" asked Josie. "Daddy would like to come on a picnic and play hide and seek as well."

Sarah forced back the tears as she thought of Pete. Josie was right. He always enjoyed playing games with the children. "He'll be here soon," was all she could say.

Becky, hearing the word 'Daddy', thought her father was close by. Looking out of the window, she called out for him. "Dadda, Dadda," she squealed, bouncing around on her mother's knee.

Andy suddenly felt the odd one out. Sarah and the children were all looking for one man – Pete. To them he was everything. Until that moment, he had never thought of himself as being a family man. His plan had been to work hard and keep his nose clean and hopefully he might be recognised as an outstanding officer. It could lead to a promotion. For him that could only mean Scotland Yard, nothing less would do. But thinking it through, at the end of a hard day would there be anyone waiting for him? He had never thought about it before, but even the chief constable must have someone who...

"Andy, are you feeling alright?" Sarah interrupted his thoughts.

"Eh... yes. I was trying to think of somewhere to stop for an hour or so."

Privately, he would have preferred to stay on the road. If it hadn't been for that old fool, Bob, they could have been much further south by now. However Sarah looked pale. Perhaps a break would do them all good. The children had been very quiet up until now. Why risk making them agitated?

"I know a rather nice spot, by the river," he suggested. "We could have something to eat and the children could even play around for a while before we move on."

"That sounds good, doesn't it girls?" Sarah hugged her daughters. "Let's go."

However, turning back to restart the car, Andy was startled to see another army vehicle heading towards them. In his reversing mirror, he saw Sarah talking to the children. She didn't appear to have spotted it yet.

Starting the engine, he carefully pulled out into the road. It was possible the soldiers hadn't seen them. They might simply be scouting the area, still unaware of their presence in the town. But he couldn't take the chance. Indicating right, he slowly turned into a side street, not wanting to draw attention to the vehicle. However once around the corner, he hit the accelerator hard.

Hardly daring to breathe, his eyes danced between the wing mirror and windscreen as the car screeched down the road.

"Andy! Stop! What are you doing?" Sarah was almost flung from her seat. She grabbed her children and tried to hold them steady as they were swung from side to side.

Andy didn't answer. If only he could reach the junction at the bottom of the road without being seen, they might be in with a chance. The soldiers wouldn't know which way they had gone and it would take them a few seconds to decide what to do. But the junction seemed a long way off – would they make it in time?

CHAPTER EIGHT

Pulling a handkerchief from his pocket, Pete mopped his forehead.

"This is hopeless." Josh threw himself down onto one of the boulders. "We've been heaving at these wretched rocks for over an hour and we don't seem to have made any difference at all."

Pete peered at his watch. They had actually been working off and on for almost four hours. However, Josh was right about one thing, the entrance was still well and truly blocked. He sat down next to his friend.

"We'll take a break before trying again." He glanced around the dimly lit cave. "Perhaps this isn't the only way out."

Following Pete's gaze, Josh looked towards the tunnels. The darkness loomed out at him and he felt the blood drain from his face. "You don't mean we might have to go through those tunnels," he gulped. He turned away so Pete wouldn't see the fear in his eyes.

Faced with being confined in a small, dark space filled him with absolute horror. It was this phobia that had led him to farm work in the first place. Open fields had no doors to shut you in.

Again he glanced at the tunnels. This cave was bad enough, but at least he had room to breath. Down there in the darkness, the walls or ceiling might close in and... Raising his hands, he clutched his head. Stop! Even thinking about dark tunnels made him gulp for air.

Unable to remain seated any longer, he leaped to his feet and began to tear at the boulders. "I think we should carry on. We can't waste time sitting around."

Alarmed, Pete hurried across to him. They needed to get out of here before his friend did something stupid. However before he could say anything, he noticed the sheep were starting to move around the cave. It seemed they had become bored watching the men tug at the rocks and were seeking some other form of amusement.

Concerned they would stumble and break their legs, Pete called on the dogs to shepherd them back towards the far end of the cave. But the sheep stubbornly continued to walk towards one of the tunnels. Both men could only stand back and watch as they disappeared into the darkness.

Pete suddenly felt something rubbing against his legs. Lowering the light, he saw Daisy pushing her head against him. Belle was standing close by. "Daisy, old girl, I hadn't seen you among the rest of the sheep."

He moved to one side to allow her to pass, but Daisy still kept nudging him.

"Do you think she wants us to follow them?" asked Pete, after it had happened for the third time.

"I don't know." Looking into the dark tunnel, Josh shivered nervously. He wasn't keen on following anything down there, least of all a bunch of sheep. They weren't known for their intelligence. "Maybe she's gone a bit stupid being trapped in here." He could empathize with that!

"I'm not so sure." Pete moved a couple of feet towards the tunnel and then stopped. Daisy began to push him again.

"See, she only stops pushing me when I move towards the tunnel. I think we should give it a go. Perhaps there's another way out. After all they knew about this cave, didn't they. They've probably been in here several times. You said that yourself a few hours earlier."

Josh still looked unconvinced.

"Come on, Josh," Pete continued. "Let's follow them. Besides, it strikes me we're going to have to try something else. Heaving at the rocks hasn't worked."

Josh glanced back at the blocked entrance. What Pete said was true, but why was following a flock of sheep down an extremely dark tunnel their only option? Already he could feel himself beginning to tremble. Truthfully, he would rather wait for help to arrive. But they could sit here for a hell of a long time before anyone raised the alarm, and even then it would take some time to unblock the entrance from the other side – the rock fall was at this end of the narrow tunnel. He took a deep breath. There was nothing else for it: he would have to go down the tunnel.

"Okay." He grabbed Pete's arm. "But you've got to promise me something, if I panic, don't let me hold you back. You must keep going. You've got a wife and kids, I haven't." He forced a laugh. "You can always come back with reinforcements later."

Pete nodded. But he knew he could never leave his friend all alone down here. "Come on then," he said, cheerfully. "Let's go before Daisy gives up on us both. The rest of the sheep have already gone on ahead."

Gathering together what was left of the wood to serve as torches, they followed Daisy into the tunnel. Arriving at the fork the men had encountered earlier in the day, the sheep knew instinctively which tunnel to take. However it was as Josh had feared. A few yards further on, the tunnel narrowed and the roof suddenly dropped in height. The men were forced to bend double to pass through.

Behind him, Pete could hear Josh gasping for air. But there was nothing else for it – they had to go on. There had to be another way out of these tunnels and if the sheep knew it, then they must follow them.

"It can't be much further. I think we're doing well. Who'd have thought we'd be saved by a bunch of sheep, eh?" Pete laughed, trying to keep his friend's spirits high. If Josh lost control now, it would be all over.

"If you remember, it was this same bunch of sheep that got us here in the first place," replied Josh, sullenly. He could feel the walls closing in on him. It was all he could do to stop himself from screaming out in terror.

He wiped his face with an old rag he found in his pocket. It was warm in the tunnels and he tried to convince himself that if it had been cooler he would have coped better. But he knew it wasn't true. Even if it were ice cold down here, he would still be burning hot and terrified.

He recalled the nightmares he used to have a few years ago. He was always trapped in confined spaces. Sometimes he would find himself in a lift. The power having suddenly gone off, he would be left there alone in total darkness. Others times, he would see himself in a small windowless room. But mostly he was lost in a dark tunnel, exactly as he was now. He had moved to the country in an attempt to free himself from his fears and so far it had worked. Even the nightmares had stopped. But now it was all happening for real.

He tried to remember how each fearful dream had ended; perhaps he would find it helpful. However, on reflection the dreams had never come to a conclusion. He had simply awoken to find himself screaming out in terror with sweat pouring from his body.

Having caught up with the sheep, Pete and Josh continued to follow them through the maze of dark tunnels. At each fork the animals never hesitated, they seemed to know exactly which way to go. Suddenly the men found themselves climbing upwards. Though the slope was gentle at first, it soon became much steeper and the solid floor gave way to loose gravel. The men stumbled and slid, as they desperately tried to keep up with the sheep.

To lose sight of them now would be fatal: neither of them had any idea of the way back.

But then the roof of the tunnel lowered even further, making it more difficult to move around. Now crawling on all fours, it became too much for Josh. He clawed frantically at the walls. He had held on for as long as he could, but now he felt he was being crushed from all sides.

"I can't make it!" he screamed out, gulping for air. "I can't go any further. You must go on without me."

"Oh course you can make it." Somehow Pete managed to turn and look back. He stretched out his hand. "We must be nearly there. For God's sake hold on, Josh. Take my hand, I'll help you." He desperately hoped they would soon be out of here. This was their last torch. The light was dim, but to have none at all...

Grabbing Josh's arm, Pete pulled at him. "Come on. Try again. We can't afford to let the sheep get too far ahead. If there's another fork, we need to know which tunnel they take."

Now dripping with sweat, Josh looked at Pete and nodded. "Okay." He heaved himself forward, but there was so little room. "I'm okay. You go ahead, I'll follow." He wiped his face. "At least that damn whirring sound has gone, but why does it have to be so damn hot?"

Pete listened. Josh was right. He had been concentrating on keeping up with the sheep, but now that his friend had mentioned it, he realised he hadn't heard the noise for quite some time. Holding the torch out in front of him, he tried to see where the sheep had gone. He breathed a sigh of relief when he saw them a little way ahead. They had come to a halt and were all bunched together. Was it a dead end? Had they followed the sheep here only to find there was no way out?

However moving closer, he held up the torch and found the tunnel had narrowed even further and the sheep were squeezing through the gap one at a time.

"Oh my God! If it's like this for the rest of the way, I can't go on." Peering over Pete's shoulder, Josh could see what was happening up ahead.

"Wait! I'll go first and take a look, it might not be so bad." Pete pushed himself along the narrow tunnel and stuck his head through the small opening. "It's okay, Josh," he yelled out. "It's not a tunnel; it opens out on the other side. It's a cave rather like the one we left back there." He pushed himself through and held the torch aloft. "Come on, Josh, I promise you it's alright."

Josh crawled up to the gap and peered through. He ran the back of his hand over his brow. Thankfully Pete was right, it was a large cave. Behind him, the two dogs nuzzled at his ankles, they were impatient to follow their master. Closing his eyes, Josh squeezed his large frame through the gap.

Meanwhile, Pete was trying to locate the sheep. He and Josh needed to stay close to them. Their last torch was almost burned through and from what he could see, there wasn't any wood in this cave.

Catching a glimpse of the animals a little way ahead, he moved forward. They couldn't afford to lose sight of them now. He marvelled at how the sheep had ever found their way through this tunnel in total darkness.

"Come on, Josh, it won't be long now," he called out. "The sheep are a little way up ahead and we really must keep up with them."

Stumbling across the cave, the two men followed the animals through another tunnel with the dogs bringing up the rear. At first the tunnel seemed wider than the others, but after several yards, it began to get narrower.

The torch flickered and dimmed: it was going out. Straining his eyes, Pete looked up the tunnel, searching for what lay ahead, but then the light faded and died. Now it was pitch black.

Josh screamed out as the fingers of darkness enveloped him. His nightmares were coming true. He hadn't escaped his fate after all. The tunnel, the darkness, they had both been here all the time, quietly waiting for the day when he would be forced to face them both. Gasping for air he thrashed out, grazing his hands on the walls of the tunnel. He felt hot and cold at the same time.

"Get me out of here," he gulped. "Pete, for God's sake, please get me out of here!"

Feeling around in the darkness, Pete managed to grasp Josh's flailing arms. "Stop it! Stop it!" he yelled, shaking him hard. "We're going to get out of here, but we must keep our heads."

Josh stopped shouting and tried to control himself. He was still breathing deeply. "I'm... sorry, Pete... I'll try."

"I'll let go of you now, but stay close and for God's sake, stay calm."

Slowly moving along the tunnel, Pete pressed his hands up and down against the walls. He was beginning to despair of ever finding his way out of this accursed place, when he felt the woolly coat of one of the sheep. Trying desperately to keep up with it, he stumbled and hit his head on the roof and crashed to the floor.

Josh heard Pete groaning. "Pete! Pete! Where are you?" He tried to feel his way along the wall. "Where are you? I'm coming."

"I'm okay! Stay where you are!" Pete yelled. Rubbing his head, he felt something warm and sticky running down his face. Blood! "Don't move, Josh, you might fall over me."

His head still hurting from the blow, Pete slowly rose to his feet. The sheep would be long gone by now. Without any light, he and Josh couldn't chase after them. They could only stumble forwards. But if there were another fork in the tunnel, which one would they take? Without the sheep, they could stagger around these tunnels forever.

Just then, he felt something brush against his leg. Bending down he again felt the thick woolly coat of a sheep. "Thank God," he murmured. "Josh, I have one of the sheep here, stay close to me. Are the dogs still behind you?"

"Yes, I hear them." Josh's voice was but a whisper. He couldn't take much more. He could barely breathe: the darkness was crushing him. Somehow he managed to tuck his hand in Pete's belt.

"We need to take it slowly. I pray to God this sheep knows the way." Pete took a few steps, but then he slipped on the gravel, hitting his head on the wall of the tunnel as he fell. "Damn! I've lost my grip on the sheep," he said, rubbing his wound.

Josh let out a piercing yell as his legs buckled beneath him and he crumbled into a heap on the tunnel floor. For him, this was the end! "We're going to die!"

Shutting his ears to Josh's wails, Pete groped around in the darkness. If he could find the wall he might lever himself up. But instead, his hands fell on the soft coats of two sheep.

"Josh! Hold on a while longer! There're two sheep here. I'll try to hang on to them this time."

Slowly they made their way along the tunnel. At one point the sheep stopped for a moment, but then began walking again. Pete had the feeling they were veering towards the left. A few yards further on they stopped again, but this time neither sheep made any attempt to move.

"What's happened?" gasped Josh.

The sweat was pouring from him. He would quite happily lie down and wait for the inevitable. But despite the pact they had made earlier, he knew Pete was not the sort of person who would leave him here alone. He must try to carry on or they would both perish. However one thing was certain, if he got out of here alive, he would never ever set foot in this God forsaken place again.

"I don't know," Pete answered. "They've both stopped. Don't move, I'll feel around."

Carefully releasing his grip on the sheep, he began to grope around the walls. But it all seemed to be solid rock. Could the sheep have lost their way? Had they come to a dead end after all? Not wanting to believe that, he continued to run his hands frantically up and down the rough walls of the tunnel.

Nothing! He was beginning to lose heart, when his fingers slipped through an opening.

"There's something here!" he called out, swirling his hands up and down the void. "I think there's a gap! Let go of my belt for a minute, I'm going to crouch further down and feel around to find out how big it is."

Down on his knees, he found the hole was larger than he had first thought. He peered through. There appeared to be another long tunnel filled with darkness, but at the end of it – glory be, there was daylight. He gave out such a yell, that Josh thought something had happened to him.

"What is it? Are you alright Pete?" Josh crashed around in the darkness.

"Thank God! We've made it, Josh." Pete fumbled around until he found his friend's arms. "There's a gap here and a long tunnel, but at the end of it I can see daylight."

The men heard the two sheep scuffling along the tunnel.

"You go first, Pete. I need a couple of minutes, to pull myself together."

Pete heaved himself through the tunnel and tumbled down onto the earth outside. Dazzled by the sudden glare of daylight, he covered his eyes, but he could hear Josh scrambling along the tunnel. Then there was the sound of a dull thud, as his friend fell onto the earth beside him.

Once their eyes became accustomed to the light the first thing they saw was Daisy and behind her stood Belle. Both sheep were looking down on the two men.

"Daisy! Belle!" Pete exclaimed. So it was you who waited for us back there. What I can't figure out, is how you sheep ever found your way through the tunnels in the dark?"

"Don't bother to try." A wave of relief swept over Josh. Deep inside the tunnels, he fully believed he had met his destiny and was about to die, but it wasn't to be. He had escaped. "Let's simply be thankful they knew the route. I really never thought I would ever be grateful to a couple of sheep."

However, looking back through the small gap in the hill, he shuddered. It was still difficult to believe he had survived those dark tunnels beneath the surface.

Glancing around to get their bearings, the men were horrified to find the land was burnt to a crisp. So preoccupied were they with their escape that they hadn't notice it before.

Speechless, Pete and Josh looked out across the valley. The fields, the crops, the trees, everything had gone.

"What on earth has gone on here?" uttered Pete, finding his voice.

Turning towards the hills again, he saw his truck in the distance. Even from here, he could tell it was a mere shell.

Pulling his mobile phone from his pocket, he tried to ring Laura. But for some reason, he couldn't he get through. The signal looked good, but there was a hissing sound. He tried ringing Sarah in Alnwick, but again there was only the same strange sound. A cold feeling swept over him, as each number he tried brought the same response.

"I must get down there Josh! I need to find my children."

Thrusting the phone into his pocket, Pete called out for the dogs and tore off down the hill.

"Wait for me." Josh caught up with Pete. "Take it easy, I'm sure they'll be okay." Now it was his turn to be the comforter.

The men hadn't gone far before they came to the fields where, only yesterday, sheep and cattle had grazed contentedly in the warm sunshine. Horrified, they gazed at what remained of Pete's pedigree animals. Moving closer, they saw that the skeletons of the beasts were lying in pools of some sort of thick sludge. Both turned their heads away, sickened at the sight.

"What on earth could have happened to cause this?" Pete murmured, more to himself than to Josh.

One hand clenched over his mouth, Josh slowly walked towards one of the skeletons. "What's this treacle-like stuff?" he asked, peering down at it.

"I don't know. But how can the bodies have decomposed so quickly? Only yesterday everything was fine. Something like this simply can't happen overnight."

Josh didn't reply. He was still bending over the thick, pink-black liquid surrounding the skeleton.

Pete turned and looked across the fields. Skeletons stretched as far as he could see. A sudden movement caught his eye and he saw a field mouse run by the side of one of the remains. Its tiny feet trod in the thick liquid. The rodent squealed out in pain.

Unable to move, Pete could only watch in horror as the mouse writhed in agony before dying. But then, when he thought it was all over, its fur seemed to disintegrate and flesh began to drip down onto the grass from the tiny bones. Shocked, he took a few deep breaths to rid himself of the sickness rising in his stomach. In God's name, what was going on?

Turning his head, Pete saw his friend crouched over a skeleton. His hand outstretched, he was about to dip his fingers into the liquid. "Stop!" he yelled. "Stop! Don't touch it!"

Josh drew his hand back sharply. "Why? What is it?"

Pete stabbed his finger towards the mouse. "It caught its foot in a fragment of the thick liquid."

Josh paled when he saw what had happened. "And I was about to..." He couldn't finish. Looking away, he was violently sick.

Gazing across the fields, Pete noticed skeletons lying outside the farm cottages. Treading carefully, he went to take a closer look. He cried out in dismay when he realised they were human. They were the remains of his farm workers. People he had known and worked with for several years were lying here – all dead.

"Josh! Josh!" he called out. Squatting down on the burnt out land, he lowered his head into his hands.

Running across to join him, Josh sank to his knees at what he saw. Was this all that was left of his friends? "I can't believe it." He hung his head and sobbed. "We were only away for one night. What happened?"

Rising to his feet, Pete looked down at the bare, white bones. But then he quickly turned his attention to Laura's house. The colour drained from his face as he thought of his children.

"Oh my God! Not my family!"

He began to run towards the cottage Laura shared with Dave. Outside there appeared to be only one adult skeleton. Carefully making his way inside, he looked for the remains of his two children. But there were no skeletons at all. For some reason, no one had been inside the house when this awful thing took place. Where were Josie and Becky?

Running in and out of the other cottages, he found the remains of adults and older children outside. Inside, tiny skeletons lay in beds and cots. Were his children among them? And even if they were, how would he know?

Closing his eyes, he tried to remember how many children there were in the valley. Frantically darting from house to house, he tried to count the small skeletons. But his mind was in turmoil; he couldn't concentrate. Besides, how could he know for sure how many children there should be? The people living here often had young relatives staying with them. Nephews, nieces and grandchildren; they came and went all the time. Searching for answers, he wondered if his children were up at the farmhouse. If Sarah had heard this terrible thing was happening, she would have come back for the children. Then another thought hit him like a punch in the stomach. Oh my God! Was she, too, lying dead up there?

But how could she have known what was going on here? Alnwick was some thirty miles away. He began to run blindly towards the lane leading to the farmhouse. He had to know if she and the children were up there.

"Sarah! Sarah!" he screamed hysterically, as he dashed across the field. "Sarah, can you hear me? Please answer. Tell me you're alright."

Jumping to his feet, Josh chased after his friend. "Wait for me!" he called out. If Sarah was dead... Josh pushed the thought from his mind. Even he couldn't bring himself to think about it. Sarah was a lovely young woman. Her warmth and friendship towards the farm people had touched their hearts.

"Wait for me! I'm coming with you."

But Pete kept on running. It was only when he came to another skeleton in the lane that he stopped.

"No, no. Please, no." Filled with grief, Pete mumbled the words over and over. "Don't let it be Sarah." This couldn't be his beautiful young wife. Sobbing, he sank to his knees.

Now having reached the scene, Josh peered at the remains. "It's not Sarah," he said at last.

Pete didn't hear. Frozen, he continued to stare down at the skeleton. Had Sarah been on her way to Laura's to collect the children? Were his babies down there after all?

Grabbing Pete by the shoulders, Josh shook him. "Listen to me, this is not Sarah!" He pointed at the skeleton. "Do you hear me? This is not Sarah!"

"Not Sarah?" Pete slowly turned to look at Josh. "How do you know? How can you tell?"

Josh pointed to one of the skeleton fingers. "The ring! Look at the ring! It's Dave's ring. Laura gave it to him on their wedding day." He lowered his voice and tears filled his eyes. "I was at their wedding. He showed it to me."

Pete stared down to where Josh was pointing. It was true. It wasn't the ring he had given to his wife.

"Thank God it's not Sarah," he murmured.

He was sorry this awful thing had happened to Dave, yet if this wasn't Sarah, where was she? Would he find her lying in a similar state at the farmhouse? Suddenly he began to run again, screaming out her name as he went. "Sarah! Sarah! Answer me."

But he stopped abruptly by the farm gate and stared up towards the house. What would he find inside? His wife? His children?

Josh came alongside him. "Would you like me to go in first?"

"No. Thanks, Josh, but I've got to do this."

Pushing the gate open, he walked towards the house. Josh followed a few yards behind. Despite what Pete had said, he might need him.

By the door, Pete hesitated. He looked at Josh for a few seconds before disappearing inside.

While he was waiting, Josh glanced around the farmyard. The fields at the front of the farm were empty of livestock. Why weren't there any skeletons lying there? Pete kept his most prized herds near to the house. It was then he noticed something else and he hurried forwards to take another look. Rubbing his eyes in disbelief, he looked again, but it was true.

"Pete! Pete! Come out here and take a look!" Josh ran back to the farmhouse.

Inside, Pete tore in and out of the rooms, dreading what he might find. But the house was empty. His wife and children weren't here. Were they among the remains at the farm cottages after all? He tried ringing Sarah's friend in Alnwick, but though someone answered, he couldn't hear properly, because of a continual hissing sound.

It was then he heard Josh calling out for him and he ran outside. "They aren't in there! Have you...?"

"Pete, look at the grass!" Josh interrupted. "Look at the fields!" He gestured madly towards the fields around the farmhouse, hardly able to contain himself.

Pete looked to where Josh was pointing. At first he couldn't see what his friend was getting at, but then slowly it dawned on him. The fields around the farm weren't burnt like the others.

Now excited, Pete ran across to Josh. "It didn't reach the farmhouse." He yelled out, punching the air in delight. "Whatever it was didn't reach the farmhouse. So if they were up here, they could've been spared."

"Yes! Yes! If Sarah came back from Alnwick and brought them up here, then they might be alive!" Josh was almost as excited as Pete. "And look, the herds have been moved out of the fields down here: they're all up on the pastures behind the farmhouse. Perhaps Sarah moved them before she left. She's probably gone into Wooler to report what's happened out here."

While Josh was talking, Pete looked frantically around the farmyard for further proof that Sarah and the children were still alive. After all, one of the farmhands may have moved the herd long before the devastation took place. If Sarah was unaware of what was going on, she would still be in Alnwick, which would mean the children may be among the dead down there in the valley.

On the other hand, if she had come back she would have gone down there to find the children. And that being the case, all three could be dead. Pete's mind was racing: piecing together every possibility. Yet they all ended the same. His children were dead and maybe his wife, too. Tears in his eyes; he looked towards the heavens. "Please let them all be safe," he murmured.

Wiping his eyes, he turned back to Josh. "I'll get the old car out of the garage and we'll go into Wooler and try to find out what's happened."

"But first, I think you should do something about those wounds." Josh pointed to the dried blood on Pete's forehead. "It's where you banged your head in the tunnels."

"I'll grab a couple of wet towels while I'm getting the keys to the car. We could both do with a good wash, but I really don't want to waste any more time."

A few minutes later, they were driving up the lane towards the town.

"What's that up ahead?" Josh put down the towel and, leaning forward in his seat, peered through the windscreen. "It looks as though there's been an accident."

Driving closer, they found a police car had run off the road and crashed into a tree. Pete pulled over and both men stepped down to take a closer look. Perhaps they could help. On Pete's command the two dogs stayed in the car. Josh drew back sharply when he saw the remains of two men inside. They looked the same as those in the valley.

"Perhaps they came out here on patrol and touched something," said Pete, after a long pause. "Their car isn't burnt out like my truck – or any of the other vehicles around the cottages."

"Yes." Josh spoke quietly. He was thinking how easily the same thing could have happened to him when he very nearly dipped his fingers into the thick slime.

"I think we should go, there's nothing either of us can do here." Josh looked around nervously. He didn't want to stay here any longer. This place and the two skeletons in the car were giving him the creeps.

Pete agreed. He was still anxious to find out whether Sarah was still alive. The phones in Wooler might be working, he could ring Sarah's friend in Alnwick. However, as they were climbing back into the car, they heard the sound of another vehicle. Looking up ahead, they saw an army truck approaching them.

For a moment, they were relieved: help had arrived. However, their relief quickly turned to alarm when soldiers jumped down and waved guns in their direction.

"I'm Captain Saunders." The voice came from an officer stepping down from the truck. "This is Sergeant Patterson." He jerked his head towards the soldier behind him. Both men were holding a cloth over their face. Keeping well away from them and the police car he continued. "What are you doing here?"

"I live here. I'm Pete Maine, this is my land." He nodded towards Josh. This is Josh Davies. What's been going on here?"

The officer ignored the question. "What have you seen down there?"

"Things we hope, we'll never see again. Now will you tell me what's been going on here?" Pete was beginning to feel uneasy. The soldiers still had their guns trained on Josh and himself. Surely they didn't think they had caused all this devastation.

"None of your damn business," answered the officer. "I'm asking the questions. Is the woman, Sarah Maine, down there? She's your wife, I presume?"

"None of your damn business." Pete spat out the words. "And there's no need for all this." He pointed to the soldiers. "We haven't done anything."

Saunders took a step forward. "Move away from your car!" he ordered, nodding to one of his men.

Obviously the nod meant something to the soldier, as he ran to the back of the truck and called out to the men inside. Pete and Josh looked at each other as five men in thick, protective, silver coloured clothing complete with helmets and some sort of gas masks, stepped down from the back of the truck. Forced to walk slowly due to their restrictive suits, they made their way over to the police car.

"I wouldn't like to meet one of them on a dark night," whispered Pete.

Though the men examined the police car very closely, they refrained from touching anything. Turning back to the officer one of the men reported that two skeletons were sitting in a thick liquid. His voice, distorted by the headgear, sounded menacing.

Lad and Bob, still in the back of Pete's car, growled threateningly.

"Tell them to stop or I'll have them shot," said the officer.

Pete didn't say anything. He didn't like the look of this. All he wanted to do was to get away from here and find out whether his wife and children were still alive.

Saunders raised his hand and the soldiers turned their guns towards the dogs. Alarmed, Pete called out for them to be quiet and they obeyed instantly.

"A wise decision." Saunders gestured to his men to lower their guns. "Did you go near the police car?"

127

Surprised at the question, Pete looked at Josh. "Yes, we thought there had been an accident and wanted to help. But when we looked through the window, we saw the two skeletons."

Keeping a safe distance, Saunders walked around the two men. "So, you've been in the valley and up close to the car. Yet, you're both still alive. Do you feel alright?"

"Yes, we feel fine. What's all this about?" said Josh.

Lowering the cloth covering his nose and mouth, Saunders turned to the men in the protective gear. "It would seem it's safe to take off your helmets." He looked back at Pete and Josh. "You'll both have to come back with us."

"If it's all the same to you, we'd rather not." Pete tried to sound matter of fact. "We can't help you. We don't know anything."

He reached out to open the car door, but he heard the soldiers take a step forward. Their guns were poised, ready for use.

"Like I said, you'll come back to Headquarters with us." The captain called out to one of the soldiers. "Corporal, you stay here and keep an eye on them while we drive down into the valley and assess the situation. We'll also check out the farmhouse." He glanced at Pete and laughed. "If the woman's there we'll find her. I'm sure she'll amuse my men." He turned and walked towards the truck.

"She's not there," Pete called out. He was afraid Sarah might have somehow eluded them and returned to the farmhouse. "No one's there."

He began to run after the officer, but was brought to a sudden halt when the butt of the corporal's gun was thrust into his stomach.

"We shall see for ourselves," said the captain. He glanced at the corporal. "You have your orders."

"Sit down over there." The soldier ordered, pointing to a large rock.

Still winded from the blow, Pete staggered across the road with Josh's help and sat down.

Sneering at the two men, the corporal reached into Pete's car, and pulled the keys from the ignition. "Just in case either of you get any ideas about trying to drive off. Anyway, my buddies won't be long. Once they get hold of your missus and had a little bit of fun, they'll be back." His laugh was coarse. "Hopefully, they'll leave some for me."

Making sure the officer was well out of sight, he lit up a cigarette. "Have you seen those two in there?" He flicked some ash towards the police car.

Pete was too angry to respond. He was thinking of Sarah, hoping she hadn't taken another route back to the farm.

"Yes we saw the two skeletons," said Josh. "But we don't know what caused it. Do you?"

The soldier shook his head. "No and I don't want to."

"But don't you care?" Josh uttered. He was amazed. "All those people and animals lying dead down there and you don't want to know why." He looked away in disgust.

Shrugging his shoulders, the soldier drew on his cigarette. "Why should I care? Like Captain Saunders says, it's none of my business. I'm just here to clear up the mess."

"And how do you propose to do that? As far as I can see, if you touch anything you'll end up like them." Pete jerked his head across to the police car.

The soldier looked up sharply. "Found your tongue, have you?" He sniffed and flicked his cigarette. "Anyway you told Captain Saunders you didn't know anything!"

"We don't. Neither of us knows anything about this." Pete wished he hadn't said anything. "We saw a rodent run into the liquid lying around one of the bodies and within a few seconds, it was transformed into a skeleton."

Swallowing hard, the soldier moved a little further away from the police car. Why take unnecessary risks? Throwing down his cigarette, he ground it into the road with the sole of his boot. He and the others had been warned not to touch anything out here, but he hadn't expected anything like this. He glanced back towards the grisly contents of the police car. Fighting the enemy when it was someone you could see, was entirely different to fighting something, which could turn you into a skeleton in a matter of minutes.

Seeing that the soldier was momentarily distracted, Pete wondered if they could make a dash for the car. Moving his elbow slightly, he tried to nudge Josh, but the soldier saw him and raised his gun.

"Move again and I'll kill you both."

"Kill us!" Josh was astounded. "What the hell for? We haven't done anything."

"You would say that, wouldn't you? The captain says you're to be taken in for questioning, which means you're suspects. Trying to escape will prove he's right."

Pete couldn't believe it. He thought back to the burnt grass and the bodies. How could anyone accuse them of causing that? There was nothing else for it, but to go along with the soldiers and sort it all out. But then another thought struck him. Why were they so intent on finding Sarah? What had she to do with it? Thinking back, Captain Saunders had spoken of her by name. They had come here looking for her especially – why?

Shortly afterwards, the soldiers returned. The captain strode over to Pete and Josh. "She's not there. Do you know where she is?"

"No. I have no idea." Pete was being truthful. He still didn't know for certain if she was alive or dead.

Saunders was furious. Without a word, he strode across to the truck and picked up the radio. Pete strained his ears, trying to make out what was being said, but he couldn't hear very clearly.

"There's no one at the farm. Either the constable was right and she went somewhere else, or he's fooled us. I'll go back to the police station and check it out and get back to HQ as soon as possible." Glancing at Pete and Josh, he turned away and lowered his voice. "We've found another couple of live ones; it seems they've seen everything. One is the owner of the farm; I think the other is a farmhand. What do you want us to do with them?"

There was a pause, as the captain waited for his instructions.

At the other end of the phone, General Lewis took a deep breath. This was important. He was answerable to the Prime Minister himself; he couldn't afford to screw this one up. "Bring them straight here, Saunders," he said at last. "Forget the police station until you've delivered them to me. But whatever you do, don't let them get away. You're one of the few men who's privy to the Prime Minister's orders. For God's sake don't let me down. As for the woman, I'll get a series of road-blocks set up right away. One stupid woman with two small children in tow won't get far."

"Yes sir, I understand. Leave it to me." Saunders threw the receiver into the truck and walked across to Pete and Josh.

"I have orders to take you in. General Lewis is waiting to question you." He ordered the corporal to escort them into the truck.

"What about my dogs?" Pete asked. "I can't leave them here."

Without even looking at the dogs, Saunders nodded towards two of his men. "Shoot them!" he ordered.

"No!" Pete yelled. "I won't let you." Pushing himself away from the soldiers, he ran across to the car door and yanked it open. "Go! Go! Go!"

The dogs jumped out of the car and ran across the fields. Two soldiers took aim, but before they could fire, Josh managed to hurl himself at them. The shots flew into the air and by the time they were in position to try again, the dogs were out of range.

Several men rushed forward and knocked Pete and Josh to the ground.

"You bastards! You're going to pay for that," said one, kicking Pete in the stomach.

"That's enough!" Saunders intervened. "We haven't got time for this. Forget about the dogs. They'll probably run through the stuff and die anyway." He pointed towards the truck. "Get them in there. We need to get back to HQ as soon as possible: the general's waiting."

On the outskirts of Wooler, the truck pulled up at a large old building. Pete recognised it at once. Several years ago, it had been the home of a country squire. However when he died without an heir, it had remained empty until the Ministry of Defence took it over. Now it was used as Military Headquarters when they were training in the area.

Hauled from the truck, Pete and Josh found themselves being bundled inside. They were led into a large room; the general was sitting at one end.

After his talk with the Prime Minister, General Lewis had flown straight here with several troops. Most were from an elite squad, ruthless but dependable. They had been trained to guard the British Isles to the end, without question. However also among the ranks were ordinary soldiers, brought in to camouflage the real reason for the army's presence. To inquisitive eyes, it would look like another training exercise.

"Sit down, gentlemen." General Lewis offered the men cigarettes; they both declined.

"The reason you're here is because you've seen what's happened out there in the hills." The general took a cigarette from the box. "We need to know everything you know. Anything you can tell us, no matter how trivial it may seem, could be of vital importance." Lighting the cigarette, he sat back in his chair.

"But that's just it. As we told your Captain Saunders, we don't know anything." Pete sighed. "We're as shocked as you are."

"I see." Unconvinced, the general leant forward. "What were you doing out there and how is it that you're both still alive?"

Pete was taken aback. "We live out there. The land belongs to me."

He paused, realising they weren't going to get out of here until they told the general something. Briefly, he explained how they had followed some sheep into a cave, only to become trapped.

"By the time we got out, all this had happened. So you see we really don't know anything at all. Perhaps we can go now?"

"Have you told anyone about any of this?" asked the general.

"No. No one at all. We didn't even see anyone alive, until we met up with your men." Pete was starting to feel agitated. What was going on? Why was the army so interested in whether they had spoken to anyone? Was it possible it was they, who had caused this while on one of their damn exercises and were now looking for a scapegoat?

"You're quite certain you've spoken to no one?"

"Damn blast you! Haven't we told you and your wretched captain several times over? We didn't speak to anyone!" Pete leapt to his feet. All this talk wasn't getting them anywhere. No one was listening. "Come on Josh, we're out of here."

"Sit down, Mr. Maine!" The general's voice was cold. "I'm in charge here! You'll leave when I say so."

Pete sat down automatically.

"Thank you." The general smiled. "You've told me everything I needed to know."

He pushed a button and Sergeant Patterson came in.

"Take them." The general gestured towards Pete and Josh. "You know what to do."

The soldier saluted and quickly shepherded the men out of the building. Outside, the sergeant and two men, still wearing protective clothing, used their guns to push them towards a covered truck.

"What's going on?" Josh wanted to know. "Where are you taking us?"

"Never mind," said the sergeant. "Just get in."

Pete tried to break free, but was knocked to the ground by one of the soldiers, while another jabbed at his forehead with the butt of his gun. Picking himself up, Pete wiped away the blood from the wound on his head.

"I said get in," the sergeant repeated.

Josh helped Pete into the truck. "They're going to kill us!" he whispered.

Pete looked at Josh in amazement. Why would they want to kill them? These were British soldiers, weren't they? Or had Britain been invaded while they were trapped in the tunnels? He shook his head. No of course not, that was a ridiculous notion. Nevertheless, a lot of strange things had happened during the night.

Still wielding his gun, the sergeant climbed in behind them, while one of the men in protective gear hauled himself into the driving seat and started the engine. The canvas on the sides of the truck was rolled down so neither Pete nor Josh had any idea where they were going. But it wasn't long before they found out. Shortly after starting off, the truck pulled up sharply and the two men found themselves back beside the crashed police car.

"Get out and stand over there." Sergeant Patterson waved his gun in the direction of the wrecked car.

Pete and Josh glanced at each other as they climbed down. The same thing was running through both of their minds. There were only two men guarding them. Would it be possible to rush them before they could fire their guns?

"Now you could make this less difficult for us and yourselves, if you were both to put your hands through the car window and touch some of that muck in there." The sergeant looked across at the other man and laughed. "What do you say, Jones? We could have a cigarette while these two give us a floorshow. It's been a long time since we've seen a real horror movie."

Without answering, Jones threw his gun into the back of the truck and pulled out a knife.

"But it doesn't really matter," the sergeant continued. "Because you'll end up looking like them anyway, so which is it to be?"

Pete glanced around. Now there was only one gun pointing at them. If they were going to do something it had to be now. As he was nearest to the man with the gun, he lunged forward. But the sergeant was too quick for him and stepped smartly to one side. Pete hit the ground with a thud.

The sergeant raised his gun. "What the hell," he said. "Let's shoot the bastards. Does it really matter if they find a bullet lying in the slime? It's our men who'll be clearing up anyway and they're not going to say anything."

Still lying on the ground, Pete waited for the gun to go off. This was it then – the end. In a moment or two, it would all be over. During those few seconds, his life played out before him like a film. His wife, his children: pictures of them flashed through his mind as he braced himself for the inevitable. The sergeant wrapped his finger around the trigger and began to squeeze. Pete closed his eyes... But there was only a click. Mercifully, the gun had jammed.

"Damn!" The sergeant cursed as he fumbled with his gun.

Seizing his chance, Pete leapt to his feet and smashed his fist into the soldier's face, causing him to fall to the ground. Jones, still holding the knife, moved towards Pete, but the thick protective suit slowed him down.

Seeing what was happening, Josh hurled himself at the moving soldier and manhandled him down onto the road. "It seems things have taken a new turn," he said, picking himself up.

"What are we going to do with them?" asked Pete, rubbing his fist. The sergeant's jaw had turned out to be much harder than he had thought. He picked up the gun that had flown from the sergeant's hand as he fell.

"Don't kill me. I've got a wife and two kids," wailed the sergeant.

"So have I," said Pete. "But it didn't seem to bother you too much." Though sorely tempted, he knew he couldn't kill them. Yet neither could he let them run back to Headquarters. At least not until he and Josh were safely away from the area.

"I was only obeying orders," sobbed the sergeant.

"And what have you got to say for yourself?" Josh looked towards Jones.

"What can I say?" He shrugged. "What Sergeant Patterson said is true. We were ordered to kill you. But he lied about having a wife and kids." He pointed towards the knife on the ground. "There were to be no bullets. Once you were dead, I was to dip your hands in the slime. This is supposed to protect me." He gestured towards his thick suit. "No one would have been any the wiser. I can't say I was happy about it, but orders are orders." He paused. "We're guilty and that's an end to it."

"Shut up," yelled the sergeant. "I don't want to die." He looked towards Pete. "Please have mercy. He doesn't know what he's talking about. I was really on your side. If he hadn't been with me, I'd have let you go."

Pete lowered the gun. "Sergeant, you're an evil, lying bastard. Your man here has more decency than you'll ever have. At least he's honest. You don't know the meaning of the word." He looked back towards Jones. "I don't want to kill anyone. I only want to find my wife and children."

"I honestly don't know where they are," Jones said. "All I can tell you is that calls in and out of this area are being blocked. Early this morning our men listened in on the police radio and learned how two police officers had gone to investigate something Mrs. Maine had reported seeing. Captain Saunders went to the station to pick her up. But she'd left." He shrugged. "Apparently the constable's wife and children were in the police station, so the captain didn't make too much fuss. However the constable did say Mrs. Maine was going back to the farm. That's why we came down here. But as you know, he didn't find her. What happened to her after she left the station is anyone's guess. She might have come back here and touched one of these." He gestured towards the skeletons in the police car. "And then run off somewhere across the fields to die. Or she could even be one of those down there in the valley."

Pete didn't want to hear any more. He couldn't bear to think she was dead.

"Thank you. But I must keep on looking. I've got to find her." He turned to Josh. "Come on, let's go."

"What'll we do with these two?" Josh pointed to the two soldiers. "We can't just leave them here. They'll tell their superiors we've escaped. We should do to them what they were going to do to us."

"Tempting," said Pete, staring at the sergeant. "But if we kill them, then what? Sure, two more skeletons will be found here. But if they're supposed to be you and me, then someone will wonder what happened to these two. It wouldn't take long to figure it out. Besides Josh, we're not murderers."

Josh hung his head. He felt ashamed. "Yes, you're right. But I was so angry, I wanted to see them dead."

"Come on. The car's still where we left it." Pete didn't want to linger any longer. "Let's get away from here. There's a spare set of keys in the glove compartment." He grinned. "There was no point in letting that be known earlier."

They had almost reached the car, when they heard a noise behind them. Looking back, they saw Sergeant Patterson had taken a knife from the side of his boot and was about to throw it. However, Jones lashed out and knocked him off balance. Pete started to run back as the sergeant reached out for the knife. But, despite his bulky suit, Jones managed to pull him away.

In a desperate effort to stay on his feet, the sergeant grasped out at the police car, only to find his hand disappearing through the open window. Unable to pull back quickly enough, he felt his fingers sink into the thick melted flesh of what was once a policeman.

"Get it off me! Get it off!" he screamed, as he pulled his arm from the car. He hopped around the road in agony; already his fingers were beginning to blister. Holding out his arm, he turned towards the other soldier for help.

But Jones took several steps backwards. "Keep away," he shouted. "Stay away from me!"

The men could only watch as the flesh on the sergeant's fingers began to melt and drip to the ground. There was a slight hiss as it hit the road's surface. Pete closed his eyes. Could the very same thing have happened to his wife and daughters?

Jones continued to back away, the colour draining from his face. Suddenly, he made a dash for the ditch.

"Come on, let's go." Josh too, felt sick. He needed to get away from what was happening here.

"Yes..." Pete took a step backwards. "... there's nothing any of us can do for him."

But then he noticed a notepad lying on the dashboard of the police car. It was clean: none of the melted flesh had reached it. Wondering if it might be useful, he very carefully reached through the open window and picked it up. Deciding to read it later, he tucked it into the breast pocket of his shirt and went to join Josh who was already sitting in the car.

Starting the engine, he looked across at Jones; still leaning over the ditch. "Will you be alright?" he asked.

One hand still over his mouth, Jones looked up and nodded. "Go," he mumbled, before turning back to the ditch.

By now, Sergeant Patterson had sunk to his knees. He screamed out in terror as the flesh on his hand continued to melt. Steadily the evil chemicals began to creep up to his wrist. He stretched his arm out in front of him and pulled his head away in a futile effort to stop the process from reaching his neck and face.

Pete couldn't bear to watch any longer. Ramming his foot down hard on the accelerator, he set off in the direction of Wooler. Obviously they would need to avoid the town itself; a detour that would take them out of their way by a few miles. But if they were to remain undetected, it was their only option. "I hope the petrol holds out until we can find a filling station."

A couple of miles down the road, Pete spotted his two dogs in one of the fields. Bringing the car to a halt, he called out to them. Delighted to see their master again, they leapt into the car. Pete also noted there were several sheep in the field. Looking closer he was able to make out the markings on their coats. They were the sheep from Top Meadow. How could they have got down here without touching the dead animals on the way?

He was about to pull away, when he saw Daisy and Belle watching him. Pointing them out to Josh, he gave a mock salute. Could it have been them who guided the others down here? It certainly wouldn't have surprised him.

That was a good tackle back there," said Pete, once they were back on the road.

Josh laughed. "I was very keen on rugby when I was at school. Being a big lad, everyone wanted me on their team. At one time I thought I might make a career of it, but I wasn't good enough. It's some years since I played, but it seemed to come flooding back." He paused "Mind you, it was quite a smack you gave the sergeant; I almost felt it myself. Don't tell me you were into boxing."

"Me? Boxing?" Pete chuckled. "No way, it was a lucky punch. I was more a football man. Quite good too, or so I was told. But as a career – no way. Once I saw my grandfather's farm, I knew I wanted to be a farmer. Nothing else would do. I used to love to come up here during the school holidays. Granddad and his men taught me everything about farming. I couldn't wait for each holiday to come around. I guess that's why he left me the farm: he knew I loved it and wouldn't change anything." He grinned, as he recalled his brother's reaction. "James thought I was mad to take it on and tried to talk me out of it. But then it wasn't his scene, he was into big business and I have to say, he's done very well for himself. Strangely enough though, it was through him I met Sarah."

He fell silent.

"Where do you think Sarah might have gone?" asked Josh.

"I really don't know." Pete was thoughtful. "She doesn't have any relatives up here, only a friend in Alnwick. Her parents live in London so she might try to get down there." He sighed. "All we know for certain is what Jones told us. She went into the police station to report what she saw and then left." He paused, as he thought it through. "I wonder if she knows the army is after her. I can't ring the police. The soldier said all calls in the area are being blocked. That's probably what all the hissing was on my phone."

Suddenly Pete pulled off the road.

"What is it?" Josh asked, anxiously. He looked around half expecting to see an army vehicle behind them.

"I'm going up there." Pete pointed to a ledge on the hillside. "There's an old telescope in the glove compartment, I might be able to look across the fields and into the town and see what's going on."

Pete leapt from the car and climbed up to the ledge. Sweeping the telescope back and forth, he could see most of the town. There were a few military vehicles moving around, though the police station looked quiet enough. But then he saw Sarah's car and his blood ran cold. Had she gone back into the town? If so, she could now be in the hands of Captain Saunders.

"What do you see?" Josh called out from below.

"Sarah's car, it's parked near the police station!" Pete continued to peer through the telescope, hoping to catch a glimpse of his wife. Why would she go back to the station – but then why not? She probably didn't know the army was after her.

He tried to remember what the soldier had told him. Something about Sarah going back to the farm... Well he and Josh hadn't seen her, nor had the captain. What else had the soldier said...? He slapped his head with the palm of his hand. Think man – think! ... Hadn't he mentioned how the constable's wife and children were in the station, which was why the captain left without making a fuss...? That didn't help much. Wait a minute! The constable's wife and... Suddenly, something clicked and he rushed back down to Josh.

"Josh! Josh!" he called out excitedly, as he slid down the loose gravel. "I think Sarah and the children have escaped in someone else's car."

"Slow down, Pete, I can't make out what you're saying."

"Remember what the soldier said," continued Pete, breathlessly. "He told us the constable's wife and children were in the police station."

"So?" Josh scratched his head.

"So – don't you remember? The constables aren't married! Neither of the two constables are married!"

"You're right," said Josh, laughing. "You're damn well right."

Pete carried on excitedly. "Perhaps the constable on duty was suspicious and said she was his wife, to protect her and..."

"And he took her and the children off somewhere, because if the captain came back from the farm empty-handed, the constable himself might also be under suspicion," finished Josh.

"Exactly!" Pete threw himself back into the car. "It wouldn't take long for the army to find out that both constables are still single." He looked around to get his bearings. "Well if we're right, he's probably decided to take the forest road out of Wooler." He looked around. "If we stay on this road, it'll take us to the edge of the forest – near to where they should have come out. Once there, we'll decide which road they might have taken next. Keep your eyes peeled for the military, Josh."

Pete looked at his watch and for the first time in hours, he laughed heartily. "It's been one hell of a day, yet it's still only twelve noon."

CHAPTER NINE

Andy pulled up a couple of miles south of Alnwick Castle. Fortunately, either the army truck hadn't been chasing them after all, or he had managed to give them the slip. Looking around, he decided this was the ideal spot for their picnic. There were plenty of trees to give them cover.

"I think we should be okay here for a while." Pulling a rug from the back of the car, he laid it on the ground.

Sarah nodded and after helping the children down from the car, she set out the food they had found in the police station fridge. Normally, she enjoyed a picnic with the children, but without Pete it wasn't the same.

Once they had finished their meal, Sarah suddenly felt very tired. The trauma of the last twelve hours was taking its toll. Lying down on the rug, she closed her eyes. Was it really only last night that she had seen the light in the sky? Looking back now, it seemed a lifetime ago.

A few yards away, Andy was playing with the children. He had found an old ball in his car, something he had confiscated from a group of youths a few days earlier. Now he was throwing it for the dog to fetch. The children were squealing with excitement. Even Becky was joining in.

Andy was a great guy. He was doing his best to look out for her and the children, but... he wasn't Pete and she yearned for her husband. If only he were here with them, everything would be alright.

"Pete. Oh Pete, where are you?" she sobbed. "What's happened to you? You should have been home long before the light appeared in the sky. If you had come home, you would've been safe."

Her thoughts drifted back to the last time she had seen him. Holding her close, he had kissed her before setting off for Top Meadow. She placed her fingers on her lips: she could still feel the tingle of that last kiss.

"Play hide and seek. Play hide and seek." Josie's voice interrupted her thoughts.

The child sounded so excited. It was a game she and Becky played with their father. The two of them would go off somewhere to hide, Becky trying so hard to keep up with her sister. Pete would then go to look for them.

Sarah smiled through her tears. Of course he always knew where they were, Becky always gave the game away. She giggled every time Pete got close, though he pretended not to hear.

"Mummy, Mummy, we're going to play hide and seek." Sarah sat up and saw Josie jumping up and down. Becky tried to copy her, but kept falling over. "We're going to play hide and seek."

Sarah glanced at Andy. "You don't have to. I can settle the children."

"I don't mind. I'm enjoying it," he answered.

And it was true. Yet if anyone had told him a couple of weeks ago that he would be playing nursemaid to a couple of kids and having a whale of a time, he would have told them they were mad. But since meeting Sarah and her children, he had come to realise there was more to life than police work.

Sarah watched as he knelt down by the two little girls; his voice floated towards her on the soft breeze.

"I think your mummy's tired and needs a nap. We'll play quietly. I'll cover my eyes and count to ten, while you go and hide. Then I'll come to find you. But don't wander off too far. Remember, I'm older than you and get tired quickly."

"But Daddy doesn't get tired," argued Josie. "Even when he carries Becky, he's not tired. He takes us out for walks over the fields and shows us the sheep and the cows and everything."

"Why did I have a feeling you were going to say that?" Andy smiled. "But you know I'm not your daddy and as he couldn't be here himself, he asked me to stand in for him. I'm doing my best."

Sarah grinned, as Josie thought about what Andy had said. Her tiny lips pressed tightly together in concentration. "Okay, Andy," she said at last. "We'll not go far."

Hiding a smile, Sarah lay back down on the rug. The sun was warm and the children's voices bubbled somewhere in the background. Everything was calm and peaceful. For the moment she felt safe and... and...

Suddenly someone was shaking her.

"Sarah, Sarah."

She opened her eyes to find Andy looking down on her.

"I think we'd better move on. It's not wise to hang around too long. I've put the children and the dog in the car."

Sarah sat up with a jolt. "What time is it?"

"Nearly four o'clock."

"What!" She leapt to her feet. "Why did you let me sleep so long?"

"You looked tired. You've been through a lot." Andy smiled. "I thought the rest might do you good." He picked up the rug and folded it.

"Thank you. Yes I was tired. I hope the children didn't wear you down." Sarah laughed. "I bet when you went on duty this morning, you never thought you would be looking after a couple of toddlers by the afternoon."

"No, I didn't. But they're good kids. Even if they do keep telling me I'm not as fast, or as strong or as tall as their daddy."

After checking the map, Andy set off down another unclassified road. It was narrow and very uneven, making the pace extremely slow. But the last thing they needed now was a flat tyre.

While Andy kept his eyes firmly on the road, Sarah looked out for army trucks. Neither of them believed the military had given up the search and it wouldn't take long for them to realise the fugitives were keeping away from the main roads. Once they did, they would catch up in no time: they had the right vehicles for this kind of terrain.

"What are we going to do when we reach the outskirts of Newcastle?" asked Sarah, thinking ahead. "The suburbs stretch out for miles. We'll have to take a large detour if we're to go around the City."

Andy didn't answer. He had already thought of that. However, at the moment he was more concerned with putting a few more miles between themselves and the soldiers. But then another thought struck him. It was possible they were already in front of them. They probably hadn't stopped to play a few games or take a nap. If the military had already reached the City, might they not try sending a few men back north, using one or two of the quieter roads?

"Sarah, perhaps it would also be a good idea to watch the road ahead."

She gave him a puzzled look. "Why do that? We're still ahead of the army aren't we?"

Trying to sound calm, Andy explained his fears.

Sarah's stomach turned over. She had just begun to feel a little more relaxed. "Oh no!" she gasped. "I thought everything was going to be alright now." Leaning forward, she peered through the windscreen.

"I could be wrong." He tried to reassure her. "It was only a thought."

"But you might be right! You have the annoying habit of always being right." A little further on, Sarah pointed towards something in the distance. "Could that be an army truck?"

They couldn't afford to wait to find out. Andy scanned the road ahead, desperately searching for somewhere to hide. Fortunately a few yards further on, there was a turn-off. If they could reach it before anyone saw them, they might be in with a chance. But as they had seen the soldiers, it was more than likely they had also spotted them.

Andy swung the car into the narrow lane only to find it was in even worse condition than the previous one. Being a farm road, it would be no trouble at all to a tractor – or an army vehicle. But an ordinary car was a different matter entirely! He slowed down to a crawl.

Sarah turned to look out of the rear window. Whatever the vehicle was, it wasn't in sight now. She recalled it had been some distance away, so with a bit of luck they may not have been seen turning off down here.

"Can you see anything?" Andy's eyes were firmly fixed on the lane ahead. It was filled with potholes, making it impossible to drive any faster than a snail's pace. A little further on were some trees and a few bushes. If he could reach them before the truck appeared, they might get away with it.

"No! Not yet. But hurry!"

A note of tension had crept into Sarah's voice and though Andy himself was very worried, he tried to sound calm. "Good. Keep looking back there. I'm going to try to reach the trees."

"Mummy, where are my pictures?" Josie had suddenly discovered her drawings were missing.

"Hush, Josie! Not now," Sarah said, sharply. "We'll find them in a minute."

"When is a minute?" the child persisted.

"When I say so!" Sarah almost shouted, not taking her eyes off the road behind. Realising the sharpness of her tone, she sighed. "Please darling, hush. We're playing hide and seek."

Putting her finger to her lips, Josie looked at Becky. "Sssh, we're playing the game again."

"I still can't see anything." Sarah turned back to Andy. "Perhaps it wasn't an army truck after all. It could have been a tractor and trailer picking up something from one of the fields."

Andy pointed to the trees. "I'll reverse in there. We'll keep watch to see if the vehicle follows us." He carefully manoeuvred the car into the trees, but he was only just in time, as a few seconds later an army truck stopped at the end of the lane.

Sarah held her breath, hoping the soldiers hadn't seen them turn off. But the truck turned into the narrow road and began to edge its way down the track. Swallowing hard, she turned to face the children.

"This is very important," she whispered, placing a finger to her lips. "We must all keep very quiet indeed – not even a whisper."

She hoped the dog wouldn't suddenly decide to stand up and turn around. Any sudden movement could cause them to be discovered. "Still, Betts. Still!"

Grinning, the children looked at each other and placed a finger over their lips.

The truck came closer and Sarah held her breath as two soldiers, both holding guns, jumped down and began to walk alongside the vehicle. Trembling, she reached over and grabbed Andy's arm for support. Surely the soldiers couldn't help but see them. They weren't very well hidden: the trees and the undergrowth had begun to thin out with the coming of autumn.

By now the truck was almost upon them. The two men on the ground had been joined by a couple more and they were fanning out. Another few yards and they would be on top of them. Sarah saw Andy move his hand towards the ignition key.

Already having made up his mind they weren't going down without a fight, Andy had decided he would start the engine and make a dash for it. Ramming everything in sight if necessary.

Inch by inch, the men moved closer, one was almost upon them. Sarah's heart pounded so strongly, she felt sure the soldier would hear it. Hardly daring to breath, she very slowly turned to face the children. If one of them were to make the slightest sound now, the game would be up. Placing a finger to her lips again, she shook her head.

The soldier came closer still. Only a few more steps and he would see them. Andy's fingers tightened around the ignition key. Sarah braced herself for the inevitable. Slowly and carefully she pulled her seat belt even tighter. She knew the children were safely fastened in the back.

Suddenly the driver of the army truck rammed the horn. Sarah jumped, feeling sure they had been spotted. But he was pointing to something further up the track. "False alarm", he called out. "Up ahead – it's only a farmer."

Sarah and Andy followed his gaze and sure enough, a vehicle was parked by a gate leading to one of the fields. A man with a dog had stepped out and was making his way into a field full of sheep.

The lead soldier nodded and motioned to the others to move back. Once they were all on board, the truck slowly reversed down the narrow lane.

Still watching, Sarah breathed a sigh of relief. "I don't know where the farmer came from, but thank goodness he arrived in the nick of time." She looked at Andy. "I saw you reach for the ignition, what were you going to do?"

He grinned. "I was going to blast my way through."

"Like James Bond?" said Sarah.

"Yes, something like that."

"Would the car have taken it?" she asked thoughtfully.

"I've no idea. But wouldn't it have been great finding out?"

Leaning forward, Andy looked down the lane. The truck, having reached the junction, had turned and was continuing its journey north.

"Yes, I suppose so." Sarah shrank back in her seat, relieved the ordeal was over – at least for the moment.

"Mummy," Josie whispered. "Can we talk now?"

"Yes of course you can, sweetheart." Turning to her daughters, she forced a laugh. They must never know of the dangers they were facing. "The men didn't find us. We fooled them didn't we?"

"Will they come back to look for us again?" Josie asked.

"No, I don't think so." Sarah hoped not. That had been a close call.

Andy waited for a few more minutes before starting the car. At the end of the lane, he edged forward and looked up the road to make sure the army vehicle had gone. It wouldn't do to pull out only to find the men had parked a few yards away. To his relief, it had disappeared.

"It's okay." Andy pulled out into the road. "I only hope we don't meet any more of them."

"Me too." Sarah swept the back of her hand across her forehead. "I don't want to go through anything like that again."

She kept a careful watch in every direction for the next few miles.

Just outside Newcastle, Andy pulled into a lay-by. "We can't risk going through the City. The soldiers could be waiting for us."

"I know." Sarah paused and swallowed hard. "When do you think it'll be safe to telephone my father? Surely it would be alright if I was to use a public telephone now. We're a long way from the farm. They can't have bugged every phone in the country."

Andy wasn't so confident. They might have bugged her father's home. Especially if they knew he had a daughter in the affected area. But he realised Sarah was desperate to speak to her parents. "Wait until we get around to the other side of the City. Then we'll be able to shoot straight down the road. I would hate to be caught here and have to dodge our way through the traffic. Even the outskirts of the City can be busy at times."

He glanced at the petrol gauge: they were low on fuel. "I'll need to stop for petrol soon. Perhaps you could phone then?"

Sarah turned around and smiled at her children. "I'm going to telephone Granddad and Grandma shortly. You can tell them we are on our way for a visit." She knew how her daughters loved their grandparents.

"Yes and I'll tell Grandma about my pictures." Josie suddenly remembered she hadn't seen them for a while. "Where are they, Mummy? I want to show them to Grandma."

"I have them safe, darling. You're right, Grandma will want to see your lovely pictures, so we must keep them nice and clean until we get there."

Sitting back in her seat, Sarah wondered if they would ever reach her parent's home. If only she could talk to her father. He would be furious that such terrible things were happening here in Britain. Not only would he ask the Prime Minister to find out who was responsible for all those horrible deaths, but he would also make sure the military stopped chasing them. She felt easier in her mind, knowing she would be able to speak to him very soon.

It took nearly two and a half hours to drive around the City outskirts. Andy was beginning to despair of ever reaching a quiet road leading south. He had forgotten Newcastle and Gateshead, another large, sprawling City, were only separated by the River Tyne.

It was beginning to get dark and the bright orange street-lights seemed to go on forever. Sarah gazed out at them as they lit up the night sky above the two cities. It reminded her of London and she wished they were safely there. Finding a petrol station, Andy pulled in.

"You can use the phone over there," he said, as he began to fill the petrol tank. "But Sarah, please be careful. If you hear any strange noises on the line, hang up immediately. You can't be too careful."

"Stop it, Andy! You're frightening me." Sarah turned away to help her children out of the car. "Come along, we're going to speak to Grandma and Granddad."

In the small booth, she dialled the number. She didn't have much change, but no doubt her father would phone her back and she could tell him what had been happening over the last twenty-four hours.

The phone rang for some time before anyone answered. "Is that you, Dad? It's Sarah." She could hear someone breathing at the other end of the line, yet no one spoke. What was going on?

"Dad! Mum!" She yelled down the line. "Can you hear me? For goodness sake, say something."

CHAPTER TEN

Before leaving the laboratory, Charles Hammond spent several hours examining the machines. He was desperate to learn why they had gone out of control so suddenly. Obviously with the safety guards turned off, there was nothing to shut them down once it happened and again, that was something else he needed to look into. But for the moment his concerns were on finding out the cause of the eruption.

Finally, he went home to shower and change or at least that was what he told his staff. The real reason being he needed to speak to Irene. She was still unaware of what had happened. He was dreading the prospect of telling her about the fate of their daughter and her family. Yet he had to do it. He couldn't allow her to hear it from someone else.

John Shaw also took the opportunity to go home for an hour or so, promising to return as soon as possible. He had been on duty at the time of the crisis and felt responsible, though Charles insisted he had no reason to reproach himself.

The two men had gone over the figures and checked the machines several times. While John was at a loss as to what had happened, Charles had made an amazing discovery. But he decided to keep it to himself, hoping to catch the culprit. He had to admit, the problem had been well hidden. Even as he drove home, Charles still pondered over the matter.

Most of his staff were reliable – people he could trust. True, there were a few he needed to keep an eye on. However, he would never entrust anything as dangerous as Trojan to anyone he considered flippant. But then if it had been entirely up to him, such people wouldn't have been given the job in the first place. Yes, he was part of the selection committee, but it was that ferret-like creature, Alan Crisp, who took charge. Many a good applicant had been turned down because the silly little man's head had been turned by a flash of thigh or a promise of free membership to some exclusive men's club.

Charles was almost home. A few more turnings and he would come face to face with Irene. Surprisingly, the traffic was busy and it was taking longer than usual to reach his house. Glancing in the mirror, he indicated to turn left. The car behind also followed him around the corner. Charles vaguely remembered seeing the same car a while back.

He indicated again and once more the car followed suit. Was he being tailed? No! Of course not! That was ridiculous. Now he was being paranoid. Why would anyone be watching him? Nevertheless the car followed him right into his own street.

Charles pulled into his drive. The car behind carried on towards the end of the road, but a little way past his drive it began to slow down. He didn't recognise it as one of his neighbour's cars. But it still didn't mean he was being watched. Perhaps there was a simple explanation – one of his neighbours might be expecting visitors.

Having heard the car pull into the drive, Irene was already waiting at the front door. As Charles walked towards her, she didn't fail to notice how her husband's shoulders drooped even more than usual. However, she didn't let it show and greeted him with a kiss, just as she did every day when he came home.

"Shall we go inside?" Charles sounded weary.

Irene led the way down the hall; bracing herself for bad news.

"I have something to tell you," said Charles. He paused, glancing cautiously around the living room. Could his house be bugged?

"Have you been out today?" He tried to sound natural. "Did you go shopping?"

Irene looked at her husband and frowned. Charles didn't usually ask questions of that nature the moment he got home. They were left until later, over dinner or while relaxing with a drink during the evening. "No. I've been here on my own."

"No visitors? No one called?" Charles raised his eyebrows.

"No. No one at all. Like I said, I've been on my own all day. In fact, I haven't seen a single soul." She studied her husband. Was the job beginning to grind him down? "Why? Should I have gone out for something?"

Charles shook his head. "Sit down, Irene I have something to tell you."

Irene slowly lowered herself into a chair, her eyes never leaving her husband's face. She had never seen him like this before. Though she had been expecting bad news, this sounded as though it was going to be worse than she thought. "What is it?" Her voice was strained.

"I have something to tell you." Charles repeated. He hesitated. "You're not going to like it."

"For goodness sake, get on with it." Irene was anxious. Charles hadn't fooled her earlier when he said the meeting with the Robert Turner had gone well. The Prime Minister didn't demand you attend Number Ten at four in the morning, simply because he couldn't sleep and was in need of a chat.

He hesitated, not knowing where to start.

"Charles! For heaven's sake, tell me what's going on!" Irene slammed her hand on the arm of the chair. This nonsense had gone on long enough. She wanted to know what had happened.

"It's the project I was working on." He paused. "It's all gone wrong."

"What do you mean – gone wrong? What happened?"

"It blew up." Until then Charles had remained standing, but now he sank into a chair and hung his head. "It blew up, Irene." He paused. "Well, as good as, for some reason the damn thing imploded allowing the contents to escape. The result is the same: hundreds of lives have been lost."

"Blew up! What do you mean – blew up?" Irene shook her head. "I didn't hear anything. Wouldn't I have heard something?" She raised her voice slightly. "Wouldn't all of London have heard something?"

Charles lifted his head and looked at his wife. Taking her by the hand, he said. "It wasn't here in London. It was in Northumberland."

For a moment, Irene was puzzled. But then the full impact of what Charles had said, sunk home.

"Oh, my God, Sarah!" She pulled her hand away. "You're not telling me that Sarah... Pete... the children..." Unable to finish, she stared at him for confirmation.

"I don't know."

"You don't know! Haven't you tried to ring them?" Irene leapt to her feet. "What's wrong with you? It's our daughter we're talking about and you haven't even tried to call her?" She rushed across to the phone and picked up the receiver.

"No!" Charles yelled, jumping to his feet. "Put it down."

"Why? Surely we...!" Irene saw her husband put his finger to his lips.

Charles hurried across to his wife. Gently, he took the receiver from her hand and replaced it on the cradle. "I think it's bugged."

"Bugged?" Irene looked at her husband. Had he gone mad?

"I think so. When I called you earlier, there was a distinct click after you had hung up."

"But that's ridiculous, Charles. Who on earth would want to bug our phone?"

"The Prime Minister." Charles led Irene across to the sofa. "He wants this business hushed up. I overheard him talking to some of the members of his Cabinet when I left the room."

"But Sarah and all those other innocent people up there; how can he even think of hushing up a catastrophe like this?" Unable to control herself, Irene was shaking as she looked up at her husband for answers. "How on earth could you allow yourself to become involved in anything so evil?" After all the years they had been together, did she really know this man? She began to cry. "I'll never forgive you for what you've done."

Charles sighed. "I can understand how you feel. Once this is finished, I never want to have anything to do with it again."

"What do you mean, once this is finished?" Irene sobbed. "Surely you're not going back to the laboratory? We must go up to Northumberland and look for Sarah and her family."

Charles gazed down at his wife. "I can't go anywhere. I think I'm being followed."

"Followed? What on earth for?" This was going from bad to worse. "Who could blame us for wanting to find our daughter?"

"Irene, haven't I just told you, the Prime Minister wants this hushed up." Charles relayed what he had overheard while standing outside the Cabinet Room. "He doesn't want any survivors. That's why I didn't dare ring her. While there is the slightest chance that she, Pete and the girls are still alive, we must keep silent. No one must know they were anywhere near the scene."

Irene sank back into the sofa. "This is a nightmare. When will we know whether they're dead or not?" She closed her eyes. "When they find the bodies, I suppose."

Charles sat down beside his wife and put his arm around her. "We'll only know if we don't see or hear from her ever again."

Irene looked at her husband. "What are you saying?" She spoke slowly. "Is there something you haven't told me?"

Charles took a deep breath. "The bodies will be beyond recognition." He closed his eyes. "They'll have melted." Charles gave her a brief account of what would have happened to the people caught up in the light and the gas.

"What! May God forgive you!" Irene screamed out at her husband. "Never in a million years would I have believed you'd even think of creating something so monstrous."

Charles reached out and touched her hand. "Irene, please. I understand how you feel. But they may still be alive. You know Sarah, she's a fighter."

"In God's name, Charles, how could anyone fight something like that?" Irene pulled her hand away. "Go on, explain it to me. From what you've told me, there's nothing anyone could have done to save themselves."

"Hopefully they might have escaped the light and the gas..." Charles began.

"But then what?" Irene interrupted. "You say soldiers have been sent to deal with anyone who might have seen what happened. Those who survived will think the army has come to their rescue and..."

Just then the phone began to ring. Irene glared at her husband with disgust. "You answer it, it'll probably be for you anyway. It's most likely the Prime Minister, with another of his little schemes for national security."

Charles slowly lifted the receiver. He couldn't bear to hear any more bad news. He had heard enough to last a lifetime. But before he had a chance to speak a voice came down the line.

"Is that you Dad? It's Sarah."

Charles swung around to face his wife. He was jubilant. His daughter was alive! Oh my God, Sarah was alive! Trembling with relief, he wanted to shout with joy, yet he didn't dare. Someone out there may be listening to his every word.

Seeing the expression of amazement on her husband's face, Irene began to make signs. She wanted to know who was on the phone. He placed his hand across the mouthpiece. "It's Sarah," he whispered.

Irene caught her breath and ran across to Charles. Was it really possible that Sarah was alive after all?

Charles heard his daughter's voice again. He was going to have to say something. The faceless person listening in would get suspicious if he didn't answer her.

"Sarah, darling," he said at last. "What a surprise. It's so lovely to hear from you; I thought you were on holiday for another week. I must have got the dates wrong. You and the family must come here and tell us all about it." His heart was in his mouth as he waited for her response. Silently, he pleaded she wouldn't say anything that might arouse suspicion.

Sarah paused. Holiday? What was her father talking about? They were on holiday months ago. He had obviously been working too hard.

"Dad, what are you talking about? You know that..." she broke off. There were some faint clicks on the line.

Was Andy right? Was someone listening in to her father's calls? If so, did he know about it? Was that why Dad was talking in riddles? She decided to play it safe.

"Sorry about that Dad, one of the girls dropped something. What was I saying, oh yes, you know we go there every year and you've heard it all before. But we'll come over to see you. The children want to show you all the photos."

"That would be really great. You know how much we love seeing you all. Make it soon, won't you?"

Sarah noticed the relief in his voice. "Yes, we hope to call on you sometime tomorrow." She paused. "It'll probably be late as we still have so much to do. Is Mum alright?"

"Yes, she's here, do you want a word with her?"

"Yes, but I'll have to be quick. It's been a long day for the children. Travelling is very tiring."

Handing the phone to his wife, Charles covered the receiver. "Be careful what you say."

"Sarah, my darling it's so lovely to hear from you." Though she was trembling with a mixture of fear and relief, Irene tried to sound natural. "As your father said, we're both looking forward to seeing you all again."

However, Sarah detected the note of tension in her mother's voice. Something was very wrong at home.

"Yes, Mum, we had a super time. The girls always enjoy their holiday."

She glanced across to where Andy was filling the car. He was waving at her to hurry up.

"I'd better go, Mum, the children are tired. I need to get them into bed. I'll see you tomorrow. I simply wanted you to know we'd arrived back in England."

"That's fine, darling. We'll look forward to seeing you, Take care."

Tears ran down Irene's cheeks, as she replaced the receiver. "I thank God they're alive Charles. From what you told me, I really believed we'd never see them again."

Charles stroked his chin nervously. Obviously Sarah still had some way to go. She had hinted at that when she said they would be late, still having so much to do. She wasn't out of the woods yet. So many things could happen between Northumberland and London. However he wasn't going to mention his fears to his wife. Now that Irene had found a straw to clutch on to, he wasn't about to pull it away.

CHAPTER ELEVEN

Sarah was thoughtful as she walked back to where Andy was waiting. Without saying a word, she strapped the children into the car. Josie grumbled about not having spoken to her grandparents.

"That's a shame." Andy glanced at Sarah. "Weren't they at home?"

"Yes they were," she replied, climbing into the front seat. "But my father was acting very strangely. He was talking about us being on holiday. At first I thought he had gone mad and was about to say so, but then I heard a couple of faint clicks on the line. After what you had said, I wondered whether his phone was bugged and he was trying to stop me from saying too much. That's why I didn't dare let the children speak to him. They might have said something about you being with us."

"Your father's phone is bugged?" Andy's eyes widened and he caught his breath. Alarm bells were ringing. "Why would anyone do that, Sarah? Do many people know that he has a daughter living in the north?" He fired questions at her.

"I suppose a few do: family and friends," said Sarah, thoughtfully, not appearing to notice the panic in Andy's tone. "But I don't think his work colleagues know. My father has never been one for mixing business with pleasure." She paused. "Except with Rick, but then he's also a friend."

"What does your father do?" Andy tried to make the question sound casual.

"He's a scientist for the government." She sighed. "I don't know much about it. It's all very hush-hush."

"A bit like 'Q' in James Bond?" said Andy.

"Yes, something like that." Sarah smiled. "You're obsessed with James Bond."

"By the way, I picked up a newspaper while I was paying for the petrol. Check through and see if the incident back there is mentioned."

Sarah swiftly looked through the pages of the newspaper, but there was nothing. Desperately she turned back to the front page and thumbed through again, but there was definitely no mention of the catastrophe in Northumberland.

"Oh my God, Andy, they don't know. All those poor people lying dead and still no one knows anything about it."

She turned towards the window to hide the tears trickling down her face. "Pete. I won't let them get away with it," she murmured. "I swear to you that once the children are safe, I'll tell everyone what happened up there."

Andy didn't say anything. It was as he had suspected all along: a cover-up. Why else would they be fleeing for their lives? But now he had something else to occupy his mind. Sarah's father was a government scientist. His job was very hush-hush and now his phone was bugged. Was it possible that...?

"Andy, you've gone very quiet." Sarah interrupted his thoughts. "Are you alright?"

"Err... yes, I was just thinking."

"What about?"

"I was simply trying to piece everything together." He glanced across at her. "Why would they bug your father's phone?"

"I really don't know, but he's not a threat to the security of the nation. He wouldn't run off and sell secrets to foreign countries, if that's what you're thinking." Folding her arms, she sniffed and looked away. Her father was no traitor and she wasn't going to allow Andy to say he was!

"No, of course he wouldn't. But what if they thought he might want to leak this disaster to the newspapers?" Glancing at her again, he saw her frown. "I didn't mean for money," he added, hurriedly. "But if he didn't agree about this business being hushed-up, they might suspect he'd tell someone." He sighed. "I'm sorry; I'm not making a good job of this."

"I think I understand what you mean," Sarah relented. Her father was an honourable man, if he believed the country should know about something, perhaps he would tell. What other explanation could there be for bugging his phone. Yet, if the incident were being kept quiet, how would he know about it? Surely only those connected with this terrible thing would be informed? Her father couldn't possibly be involved in something like this.

She looked back at Andy. What was he really thinking? But he gave nothing away; his eyes were fixed on the road ahead. Having rejoined a side road, it was very uneven and needed his undivided attention.

"We'll have to find somewhere to stop for the night." Changing the subject, Sarah smiled at her two children. "They need somewhere to sleep. Couldn't we pull into one of those motels?"

"But they're all on the main roads," Andy didn't dare to take his eyes off the road. "I don't think we should chance driving on the motorways."

"Well we're going to have to stop somewhere. The children are tired, I'm tired and you must be too."

He opened his mouth to say something, but she got there first. "Don't argue! Of course you are. You've been driving all day." She stabbed her finger towards the window. "Look out there! What do you see?"

"What! Where?" Andy strained his eyes. "What can you see? There's nothing out there but the beams from our headlights."

"Exactly! This is the only car on the road. Our headlights can probably be seen for miles. They're a dead giveaway. Who else would be foolish enough to drive on this road in the dark, especially in a car like this?" She laughed. "Only people like us, people on the run."

Andy quickly pulled up and turned off the headlights. Sarah was right on both counts. He was very tired and it was true, the main beam would be seen from a long way off. He glanced at the two children in the back. They had been so good: not crying or screaming for attention, like some he had come across. But now they were tired and in need of a proper bed.

As he saw it, they could do one of two things. They could find a turn off which would lead them onto a main road where they could blend in with the other traffic until they found a motel, or they could spend the night in the car out here and try to make the best of it. Either way, they were going to have to stop, which was the one thing he had tried to avoid all day. If only they hadn't met that wretched man earlier, they could have been miles further on by now. He had taken them miles out of their way. But at least they had got this far and that in itself was a real achievement.

"Alright, Sarah, you win. We'll look for a motel. But we'll need to rise early and make our way back onto the side roads before anyone sees us. By the way, do you have any cash? That was the one thing I forgot to pick up when I went home to get a change of clothes. I've spent most of what I had on the petrol."

"I've got some, but not a lot. I've got a couple of credit cards, though." Sarah rummaged around in her bag.

Andy looked doubtful. "I'm not keen on using those. By now, they'll be using every method at their disposal to find us. Credit cards could easily be traced back to us, telling everyone where we are."

"Yes, I've seen that film too." Sarah laughed, but then she frowned. "You don't really think it's possible, do you?"

"Yes I do. At the police college, I learned how hackers can do all sorts of things nowadays. This is the age of technology, we can't be too careful."

Sarah wasn't really convinced, but there was no point in taking a chance. "Well I've probably got enough cash for a couple of rooms and..."

"One family room." Andy corrected her. "We've got to act like a family."

Sarah sighed, he was right. "Okay, a family room," she said slowly. "But I still need to get some money from somewhere. We might need it further on. Perhaps we could find a bank."

"We'll see." Andy hoped they would be in London before they needed to use any more cash.

The dim light in the car was bright enough to look at the map. It seemed they weren't too far from a turning, which would take them to the main road. Starting the engine, Andy switched on the headlights, hoping he might manage without the main beam. But it was too dark. He couldn't take the risk of running off the road and ending up in a ditch.

Thankfully it didn't take too long to join the motorway and a few miles further on, they came to a motel. Between them they found they had enough money for the room with a little left over for some supper and breakfast the next morning, plus a couple of cans of food for Betts.

While Andy took the dog for a walk, Sarah bathed the children and put them into the small bed at one side of the room. Though they had slept a great deal during the day, they were still tired and fell asleep instantly.

Tears formed in Sarah's eyes, as she gazed down on the two innocent faces. It wasn't fair, why did this have to happen to them? Tracked by soldiers bearing guns, the poor mites had been dragged through the countryside and none of it was their fault. She quickly wiped her eyes when she heard Andy open the door.

"Betts seems okay," Andy said as he came in. "Though she could probably do with something to eat." He looked towards the sleeping children. "Are they alright?"

"Yes, I think so." Sarah stood up. Her voice was choked. "Would you mind feeding the dog while I have a bath?"

"Yes of course I will," said Andy, looking around. "But we haven't got a bowl..." Seeing the tired expression on Sarah's face, he quickly added. "You go ahead; I'll find something."

Sarah sank into the hot water and closed her eyes. Never had a bath felt so good. The aches and pains of the day slowly ebbed from her. The water was relaxing. She could feel herself slipping away... sinking into a world without horror and sadness, a world where she and Pete were back on the farm playing with the children...

Suddenly she was aware of a loud banging on the door. "Sarah! Sarah! Are you alright. For God's sake answer me, are you alright in there?"

"For goodness sake, keep your voice down or you'll wake the children." Reaching out, Sarah picked up her watch and was amazed at how long she had lain there.

"I'm sorry Andy." Her tone was softer. "I didn't realise the time: I must have dozed off. I'll be out in a minute."

"It's fine. No rush. I was just making sure you were okay."

Sarah noted the relief in his voice and she puzzled over it for the next few minutes. What had he expected? Surely he hadn't thought she had slit her wrists? She sat up so quickly, the water slopped over the sides of the bath.

No way would she do that! Especially with her children lying asleep in the next room. They needed her now more than ever. Jumping out of the bath, she quickly got dressed.

In the main room, she found Andy watching the television; the volume was turned low.

"It's all yours." She pointed to the bathroom, before walking across to small table where a selection of tea and coffee was laid out. "Do you want anything?"

"Thanks. But I'll wait until I've had a bath," said Andy rising to his feet.

Sarah made herself a hot drink and after checking the children, she slipped out of her jeans and climbed into bed.

Andy found her asleep, still holding the mug of tea. He was removing it from her hand, when she awoke.

"Sorry, I didn't mean to wake you, but..." He pointed to the mug.

He took the mug to the bathroom and rinsed it out. On his return, he pulled a blanket from the cupboard and sat down on the chair. "Wake me if you need anything."

Sarah snuggled down under the covers. The bed was warm and comfortable. Andy certainly didn't look very comfy over there in the chair. She could hear him wrestling around and felt guilty at having the king size bed to herself.

Five, then ten minutes passed. She could still hear him moving about. If only she had thought about it earlier, she could have put the girls in this bed with her. Andy could then have had the smaller one. She toyed with the idea of moving the children. But they were sleeping soundly; it would be a shame to wake them. They had fallen asleep the instant their heads had touched the pillow.

Andy shifted his position yet again. It was no good. She was going to have to share this bed with him. But he must understand that this was only because of the extenuating circumstances.

"Andy," she whispered, sitting up.

"Yes." Andy stood up quickly. "Did you hear something outside?"

"No. But I can hear you moving around in that chair. I guess you're having trouble getting to sleep." She paused. "You can share this bed with me. But only if you promise to stay on your own side."

"Of course I promise. I tell you, Sarah, I'm too damn tired to even think about anything else."

The darkness hid the smile that played around her lips as she lay down. She heard him stumble and then the low growl of Betts.

"And mind you don't fall over the dog," she whispered, still smiling.

The bed rocked gently, as he climbed in beside her. "Goodnight Sarah, and thanks."

"Goodnight Andy." She laughed. "I hope you don't snore."

"Of course I don't snore." Andy was indignant. He paused. "At least I don't think I do."

"I'll tell you in the morning," said Sarah, snuggling down under the covers.

CHAPTER TWELVE

Luck was smiling favourably upon the Prime Minister. So far, the news of the catastrophe in the north had not leaked beyond the four walls of the Cabinet Room. Since the meeting during the early hours of the morning, he had checked every newspaper and news bulletin. He knew it would only take one up and coming journalist to hear the slightest snippet of information and the whole of his hush-hush plan would be in jeopardy.

It was unfortunate that some of the soldiers being sent to sort out the 'little problem' had to be informed of the incident. But Turner had warned the two generals to handpick their most trusted men to help in clearing up the affected area. Most of the other troops were only there as camouflage and knew nothing of the real reason for their deployment. They believed they were on some new sort of training exercise.

That same day, some twelve hours later, Robert Turner called another meeting at Downing Street. He invited the same group of people, with a couple of exceptions. One was Arthur Goodwin. At the Prime Minister's request, Brian Tate had not informed his minister of the meeting.

"Don't involve him further," the Prime Minister had told him, privately. "The man is too honest for our good."

The other person missing was Sir Charles Hammond.

Obviously General Lewis was also not present, having flown to the north-east immediately after the previous meeting. However, using a scrambling device, he had telephoned his report to General Bainbridge who promised to relay it to the Prime Minister personally. Why take the slightest risk of using an adjutant when so much was at stake?

There was however, one extra person there – the Chancellor of the Exchequer. He had been unable to attend the previous meeting, due to a former engagement, which had meant spending the night away from London.

General Bainbridge's eyes gleamed at the sight of the all-important man from the Treasury. The Prime Minister had promised both generals extra troops and weaponry as well as a financial reward in exchange for their co-operation. Not wanting to miss out on a deal like that, the generals had agreed to work closely together.

The general took the chancellor's presence to mean he was prepared to discuss money. Delighted though he was, he wished Lewis was here. It would be easier with the two of them. It was well known that chancellors could run rings around people. They hated parting with taxpayers' money: treating it as though it was their own. Nevertheless, the Prime Minister had made them a promise and if clearing away a few skeletons up there in the back of beyond would get them the much-needed equipment, not to mention a healthier bank balance, then so be it.

The thought of the skeletons made Bainbridge shudder. Tomorrow he was flying north to meet up with Lewis. And from what he had already heard from his colleague, he didn't relish the prospect. However, Lewis had promised there was no need for either of them to go near the bodies.

"Even I haven't seen them yet!" he had bellowed down the phone after giving his report. "I'm relying on my officers for information. After all, isn't that what the men are for?"

But Bainbridge wasn't so sure. Perhaps it would be a good idea if they took a peek for themselves in case the Prime Minister ever asked them about it. But another reason lay behind his thinking. Surely it would be good for the men to see the generals getting their hands dirty, so to speak. To his mind, the morale of the men should always be the priority of any general worth his salt. Without the men's support, they wouldn't get anywhere. Besides, he and Lewis didn't actually need to touch anything. Simply being seen in the right place would be enough.

"Right gentlemen, now we're all here, I suggest we get down to business." The Prime Minister's voice interrupted his thoughts. "I understand General Bainbridge has heard from Lewis. Isn't that so?"

The general rose to his feet. "I'm sorry, Prime Minister, but aren't we waiting for Sir Charles? I was hoping to have another word with him."

"Sir Charles will not be attending this meeting." The Prime Minister's voice was cold.

He was desperate for news and here was Bainbridge, waffling on about Hammond. But remembering he was relying heavily on both this man and his counterpart, he engaged his most winning smile and softened his tone. "Please carry on." He gestured to the people around the table. "We're all very anxious to hear what General Lewis has to say."

"Err, yes, Prime Minister." Bainbridge shuffled his feet. He would have preferred a private audience with the Prime Minister, the news being less than favourable. But Robert Turner had insisted he should speak to all the people present.

"Oh I think you can call me Robert while we're in here." Smiling broadly, Turner looked at the others. "That goes for you all. As we are working so closely together on such a delicate matter, a little less formality would be a good thing, don't you think?"

He nodded to the general, "Do carry on."

"Yes. Thank you... Robert."

The general felt uncomfortable. To him it was unnatural to call anyone above his rank by their Christian name. He looked down at the paper in his hand.

"As I was about to say, General Lewis reports that the men have started the mammoth task of clearing up the..." He coughed. "...the remains. This will take some time, as the men can only work very slowly." He glanced around the table. "Quite apart from the... dangerous nature of the problem, the thick suits are most cumbersome." He smiled. "However, I'm happy to be able to say, the air is not contaminated. The men wear masks because of the risk of splashes to the face."

He paused and took a deep breath. Now for something the Prime Minister wouldn't like. "General Lewis also tells me a woman came across a skeleton near where she lived and reported it to the police. He learned of this incident because the police went out there to investigate and used their radio to report back to the police station. Fortunately our men, who were jamming all forms of communication, intercepted the message and blocked it. Captain Saunders quickly drove to the police station with the intention of taking the woman into custody."

The general paused and swallowed hard before continuing. "However, when he arrived, the woman wasn't there. The constable said she had returned to her farm. Captain Saunders would like to have questioned him further. But the constable's wife chose that very moment to arrive at the police station, and not wishing to arouse suspicion needlessly, Captain Saunders left. After all, there was no reason to doubt the word of the constable." Pausing, he looked up at Robert Turner.

"Quite." The Prime Minister nodded. "Do carry on."

General Bainbridge hesitated, hardly daring to read out the next part. "However when Captain Saunders reached the farm, the woman wasn't there. Lewis has reason to believe the constable fooled his officer, as both he and this woman have since disappeared. Further discreet enquiries have shown that the constable isn't married."

Bainbridge shuffled his papers uneasily. He recalled picking up a distinct feeling from Lewis that there was more bad news. But as the general hadn't said anything further, Bainbridge had left well alone. This was enough to be going on with.

"Of course our men are in pursuit," he continued. "All major roads have been blocked and suitable vehicles have been dispatched to search all unclassified roads in the area. I can assure you, Prime Minister, they will not escape."

Pleased his report was over, the general was about to sit down, when he thought he heard something. He looked towards the door, fully expecting to see someone walk into the room. But it remained firmly closed.

Puzzled, he slowly lowered himself into his chair. He was still quite sure he had heard something. However, glancing around the table, he noted no one else seemed to have noticed anything. He shrugged. He must be hearing things. But then, quite suddenly, a cold shiver ran down his back. He had a strange feeling there was someone else in the room. What was going on? Was his imagination working overtime?

Looking around, he noticed for the first time that there was a large wing-backed chair in the far corner. From his position, all he could see was the back of the chair. Nevertheless, he felt sure someone was sitting there listening to every word, yet not wishing to be seen – not by him, anyway.

"General Bainbridge." The sudden boom of the Prime Minister's voice made him jump. "Your report has given me no comfort. I had hoped I'd made myself absolutely clear at our last meeting. No one. I repeat; no one was to be left in a position to inform the public of what had happened in Northumberland. Now I'm told there are at least two people roaming around the countryside that could pass on this information. May I ask how many more has escaped your net?"

Robert Turner closed his eyes. Already he could see the luxury of another term in office slipping away from him. He was enjoying his role as Prime Minister and why shouldn't he? He had given up a great deal to achieve his goal.

Out there on the campaign trail, he had done everything expected of him – and more. He had covered more ground in the space of a few days than he ever thought possible. It sickened him when he recalled the number of babies he had kissed and the work-worn hands of men and women he had shaken. Always at the beck and call of the Party, he had lost most of his friends when his ambitions had forced him to let them down so many times. Then, when it seemed he and the Opposition were neck and neck in the race for Downing Street, he had gone all out and promised voters far more than he knew he could ever deliver. All that had been a necessary evil. Yet there was more – he was locked in a loveless marriage.

Running for Prime Minister didn't come cheap. Despite the Party's principles, he knew that the odd few thousand pounds quietly dropped in the right quarter would certainly make a difference to his campaign. Therefore he had entered into his marriage purely for the sake of his career. With his father-in-law being powerfully rich and agreeing to pour money into his bank account whenever he needed it, he couldn't fail to succeed.

But now his wife Annabel, first lady of the land, had lost what little interest she had in him and was never at home: always gracing some function or another with her presence. While her father, having been elected to even further directorships, was richer than ever. Turner knew it would only take one slip on his part and they would all plummet from the scene forever.

Since the election, only his quick wit at the dispatch box had allowed him to divert attention from the fact that most of what he had promised was unfulfilled. His silver tongue ran rings around the opposition leader. But now it seemed everything he had worked and schemed for could be lost, because one stupid woman had managed to survive and report her findings to the police.

Why hadn't the wretched woman died with the others? Why couldn't she have touched one of the bodies in a gallant effort to help the victims, only to be reduced to a pool of slime? Because of her, the very foundations of his government could be destroyed and he would go down as the most infamous Prime Minister in history. A Prime Minister who had secretly encouraged chemical weapon research in the United Kingdom, while telling the rest of the world they should disarm.

He gritted his teeth. No, he wasn't going down without a fight. He would do whatever necessary to keep this off the front pages. He had succeeded before and he could do it again.

Opening his eyes, he looked around the table. "Do you realise the press will have a field day with information like this? With an election only a few weeks away, we must all do our utmost to stop these people from talking to anyone, let alone the press." He slammed his fist down onto the table. "Am I making myself clear?" Robert Turner looked at each of the people seated around the table in turn, before his eyes rested on General Bainbridge.

"Of course, Robert." The general felt obliged to confirm the Prime Minister's last sentence. "I'll be flying to Northumberland to join General Lewis directly our meeting is over. I assure you that together we'll find the people involved and take them back to the area." He looked away. "We know what must be done."

Robert Turner smiled. "That is good news, General Bainbridge, I'm sure we'll all be delighted to hear from you when you have succeeded in the task." He glanced at the Chancellor. "Perhaps you and the general would like to have a little chat about the money involved in this... clean-up operation." There was no point in letting the others know of the special arrangement he had made with the military.

"Yes... er... thank you, Prime Minister," the general blustered. "I can speak for General Lewis, of course."

"But of course." The Prime Minister gestured towards the door. "You can talk in the room across the hall."

Once the chancellor and the general had left the room, Robert Turner turned to the others. "Has anyone got anything to say?"

As there was no response, his eyes rested on Brian Tate. "What about you? Are you satisfied everything is being done to put an end to this disaster? Or is there something we've forgotten?"

Tate shook his head. "There's nothing else we can do. We're all in the hands of the two generals."

"And what about you? Do you wish to say something?" Raising his voice, the Prime Minister looked across towards the large chair in the corner of the room.

The chair revolved to reveal a dark haired man. "No, I have nothing to add to my report."

The man slowly crossed his long legs, making himself more comfortable. "As I said, it appears Sir Charles turned off the safeguards and left instructions stating he didn't want to be disturbed. How can you trust a man who would do something like that?" He paused, allowing his words to sink in. "I understand it was your own minister, Alan Crisp, who alerted you to the incident."

"Yes, that's right." Alan interrupted. Here was his chance to get back at Charles for not involving him in his briefings. "I called at the laboratory to speak to Sir Charles, but he wasn't there. I found the place in turmoil. The man's a disgrace. If you ask me, it was his negligence, which caused the whole problem. I think..."

"Yes, yes, Alan." Without as much as a glance in his direction, the Prime Minister silenced him with a wave of his hand.

Turner disliked the man intensely. Alan Crisp was a man who was always looking to pull someone down, especially if it was to his own advantage. It wouldn't surprise him if he himself were Crisp's next target. Nevertheless, he realised the wretched man could be useful at times – so long as you kept your back turned away from him.

Turner again addressed the man in the chair. "You've spoken to me of Sir Charles before, but I always thought him to be very thorough."

Uncrossing his legs, the man rose to his feet. He was still unsure of how this was going to workout. Therefore he needed to think very carefully about his position. While it was true Charles had his uses, the Prime Minister could do so much more for him. Perhaps for the time being, he should play them one against the other.

"Yes, I agree. Charles is a very meticulous man." He ambled across to the table. "I've worked with him for some time now and I don't want to speak out against him. Perhaps he was simply having a bad day. Mercifully this incident didn't occur in the London area..." He shrugged.

Robert Turner shivered at the thought. "Yes. You're absolutely right." He turned to the group around the table. "Gentlemen, for those of you who don't know him already, may I introduce Rick Armstrong. I strongly believe he should take over the laboratory as from now. Do you all agree?" He looked around the table. "Motion carried," he added, as everyone nodded in silent agreement.

****

Rick smiled to himself as he strolled out into the hall of Number Ten. He was head of all Government Scientific Affairs. It was the top job in his field and the title rested well on him. It had a certain ring to it.

Yet it had all been so easy. With the help of that little shit, Alan Crisp, he was at the top of the tree. In time it would probably mean a knighthood. The thought excited him and he rubbed his hands together.

For a fleeting moment he felt sorry for Charles. It needn't have happened like this. He would have been prepared to wait until Charles had retired, if only the man had listened to him and given his ideas some credence. Instead Charles had told him he was impatient and foolhardy. Foolhardy indeed! Rick grimaced. He knew exactly what he was doing. He had worked hard on the project. There was no need to wait any longer. He was a man of vision – Trojan was ready.

The experiments he and Sir Charles were working on would put the United Kingdom at the forefront in chemical weapons. With a weapon such as this, the country would be back where it belonged – on top: second to none.

The Prime Minister was yearning for the power of having such a weapon at his disposal. Yet Charles was hesitant, cautious – too cautious, always checking and double-checking everything.

Rick recalled how he had hung back and waited. Biding his time, he had allowed Charles to do all his checks, while waiting for exactly the right moment. He wasn't in a hurry and would have waited even longer. But a few weeks ago, something had forced his hand: he had seen Sarah again. He had been invited to dinner when she was visiting her parents and chatting to her had been like a blast from the past.

Since her marriage to Pete, he had tried to get over her. My God, how he had tried! But at that moment, there in her parent's home, he knew he still loved her. She would have been his years ago, if that bloody farmer hadn't come along and turned her head.

He remembered how the day he saw her, had been the very same day her father had once again rejected his plea to test the new weapon in a confined atmosphere.

"It's too soon. Trojan is unstable," Charles had told him. "If something were to go wrong, we might not be able to stop it. Give it a few more months and we'll talk again."

In the end, Rick had lost his temper. "You're an old fool. At this rate, we'll still be talking ten years from now." Unable to restrain himself he had stormed out in a fit of rage.

But there had been a moment before the argument, when Charles had been called from the study. Waiting there alone, Rick's thoughts had drifted back to Sarah. Absentmindedly, he wrote her name on a piece of paper, even adding the date she had said she would be staying with a friend. When Charles re-entered the room, he stuffed it into his pocket. Back home, he had come across the paper while removing his jacket. Seeing Sarah's name reminded him of how much he still yearned for her. From that moment he began to hatch a plan to bring her back to him.

He would use Trojan. It was sitting up there in the hills, waiting to be tested. Still unsure how far the rays and gas would reach he would need to work it all out very carefully, not wanting Sarah to be caught up in them. But then the date on the paper stared up at him. That was it! He clapped his hands with joy. It was the date Sarah was staying away overnight; leaving the children with a friend. Pete was picking them up later in the day.

It couldn't be more perfect! It wouldn't matter how far the wretched weapon reached. With Sarah safely out of the way, he would kill Pete and his two brats. With them gone and the land devastated for years to come, Sarah would be forced to leave the farm and return to her parent's home.

Naturally he would be there to comfort her: to grieve and sympathise at her loss. He would give her time to get over the death of her two children and her husband. And when she did – he would be there for her. Then, when the time was right, he would ask her to marry him and she, realising the mistake she had made in marrying Pete, would agree. Together they would have children – his children. He had always wanted to be a father.

He would also show sympathy towards Charles. As the perfect son-in-law to be, he would raise his hands in mock horror at the government's findings. He would tell them all how, on reflection, Sir Charles was not the sort of person to tamper with the machines.

Rick knew the deadly weapon would kill every living thing in all the valleys around the old power station and devastate the land for years to come. But it was a small price to pay to get even with the farmer who had come between him and his beloved Sarah.

Now walking down the hall of Number Ten, his heart pounded with excitement. All his plans had worked out perfectly. He chuckled at the thought of Pete and his two kids now lying dead; their skeletons exposed to the army personnel. There would be no words said over them. The soldiers would simply shovel up their remains with all the others and drop them into a concrete pit.

According to General Bainbridge, it was a young woman, who had reported the incident. In his heart Rick knew it was Sarah. It had to be her. Never would he believe it was anyone else.

By now he had reached the door and the man on duty leapt to his feet. "Good afternoon, sir," he said. "Can I order you a taxi?"

"No, that won't be necessary," Rick, answered. "I'll walk. It's a pleasant day."

Outside the door of Number Ten, the policeman saluted. Rick nodded towards him and smiled. He could very easily become accustomed to all this attention. He recalled Sarah was with a constable at this moment. The young policeman would guide her safely to him. But at the same time, that officer knew what had happened up there in Northumberland. He could be a threat to his plans. Therefore once he had delivered Sarah back to him, it was imperative the poor unfortunate man should meet with an accident.

Like Sarah, Rick would also mourn the death of the young officer who had risked his life to save her. As for Sarah, once she learned it was her father who had caused the devastation, he was sure she could be relied upon to keep the secret.

Reaching the large gates at the end of Downing Street, Rick grinned to himself as he turned into Whitehall. Yes, it really was amazing how easy it all was.

CHAPTER THIRTEEN

Pete and Josh had almost reached the edge of the forest when they heard the sound of a helicopter flying above them. Despite the thick branches of the trees, they were able to make out the markings of the military. Obviously the soldier hadn't wasted any time in alerting his HQ. From now on they would need to be very careful.

Once they were clear of the forest, they found two roads lying in front of them. Pete pulled up and they looked around. Thankfully, there was no sign of the helicopter; they were safe for the moment.

"Which road do you think Sarah and the policeman took?"

Both men looked from one road to the other.

Finally Josh pointed towards the road on the right. "If it had been me, I think I'd have taken that one. I know it's narrow and winding, but it stays well clear of the villages. The other takes you through Bamburgh, Seahouses, and all the other tourist spots. Though it's late in the season, there'll still be a number of people around and I'm sure they wouldn't have wanted anyone to see them."

"Yes, I'm inclined to agree." Slipping the car into gear, Pete headed along the narrow road. "Though they're probably well ahead of us by now, we might still catch up with them. This is a very quiet road, we're not likely to meet much traffic."

However, they had only travelled a short distance when Pete caught sight of a large vehicle parked some way ahead. "Take a look through the telescope, Josh. Could it be an army truck?"

"Yes, it is." Lowering the telescope, Josh glanced around. "And there isn't much cover here. Open fields on all sides!" He peered through the eyeglass once more. "Oh my God, I think they've seen us! Yes, they've started to move towards us."

Taking his eyes off the road for a moment, Pete scanned the area. But Josh was right, there was nowhere for them to hide. There wasn't even room to turn around and even if there was, he couldn't speed off anywhere. His car was old and had never been built for this kind of terrain. On the other hand, the army truck was a modern vehicle – ready for action in any part of the world. It would catch them in no time.

"What are we going to do?" Desperation showed in Josh's voice. "You know what happened the last time they caught up with us. If the gun hadn't jammed..."

Pete wasn't listening. He slowed down. There had to be some means of escape. But if there was, he still couldn't see it. The truck was closing in. Any minute now it would be upon them. Already two soldiers had jumped down to the ground. They were holding guns and meant business.

"Pete, if you've come up with a good idea, now's the time to let me in on it." Not once taking his eyes off the soldiers, Josh ran his tongue around his lips. "I can't think of a single thing except to leg it and quite frankly, I don't think we'd get very far. These guys look fit."

Pete's eyes darted back and forth, frantically searching for a slip road – anything that would get these guys off their backs. But there were only endless fields of sheep... Sheep! That could be the answer. "Josh, I've just had a thought."

"Well spit it out. Will it get us out of here?" Josh gasped, recalling their last episode with the military.

"It might." Pete spoke quickly. "It's possible these soldiers don't know what we look like. Only Captain Saunders and that soldier, Private – whatever his name was – the guy who escorted us back to the farm." He shook his head, unable to recall the man's name. "Anyway they're the only two people who might recognise us. Pray neither of them are with this group." He pulled alongside a gate leading into one of the fields. "Follow my lead. Do exactly as I say or do."

"You bet!"

Pete stepped out of the car. By now the truck had reached them. The two soldiers with guns stood alert while the officer climbed down from the cab. Pete was relieved to see it wasn't Captain Saunders, so far, so good. "Hello there; out on manoeuvres?" Pete tried to hide the tension in his voice. "Aren't you a bit far south? I understand you're usually based a little further north." He laughed, but even to him it sounded strained. "Or have you lost your way?"

The officer forced a grin. "No, we're tracking a couple of our men. It's a sort of exercise; something new. Two of our men are dressed as civilians and have escaped in a car." He gestured towards his men. "We have to track them down. You didn't come across anyone back there, did you?"

"Sorry no." Pete trembled as he glanced across at Josh. "You didn't see anyone did you, Jim?" Pete looked back at the officer. "I need to keep my eyes on the road when I'm using this otherwise I end up with a flat tyre." He pointed towards the car. "My son has the 4x4. Since he got his license, I never see it."

"No, John. Didn't see a soul." Josh stopped himself from wiping away the beads of sweat gathering on his forehead, not wanting to draw attention to his nervousness. "I haven't seen any other vehicle."

"Purely as a matter of interest, what are you men doing out here?" The officer swatted the flies buzzing around his head. He hated the countryside with its insects biting and stinging him all the time. He much preferred the base near London: it was more civilized.

"We're checking the sheep." Still trembling, Pete opened the rear door to his car, allowing the dogs to jump out. If the real farmer showed up now, it would be the end. "We have all these to check out before dinner." He opened the farm gate and allowed the dogs to go inside. He issued a command and the dogs ran towards the nearest group of sheep and crouched down. "We've had a few problems with a fox recently, therefore we need to keep an eye on them. You couldn't spare a couple of your men, could you? Those guns would keep the fox at bay. We'd certainly appreciate the help. Especially Jim here." He gestured towards Josh. "Being a newlywed, he's itching to get back to his wife."

The officer gave a thin smile. He was unfamiliar to dealing with jovial civilians. "No. I'm sorry. We're all far too busy to mess around with a flock of sheep. Military business, you know." He looked back towards the truck. "Private Jones, step down."

Pete's heart missed a beat. Private Jones! It all came flooding back. He was the soldier, whose name he had forgotten earlier. No doubt he would recognise them in an instant. How could he have reached here ahead of them? The last time they had seen him he was bending over a ditch heaving his guts out. But then he recalled seeing a helicopter. They must have flown Jones down here to join the search. He could only watch in dismay as the soldier stepped down from the truck.

"Private Jones," the captain's voice rang out. "Are these the two men we're looking for?"

Pete felt dizzy with fear. He put his hand on the fence to steady himself. Jones was almost upon them. Any minute now the game would be

173

up. Looking around, he wondered whether he and Josh could make a dash to the car. But it seemed the captain had anticipated such a move and was standing in front of the driver's door. There was no escape. They had reached the end of the line.

The first time they found themselves in trouble, the sheep had shown them the way out. Then the sergeant's gun had jammed. It was too much to expect they would escape death for a third time. Pete now felt certain he would never see Sarah and the children again. But hopefully his family was still alive and he gave a silent prayer that the man escorting them would get them safely away from the area.

Private Jones stepped forward and peered at the two men. Turning his head from side to side, he studied them carefully. Pete wanted to scream out, 'yes, it's us', but he fought to remain calm while Jones continued to stare at them. Why was he taking so long? Surely he must recognise them. Was he playing cat and mouse? Could he be getting some sort of perverse pleasure from prolonging their agony? Pete felt his legs giving way beneath him, but he tightened his grip on the fence. A quick glance at Josh told him his friend wasn't fairing much better: not for the first time that day, his suntanned face had paled in colour.

"Come along, man! Are these the two men or not?" Even the captain was beginning to get impatient.

"Sorry, sir." Jones turned and looked at his captain. "But I had to make sure. No, these are not the men. Similar build, but it's not them."

"Are you absolutely sure?"

Moving his head closer to Pete and Josh, Jones peered at them again. "Yes sir. I'm positive. These are definitely not the men we're looking for."

Pete gulped. Jones must have recognised them. They had stood as close to him back there as they were now, for goodness sake.

"Very well, Jones, that will be all." The captain dismissed the soldier.

Without another word, Jones saluted the office before walking back towards the truck. Of course he recognised them. But he couldn't give them away. As far as he was concerned, they had done nothing wrong. They were being hunted down simply because they had survived the horror in the valley. He smiled to himself as he climbed up into the truck. Some of his fellow soldiers had already renamed it, Death Valley.

He glanced back towards the two men. The captain was still talking to them, probably spinning them the yarn dreamed up by the general. But they had spared his life when they could very easily have killed him. He couldn't give them away. He owed them that much. Now they were even. His thoughts drifted back to Sergeant Patterson. Even he would still be alive, if he hadn't acted so foolishly and drawn the knife. Heaving himself into the truck, Jones sat down and looked at the soldier next to him. He shrugged. "It wasn't them."

"Sorry about that." The captain struck his baton against his legs. "But I had to be sure. The two men on the run have been instructed to behave exactly as they would if they were really running for their lives. We're not to believe everything we see or hear."

He smiled. This time his smile was a little more friendly. "For the sake of authenticity, only a few men were allowed to see the men on the run. One of those men is Private Jones." He paused. He had said enough. "Well I'll let you get on. You said you had a great deal to do." Turning to Josh he punched him playfully on the shoulder. "Mustn't keep you from your new wife – eh – what?" Without waiting for an answer, he turned and climbed up into the front of the truck.

Pete and Josh watched the vehicle trundle up the narrow road. At the back, the canvas moved slightly and for one brief moment, Jones's face appeared. He gave a thumb up sign, before dropping the canvas back into place.

"I felt sure we'd had it," said Josh. "I wonder why he didn't give us away."

"Perhaps it was because we spared him, but who cares? I'm just grateful he didn't speak out against us."

Pete called out for the dogs to get back into the car. He wanted to get away from this place before the officer decided to check them out again. Climbing into the car, he noticed the fuel was low. They would need to fill up very soon. But one thing was certain: they wouldn't find a petrol station out here. They needed to make their way back onto the main road. Besides, the sun was going down. It wouldn't be wise to stay on this road after nightfall. He was also beginning to feel tired and hungry. Until now, he had been too preoccupied to notice it. "I could do with something to eat Josh, how about you?"

"Yes," Josh laughed. "Earlier I was pleased I hadn't eaten. I really thought I was going to throw up when I saw Jones step down from the truck, but now I could eat a horse." He paused. "I believe the nearest town is Alnwick, isn't it? That's pretty large. I imagine there'll be quite a few soldiers there." Glancing at Pete, he frowned. "I'm not sure we should risk it. We've been pretty lucky up to now."

Like Josh, Pete didn't want to go into Alnwick. With so many soldiers around, it was possible Captain Saunders would be there. They wouldn't stand a chance if they met up with him. He would give them away instantly.

Saunders was probably spreading the same story: the army was on some new kind of manoeuvres, looking for two civilians. No doubt the locals would be happy to help by pointing out unfamiliar faces. As neither Pete nor Josh visited Alnwick very often, they would both stick out like sore thumbs.

"Yes, you're right; we should give Alnwick a miss and go to a service station on the main road," Pete said at last. He glanced at the petrol gauge and hoped they would have enough fuel to last until then. "We might even try to get a few hours sleep in one of those motels. No point in drawing attention to ourselves travelling on the roads in the middle of the night."

Once on the main road, they would be able to blend in with the other commuters. If luck was on their side, they might even get south of the Tyne before they needed to stop. The further they were away from Northumberland the better. It was only then that Pete remembered he didn't have much money with him. When starting out yesterday morning, he had only been going as far as Top Meadow. Money wasn't an issue up there. He slapped his hand on the steering wheel. If only he had thought about it when they were back at the farm. But he recalled he had been too anxious to find Sarah, to dwell on what they might need on the journey.

Turning out his pockets, Josh found he, too, had very little cash. In the end they could only muster enough for some petrol and a snack.

"So much for a restful night's sleep, Josh. It looks as though we'll have to spend the night in the car."

"It could be worse," mused Josh. "We might just as easily be dead."

"It's not over yet." Pete pointed up ahead. "What's that? Is it another army truck?"

"Oh my God, I hope not." Josh peered through the windscreen. Already he could feel his heart pounding against the walls of his chest. Surely not again – yet from here, it certainly looked like one.

CHAPTER FOURTEEN

The sharp ring from the doorbell echoed throughout the hallway.

"Now what?" Irene mumbled, as she hurried towards the door.

The bell rang again. This time the caller held their finger on the button – someone was impatient.

She frowned, hoping it wasn't another delegation from MI5: two men had already called that morning. Though they were polite, their eyes had been cold and their manner brusque and unfriendly. They had questioned her husband for two hours. Why couldn't they leave him alone? Whatever they might think, she believed he wasn't to blame.

Opening the door, her face broke into a smile. "Do come in," she said, stepping aside. "Charles will be so pleased to see you."

Rick strode into the hall. "I simply had to call. I know how upset Charles must be by all this business."

Irene paused and looked towards the study door. "Yes he is. I'm very worried. He shuts himself in his study, only coming out at meal times and even then I have to persuade him. Sometimes he's so deep in thought, he doesn't even notice when I walk into the room. But I'm sure seeing you will do him a power of good."

"I do hope so," Rick gushed. "You know I'm here for you both. Any time you need a friend, simply pick up the phone."

"Thank you Rick, you're so kind." Irene led the way into the study. "There's someone to see you." She gestured towards Rick. "He thought you might like to see a friendly face." She smiled. "I'll bring you both some coffee."

"Sit down. It's good of you to call." Charles watched Rick lower his lean frame into the chair. "I suppose you've already heard what they're saying about the night of the incident – that I left instructions I wasn't to be disturbed?"

"Yes." Rick put on his most sympathetic expression. "But I really don't believe it. I know you would never do anything like that. That's why I came to see you. There must be something I can do."

He paused and shuffled around in the chair, making himself more comfortable. "Like I said to Irene, I want you to know I'm on your side. I'll always be around if you need me."

Charles leaned across his desk. "Thank you, Rick. I appreciate your concern, but I'm not sure there's anything you can do. Someone turned off the safety guards and forged my handwriting." He thumped his fist on the desk. "Can you believe it? Someone forged my damn signature! Who the hell would do that? You know I'd never turn off the safety guards and then leave instructions that I wasn't to be disturbed. Someone has gone to a lot of trouble to make sure I'd be blamed."

Rick uncrossed his long legs. "I agree. It's very puzzling. Believe me, I've thought about it over and over again, but I haven't been able to come up with a name. Your men are so loyal." He paused and leaned forward. "Perhaps you were tired... You haven't been your old self of late. Is it possible you might have...?"

"What are you saying, Rick?" Charles leapt to his feet. "Are you suggesting I was negligent? How can you even think it? I've always been very cautious. If you remember, it was me who held back, never wanting to move on too quickly. You were the impatient..."

"Yes, yes, of course. I know you checked and double-checked everything." Rick was quick to reassure him. Charles mustn't think he was against him. That wasn't part of the plan at all. If he was going to win Sarah back, then both she and her father must believe he was totally on their side.

"But you've been working very hard on the Project: arriving early and staying late. I simply wondered whether you were overtired. It may have caused you to become a little absentminded. With the Prime Minister impatient to see results, perhaps you over-stretched yourself."

Unconvinced, Charles stared at him.

Rick felt uncomfortable. This wasn't going well at all. He was relieved when Irene appeared with the coffee. For the moment the pressure was off, but from now on, he would need to think very carefully before he spoke.

"There you are." Irene set down the tray. "I'm sure you're both ready for a coffee."

"Yes, thank you, Irene." Rick smiled, warmly.

Irene turned to face her husband. "Would you like me to pour, or will you see to it?" There was no reply. "Charles, would you like me to pour?" she repeated.

"Eh... What?" Charles looked down at the tray. "Oh, we'll help ourselves. Thank you my dear."

He had been thinking about what Rick had said. It was true he had been working hard, but absentminded? Was he doing things without realising it? No! It was impossible. He was quite sure he had not turned off the safety guards, nor left any note saying he didn't want to be disturbed. Surely he would have remembered doing something like that!

"Shall I pour?" Rick interrupted his thoughts

Charles looked up. "Yes – thank you, Rick."

Pouring the coffee, Rick pushed a cup towards Charles "As I said, I'm with you all the way. I'll say anything you want me to."

Lifting the cup to his mouth, Charles returned it to the saucer so quickly, coffee spilled out over the rim. "I'm not asking you to lie for me, Rick. I'm quite happy in my own mind that I didn't do anything to cause the implosion."

"No, of course you didn't." Rick shuffled around uneasily in his chair. Everything he said sounded wrong. He had felt certain the old boy would happily jump at his suggestion of over-tiredness: it sounded plausible enough. But more importantly, it would have made it much easier for him to tell Charles that he had been asked to take over at the laboratory.

Sipping his coffee, Charles eyed Rick from across the desk. It struck him how on edge his colleague seemed. Continually crossing and uncrossing his legs, it wasn't like him at all. Rick was usually so sure of himself. Why exactly had he come here today?

He recalled how Rick had been at the laboratory on the night of the catastrophe. He had still been there when he himself had left. However, from what the staff said, once Rick left the building, he had simply disappeared. Rick knew all the codes. Had John Shaw been able to contact him, he could very easily have switched on the guards. It suddenly occurred to Charles how strange it was that both he and Rick should be totally out of reach at the same time. Why was that? Could he somehow be involved?

No! Of course not! Now he was being paranoid. Rick wasn't devious: he wouldn't do something like that to him! Hadn't he treated him like the son he never had? There must be some rational explanation why he couldn't be contacted. He had probably been visiting a young lady. Rick was a handsome, virile, young man. He was as much entitled to a life as the next man. Who wouldn't switch off their mobile phone, while escorting a lovely, young woman out for the evening? Yes, someone had betrayed him, but he had no reason to believe Rick was responsible.

"I'm sorry Rick," he said. "But you can see how I'm placed. It seems everyone is against me. I know the valves had been tampered with. If the guards had been on, everything would have shut down, but as it turned out..." Charles looked away, "... as it turned out, a great number of people died a horrible death."

He paused. "The Prime Minister believes me to be responsible, but I'm not." He banged his fist down on the desk so hard, his cup rattled on its saucer. "And I'm damned if I'm going to take the blame. If I have to spend the rest of my life proving it, then so be it." He sighed. "If only you hadn't turned off your mobile..."

Rick felt a cold shiver run down his back. This was not what he wanted to hear. So Charles knew the valves had been altered. He thought he had covered his tracks well, having been most careful when he himself had adjusted them. By fixing the dials on the machines, no one would have thought to check the valves. There was no need. With the dials continuing to show the correct figures until the last moment, no one could have guessed where the problem lay. And without the security codes, nothing could have prevented the plant in Northumberland from imploding.

Leaving it as long as possible before switching on his mobile, Rick had claimed that the signal was poor. "What? Say again... I can't hear... what do you mean – a problem? Tell Sir Charles I'll come, but..." he had yelled into the phone, implying he believed Charles was already there. Though he knew that, from the note he had so carefully forged, no one would have sent for him. "It's no good. I can't..." After those few words, he had switched off again, so no one would be able to trace his whereabouts.

Biding his time, he had arrived at the laboratory after both Charles and John Shaw had left to freshen up. He learned Charles had reset the codes to the safety guards and everything was back to normal, except that the northern edge of Northumberland had been almost wiped off the map.

With the two top men out of the way, he had found it easy to reset the valves to their normal position without anyone noticing. Slipping into his office, he had telephoned Downing Street, and requested an urgent meeting with Robert Turner.

"I was shocked to find someone had altered the valves," he had told the Prime Minister. "Being a very complicated business, it had to be someone who knew exactly what to do. Obviously this excludes most of the staff, as they wouldn't know where to start. Once I'd re-adjusted them, I came straight to you." Though he hadn't mentioned Charles by name, he had installed a seed of doubt in Robert Turner's mind.

Horrified, the Prime Minister had thanked Rick for his discretion. His chances of re-election would be slim if journalists were to catch even the slightest whiff of trouble at the laboratory. But to learn it had been a deliberate act... he shuddered at the thought.

"At this stage, I don't think there's any need to inform Sir Charles of your discovery," he had told Rick. "There's no point in worrying him further."

But the look on the Prime Minister's face had said it all: Sir Charles was no longer a man to be trusted.

Rick watched closely, as Charles sipped his coffee. His mind was racing. Surely Charles would have reset the valves himself, if it had been he who discovered they were at fault. Or could it be that someone was keeping him informed? It was a definite possibility. Charles was well liked and had a great number of friends both in and outside of government circles. Nevertheless, if that was the case, then this 'someone' was risking everything when they disobeyed Robert Turner.

"But I didn't turn off my mobile," Rick lied. "I was feeling a bit low and drove around for a few hours, before ending up in one of those all night cellar bars. I suppose there can't have been a signal down there. I found a corner booth and had one drink too many and fell asleep. You have no idea how bad I feel about it. If only I..." He paused, lowering his head for effect. "I completely understand how you feel, Charles. I know how hard you've worked for the government. You did your utmost to prevent something like this from happening. Naturally you can rely on my support."

He hesitated. "I feel really awful about this, but I think you should know, the Prime Minister has asked me to replace you at the laboratory. I hasten to add, it's only in the short term. Turner is only thinking of your welfare. He believes you should take a break until things settle down."

For a moment Charles was speechless. Taking a deep breath, he looked across the desk and saw Rick shift uncomfortably in his chair. So that was it! The Prime Minister had relieved him of his position at the laboratory and put Rick in his place. The short term indeed! He was being thrown out for good and they all knew it. Why hadn't the Prime Minister the decency to tell him himself?

"I see," Charles said at last. Though seething inside, he tried to keep his voice steady. "Well thank you for telling me. I'll call in later and collect my things from my... from your office."

"There's no rush, Charles. I'll use my own office until you're ready to..."

Charles interrupted with a brush of his hand. "No. I'm sure you'll want to get settled in quickly." He reached across the desk. "May I be the first to congratulate you on your promotion?"

"Thank you." Smiling, Rick grasped Charles's hand. "I'll never forget all you've taught me over the years." Sitting back in his seat, he pulled out a packet of cigarettes. "You don't mind, do you?" he asked.

"No, carry on." Charles pushed an ashtray towards him.

Drawing hard on his cigarette, Rick turned back to Charles. "I know how worried both you and Irene must be about Sarah. Have you heard anything from her? She's been on my mind constantly since it happened."

He had been fairly sure Sarah was the woman the general had spoken of: the woman who had escaped with a constable. But now he knew for definite she had been spared. If Sarah had not been in touch with her parents, Charles and Irene would have been inconsolable. His former boss wouldn't have cared a toss about his own reputation in the light of his daughter's horrific death. But as it was, he was hell bent on clearing his name, while Irene had been quite chirpy.

Charles hesitated, unsure how to answer. He wanted to keep the news of Sarah's escape between Irene and himself. Yet on the other hand, Rick was an old and trusted friend. A few years ago the man had loved her for God's sake and probably still did. Rick would never give her away. It was even possible he could help, should she need assistance before reaching London.

Impatient at Charles's lack of trust, Rick leant forward. "You have my word I won't let anyone know she was living up there."

Charles nodded. "Thank you, Rick. I know we can rely on your discretion. Yes we've heard from Sarah. Thank God, she managed to escape. She should be here soon."

Rick was jubilant. "That's splendid news." Smiling broadly, he leant across the desk. "Both you and Irene must be very relieved. What about Pete and the children?" He felt it only proper to enquire about them.

"We don't know about Pete." For a moment Charles looked sad. But then he smiled. "However, Sarah had the children with her. She was only on the phone for a couple of minutes so we didn't get much chance to ask about her husband.

Though stunned, Rick forced the smile to stay frozen on his lips. "That's... wonderful," he uttered. How could Pete's kids have possibly escaped? He had planned it down to the last detail. The children should be dead.

"You must promise to keep this quiet, Rick." Charles spoke anxiously. "No one must ever know Sarah was living up there during the disaster."

"Of course. I promise the secret is safe with me." It was true: he wouldn't give her away. He had waited too long for her to come back to him, to betray her now. But he would have to deal with the children in some other way – an accident, perhaps.

"And be assured, Charles, if you think Sarah needs help, please give me a call. You can count on me." He stood up. "I think I should leave now. I've already taken up too much of your time."

"You don't have to go Rick. Why not stay and have dinner with us?"

"That's very kind of you." Rick stretched his arm across the desk. "Perhaps another time; I have a few things to do at the moment. But don't forget, any time, any place, I'm always there for you. And be sure to let me know when Sarah gets back. I'd love to see her again."

Charles rose to his feet, but Rick motioned him to sit down. "I'll see myself out."

Rick walked across the hall towards the front door. His face was contorted with anger. How had those blasted kids of Pete's managed to survive? He sighed. Never mind, he would deal with it. He hadn't come this far to lose out now. One way or another, he would dispose of them and the policeman. Pausing to open the front door, he grinned. A plan was already beginning to form in his mind.

Charles was thoughtful as he watched Rick back his car out into the road, almost colliding with a parked car. Of all the bars both in and outside of London, why on that night of all nights, had he chosen to go into one where there was no signal on his mobile? He sighed. But then why shouldn't he? Rick was a free agent. How could he possibly have known something terrible was going to happen? About to turn away from the window, he saw

Rick wave at two men sitting in a parked car. That was strange: did he know them? It was only then he noticed something even more significant.

A green government pass was fixed onto the windscreen of Rick's car, only a select few were given those. As head of Government Scientific Affairs, he himself had one, so did some top members of the Cabinet. However Rick had not been issued with such a pass.

It was true, now as head of the laboratory, he would be entitled to one, but that was not the issue. What really concerned Charles was that under normal circumstances anyone, even a new incoming Prime Minister, would have to wait almost two weeks before receiving it.

Forms had to be filled in and checks had to be made, the list was endless. How had Rick received his so quickly? Had he known what was about to happen and applied in advance? Shaking his head, Charles dismissed the notion. That was impossible.

He watched Rick's car until it disappeared around the corner. The men in the car parked near his house were still there. Who were they? Rick had waved to them, but that was because he had almost bumped into them. Or was it? Did he know them? More alarmingly, were they watching the house?

He shrugged. Of course not, why should they? But then he recalled his phone was bugged and he was sure he had been tailed the other day, so it was a possibility. His heart was pounding as he moved away from the window. Quite suddenly he wished he hadn't said anything to Rick about Sarah.

In the kitchen, Irene heard the front door close. She was surprised Rick had left so early. He could have stayed for dinner; heaven knows there was plenty to eat. Peering around the study door, she was alarmed to see Charles holding his head in his hands. What had happened? Surely Rick could do something to help her husband. He of all people couldn't possibly believe the rumours being bandied about.

On that fateful day, she had been so angry with Charles. How could he have been a party to anything so terrible? All those people lying dead, even now she trembled at the very thought of it. At first she had sworn she would never forgive her husband for his part in Trojan, but watching him slowly destroy himself, she had relented. How could she continue to torment him when he was already torturing himself?

She knew they had been lucky. Their daughter Sarah and her children were coming home. Other people dotted around the country were still oblivious to the fact that their relatives in the north-east had died a most horrible death. When would those poor people know what had really happened? Probably never, if the Prime Minister were to have his own way. Even now he and his cronies would be working out plausible answers to the questions that were bound to come sooner or later.

Tactfully, Irene stepped back out into the hall and rattled the door handle before re-entering the study. By the time she opened the door for the second time, Charles was sitting up in his chair shuffling some papers on his desk.

"Has Rick gone already?" she asked, looking around the room. "I thought he might have stayed for dinner."

"He had some business to see to." Charles hesitated. "Irene, why do you think Rick came here today?"

"To see you," she answered, breezily. She collected the coffee cups onto the tray. "He knows the strain you're under and came to give you his support." She paused, sensing something was troubling her husband. "Why do you ask? Is there a problem? What did he say?"

"No. Nothing I can put my finger on. I simply wondered if..." Charles sighed. "Never mind; you're probably right. I'm so worried about this whole affair I'm beginning to get jumpy." He forced a laugh. There was no point in upsetting his wife further. Nevertheless, he decided to call in at the laboratory when Rick wasn't there.

On the morning of the disaster, he had found someone had very cleverly tampered with the valves. Foolishly, he hadn't mentioned it to anyone, not even John Shaw. Leaving everything as it was, he had hoped to catch the culprit in the act of changing them back. But that someone had corrected them in the short time he and John had gone home to change. So now he didn't even have proof they had been altered in the first place. However, what if he were to go back there and take another look around? Might he find something that would give the perpetrator away?

CHAPTER FIFTEEN

When Sarah opened her eyes, it took her a few seconds to realise where she was. Andy and the children were sleeping soundly. Perhaps it was still very early. Surely a few more minutes wouldn't hurt. But then the sound of vehicles outside caught her attention and reaching for her watch, she was horrified to find it was nine thirty. Andy had hoped to be well on their way by now.

"Andy!" Scrambling out of bed, she pulled on her jeans. "Wake up! We've overslept."

Andy groaned and pulled the covers over his head. It was too early. He was still tired and why the rush anyway? But then he remembered where they were, and sat up quickly. "My God; what time is it?"

"It's half past nine. I'll see to the children, while you take Betts out. I don't think a man walking a dog will draw too much attention."

While Andy walked Betts, Sarah washed and dressed the children. There was no time for a proper breakfast. They would have to make do with some sandwiches from the take-away café.

Deep furrows dug into Andy's forehead as he scanned the road ahead. Having checked the map before leaving the motel, he was anxious to find the turning that would take them away from the motorway. It was definitely along here somewhere.

"Keep a look out for the road I mentioned earlier," he said anxiously. "We can't afford to miss it, the one after that is several miles further on."

Looking up ahead, Sarah saw a large blue road sign. "There's a sign coming up. This might be it."

She peered through the windscreen, but the sign was still too far away, to make out the road number.

"I don't believe it!" The tone of Andy's voice told her something was wrong.

"What is it?" Sarah looked from him to the road ahead, in turn. "What can you see?"

"Up ahead." Lifting one hand from the steering wheel, Andy pointed to an army truck. "Just before the turn off there's a road-block. It looks like soldiers are pulling over some of the cars."

So intent on trying to read the road sign, Sarah hadn't noticed the parked truck. "Turn around!" she screamed.

"What do you mean, turn around?" Andy yelled. "We're on a bloody motorway for heaven's sake. How can I turn around?"

Sarah didn't answer. All she could see was the road-block looming towards them. The soldiers had spread themselves across the carriageway to slow down the traffic. There was no way they could pass without the soldiers peering into the car.

Andy glanced across at Sarah. "If you have another suggestion, I'd be delighted to hear it."

"Can't we simply bluff it out?" Sarah was unable to think of a better idea.

"Bluff it out?"

"Well, think about it Andy. Hopefully, the soldiers won't know what we look like." She gestured to the other cars on the road. "Look at all this traffic; they can't stop everyone."

Andy looked around. It was true. If they stopped every car, there would have been a long queue by now. But though the traffic was moving slowly, it *was* still moving. It seemed the soldiers were only picking on certain vehicles – but which ones?

Frantically he glanced into the passing cars, looking for an answer. What was different about each of them? Come on! Think! Think. They were getting closer to the road-block. It wouldn't be long before they reached the soldiers. He looked at the cars again. Most of them contained only one or two people, but there were a few like this one carrying adults and children.

Andy suddenly felt like he had been hit by a thunderbolt. Oh my God! That was it! They were looking for a man, a woman and two children. Cars with more than two people on board were being pulled over.

"Sarah! Quickly, get the kids out of sight."

"What?" Sarah looked at him in amazement. "How can I?"

"I don't know! Tell them to lie down on the floor, anything, but get them out of sight." Gently, he put his foot on the brake and moved into a slower lane.

"Whatever for? Why...?"

"Never mind why!" Andy interrupted. "For God's sake, Sarah, don't argue – just do it!"

Her hands trembled as she reached behind to the children and unfastened their seat belts. "Lie down on the floor." She tried to keep her voice calm, not wanting to alarm the children. "We're playing hide and seek again. Don't make a sound."

"Hide and seek," squealed Josie, sliding down behind Andy's seat. She reached out and touched her sister's hand as Sarah struggled to lower Becky to the floor. "Ssh, we're playing a game again."

"Yes," said Sarah, pulling a blanket over them. "You must both be very quiet, like little mice. Just like when you play hide and seek with Daddy."

"And Andy," whispered Josie.

Despite the desperate situation, Andy smiled at her remark. It seemed he had been accepted at last. Now almost alongside the military personnel, he slowed down even more. "I hope this works," he said.

Sarah took a few deep breaths. Would they never be free of these wretched soldiers? They were approaching the blockade. She wanted to check the children were still well hidden, but she didn't dare turn her head. Up ahead, a soldier gestured to the driver of the car in front to pull onto the hard shoulder.

Drawing closer, Andy smiled, trying to look as natural as possible. "I hope he doesn't look too hard," he muttered to Sarah. "With a bit of luck, he'll only see the two of us."

Sarah was still watching the car that had been pulled over. The occupants were being instructed to climb out. She noted there were two children amongst them. Ushered to one side, the adults placed their hands behind their heads, while the soldiers checked them over. She shuddered and quickly looked away. Would they too, be asked to pull over to the side of the road? She gripped the map tightly to stop her hands from shaking as they came alongside one of the soldiers.

Bending down, he looked through the window. Becky's car seat was still in place. Would he question them about it? The soldier glanced at them briefly and then waved them on. Sarah smiled at him before looking down at the map on her lap.

"This is our turning coming up Andy," she said. "With a bit of luck we're going to make it."

But as she finished speaking, the soldier moved forward and signalled them to stop the car.

"Oh my God," she murmured, as Andy pulled over. "Did he see the children after all?" Without turning her head, she whispered to her daughters. "Not a sound."

Stepping out of the car, Andy stood alongside the back passenger door in an effort to hide the children. "What is it? What's the trouble?" he asked.

The soldier moved closer and peered inside the car. By now Sarah felt sure he would hear her heart pounding.

"I saw your wife looking at the map. I know this area quite well, perhaps I can help." The soldier smiled.

Sarah wanted to haul the children out of the car and run for all she was worth. Instead she forced a smile to her lips. "Thank you." She glanced at Andy. "My husband thought it would be rather nice if we saw some of the countryside, so I was looking for the best route. I see there's a turn-off up ahead."

Leaning across the driver's seat, the soldier gazed at the map.

Andy held his breath as Sarah traced her finger along the road shown on the map.

"We're here, I believe." She spoke loudly, hoping to drown any sounds the children might make.

"Yes," he said, pointing to the junction. "If you turn off here and take the unclassified road you'll find the scenery quite breathtaking, but I should warn you the road is very narrow."

Backing out of the car, he looked at Andy. "Still, I'm sure you won't mind that."

"No. Not at all." Andy climbed into the car.

All he wanted to do now was get away from here. Out of the corner of his eye, he could see the other soldiers were beginning to take an interest in what was going on.

"In fact it sounds like the sort of road my wife and I are looking for. You miss so much if you stay on the motorway." He started the engine. "Thank you for your help."

Sarah sank into her seat as they moved away. "I really thought he would see the kids." She turned and looked out of the back window. The soldiers were grouped together, no doubt wanting to know what had transpired. "Josie, Becky, stay where you are for a few more minutes." She didn't want to risk anyone spotting the children climbing back into their seats.

Glancing in his wing mirror, Andy was relieved to see that no one was following them. It seemed they had got away with it – this time. He signalled and turned off the Motorway.

"I don't think we'll take this side road after all," he said. "But we'll let them think we have. We'll re-join the motorway and carry on until the next turn-off. Though I recall it's several miles on and it looks even more of a cart track."

Once they were out of the soldier's field of vision, he pulled up and helped Sarah fasten the children into their seats before heading back onto the main road.

Sarah didn't say anything. She wished this nightmare journey was over and they were all safely at her parents' home. However, on reflection, there was still the matter of their phone being bugged. She hadn't figured that out yet.

Anxious to rid themselves of this road and the soldiers, Andy put his foot down hard on the accelerator and they soon found themselves on the side road. However, as he had anticipated, it was extremely narrow and rather winding, making it impossible to gather up speed.

At every bend in the road, Sarah held her breath; fearing lines of soldiers were lying in wait for them. Only after travelling several miles, did she begin to relax. Perhaps they had seen the last of them. The troops may not be searching this far down the country. Taking her eyes off the road ahead for a fleeting second, she suddenly felt herself being propelled forward: Andy had rammed his foot on the brake. Looking through the windscreen, she caught her breath – a small military vehicle was blocking their path. Two soldiers armed with guns began to walk towards them.

"Oh my God, Andy, what are we going to do?" Sarah's voice trembled. After finally beginning to believe they had escaped the clutches of the army, she now found they were yet again, caught in their ever tightening net.

"I don't know." Andy swallowed hard. He had run out of ideas. Climbing out of the car he whispered. "If there's any trouble, move into the driver's seat and get the kids out of here. Don't wait for me, just go. There's a small gap at the front of their vehicle, it's possible you could get the car through."

Her heart pounded as she watched Andy walk across to meet the soldiers. Their guns were poised. Though she couldn't hear what was being said, she could tell from their expressions that they weren't convinced. One of the soldiers kept looking towards her and the children.

Andy turned as if to walk away, but a soldier grabbed out at him.

"You're all coming with us!" he yelled, gripping Andy's arm.

As the other soldier started moving towards the car, Andy lashed out with his foot and knocked him to the ground. "Get out of here Sarah," he screamed. "Leave me, get the kids away."

For a split second Sarah froze, unable to move as the scene before her played out in slow motion.

"Sarah! What are you waiting for? Get the hell out of here!" Andy yelled again.

The urgency in Andy's voice forced her to her senses and she scrambled into the driver's seat. Her hands were shaking, as she fumbled with the ignition key. The car refused to start on the first turn and again on the second. She stabbed her foot up and down on the accelerator "Come on! Come on, damn you!" She slammed her hands on the steering wheel in frustration.

Looking up, she saw the soldier had leapt to his feet and was running towards the car. It was now or never. Turning the ignition again, the engine sprang into life.

She looked at the gap between the Jeep and the hedge. It was narrow, but Andy was right: the car would go through there. Turning back, she saw him struggling with his captor; the other soldier was almost upon her. Quickly, she rammed down the door locks – at least the bastard couldn't get in.

Still struggling with the soldier, Andy called upon every ounce of his strength and wrestled him to the ground. Meanwhile, fearing his mate was in trouble, the soldier approaching Sarah, ran back to help him.

After kicking Andy in the stomach, the soldier then held his gun to his head. "Get out of the damn car, bitch or I'll kill him right now!"

"Go! Go!" yelled Andy. "Get out of here."

The other soldier, having recovered, jumped to his feet and began to punch Andy. "Tell the bitch to get out of the car!"

Breathing heavily, Sarah's mind was racing. She looked up ahead at the gap. She could do this. In a few minutes, she and the children would be safely away from here. But looking back at Andy, she saw the soldier was still pressing the gun against his head. The tiny space between the Jeep and the hedge beckoned her. Once through there they would be free from these terrible men. What was she waiting for? Why didn't she go?

But how could she leave Andy? Heaven knows, she wanted her children safe, yet he had done so much for them. They would never have got this far without him. Noting the children were tightly strapped into their seats, she turned back towards the front. Taking a few more deep breaths, she pulled her own seat belt tighter before slamming her foot down hard on the accelerator. The car shot forward towards Andy and the soldiers.

She was coming up close to the men. What would she do if they didn't move? Andy was going to die anyway: there was no doubt they would shoot him. But would she run him down if the soldiers held their ground? Fortunately she didn't have to find out. As she had anticipated, fearing for their lives the soldiers threw Andy to the ground and scrambled away.

"Get in Andy!" she yelled, as she undid the locks and brought the car alongside him.

"You mad bitch!" yelled one of the soldiers, as he leapt to his feet and looked for his gun.

Wrenching open the car door, Andy jumped in. "Let's get the hell out of here."

But Sarah wasn't finished. Having got this far, she didn't want the soldiers chasing them. Their Jeep was better equipped for this type of road and would catch up with them in no time.

Backing up a little, she rammed the car into first gear and revved the engine. Taking a deep breath, she stabbed her foot on the accelerator and plunged the wing of the car into the grill of the army vehicle. The wheels of the car spun, as she thrust the gears into reverse and backed away. Repeating the operation, she smashed into the vehicle again. This time there was a loud crack as the Jeep's radiator burst and water spewed to the ground.

Satisfied the soldiers couldn't follow, she hurled the car through the narrow gap and sped from the scene. By now the children were screaming and the dog was barking for all the poor beast was worth.

"Shut up! All of you, shut up!" yelled Sarah, still speeding away. The car bounced over the potholes, throwing them from side to side. Terrified, yet relieved, she was now in a state of shock. She felt cold and was trembling violently.

"Slow down!" yelled Andy. "We'll get a puncture! Why didn't you go when you had the chance? They could have caught you and the kids."

"You think I don't know that?" Sarah cried, slowing down a little. "But I couldn't leave you with those men. They'd have killed you."

"Yes, I know." Andy's voice was barely above a whisper. A few minutes ago he had come face to face with death, yet he was still alive. He glanced at the children. Though they had stopped screaming, they were still crying. "I think you should pull up and let me take the wheel. Your children need you." His statement was a cop out. She had saved his life, but he didn't know what else to say. This plucky young woman could so easily have driven away and left him to die.

"Yes, you're right." Sarah brought the car to a sudden halt. She felt drained and wanted to cry, but she forced back the tears.

Andy checked the front of the car, while she settled in the back with the children. "I'm amazed, but the car isn't too bad at all. Where did you learn a trick like that?" he asked.

Sarah hesitated. "Dad would have been furious if he'd known, but several years ago, when I was learning to drive, one of his friends gave me a few lessons. He was a stock car racing driver. James often took me to the racetrack when no one else was there. It was against the rules, but it was fun. He showed me a few tricks of the trade. The idea is to wreck your opponent's car without making too much of a mess of your own. It was a long time ago, but it suddenly came back to me." She paused. "Mind you, I'd never actually done it myself. Today was the first time. James only showed me how it was done. He was a bit of a show off really – a bit like your James Bond."

Sarah suddenly went quiet again. Glancing in the rear-view mirror, Andy saw how pale she looked. If she were to break down, how would he cope with her and the children?

"I'm beginning to wonder if we might be better on the main roads. This route hasn't proved to be a success."

"Do whatever you think best," said Sarah, weakly. She leaned forward. "Shall I check the map?"

Andy passed the map across to her and she studied it for some time.

"There's a road ahead, which should take us to the motorway." She traced her finger down the road shown on the map. "Once on the main road, we should reach London in a little over a couple of hours." She paused. "Unless we meet up with the army again."

She fell silent. The thought of meeting more soldiers frightened her and she clutched her children. She had been stupid to pull a stunt like that; she could have killed them all. But how could she have driven away?

"Once we're back on the motorway, we'll stop and have something to eat." Andy hoped it would cheer her up a little. Though he would rather have kept going, he realised Sarah needed a break. From the look of her, she could do with a stiff drink.

"Yes, I think we could all do with a breather." Forcing a smile, she looked at the children. "We're going to stop soon and have large ice-creams with lovely chocolate flakes," she told them. She was determined they were going to have a treat, even if it meant using her credit card.

"Will Daddy be there?" asked Josie, excitedly. She fumbled around the seat and found her drawings. They were beginning to look rather tattered. "He still hasn't seen my pictures."

"I don't know darling." Sarah fought back the tears. "But he might be. We'll have to wait and see."

Becky, hearing the word 'Daddy', held out her arms. "Daddy, Daddy."

"I hope so," said Sarah. Pulling her daughters close, she buried her face in their hair. "I truly hope so," she sobbed.

CHAPTER SIXTEEN

Pete and Josh pulled away from the service station. After pooling their resources the night before, they found they only had enough money for some petrol and a few sandwiches. With a room in a motel being out of the question, they had been forced to spend the night in the car.

"Where do we go from here Josh? Should we stay on the main road or try to find another country track?"

On the main road, they might blend in with the commuter traffic, but there could be more army personnel around. On the other hand, if they were pulled up on a country road no matter what they said, they could be hauled in for questioning. After all, people on the run usually take the back roads.

Twice yesterday they had been lucky. When stopped by the military, they had spun a yarn about inspecting a field of sheep and had got away with it. Even so, if Private Jones had spoken out against them, what could they have done? Fortunately, the second vehicle they had spotted had turned out to be nothing more than a tractor pulling a trailer.

After a short discussion, they decided to stick with the main road. If they were stopped again, they would simply have to do their best to bluff it out. Though, having to make do with a wash in the facilities provided by the service station, they could hardly pass themselves off as travelling salesmen. Their unshaven faces, crumpled, dirty shirts and torn trousers, made them look more like a couple of tramps rather than men trying to win the confidence of prospective customers. Nevertheless, being on the main road meant they could drive faster. Pete felt they had wasted enough time already.

Taking the side road to Morpeth last night had slowed their progress. With its twists and turns, the road seemed to go on forever making them dangerously low on fuel. They couldn't take the chance of that happening again.

Despite the early hour, there were a number of cars already on the road leading to the Tyne Tunnel, yet there didn't seem to be any military personnel. Pete was a little uneasy. Yesterday the army had been hell bent on finding them. He couldn't believe they had given up already. But arriving at the tunnel, they found a large number of military trucks parked around the entrance.

"Of course!" Pete slammed his fist on the steering wheel. "We should have guessed they'd all be waiting here. What better place to catch anyone trying to escape?"

The soldiers at the front were instructing the cars to slow down and a queue was beginning to form. For one brief moment, Pete considered turning around and heading back. However glancing in the reversing mirror, he quickly dismissed the idea. Several cars had already lined up behind, making it difficult to move out of the queue. But more than that, it would look jolly suspicious.

The two men watched as the soldiers peered into each of the cars. Some they waved on, while others were asked to pull over to the side of the road.

"It looks like a random check. These guys don't know who they're looking for, remember?" Pete paused. "If they pull us over, what'll we say? We've got to have the same story."

"I don't know." Josh sounded worried. "But like I've said before, it's got to be plausible or I'll give the game away. I was never very good at telling lies. As a kid my dad always knew when I was fibbing."

"We could say we are farming equipment engineers." Pete looked down at his badly stained shirt. "At least we look as though we've been crawling around a farmyard and we do know all about farming machinery."

"Good idea!" Josh exclaimed, sounding relieved. He could go along with that; he had often helped to mend the tractors on the farm.

"Right, that's our story. Let's get it straight. We were on a job at one of the farms in Northumberland." Pete paused. "But now we're on our way to a warehouse, as we need some parts."

"Fine." Josh glanced at Pete. "However, if they ask, where are we going for these spares? You should have some ideas, as you buy these things all the time."

"I order by phone, but I believe some of the parts come from a large trading estate somewhere down here." Pete thought for a moment. "I have it, it's the Team Valley Trading Estate. But on second thoughts, aren't we on the wrong road for that?" He sighed. "Hopefully, the soldiers are strangers here and won't know the difference."

Both the men held their breath, as one by one the cars inched forward. It was almost their turn. They watched nervously as the soldier up ahead signalled the driver in front to pull over. Glancing at Pete and Josh, he waved them on.

Unable to believe their luck, Pete was about to sigh with relief, when an officer moved forward and motioned them to stop.

"Oh my God, I don't believe it," whispered Josh. "It's the officer we met yesterday."

Pete toyed with the idea of ramming his foot down on the accelerator and making a dash for the tunnel, but he decided against it. They probably wouldn't get very far anyway. The captain gestured to him to roll down the window.

"So we meet again." Pete noted the officer's voice was cold. "Heading south are you?"

"Yes." Pete laughed nervously. "We need some spares."

Josh coughed to hide his fear. He suddenly felt sick and wanted to get out and make a run for it, yet somehow he forced himself to stay seated in the car. He saw the captain staring at him. "Sorry," he muttered. "I seem to have a tickle in my throat."

The officer turned back to Pete and glared at him. "Is it usual to take the dogs with you when you pick up spares?" His tone was sarcastic.

Lost for words, Pete remained silent. He could feel beads of sweat forming on his forehead. He should say something – but what? However, to his relief, he heard Josh's voice.

"Absolutely! The dogs know exactly what we're looking for. We never buy a single spare without consulting them first." Josh paused and laughed. "No, I'm sorry. I shouldn't be so flippant. Seriously, we were out in the fields this morning, when a message came through saying some parts were needed urgently." He held up Pete's mobile phone. "There was nothing else for it but to bring the dogs with us."

For a moment the officer didn't answer. He looked from one man to the other. Pete's foot hovered nervously over the accelerator. He was still tempted to make a run for it. But would he be able to make it to the tunnel before anyone realised what he was doing? And even if he did, there would probably be soldiers at the other end waiting to gun them down.

By now Pete could feel sweat trickling down his face. He wanted to wipe it away, but it would only draw attention to his nervousness. He swallowed hard, not daring to look at Josh. Why didn't the captain say something? What was he thinking?

So deep in thought, he almost jumped out of his seat when the officer laughed heartily.

"Consulting the dogs – yes I see." The captain slapped his leg with his baton. "Very good! Okay, you can go. Might even see you on the way back, at this rate I'll still be here." He gestured towards one of the soldiers. "Escort them through," he said.

"There's no need." Pete looked up at the captain. "We'll be fine." All he wanted to do was to get as far away as possible from anyone in a military uniform.

"You don't want to be stopped again, do you?" The officer stepped aside as the soldier's motorbike swerved past him and came to a halt in front of the car. "He'll see you through to the other end." Moving away from the car, he nodded to the soldier up ahead.

Pete rolled up his window and began to move forward, but then the captain put up his hand and stepped back in front of the car.

"Now what?" murmured Pete. He wiped his hand across his brow. Was this man playing cat and mouse with them?

The soldier on the bike pulled up and turned around. Nudging Josh, Pete inclined his head towards the young soldier. Following Pete's gaze, Josh was alarmed to see the soldier's hand resting on his sidearm.

Stepping up to the car, the officer reached into his pocket. "I've had a thought. I'll give you a pass. It'll be of some help should you encounter another road-block somewhere on the other side of the tunnel."

Pete glanced at Josh out of the corner of his eye. "Too right," he muttered.

The captain tore the sheet from the pad and handed it to Pete. "Can't have you being held up all the way to... Where did you say you were going?"

"The trading estate. It's not too far from here."

Still unable to believe their good fortune, Pete stared down at the sheet of paper. It stated that the bearers were not the men in question and should be allowed to pass. The officer had signed his name boldly – Captain P. Rankin. What would the captain say when he learned that, not only had he allowed the two fugitives to slip through his fingers, but he had also given them a pass?

"Thanks a lot. You have no idea what this means to us," said Pete. "Especially to my friend here, he doesn't want to be away for too long. You may recall he hasn't been married very long." He tapped his nose. "Need I say more?"

"I'm only too pleased to be of help!" The captain slapped his baton against his thigh. "Must get the lad back to the little wife – eh?"

While grinning at Captain Rankin, Pete muttered a few words under his breath to Josh. "I can't believe it. Let's get out of here."

The captain took a step backwards and motioned to the soldier to advance. "Good luck with the spares," he called out, as Pete put his foot on the accelerator and moved forward.

"Thanks a lot." Holding his hand out of the window, Pete waved to the officer. But it was only when they were out of sight that he sat back in his seat and began to breathe easily. "Thank goodness for your quick thinking about the dogs, Josh. I'm afraid I panicked. All this is really getting to me now. I was lost for words."

"So was I at first, but we'd come this far, I had to try something." Josh laughed.

Pete didn't reply. His thoughts were with Sarah and their children. Had they also escaped through this network of road-blocks? He desperately hoped the young policeman had managed to get them to safety.

Tears filled his eyes as he thought of his family. It was only a few hours ago that he had said goodbye to Sarah and wished her a pleasant visit with her friend. Who could have foreseen the horror that would follow? He wiped his eyes. The tunnel wasn't well lit and he didn't need his vision to be further impaired by tears. The last thing he wanted was to plough into the soldier on the bike in front.

The tunnel seemed to go on and on, until finally a glimmer of daylight peeped in from the other side. Out in the open, the soldier drove towards the checkpoint. He spoke to the corporal in charge, while pointing at Pete and Josh.

Finally, the corporal motioned them forward. "Go through." He moved to one side and gestured to his men to raise the barrier.

Breathing a sigh of relief, Pete put his foot down hard on the accelerator. As the car swept past the soldiers, he hoped they wouldn't be stopped again. But even if they were, they had a pass signed by Captain P. Rankin. Surely nothing could stop them now.

CHAPTER SEVENTEEN

Opening her eyes, Sarah winced as she turned to look at the children. She had been resting her head awkwardly against the back of the seat and now her neck was stiff and painful. She moved her head gently from side to side, trying to ease the tension.

It was beginning to get dark and she could barely see anything. "Where are we?" she asked, rubbing the car window to clear the condensation.

"I'm not sure. The last sign said Watford Gap."

"Watford Gap!" she exclaimed. "I must have slept for ages. Why didn't you wake me?"

Sarah felt guilty at having been asleep for so long. But she consoled herself by blaming it on the large brandy Andy had forced her to drink when they pulled into the service station. Still in shock after her run in with the soldiers, the brandy had been warm and comforting; lulling her into a false sense of security. After that she had drifted off to sleep quite easily.

"You needed to rest; I was worried about you." Andy was relieved at how much better she looked. He had taken a chance by allowing her to use a credit card to buy food and a few treats for the children. But it had been worth it. "I decided to stay on the main road. Fortunately we weren't stopped, though I did see some army trucks a few miles back." He glanced at her. "I've got to tell you, I was so scared, I nearly woke you. But when I drew close, I realised the men weren't taking too much notice of the traffic and I was able to drive straight through. I guess they're all getting bored, checking out every vehicle can't be much fun."

Sarah didn't answer. It surprised her that the soldiers hadn't been more vigilant. Surely the two soldiers, whose Jeep she had wrecked back on the side road, would have radioed their base to report the incident. With helicopters and trucks at their disposal, it was amazing the military hadn't swooped down on them hours ago.

"And they were the only ones you saw?" she asked. "Don't you find it strange?"

"I did at first. But perhaps they concentrated on the side roads. That's where they caught us before." He glanced at her. "If we'd stayed out there we could well be in custody by now. I think we made the right decision after all."

Sarah's stomach turned over at the thought of meeting up with the soldiers again. Glancing out of the window, she saw streets of houses had replaced the large open fields. At last they were on the outskirts of London. Nevertheless, only when they reached her parents' house would she fully relax.

"Are you alright?" Andy's tone was anxious. She had gone quiet and he was concerned she might be having a relapse. "We shouldn't be too long now," he continued, trying to make light of the matter. "But you'll have to guide me, I have no idea where we are."

Sarah smiled. "I'm fine, I was just thinking. Follow the London signs for the moment. Once we get closer, I'll direct you."

"Your parents are going to be pleased to see you and the children again." Andy tried to keep her talking. It wasn't good for her to dwell on all that had happened.

"Yes," she agreed. "They adore the children. My father is going to be so angry when he hears what we've gone through and..." She paused, recalling that his phone was bugged.

She still puzzled over that. Her father was part of the government – well, sort of. He was well respected and certainly didn't pose a threat to anyone. "So why would anyone bug his phone?" She was mumbling more to herself rather than to Andy.

Pulling up at the traffic lights, Andy glanced at her. He had heard her last comment. "You'll be able to ask him about it very shortly." He turned his attention back to the red light. "The roads are much busier now, we must be getting close to the City."

Sarah looked through the window. "Yes. Once we go through the lights, take the turning on the left. We don't want to go through the centre of London." Now they were so close to her parents' home, she wished they were safely there. She could almost feel her mother's warm and comforting arms wrapped around her, erasing the memories of their nightmare journey south.

She led Andy down a maze of one-way streets until they opened out into an expensive residential area. Glancing at the large houses, he wondered whether he would ever be able to afford something like this. He still couldn't understand how Sarah could give up a life here to live on a remote farm.

"Here we are!" Sarah pointed to a large driveway. "Thank God we've made it!" She jumped out of the car and helped Josie climb down before picking up Becky. Hearing the front door open, she looked up to see her parents running towards them.

Andy shuffled from one foot to another as Sarah greeted her family. On the journey down he had begun to feel like one of them, but now he felt awkward and left out.

"Grandma, Granddad. I have some pictures to show you." Josie jumped up and down excitedly. "Mummy! Where're my pictures?"

"We'll see them shortly Josie. Come inside with Grandma."

Tears streamed down Irene's face as she clasped her arms around her grandchildren. "Oh my darlings, I'm so happy to see you. I never thought..." She broke off, hardly knowing whether to laugh or cry.

"We'd better go inside." Charles glanced anxiously towards the road. He now knew for certain his house was being watched. They might use different cars, but the faces were always the same. The same two guys parked close by his house every day, while another two relieved them later in the evening.

Once safely indoors, Sarah introduced Andy to her parents. However it was only after dinner, when the children were tucked up in bed, that she spoke of their ordeal.

"We wouldn't be here today if it weren't for Andy." Over a drink, Sarah explained how Andy was a constable in the police station at Wooler. She went on to tell them of the light she had seen in the night sky and how, after finding a body in the lane, she had reported it to the police.

"It was Andy who realised the military were after me. It appears they were intercepting all calls, even those made on the police radio." Tears welled in her eyes, as she relived each terrible scene. "They hounded us down like criminals simply because we had survived." She paused and wiped her eyes. "When I think back, I still can't believe it – all those poor people are dead."

She shuddered, unable to erase the vision of Dave from her memory. During the journey she had pushed it to one side, needing to have her wits about her for the sake of her daughters. But now they were safe in London, it returned to haunt her.

"You know I actually spoke to one of those poor souls before he died. It was Dave, a good friend of Pete and husband to Lorna, who used to look after the children occasionally." She closed her eyes. "I say 'used to', because she is most probably dead too. Have..."

She broke off. Opening her eyes, she stared at her parents. "Do either of you have any idea how Dave died or the agony the poor man went through? His flesh was dripping onto the road. I could see his bones. You can't possibly imagine what it was like seeing a friend lying there like that and yet find yourself unable to help him." Her voice rose a pitch; she was becoming hysterical. "I wanted to take him back to the farm, call an ambulance! Do something, anything to stop this terrible thing from hurting him further! But when I moved towards him he warned me to stay back or I would end up like him. He told me Pete was dead. But I won't accept that!"

Suddenly she reached out and grabbed her father's arm. "But you can do something! You can tell someone about what's going on up there. Tell them about the light, the cloud. Make them do..."

Sarah stopped abruptly as her father looked away and bowed his head. Puzzled, she removed her hand from his arm. "What is it?" She looked at each of her parents in turn. "Tell me! What's going on?"

Neither spoke. There was an awkward silence.

Sarah glanced across at Andy. "They don't believe me." She swung back to face her father. "You don't believe me! My God, do you really think I could make up a story like that? Tell them, Andy. Tell them I'm not making it up."

Andy shifted around in his chair. He didn't know what to say, not having actually seen the bodies for himself. However, he did know something was terribly wrong, why else were they being chased by the military? He opened his mouth to speak, but before he could say anything, Charles broke in.

"Of course we believe you." He glanced at his wife. "I know exactly what you saw." This was the moment he had been dreading. "Both the cloud and the light are part of a secret weapon the government has been working on."

"What secret weapon?" Sarah's mind was racing. "No! You don't mean... chemical weapons? I don't believe it!"

When Charles didn't answer, Sarah knew she was right. She shook her head. "But I don't understand. There must be some mistake. Surely the making of such weapons was outlawed. Didn't the Prime Minister himself stand up in Parliament and declare his government was opposed to all forms of chemical weapons?"

Unable to deny it Charles remained silent, his head still bowed.

Sarah was horrified. "Surely Robert Turner would never go against his treaty with the United Nations." However the expression on her father's face told her the Prime Minister had done just that.

"But this is terrible." Sarah was appalled. "You must speak out and tell the country what's going on. Your position in government circles would allow you to trace whoever is working on such a monstrous..." She broke off. Her father was acting strangely. He seemed very uncomfortable and kept looking at his wife. "What is it? Do you already know who it is?"

She hesitated, waiting for an answer. But none came. What was going on? Why didn't someone say something? Then it dawned on her.

"Oh my God, it's you isn't it?" she screamed out at her father. "Please tell me it's not true."

Charles swallowed hard and he looked away.

"I can't believe it. How could you? How could you be a party to anything so despicable? Have you any idea what you've done? Never would I have believed..." Sarah sunk her head into her hands. "All those people, settling down for the evening and then this terrible thing was unleashed upon them."

She shuddered as the image of Dave loomed before her. His ghost would never be laid to rest now she knew it was her own father who had caused his death.

"The blood of all those people is on your hands. And Pete: what of him? My husband, the father of your grandchildren, have you killed him too?" Her eyes flashed with anger. "If he's dead, I'll never forgive you."

She looked at Andy, suddenly remembering he was there. "I don't know what you must think. I promised you that when I told my father about it, he would sort it all out. He would see the Prime Minister and he would stop the military from..."

She began to cry again. It was all too much to take in. "And now I find it was he who devised the whole horrible thing with the Prime Minister's blessing."

"Sarah," Irene spoke for the first time. "Your father didn't allow Trojan to escape. He did everything he could to keep the experiment under control.

It was at his insistence that safety guards be installed. They were designed to shut everything down if the pressures rose..."

"Well, they failed, didn't they?" Sarah interrupted. "They damn well failed!"

"But that wasn't his fault, Sarah." Irene tried again. "Someone forged your father's handwriting. Whoever it was, not only left messages saying Charles wasn't to be disturbed, but they also turned off the safety guards and altered the codes. No one was able to switch them back on. Whoever did that also tampered with the machines allowing the pressures to rise. It set off a chain reaction that couldn't be stopped, so Trojan was released. Now your father is being blamed."

"Trojan. Is that the name of the monster?" Sarah spoke quietly, looking towards her father for the answer. Despite her mother's reassurances, she still thought him responsible. When asked to develop something like this, he could have said no! Why didn't he?

Charles nodded. "Yes. It's known as the Trojan Project." He paused. "But your mother is right. Everyone believes it was all my doing. Since the disaster, my phone has been tapped." He gestured towards the window. "Men sit in cars outside my house, but for what? What do they think I'm going to do? Unless of course, the Prime Minister believes I might defect." He shook his head. "I've even had Rick around here suggesting I may have written the note, while not realising what I was doing and then forgotten about it." He thumped his fist on the small table by his chair. "The man is saying I'm going senile. Can you believe it?" He sighed. "Even if I had written the note, why would I have turned off the safety guards and altered the codes. It doesn't make sense."

"You mean Rick was working on this monstrous thing too?" Sarah didn't know what to believe anymore. She was astounded her father had created such a horrible weapon, but to hear Rick was also involved was too much. She tried to calm herself. "What's happening at the laboratory now?"

"I don't know. I haven't been there for a couple of days. I've been relieved of my position." Charles hesitated. "The Prime Minister has seen fit to place Rick in charge of all government scientific affairs. But Sarah, you must realise I would never leave such a note, nor would I turn off the safeguards." He leant forward. "For heaven's sake, surely you of all people know I would never do that. For whatever reason, someone has framed me."

Sarah closed her eyes. She wanted to believe her father, but seriously, why would anyone want to frame him. Maybe Rick was right. Having worked with her father for a great number of years, he must know him by now. Perhaps he had reached a stage where he was being forgetful. Rick might have noticed it before but, being loyal, he hadn't wanted to cause trouble for him. But there was something else nagging at her.

Was this man really the father she had known and loved all through her childhood? How could any normal, family man devise something so horrible? Fathers weren't meant to do things like that. Had he been living a lie all these years?

She opened her eyes. Looking across at him, she thought back to her life with Pete. He was a family man; the father of two lovely young girls. Never in a million years would he have constructed something so despicable. All he wanted was a peaceful life on the farm with his wife and children.

"I really don't know what to believe anymore." She glanced across at Andy. "What do you make of all this?"

"I don't think I should comment." Andy felt uncomfortable. He didn't know Sarah's father, so how could he judge what the guy was like?

"Why ever not?" Sarah retorted. "Surely you have as much right as anyone to speak your mind! You would have been safe at the police station in Wooler, if you hadn't put yourself in danger by escorting the children and I down here. Don't forget, you were very nearly dragged off by the soldiers. We both know they'd have killed you without hesitation. And then there's Sergeant Gilmore and your friend, Constable Manners. If they hadn't already touched the melted flesh and died horribly, then the soldiers will have killed them. But either way, they're probably lying dead somewhere and you know it. No Andy! You certainly have every right to comment."

She paused for breath before looking back at her father. "And that's another thing, why is the army trying to kill us? Why aren't they out there trying to help the victims? At least they could have warned the others not to touch anything."

"The Prime Minister doesn't want the news of the catastrophe to get out." Charles knew he shouldn't be telling his daughter this, but he was tired of the whole business. "Turner's a desperate man. He's given instructions that no one should be found alive."

"But that's despicable." Sarah cried. "Why?"

"Apart from the general election coming up in a matter of weeks," said Charles. "The Prime Minister knows that if even one word of this gets out, he'll be finished."

Suddenly Sarah felt weary. She had hoped, that on reaching her parents' home, her troubles would be over. Instead, they had multiplied.

"If no one minds, I'm going to check on the children and then I'm going straight to bed," she said. The long hot soak in the bath she had thought about earlier had suddenly lost its appeal. "It's very late and I can't take anymore of this tonight." She gave Andy a rueful smile. "Sorry I shouted at you, but I'm tired and shocked. Mum will show you the spare room. Don't let them keep you up much longer, you must be as tired as I am." Without another word, she left the room.

There was an awkward silence after Sarah had gone. Andy gazed down at the patterned carpet on the floor. He was unsure of what to say.

"We can't thank you enough for bringing Sarah and the children to safety." Charles was the first to speak. "We honestly didn't think we would see any of them ever again. It was only due to your quick-wittedness that they escaped with their lives. It was a huge relief to her mother and I when we received her phone call."

Andy explained how his suspicions had been aroused when he saw soldiers carrying weapons and wearing strange outfits. "I only did what anyone else would have done." He looked away. "I'm only sorry Sergeant Gilmore and Constable Manners went out there. Neither of them came back. As Sarah said, we don't know whether..." He broke off. Until now he hadn't had time to dwell on what had happened to his friends.

He wiped a tear from his eye. "But Sarah's right, they're probably dead." He looked across at Irene. "If you don't mind, I think I'd like to go to bed."

Irene leapt to her feet. "Of course, you must be exhausted. Follow me; I think you'll find everything you need in the guest room."

She led the way up the stairs. "Here you are." In the bedroom she pointed to the en-suite. "You'll find towels and bathrobes in there. There's plenty of hot water and there are clean pyjamas in the chest of drawers." She looked him up and down. "I'm sure there'll be something in your size."

"Thank you, Mrs. Hammond, I..." Andy began.

"Please, call me Irene," she interrupted him. "And it's me who should be thanking you. If it hadn't been for you..." She smiled, leaving the rest unsaid. "I'll leave you now. I hope you sleep well."

After she left, Andy enjoyed a hot bath before slipping between the crisp white sheets on the bed. Discounting the fact it had been Sarah's father who devised the weapon, the house was under surveillance and the phone was bugged, for the first time in days he felt safe enough to sleep easily. Lying there in the darkness, he decided he would speak to Sarah tomorrow. Her father didn't seem a bad sort.

He would gently remind her how someone had to invent these weapons if the country was to remain safe. After all, in the last war, the Spitfire and Hurricane aircraft had been invented, making a huge impact on the outcome of the war. But even he had to admit, there was an enormous difference between the Spitfires and the type of weapon that would burn and melt the flesh of the enemy.

CHAPTER EIGHTEEN

The following morning, as he made his way down to breakfast, Andy heard voices coming from the dining room. Drawing closer, he could make out the sounds of Sarah and her father in conversation. But then there was another voice; one he hadn't heard before. Opening the door, he peered inside.

"Good morning Andy." Sarah jumped to her feet. "I'd like you to meet Rick. He works with my father."

"Good morning," Andy smiled at the group.

"I'm pleased to meet you." Rick stepped forward, his arm outstretched. "I've been hearing all about you. I understand we have you to thank for bringing Sarah back to us."

"I'm glad I was able to help." Grasping Rick's hand, Andy noted his smile was neither warm nor friendly and he wondered why. Having only met this man, what could he have done to upset him?

"Good morning Andy. I trust you slept well." Irene bustled into the room carrying two large dishes. "Shall we have breakfast? The children have had theirs already and are playing upstairs." She nodded across to Rick. "Have you had breakfast or would you like to join us?"

"No I haven't eaten, Irene. I came straight over as soon as I..." he faltered. "I came as soon as I was dressed." He smiled at Sarah. "I was anxious to know if your parents had heard anything more from you."

"That was very sweet of you," Sarah said. "Then of course you must stay and have breakfast with us, mustn't he, Father?"

Charles didn't answer. Sarah repeated her question, but this time she spoke a little louder. Was her father becoming senile after all?

"Father, are you listening? Rick came here to enquire if you had heard from me. He must stay and have some breakfast with us."

"Sorry!" Charles jumped. He had been deep in thought. What had Rick really been going to say? If he had simply wanted to enquire about further news of Sarah, he could have picked up the phone. There was no need for him to rush over here before breakfast.

"Yes. Yes, of course he must," said Charles, vaguely. To him it sounded as though Rick already knew that Sarah had arrived last night. However, as

209

neither he nor Irene had spoken to anyone, he could only have heard it from the report written up by the men outside in the car.

But this led Charles to another point. Any such report would go to MI5 and then to the Prime Minister. He knew Turner wouldn't have reported anything of that nature to Rick. Why should he? As head of Scientific Affairs, he had nothing to do with MI5 other than laboratory security. Therefore, for Rick to come by this knowledge, he must have bribed the men outside to inform him if a young woman with two children turned up at the house. But why would...

"Charles dear, attend to our guests." Irene's voice interrupted his thoughts. "You don't seem yourself this morning. Are you feeling alright?"

"Yes, of course I am." Charles looked around at everyone and ushered them towards the table. "Come along everyone, take your place before the food gets cold."

"Sit next to me Sarah." Rick swiftly pulled out a chair for her. "We have so much to catch up on."

"Andy, you sit here." Charles gestured to the seat alongside him. "Help yourself."

"Yes, please do." Irene smiled. "Don't be shy Andy. Heaven knows there's more than enough."

Andy had been watching Charles. It was obvious his thoughts were elsewhere. Though he had no idea what was going through the older man's mind, his first instincts told him that Sarah's father didn't trust Rick.

Still pondering over it, he heard Rick ask Sarah if she would go for a walk with him after breakfast. "You and I go back a long way, I want you to know I'm still here for you."

Sarah hesitated, so he continued. "It would help you to take your mind off the terrible ordeal you've been through. We could drive up to the West End and take a stroll through Hyde Park like we used to. There's nothing like an old friend to lean on when you're feeling low."

Though Rick spoke quietly, Andy felt certain he had been meant to overhear his last remark. Could it be that he was being warned off?

"But don't you have to go to the laboratory?" Sarah was surprised. "With all the trouble over the last few days, surely they need you there?"

"No. They can manage on their own for a few hours. Besides, everything is working perfectly now." Rick took her hand in his. "You really need a break. It must have been terrible for you, travelling through the wilds of Northumberland with a complete stranger."

"Would you pass me the bread, please, Rick?" Andy had heard enough. He pointed towards the basket of bread at the other end of the table. "You know, from being a small child, I've always loved wiping a thick slice of bread around my plate. It's the best part of breakfast."

Annoyed at the interruption, Rick removed his hand from Sarah and reached out for the bread. "Is there anything else I can get you?" he hissed.

"Well since you ask, you might just pass the toast and marmalade. It would save me interrupting you again."

Rick gritted his teeth as he pushed the rack of toast nearer to Andy, before turning back to Sarah. "What do you say? Will you come?"

Sarah thought of her children upstairs. Should she really go out with Rick and leave them?

"The girls will be fine." Rick anticipated her thoughts. He wanted to get their reunion off the ground as soon as possible and a walk in the park would be a good place to start. "I know Irene has to go out, but your father will be here and then there's Andy. I'm sure he wouldn't mind playing with them for a little while."

Andy looked up from buttering his toast. "No, not at all. You both go right ahead."

"There you are, it's all settled." Rick was pleased with himself. He had set the wheels in motion and everything was going to plan. Now all he had to do was to make Sarah realise how much she could depend on him.

But he also realised he had made one stupid mistake. Jealous of Andy having spent so much time with Sarah for the last few days, he had slipped up and allowed his feelings to show. That had been very foolish. If he was going to lure Andy and the children away somewhere without suspicion, he needed to show him friendship and gratitude for saving Sarah. He would have to make it right. Perhaps even grovel a little if necessary. The thought left a bitter taste in his mouth, but there was nothing else for it. Besides it would only be for a few days.

Once he put his plan into action, Andy and the brats would be out of their lives forever and it would be he, Rick, who would have the last laugh. With Sarah's father disgraced by the government, her husband lying dead somewhere with his guts melted, he couldn't lose. Who else would she turn to for sympathy and understanding?

After breakfast, when Sarah had gone upstairs to change, Rick sidled up to Andy. "Thanks for agreeing to look after the kids." He smiled broadly. "Sarah could do with a break and the children seem to have taken a liking to you."

"Yes," Andy replied. He was surprised at the sudden change in Rick's attitude. The man sounded almost friendly – but not quite. "We got on well while we were travelling down here."

"Perhaps you and I could have a drink together sometime?" Rick ventured.

"Yes, perhaps." Andy wasn't too keen on the idea. He couldn't quite see Rick as one of his drinking buddies. But on the other hand, the man was Sarah's friend, so he should try to show willing. Now stuck for words, he was relieved when Sarah came back downstairs.

"I'm ready, Rick."

She smiled at Andy. "Are you sure you don't mind staying with the children? You don't have to you know. Dad is more than happy to play with them and Mum won't be out too long." She shrugged. "You could come with us."

Andy wondered what Rick would say if he agreed to accompany them. For one moment he was sorely tempted – just to annoy him. But he dismissed the idea. "No, you go off on your own. I'm quite happy here." He couldn't help noticing the flash of relief in Rick's eyes.

"We won't be long." Sarah knelt down and kissed her two children. "Be good girls while I'm away."

Andy watched from the window as Rick helped Sarah into his car. Perhaps the morning air would do her good. Despite being safely back home, she still looked very pale. He waited until the car had pulled out of the drive and driven off, before turning his attention to the children.

****

Sarah sat back in her seat and closed her eyes. Rick was right. It was good to get away from the house. During their perilous drive to London, she had firmly believed that once they were at her parents' house everything would be alright.

But things were far from alright. In fact, if anything they were a great deal worse. Never in her wildest dreams had she thought her father would be in any way involved in the horrors she had witnessed in the north.

"Are you warm enough?" Rick asked. His voice was soft and comforting.

"Yes, I'm fine." Sarah opened her eyes. "What should I do?"

"What do you mean, what should you do?"

"About the disaster!" Sarah exclaimed. "My father has told me everything about the cover up. Surely I should report it. Go to the newspapers; let the country know what's going on."

"No!" Rick almost shouted.

Ramming his foot hard on the brake, he pulled into the side of the road, almost causing an accident with the car behind. But reporting Trojan to the newspapers was the last thing he wanted. The Prime Minister had put him in charge of the laboratory and he was enjoying his new position. If Robert Turner were to plummet from office through this scandal being made public, it was possible that he would fall with him. When mud splattered, it had a habit of sticking to everyone within range.

Clenching her fist, Sarah thumped the dashboard. "Why not? Surely everyone has a right to know what this government is up to!"

"But you must think about what it would do to your father." Rick spoke earnestly; he had to convince her. "Basically Charles is a good man. He did his best – introducing safety guards and all. But like some of the others around him, he's getting old. He lost his memory for a few seconds and made a mistake. If you go to the newspapers, they would crucify him. Don't you realise he could go to prison?"

"But all those people – dead." Sarah began to cry. "I don't want to believe it, but my husband, Pete, could be among them. Surely something should be done for their sake. It's up to me to spread the word and make sure nothing like this happens again."

By now she was sobbing so hard her words were distorted and Rick was having trouble understanding what she was saying. But he did hear her next remark and it filled him with alarm.

"Take me to one of the big newspapers. They'll hear me out! I need to tell them..."

"Sarah! Sarah, listen to me," he yelled, grasping her arms. "Of course the newspapers will listen to you, they're always looking for a story. But

213

talking to them wouldn't bring those people back. If it would, don't you think I'd have done it already? I know what you're going through. I understand how you feel about losing your husband. I mourn for Pete too. But what we have to do now, is think of the living."

He had rehearsed this speech a couple of days ago, when trying to anticipate her every response. Though to be truthful, he had forgotten quite how determined Sarah could be.

"Of course you're angry with Charles. But for all that, he's still your father. You can't betray him. Think what it would do to your mother." He sat back in his seat and closed his eyes. "Of course I blame myself."

"Why? You're not to blame." Sarah leant forward and rested her hand on his arm. "You weren't to know this was going to happen."

"Even so, I should have read the signs." Cunningly, Rick placed his hand over hers. "I should have insisted your father let me work more closely with him. But he resisted my help, even shutting me out at times." He gave her a sideways glance. "But I want you to know I tried. I would have done anything to have stopped this from happening."

"Oh Rick, I'm sure you did everything you could. I know how much you respected my father and all he did for you." Sarah sat back in her seat. She felt a little calmer, yet she was still unsure of what to do. One part of her wanted to bring everyone's attention to what had happened – what was still happening. After all, the killings were still going on. How many had been murdered because they saw something in the night sky? On the other hand, could she really tell the nation it was all the fault of her father?

Rick swallowed hard. Yes, her father had done a great deal for him over the years and, for one brief moment, his conscience pricked him as it tried to find a tiny chink in his armoured shell. But he swept it to one side. If Charles had persuaded his daughter to marry him instead of Pete, everything would have been so different. He would never have felt the need to go to such lengths. Therefore as far as he was concerned, all this horror was Charles's fault.

He could tell Sarah was wavering. With a little further persuasion, she would keep her mouth shut. "But they'll say I should have tried harder," he wailed. He needed to sound afraid.

"You mean they'll blame you as well?" Sarah gasped. She couldn't take this in. Rick was right. Her father might go to prison, leaving her mother devastated. But now there was Rick to think of. What would they do to him?

"But of course you mustn't let it sway your judgement. If you really feel you must go to the newspapers, then naturally I'll drive you there and come into the offices with you." Rick leant forward and wrapped his fingers around the key in the ignition. "However, remember your father is not getting any younger. The publicity, the disgrace and perhaps even imprisonment..." He paused and shook his head. "Will he ever get over it?"

"Wait!" she said.

Rick's thin lips curled into a smile as he removed his fingers from the key.

"You're right. Whatever he's done, I can't do that to him."

Tears formed in her eyes and Rick handed her his handkerchief.

"May they all forgive me," she murmured. "Pete my dearest, please forgive me."

Rick turned away and looked out the window to hide the look of triumph in his eyes. He had done it. He had stopped her from reporting the disaster. If he said it himself, he deserved an Oscar for his performance. Now all he had to do was to guide her through the next few days and then it would all be over.

"But of course they'll forgive you." Looking back towards her, he took the handkerchief from her hand and gently wiped the tears from her eyes. "What else can you do? You must think of the living. But what about your friend, Andy, will he have contacted anyone this morning while we were out?"

Rick had been forced to take the chance that Andy wouldn't report the incident while watching the children. Of course he was going to deal with the young policeman in due course. But in the meantime, it would be nice to know that he hadn't already rushed out to tell the world what had happened.

"No. I feel sure Andy won't do anything from the house," she replied. "Dad has already said the phone is tapped. I'll talk to him. I'm certain I can make him see that nothing will be gained from speaking out." She looked straight at him. "Did you know Dad's phone was bugged or that the house was being watched?"

For a moment Rick was speechless. He hadn't anticipated that. He could have kicked himself. He should have been more prepared.

"Is it?" he asked, weakly. Even he thought his response sounded ridiculous. He needed to add something else – anything. His mind raced. "Yes... I suppose it is. I'm sorry... I should have guessed. But I didn't really think about it."

"It's okay. Why should you?" Sarah smiled at him. "It was stupid of me to ask. You're a scientist, not MI5."

Rick grinned. "Quite." He breathed a sigh of relief. He had come out of a tight corner pretty well. "Come, now we've got all that off our minds, shall we take ourselves to Hyde Park and enjoy a stroll? If the teashop is open we could have cream cakes for old time's sake." He laughed. "The lady in there might remember us."

"Thank you, Rick." Sarah smiled. "You've helped me put everything into perspective. What would I have done without you?"

"That's my girl." Rick turned the ignition and the car sprang into life. "I knew you were made of sterner stuff."

Despite her earlier reservations, Sarah enjoyed her day with Rick. He was very attentive and made her laugh. Somehow, it took her mind away from the horror of the last few days.

"My goodness is that the time?" she said, looking at her watch. "It's almost four o'clock. I can't believe we've been out so long. I really must get back, the children will be wondering what's happened to me."

"They'll be fine. Your mother will be back now and then there's – what's his name. The children seem to like him."

Rick was enjoying his moment with Sarah and didn't want her to go back to the house. The handsome, young man, who had escorted her from Northumberland, might undo all the good work he had done this afternoon by telling her it was her duty to inform the public. No! The longer she was in his company, the better. It would give him a further opportunity to work on her.

"Perhaps we could do something else?" he said. "Have an early dinner and go on to a show or see a film?" He tried not to sound too anxious. "We could go back to my flat where you could freshen up. I know this lovely little restaurant..."

Sarah laughed. "Please Rick, you're overwhelming me. The man's name is Andy and you're right, the children do like him. But I can't take advantage of him – or my parents." She became more serious. "It's been fun,

Rick. Thank you for a lovely day, you've taken my mind off..." She paused. "Thank you again, but I really must get back now."

Rick tried not to show his disappointment. "Okay, I can see you've made up your mind." He smiled. "As long as you know I'm here should you need me."

"Thank you, Rick." She kissed him lightly on the cheek. "You've been so helpful already in allowing me to unburden myself upon you." She smiled. Had she misjudged him all those years ago? "Now, please say you'll come back and have dinner with us this evening. It's the least I can do."

"Sarah, like I said, I'm your friend. I'm only too happy to help you in any way I can. But yes, thank you, I would be delighted to join you for dinner." Rick held open the door as she climbed into the car. He smiled to himself. Everything was going his way. Before long he would have Sarah eating out of his hand.

CHAPTER NINETEEN

"I don't believe it! Of all the rotten luck!" Pete slumped down at the side of the car and gazed at the flat tyre. "And we were doing so well."

They had travelled quite some way since coming through the Tyne Tunnel and Pete was just beginning to feel a little more confident, when he felt a sudden jolt. The car had then hurtled across the carriageway: out of control. Only by grappling frantically with the steering wheel, had he managed to avoid a serious accident. Fortunately a lay-by had loomed up ahead and with further careful manoeuvring, he was able to pull off the busy road.

"Still, I suppose we're lucky the old girl got us this far," he added gloomily.

But what were they going to do now? This couldn't have happened at a worse time. They were on the main road to London and cars were flying past at break-neck speed. Dodging the traffic, they might have to walk for miles before finding the next turn-off.

"Haven't you a spare?" Josh lifted the lid of the boot and peered inside. "No," replied Pete without looking up. "I never use this car anymore. Well – not to travel any distance. I only keep it for sentimental reasons: it was the first car I ever had. My father bought it for me when I passed the driving test."

Pete picked up a small stone and flung it into the grass at the edge of the road. They had gone through so much, only to be beaten by a flat tyre. If the army came along now, what could they say?

"I can't even phone a garage as we don't have any phone numbers and even if I did, how would I pay them to tow it away and fix the tyre? Neither of us has any money," he said, glumly. "What a mess."

Then another thought occurred to him "If the police see us, they'll stop and what'll we tell them? We'll look very suspicious, two men with two dogs travelling without money or a spare tyre."

Josh sank down beside Pete. "Well it could be worse."

"Josh, didn't you hear what I just said?" Pete yelled. "We're stuck here with no means of transport. The military could come along at any time and even with the pass the captain gave us, they're going to ask a few questions. What on earth could we say? We've come a long way since passing through the Tyne Tunnel. Spinning some yarn about needing spares from the trading estate wouldn't wash. And if the police find us here, we'll still be questioned. So go on, tell me how it could be worse?" He hurled another stone into the grass to emphasize his point.

Josh took a deep breath. "Well, we're still alive aren't we? That has to be a bonus. If that lot back there had their way, we'd both be dead by now."

Pete nodded and smiled. "I'm sorry, Josh, I suppose you're right. It's simply having got this far I had hoped..."

"Besides," Josh interrupted. "I don't get it. If the police come, why not tell them the truth? Why not tell them we're running from the army because we saw what happened in the north-east?"

"Because, they'll still haul us in and get in touch with the army to check out our story. The police aren't going to take our word for it; not about something so horrendous." He shook his head. "Let's face it, Josh, would you believe it if someone gave you a story like that? No! You'd think the guy had been drinking. That's why I would rather get to London and find Sarah before we say anything."

"Okay, okay I get your point." Josh held up his hands in a gesture of submission. "But we can't just sit here. What if the army does come along?"

"I know all that." Pete flung another stone into the grass. "I agree we need to do something. I suppose we'll have to start walking. But the last thing I wanted, was to draw attention to ourselves and two guys with a couple of dogs walking down..."

"Need a lift?"

So engrossed in their conversation, neither had seen a lorry pull up behind them.

"Need a lift?" The man repeated. "I'm going as far as Peterborough if it would help."

Pete scrambled to his feet, annoyed at being caught off guard. While he and Josh had been talking, a large truck had pulled into the lay-by. How could they have missed it? They should have been more alert. It could very easily have been an army vehicle. He eyed the man up and down. He looked okay: youngish, round-faced and a little overweight, probably due to sitting in the driving seat all day. But more than that he couldn't tell.

"Look, do you want a lift or not?" The burly lorry driver was beginning to get impatient. "I can't hang around here, it'll be dark soon and I want to be in Peterborough before then."

"Sorry, we didn't hear you coming and you startled us." Pete realised they were going to have to take a chance. "Yes please, a lift would be great." He gestured towards the car. "I've got a flat and I haven't a spare. Stupid I know, but..." He shrugged.

The lorry driver hardly glanced at the car. "Yes, I saw the flat tyre as I passed. Hop in." He didn't think it was stupid at all; more of an everyday occurrence on this road. "I could do with a bit of company. There're usually two of us on this run, but Sam, my mate, wasn't too well this morning."

"I'm afraid we have two dogs." Pete pointed to the dogs still sitting patiently in the back of the car. "But they're very friendly."

"That's okay. I like dogs. There's plenty of room behind the seats."

"Don't say too much," Pete whispered to Josh. "Lorry drivers love to talk and we don't want him telling our story to the next hitch-hiker he picks up."

"I'm Colin, by the way," said the driver, pulling away. He glanced at the two men. "So who're you then? What are you doing out here and where are you heading?"

"I'm Pete and this is Josh." He could hardly say they were looking for spare parts. Unable to think of anything else, he decided to tell the truth or at least part of it. "We're on our way to London."

"London!" exclaimed Colin. "It's a terrible place! What do you want to go there for?"

But before Pete had time to make up a reply, Colin continued.

"Strange thing is, my sister moved down there when she got married and she loves it. She keeps going on at me to visit her. She tells me about the clubs and the theatres, but then she always was one for the bright lights. Me; I prefer the quiet life. I take this lorry to Peterborough, that's close enough to London for me. Someone else takes it the rest of the way, while I take his load back up to Newcastle. It works out fine."

He paused for breath. "By the way, do you guys want to phone a garage to have your car towed away? I tell you, it's not safe to leave it sitting there in the road. There'll be nothing left by morning."

"I have a phone here, but..." Pete got no further.

"Tell you what, call Charlie." Colin interrupted. "He'll tow it away and fix the tyre. You can pick it up on the way back. He's a good man is Charlie. I'll give you the number. Tell him you're with Colin and he'll sort it for a fair price."

"But I have the keys here." Pete jangled the keys in front of Colin. "He won't be able to get into the car."

Colin laughed. "Charlie doesn't need any keys. No, Charlie don't need keys at all. He's a regular guy is, Charlie." He went on to tell them all about his friend. "Got a place near the railway station in York, you can't miss it. Cars everywhere. You'll see what I mean when you pick up your car."

Once Pete had called Charlie and arranged to have the car taken away, Colin began to talk, hardly pausing for breath. Relieved the driver was doing all the talking, the two men allowed him to carry on.

"You guys don't talk much," Colin said after a while. He laughed. "I suppose I haven't given you a chance to get a word in. Sam says I talk too much. But what the heck, if you've got something to say, then you should say it – that's my motto."

He paused, while negotiating a roundabout. "Say, were you guys stopped by the army on the way down? Now there's a thing. We're often pulled over by the police for spot checks on tyres and the likes, but the army, that's a new one on me."

He leaned forward in his cab. "Talk of the devil, look at that. There they are again; persistent beggars aren't they? Looking for two guys in civilian clothes, some kind of new manoeuvre – or so they said."

Pete couldn't believe his eyes. Surely they weren't still looking for them, not this far south. "Err, yes," he stuttered. "We met up with a group of soldiers at the Tyne Tunnel. They gave us the same story. Didn't you believe them, then?"

Pete's mind was racing. If they were stopped, what should they do? Try to make a run for it? He glanced at Josh for support, but the colour had drained from his friend's face and he was staring straight ahead, as though in some kind of trance.

"Well you've got to admit, it sounds a bit strange. Oh-oh! They're pulling us over." Bringing the lorry to a stop, Colin rolled down the window and yelled out to the sergeant below. "What's up, then? I was stopped some miles back. Still not found your guys?" He laughed. "It certainly seems like they're giving you a run for your money."

"Yes, it looks that way," yelled the sergeant. "Where're you going?"

"Sorry, I can't hear you," Colin cupped his hand around his ear. "There's too much noise." He pointed towards the traffic.

Placing his foot on the step-up, the sergeant hauled himself up the side of the lorry and repeated the question.

"Peterborough." Colin replied. "I'll be staying there overnight and driving back with a different load tomorrow. Will you still be here?"

"Could be!" The sergeant wasn't giving anything away. He poked his head through the window and peered inside. "What about these two? Were they with you when you were pulled up further back?"

Pete glanced at Josh. This was it. Once the sergeant heard how they had only been picked up a few miles back, they would be asked to step down. The pass in his pocket would be worthless, when the soldiers checked back with Captain Rankin. Why would they be this far south looking for a few farm machinery spares?

Colin laughed as he glanced at Pete and Josh. He was about to explain how he had picked the two men up a few miles back, after finding them by the roadside. But he saw the fear in Josh's eyes.

Glancing at Pete, he stopped laughing. Something was very wrong here. Both men looked very afraid. Though they were trying to stay calm, beads of sweat had appeared on Pete's brow and Josh was biting his lip.

Colin could feel the warm breath of the soldier on his neck. No doubt he was becoming impatient. Why didn't he simply tell the sergeant what he wanted to know and get it over with? If these were the men the army were after, once they had them in custody they would unblock the roads and everyone could get on with their lives – so why was he holding back?

It was true he hadn't believed what the soldiers had told him. Perhaps the men were desperate criminals and the soldiers didn't wanted to alarm the public. If that was the case, his own life could be in danger. Yet for some reason he didn't think so. There was something about the two men that reassured him.

"Did you hear me?" the sergeant yelled at the top of his voice. It had been a long day and now he was hungry and tired. Goodness knows when he would get the chance to eat or sleep. He hadn't joined the army to stand on the A1 and check out lorries. "Were these men with you when you were last questioned?"

Pete held his breath as Colin looked back at the soldier.

"Yes," Colin replied. "Of course they were. Your guys back there were satisfied. Now can we get on? All this stopping and starting is making me late. I'm running behind schedule."

"Okay, off you go." The sergeant jumped down. Signalling ahead, he indicated the lorry should be allowed to go through.

"Thanks," yelled Colin. "I hope you find your men soon."

The sergeant didn't answer. He had already turned his attention to another vehicle.

Colin didn't say another word until he reached a lay-by a couple of miles down the road. Parking the lorry, he turned off the engine. "Okay. Let's have it. You're the two guys the army's after. What've you done?"

"Nothing!" Josh tried to sound convincing. "It's not us they want, we..."

"Don't take me for a fool!" Colin slammed his fist on the steering wheel. "I'm not stupid. I saw the way you acted back there. You were scared shitless – both of you." He sniffed. "So! What've you done that they want you so bad?"

Pete swallowed hard. "Yes." He sighed. It was no good pretending any more. "It's us they're chasing. But you really don't want to know why. It would only put you in the same danger we're in." He paused. "I'm Pete Maine and this is Josh Davies. We aren't going to hurt you, we haven't harmed anyone. All we want to do is to get to London, where hopefully all this mess will be sorted out. If you're worried, we'll get out right now and you can go on your way."

"London!" Colin exclaimed. He hit the steering wheel again. "Gee! I might have known London would figure in this somewhere. Nobody in their right mind goes to London unless they have a problem they need solving and mark my words, it's usually London that caused the problem in the first place. I tell you guys, if we got rid of London tomorrow, this country's troubles would be over."

He paused and stared at the two men. He had always hoped that just once, something exciting might happen to him on one his humdrum journeys up and down the country. He was always reading about drivers who had been seduced by beautiful blondes, or even hauled from their cabs and held at gunpoint. Until now, he hadn't believed a word. He had put it down to drivers on the road making up a story or two to make life more interesting. He could understand that. The open road was a lonely place, which was why he picked up the odd hitch-hiker along the way when Sam wasn't with him.

He cocked his head on one side. Perhaps these so-called wild stories might be for real after all. He came to a decision. Whatever these guys were up to, he wanted to be a part of it – at least until he reached Peterborough.

"Say, are you guys hungry?" he asked, casually. "I usually stop at Miss Annie's Pit-Stop a couple of miles on."

Pete looked at Josh and then back at Colin. "Are you serious?"

"Of course I'm serious."

"You mean you're not going to ditch us here in the middle of nowhere and go back and turn us in?"

"No. What would be the point of that?" Colin laughed. "They'd only place me under arrest for lying in the first place. Heaven forbid! They might even drag me to London!"

Glancing at Josh, Pete laughed. As Colin said, they might drag him and his lorry off somewhere, but they both knew it wouldn't be to London. It would more likely be back up to the north, where the horror had all begun and he would never be heard of again.

"So, are you hungry?" Colin repeated his question.

"Yes we are." Josh shrugged. "But we haven't any money. The last of it was spent filling the car with petrol."

"As it turned out, it was a waste of money." Colin grinned. "Never mind, I'm sure Miss Annie will see you right. Besides she owes me a favour."

"You go right ahead and have something to eat." Pete looked anxiously at Josh for backup. They didn't need any more awkward questions. "Perhaps it would be best if we waited in the lorry with the dogs."

"No!" Colin started the engine. "Once we get there, we'll all go in. Miss Annie is a great cook. Her steak pie is particularly good." He ran his tongue around his lips at the mere thought of it. "She'll even give some scraps to the dogs."

Turning his head slightly, Colin nodded towards the two dogs in the back. "They look as though they could do with a good meal." Looking back at Pete, he grinned. "But there's one other great thing about Miss Annie; she never asks questions."

The men ate hungrily. Miss Annie's steak pie was as good as Colin had said. As for the scraps she fed to the dogs, they would have graced anyone's table.

"Me and Colin go way back," she said over a pot of coffee. "When I was trying to get this place up and running, he told everyone he met about how good my cooking was. I've never looked back. I've even had to take on some help." She nodded towards two lads clearing tables and washing dishes.

****

It was dark by the time they all climbed back into the lorry. As the traffic was beginning to thin out, Colin believed he would make up some time.

"I'm usually there by now," he explained. "Ted likes to take the lorry straight out. It means he's back in London well before last orders." He grinned. "Likes a drink or two does Ted." He slapped the steering wheel. "Say, I've had an idea, you could ride the rest of the way with Ted. He's always on his own. Bit of a loner is Ted: he doesn't talk much. Not like me. You'll probably be able to get some sleep." He laughed heartily.

At the depot in Peterborough, Colin took Ted to one side and explained how Pete and Josh needed a lift. Ted eyed the two men suspiciously. "Why do they want to go to London?" he asked sullenly.

"They're broke and looking for work," Colin replied.

As far as he was concerned, it was all Ted needed to know. But then he thought about the army patrols. What if they ran into another one and they asked where the men had been picked up?

"By the way, were you stopped on your way up to Peterborough? The army is doing some special manoeuvres in the north. They stopped us a few times." He laughed. "No problems with me, though. The lads can vouch for that, they've been with me all the way down."

Ted didn't laugh. He wasn't the sort of person who laughed unless he had a glass in one hand. "No. I wasn't stopped at all. I can't say I saw road blocks on the other side either of the carriageway either."

Ted nodded towards the dogs. "Do they bite?" he asked.

"They haven't bitten me." Colin grinned. "Besides, they've already eaten. We stopped a while back."

Ted didn't see the joke and shuffled over to Pete and Josh. "I don't usually pick anyone up, I like being on my own. I don't like folks chattering all the time. I play the radio and if I don't like it, I switch it off. Can't do that with folks. They tend to go on and on."

"We won't say a word," promised Pete. It would suit them fine if Ted stayed silent. The least said the better.

Ted stared at them for a while longer. "Okay, get in," he grunted. "But I'm telling you, no chattering. I don't want to know your life history."

Pete drew Colin to one side. "Thanks a lot. I don't know what we'd have done without you."

"That's okay, I enjoyed your company." Colin lowered his voice. "Ted didn't see any road-blocks between here and London, but you never know. I've told him you've been with me all the way down. Nevertheless, keep your wits about you." He hesitated. "This trouble you and Josh are in; will I ever get to know more about it?"

"Oh yes, Colin. Once we get to London and speak out, you'll hear about it. It's big time. All hell will break loose and when it does, you'll know that you played a large part in helping us to put things right. But in the meantime, keep quiet; say nothing at all. Your very life depends on it."

Colin grasped Pete's outstretched hand. "Okay, I understand. Good luck to you both."

A few minutes later, Pete and Josh found themselves back on the road, to London.

CHAPTER TWENTY

Charles made his way down Pall Mall towards Luigi's Restaurant. Never before had he felt so alone. His phone was tapped and there were men watching the house, but even worse, his daughter distrusted him. To be truthful she hadn't actually said so, yet he could feel it.

He had hoped Rick would speak up for him, but though his former assistant kept making sympathetic noises, Charles felt a little uneasy. Behind Rick's wide smile, there was something not quite right.

Today, feeling even more low than usual, he had suddenly thought of Arthur Goodwin and how he regularly took lunch at Luigi's. Arthur was a fair man, if he had heard any further news, he would tell him.

Charles recalled how it hadn't been easy to lose the men following him. Good at their job, they hadn't let him out of their sight. But determined to break free, he had led them on a dull trip around his locality, hoping they would become bored and take less notice.

First, he had gone to the bank and then called at the newsagents. After a visiting a few other shops, he had called in on his tailor. Making a big display of choosing some material, he had taken it to the window and held it up to the daylight. From this vantage viewpoint, Charles had seen his plan was beginning to work. One of the men was reading a newspaper, while the other appeared to be fiddling with something on the dashboard – probably the radio.

Leaving the tailors, he had gone into a coffee shop and chosen a table towards the back. From the corner of his eye, he watched one of the men walk across to the window and pretend to look at the menu on display. Satisfied Charles was enjoying a light lunch, the man had gone back to the car and picked up his newspaper, while the other had taken the opportunity to visit the tobacconists across the road.

It was then Charles had made his move. Paying for his coffee, he left by a small side door located out of sight of the two men. Smiling to himself, he had hurried back to his car.

Now outside Luigi's, Charles peered through the window. After taking so much trouble, he desperately hoped Arthur would be lunching here today. Tomorrow it would be much more difficult to escape his tail.

Still looking through the window, he felt a hand on his shoulder and feared the worst. However, turning around he was relieved to find his friend grinning at him.

"Arthur," Charles exclaimed. "Thank goodness; I hoped you might be here today."

"Come inside." Arthur ushered Charles towards the door. "You never know who might be watching."

Once seated, Charles told his friend how he was now being blamed for the implosion. "But I suppose you already know about it."

"Yes, despite the incident being kept quiet, I have heard a few whispers. It's a terrible business." Arthur leaned forward. "However I want you to know, I don't believe a word of it. It's not the way you operate. You would never have left such instructions. I believe there's a lot more to this than meets the eye."

"You bet there is!" Charles went on to explain about how the various valves had been tampered with. "I was foolish, I should have mentioned it there and then, but I didn't. I hoped to catch the culprit changing them back." He sighed. "Unfortunately, I went home to change and when I returned, everything was as it should be." He paused, reflecting on his stupidity. "You'll have heard Rick has been put in charge of..."

"Yes." Arthur interrupted. He knew how painful this must be for Charles. "For the benefit of all those who don't know about the catastrophe, the story being put about is that you haven't been feeling well and decided to stand down in favour of Rick. It fits in with the Prime Minister's hush-hush plan." He shook his head. "Whatever you do, don't trust Rick. I never did like the man. To my mind, he's had his eye on your job for some time. Have you seen him recently?"

"Yes. He's called at the house a few times. It was he who informed me of the Prime Minister's decision. He told me how he had done everything he could to help my position, but..." Charles shook his head. "I don't know... I think you could be right. I too have a nasty feeling about him, yet I can't actually figure out why. But I've noticed a few things, which don't seem to add up."

He told Arthur about the green pass on Rick's car. "I always thought he was my friend. I even believed he was going to be my son-in-law until Sarah met Pete. Now I wonder..."

He sighed and shook his head. "What's going on, Arthur? What's happening? I don't hear anything, except what Rick feeds me. I never see anyone. My phone is tapped, men watch my house; I tell you, I had the devil's own job getting here today without being followed. Irene puts on a brave face, but I know this business is getting to her."

Arthur reached out and touched his friend's arm. "I'm kept very much in the dark. True I'm a Defence Office Minister, but on the subject of the laboratory, no one tells me anything. They're all aware that I don't agree with what's going on. In fact, I was most surprised the Prime Minister didn't have me replaced after I walked out of the Cabinet Room the other night." He shrugged. "But then he would've had to explain his reasons and as he wants this business hushed, he probably thought it best to leave things as they are for the time being. In the meantime, Brian Tate confides in his pet poodle."

Charles grimaced. "Alan Crisp."

"Precisely!" Arthur hesitated. "It's only a thought, but have you been back to the laboratory?"

"No. Not since the day I cleared out my office. After one of Rick's visits to the house, I decided to go back and take look around, but then I thought, what's the point? Whoever framed me will have covered their tracks." He paused and cocked his head on one side. "Why do you ask?"

Arthur shook his head. "I don't know. But I wondered if there might be something the perpetrator had forgotten." He shrugged. "I feel so useless. I really wish I could be of more help, but as it is..."

"You've been a great help." Charles smiled. "It's good to be able to talk to someone who is actually on my side. Now let's simply enjoy lunch together. How's your wife?"

Arthur's face brightened. "Molly's fine." He lowered his voice. "Naturally, I haven't told her about any of this business. The less she knows the better. But what about your wife and daughter..." He broke off, remembering Sarah had moved up north. "Oh Charles, I'm so sorry. I'd completely forgotten your daughter was living up in Northumberland. Have you heard from her?"

"Sarah's fine. She and the children escaped the disaster and the military, due mainly to a quick-witted police constable. We have a lot to thank him for. She's back at the house right now. We're trying to keep it quiet about her having lived up there, so I'd be grateful if you wouldn't mention it to anyone."

"You can rely on me. I won't breathe a word." Arthur squeezed his friend's arm to emphasize the point.

"Pete's still missing." Charles continued. "Sarah doesn't know what happened to him, yet she refuses to believe he's dead." He shook his head. "However, she says he was actually on one of the hills nearest to the old power station that day, and didn't return. I don't want to be the one to dash her hopes, but if he was up there, how could he have survived?"

It was then the waiter arrived with their first course.

****

"I'm going back up north. I need to know what's happened to Pete." Sarah was determined. She and Rick were in her parents' sitting room. "I've thought it through and the children are safe now," she continued. "I know you think I'm being foolish. But Pete is my husband and I need to know whether he's alive or dead."

It was the last thing Rick wanted to hear. That damned man! Even from his grave, Pete was tormenting him. Why couldn't Sarah leave things alone? They were getting on so well together.

"But Pete's dead!" He almost spat out the name. "Why can't you accept it? I'm sure he wouldn't want you to go back up there." Rick tried hard to keep his patience. Why didn't she forget about the wretched man? Hadn't he killed him so they could be together? Pete should never have entered her life in the first place, not while he, Rick, was there for her. He felt like shaking her hard to bring her to her senses. Instead he heaved a sigh. "You know, if it was me, I wouldn't want you to go back up there looking for me."

He was lying through his teeth. If there were the slightest chance he had lived through anything so horrendous, he would expect her to move heaven and earth until she found him.

"No, of course you wouldn't. You're a kind, sweet man, just like Pete. But I need to know for myself what happened to him." Sarah took Rick by the hand. "I only agreed to come away with Andy, so I could bring my children to safety. I always intended to go back for Pete. Andy knew that, I'm sure you understand."

Rick's whole body was quivering with hatred for Pete. He was all she ever talked about. He had hoped that once Pete was gone, Sarah would forget all thoughts of her husband, yet so far it hadn't happened. He would need to keep his head and stay calm. Show some sympathy for her loss. But it would be difficult. Showing sympathy for someone else was alien to Rick.

"Of course I know how you feel," he said taking her hand. "Though I really believe he's dead, I fully understand. Perhaps I could find out something from a colleague at the Ministry of Defence. The army might have seen something of him."

To Sarah, the Ministry of Defence didn't sound such a good idea. She and Andy had run into the military before. They hadn't stopped to listen. Given half a chance, they would have killed them all.

"No! I don't think so. They're likely to kill him should they find him alive."

That's exactly what Rick was hoping for. He wanted to be rid of this man once and for all. What he really wanted, was a video of Pete writhing in agony as the flesh dripped from his bones. Only then would he know for certain the damn man was gone for good. The thought filled him with ecstasy and... He pulled himself up sharply. Sarah was still waiting for a response.

"Alright, whatever you say, Sarah. You must know I only want what's best for you." He coughed to hide the note of excitement, which had crept into his voice at the thought of Pete being killed in such a horrific way.

He made a mental note to speak to Alan Crisp. If there were the slightest chance Pete was still alive, then Crisp would make sure Brian Tate knew about it. But Rick knew he would have to be very careful not to mention Sarah's part in this. Merely put forward the suggestion that someone from one of the farms might be still wandering around and if so, he or she should be dealt with by exposing them to some of the slime. He could also casually recommend they video the whole scene – all in the interest of science of course.

"Why don't you let me take you to the theatre tonight?" Rick tried to change the subject. "I'm told there's a musical on at the Palladium and I'm sure I could get some really good seats." He smiled. "I know someone there. I might even get the Royal Box."

Sarah didn't feel like going to the theatre. All this talk of Pete had unsettled her. What she really wanted to do was to pack some clothes and take the train north. However Rick was being so supportive. He had called at the house since her return in a bid to help her forget the last few harrowing days. Knowing the pain she was going through, she felt sure that if he could possibly bring Pete back to her, he would do so.

And there was another thing. Despite what her father thought, she believed Rick was sticking his neck out trying to protect Charles from the powers above. All things considered, perhaps she owed it to Rick to stay in London for a little while longer.

"Mummy, Mummy." Josie ran into the room, interrupting her thoughts. "Are you going to take us to the park?"

Sarah looked around and saw Andy following behind. He was carrying Becky. "I'll take them if you like," he offered. "I don't mind."

It was true. The children were growing on him. He had even taken a liking to the dog.

"Besides, I need to pay my way. It's very kind of your parents to allow me to stay on here."

"That's nonsense Andy!" Sarah moved across to him. "You're welcome to stay here as long as you like. I don't know what I'd have done without you." She reached up and kissed him lightly on the cheek. "And I can't expect you to look after the children every day. It's not fair, when you've been so kind already. We shall all go to the park together."

Rick turned away, his face contorted with rage. He didn't like the way this was going. Was Sarah beginning to notice that Andy was a handsome, young man? He hadn't got rid of Pete for this country policeman to step in and take his place! He had already formed a plan to get rid of Andy and the kids. It seemed it would be necessary to make his move more quickly than he had first anticipated.

"Thank you for your kind offer of a night at the theatre."

Realising Sarah was talking to him, Rick forced himself to relax and turned back to face her.

"But perhaps we could make it another night." Sarah continued. "I really should be spending a little more time with my children and of course our guest."

"Yes, you're right." Rick uttered. The words stuck in his throat, almost choking him. "I do seem to have monopolized your time, but I was just so relieved to see you back here, safe and sound." Looking across to Andy his eyes narrowed. "I trust you'll take good care of them all."

232

"Yes, of course I will." Andy felt a little alarmed. This was the second time he had felt acid in this man's tone. What did Rick have against him?

Rick shook his head. What was he thinking of? If his plan was going to work, he had to remain friendly with Andy. There was no point in frightening him off at this stage. He gave a hollow laugh. "I'm sorry. I must be getting jumpy."

Andy smiled. "That's okay."

Rick turned as if to go, but changed his mind. Perhaps he could start the ball rolling. "It's occurred to me you might like to take a look at the laboratory some time. I'm sure you would find it all very interesting."

"Well – yes." Andy was taken aback. The thought of looking around the laboratory had never entered his head. He wasn't normally into that kind of technology. However, if this was meant as a gesture of friendship, then he should respond. Though truthfully, he still had doubts about Rick. All this blowing hot and cold concerned him. "Thank you. I'd like that very much."

"Good," beamed Rick. "I'll organise something. Perhaps we could involve the children."

"Don't you think they're a little young for..." began Sarah.

"Nonsense!" Rick was determined. Having got this far, he wasn't going to let it go now. "If Andy and I take the children off your hands, it'll give you and your mother a chance to go shopping together." He smiled. "Not only would it do you the power of good, but I think your mother would enjoy it. She's been looking a bit peaky lately."

"Oh good heavens!" Sarah's hand flew to her mouth as she looked towards Andy. "I'd almost forgotten. Mum has a dress fitting this afternoon and I promised I'd go with her."

"Well you must go, of course." Andy smiled. "We'll be fine, won't we girls?" He looked down at Josie.

"In that case, I'll come with you." Rick beamed at Andy. This was working out better than he had hoped. "Perhaps we could all have some large ice-creams somewhere and afterwards I'll show you around the laboratory. What do you think?"

"Great." Andy could see no way out and he hoped his lack of enthusiasm didn't show. Rick in small doses was one thing – he could cope with that, but spending the whole afternoon with him was an entirely different matter.

"Are you sure about this?" Sarah had her doubts. The laboratory wasn't the ideal place to take the children. Not after... She shuddered. "I'm a little concerned..."

"Stop fussing, they'll be fine." Rick tried not to show his impatience, but it was difficult. Those bloody kids were all she thought about. The quicker he got rid of them the better. It wasn't as though she would be childless for the rest of her life. She could have as many children as she wanted, as long as they were his.

"Well, if you're sure." Sarah was still hesitant.

"Of course I am," said Rick briskly. He laughed. "We'll even take Betts with us. She'll love it too."

Sarah laughed. "Okay, you've talked me into it."

Rick looked at his watch. "Is that the time? I'll call into the laboratory to check the mail and other details and get back to you later." He nodded towards Andy. "Does that suit you?"

"Yes, I suppose so. If Sarah's happy, then it's alright with me."

Leaving the house, Rick rubbed his hands together. Everything was going to plan. Pete was already gone. Charles had not only been disgraced, but he had also been removed from his position and better still, his job had fallen to him – as of course he knew it would. Though truthfully, that hadn't been a priority in his mission. Originally his prize had been Sarah. The position at the laboratory had simply been an added bonus.

But when he saw the possibility of a promotion on the horizon, he had gone all out for it. The Prime Minister could quite easily have advertised the job. But why would Turner bother to go to the trouble of interviewing candidates, when the right man was already there? He liked men who agreed with him; who thought along the same lines as himself. And Rick could do that quite easily. In fact, he would agree with the devil himself, if there were something in it for him.

Over the last few months, with a little help from Alan Crisp, he had been on hand every time the Prime Minister needed something. By making himself indispensable, it was only natural the name of Rick Armstrong had sprung into Turner's mind when a new man was needed to take over at the laboratory.

In his mind, Rick had replayed countless times the singular delicious moment when he had been given the news. Each time it gave him even more satisfaction. Now, the final part of the plan was coming together. Very

234

soon Andy and the children would be history. As for Betts – well, he could tolerate the dog. Besides, he quite liked dogs. Like himself, they could be cunning and vicious if crossed, yet so docile and loving towards those who took care of them. Yes, he could empathize with dogs.

Sarah was fast becoming like putty in his hands. Very soon, she would have only him to rely on – apart from her mother. And again, Rick could cope with Irene. He liked her. To him she was everything mothers should be: kind, soft and gentle. Not like his own mother, who used to be drunk more often than she was sober. She had almost beaten him senseless with a large stick on several occasions.

Climbing into his car, he looked back at the house. All this would be his if he kept his nerve. And so far, he had done that. Yes, there had been two blips, when he had allowed his true feelings towards Andy to show through. But he had realised his error in time and made amends. All he had to do now was to smile sweetly for a short while longer.

Setting off down the road, his thoughts drifted back to his mother. If she could see him now she would never believe he was the son she had so badly abused. But then she couldn't see him. In fact she hadn't seen anything for a long time. Not since he had battered her brains to a pulp with an empty gin bottle all those years ago.

****

The house was empty when Charles arrived home from lunching with Arthur. In the sitting room he found a note from Irene informing him of everyone's whereabouts. Reading it slowly, Charles thought it strange that Sarah had allowed the children to go to the laboratory, especially the way she felt about the place at the moment. But on the other hand, Rick could be most charming and very persuasive when he wanted his own way. One comforting thought crossed his mind; Andy was there. He would watch out for them.

Charles walked aimlessly around the room. He was unused to having so much time on his hands and wondered what to do. Glancing towards the bookshelves, he decided to catch up with some reading.

Settling into his favourite armchair, he looked out of the window. The men were outside. They had been there when he arrived home. Obviously having realised he had given them the slip, they had made their way back here. He wondered whether they had reported the incident. Probably not. It wouldn't look too good on their records. He recalled Arthur telling him the dayshift men were called Grant and Jack. Well at least he now had names for the unsmiling faces out there.

He had a sudden thought. Should he make some tea and take it out to them on a small tray. He had once seen it done in a similar situation in a movie. But he dismissed the idea with a grunt. Let them get their own damn tea!

He was barely one chapter into his book, when he heard the doorbell. Sliding down in his armchair, he hoped whoever it was would go away if he didn't answer the door. But the bell rang again and again. Someone was determined to make themselves heard. He snapped the book shut. It was no good; he would have to answer it. It would only make Grant and Jack very suspicious.

"Pete!" Charles was astounded when he opened the door. "Oh my God is it really you?" For a moment he could only stand there looking at him in disbelief. But remembering the men in the parked car, he quickly ushered Pete and the other man into the house.

After a final glance at the car in the road, he slammed the door shut and turned back to Pete. "Thank God you're alive. We thought you were dead."

"Yes, we're alive, but what about Sarah?" Pete grabbed Charles's arm. "Are Sarah and the children here? Please tell me; are they here?"

"Yes, yes. They're here. Come through into the lounge." Charles led the way. "Sit down; both of you."

"This is Josh. He works with me on the farm." Pete quickly gestured towards Josh, but he was impatient to hear about his wife. "Tell me about Sarah."

"She's fine Pete. Really she is. She's out at the moment. She and her mother are shopping up town." Charles looked at his watch. "They shouldn't be long now. Andy and the children have gone to the park." He refrained from mentioning Rick; Pete would hear about him soon enough.

Seeing Pete's puzzled expression he explained. "Andy's a policeman. He was stationed in Wooler. It's only thanks to him that Sarah and the children are still alive. But what about you and..." He looked at the man sitting next to Pete. I'm sorry, but I've forgotten your name.

"Josh." He held out his hand. "I'm pleased to meet you."

236

Pete explained how he and Josh had been trapped in the cave. "All we know is something dreadful happened, because when we finally escaped, we found everyone dead." He paused and took a deep breath. His recollection of the scenes on the farm made him feel nauseous. There had been no time to think about it during the treacherous journey down here, but now the images flooded his memory. "But they weren't just dead," he continued. Their flesh had melted."

He shook his head. It sounded ridiculous even to him. Charles must think him crazy. "It was dreadful. I don't suppose you can possibly imagine what I'm saying. But it wasn't only me; Josh saw it too. The flesh was actually dripping from their bones and lying in pools on the ground. How can that be possible?"

Charles looked away. It was happening all over again. Once Pete learned it was he who had developed this... monstrous thing, he would turn against him, just as Sarah had done. But he had to tell him. If he didn't, Sarah most certainly would. In the long run, it would be better coming from him.

He took a deep breath. "Pete, I think there's something you should know..."

CHAPTER TWENTY-ONE

"You can't be serious!" Pete flopped back in his chair, hardly able to take in what Charles was saying. There had to be some mistake. Yet Charles looked deadly serious. He glanced at Josh before turning his attention back to Charles. "You're telling us it was the government who ordered the development of this terrible thing and it was you who invented it?"

"Yes. That's exactly what I'm saying. Well, me and the team that is." He paused. "But I want you to know, and I really need to make this absolutely clear regardless of what anyone says, I was not negligent. I did not leave a message saying I was not to be contacted. Nor did I turn off the safety guards. I firmly believe I was framed."

There was an awkward silence, broken only by the chiming of the clock in the hall.

"Okay." Pete shuffled uneasily in his chair. It was unthinkable anyone would actually release something so horrible on purpose. "For the moment, let's assume that what you say is true. Who do you think might have done it? Who could possibly hate you so much, they would kill all those innocent people simply to settle an old score?"

"I really don't know," Charles spoke slowly. "However, I'm not entirely sure Rick is blameless."

"Rick!" Pete couldn't believe his ears. "I thought he was your right-hand man. How does he figure in all this?"

"I don't know." Charles shrugged. "That's the problem. Nevertheless, I have this nagging feeling he knows a great deal more than he's saying." He took a deep breath. "It's no secret that I once thought Rick would be my son-in-law. But then Sarah fell in love with you and that should have been an end to it. And it was, as far as Irene and I were concerned. You're a good man and we couldn't have wished for a better husband for our daughter." He hesitated. "However, I'm not sure Rick ever got over being turned down. He's always found some excuse to call at the house whenever Sarah visited and he's spent a lot of time here since her return a few days ago." He paused. "It's true, he makes sympathetic noises in my direction regarding my predicament, yet I feel there's something not quite right. Perhaps deep down, he believes I should have insisted Sarah..." He broke off.

Pete shook his head. "I can't believe it. You're saying Rick released the weapon simply because you didn't stop Sarah from marrying me."

Charles nodded. "Yes, I suppose I am."

"But do you have any proof? What makes you even think he's behind it all?"

"No. I have no real proof." Charles shook his head. "But the day he came to tell me the Prime Minister had put him in charge of the laboratory, I noticed he had a special green pass on his windshield."

"So?" Pete shrugged, unable to see the point. "Isn't he entitled to have one, being in such a position?"

"Yes, he is. But they take at least ten days to come through. Even the Prime Minister himself would have to wait. These passes come with a personal ID that allows you into most government buildings; therefore they are very restricted. They only print them one at a time when they are needed." Charles leant forward. "So how did Rick get his so quickly? He must have applied in advance, which also means he must also have forged someone's signature. The next burning question is how did he know the Prime Minister was going to put him in charge of the laboratory ten days ago, unless he knew something no one else did?"

"I see," said Pete, thoughtfully. "Have you discussed this with anyone else? Surely you should bring this to the attention of Robert Turner."

"What would I say? I can't prove a thing. Who knows, there could be a conspiracy going on. Perhaps the Prime Minister was going to replace me anyway. I don't really believe that, but..."

"Have you been to the laboratory since all this happened?" Pete interrupted. "There could be something that might settle it."

"No, I only called in to pick up my things. I intended to go back and have a look around, but so far I haven't set foot in the place."

"But surely if you felt something was going on, you should have gone back to the laboratory and checked it out." Pete slammed his hand down on the arm of the chair as he spoke. His impatience was beginning to get the better of him. "What does Sarah say about all this?"

"I'm afraid she doubts everything I say." Charles cast his eyes downwards. "I don't think she can get beyond the fact that I, her father, created this... weapon. As far as I can tell, she seems to agree with Rick in that I wrote the note and turned off the safety guards whilst not knowing what I was doing."

"Sorry, but could we back-track a little, I think I must be missing something?" Josh had remained silent until now. "I still can't understand why Rick would have a problem with you, Sir Charles. He's an intelligent man. Surely he must realise you couldn't influence Sarah. Who she married would have to be her decision, no matter what you wanted."

"Yes, Josh has a point." Pete shook his head. "I really don't think Rick could have done this to you simply because Sarah chose to marry me. If he was still angry about that, then surely it would be me he'd..." He paused. A thought had occurred to him. "Oh my God!" he leapt out of his chair. "That's it. Don't you see? It's not you he had the grudge against, Charles – it's me! You just happened to be in the way."

****

"I suppose you and Sarah must have got on quite well together during your journey down here." Rick pushed Josie's swing. "I mean, being so close to each other for several days. It would have been a nightmare if you hadn't liked each other."

They had been in the park for some time and Andy was trying to put Becky back into her pushchair. However, the child seemed to have other ideas. He glanced up at Rick. It had sounded like a statement, so why did he feel that Rick was waiting for a reply. "Yes, we got on very well actually. Sarah is a pleasant young woman. I say would you mind giving me a hand here? Becky might be small, but she can be very determined."

With some reluctance, Rick bent over the pushchair. The less he had to do with Pete's kids, the better. "You hold her and I'll try to fasten the strap," he uttered.

Between the two of them, they finally managed to fasten the squirming child into the chair.

"Push me again. Push me again!" Josie squealed.

"I think it is time we were starting back," said Andy.

"Nonsense! There's plenty of time." Rick didn't want to go to the laboratory too early. It would be better for him if they waited until the shifts were changing. He beamed down at the children. "Uncle Andy seems to have forgotten we're all going to have ice-creams and then I'm taking you to see where I work."

"Will I be able to draw a picture?" Josie asked.

"Yes. Of course you will, I'll help you. And you can take it back to show your mummy, I'm sure she'd be thrilled." Rick could afford to be generous. The wretched child could draw what she liked as no one would ever see it. He grinned at Andy. "But I'm sure we've time for a few more minutes on the swings. What do you say?"

Andy was surprised at Rick's sudden interest in the children. Until that moment, he hadn't shown any real affection towards them. "Yes," he replied. "I think that'll be alright. Mummy knows where we are."

"You were saying how you and Sarah got on well." Rick moved closer.

"Yes." Andy's uneasiness returned. Why did Rick keep going on about it? What did he want him to say? "I think we got on as well as any two people could, when thrown together under very difficult circumstances." He frowned and then laughed. "Does that make sense?"

"I know what you mean." Rick spoke quietly to hide the bitterness in his voice.

Envious of Andy spending so much time with Sarah over the last few days, he had tortured himself wondering if they had shared a bed. So desperate to know, he was tempted come right out and ask. However, managing to control himself, he pushed the thought to one side. What did it matter now? In an hour or so, Andy would be dead and anything between him and Sarah would die with him.

He shrugged. "I just wondered. Sarah can be a very stubborn woman sometimes."

"Yes, she can, especially where the children are concerned."

"Yes," Rick muttered. But she wouldn't have that problem for very much longer!

****

Pete paced up and down the room, slamming his fist into his hand. "It was me he was after all the time."

"But wouldn't he have been taking an awful chance?" Charles didn't understand. "I mean, he could very easily have killed Sarah."

"Yes that's true, Pete. How..." began Josh.

Pete held up his hand and stopped him mid-sentence. "Let me think... Bear with me for a few minutes." He continued to walk up and down.

Suddenly, he turned back to Charles, "You say this... weapon is contained in the old power station north of my farm?"

"Yes, that's right. The government took it over when..."

"Did you know how far this... light... gas... whatever, would travel?" Pete interrupted. It didn't matter when the government had taken it over.

Charles thought for a moment. "Yes... No. We couldn't be absolutely sure." He rocked his hand back and forth. "Not down to the last mile, or even half mile. As I said, Rick could easily have killed Sarah as well as you."

"Not unless he already knew she wasn't going to be there." Pete was growing excited. "Sarah wasn't due to be home that night. She was going to spend the evening with her friend in Alnwick. What if Rick knew that?" He looked from Charles to Josh in turn. "The children should have been with Laura and I was going to pick them up from there. Josie, Becky and I were meant to die, but Josh and I survived because we were trapped in the cave. It was fortunate for us that neither the light, nor the gas was able to penetrate the hillside. If the children had still been with Laura, they would have perished. But for some reason, Sarah must have stayed home with them." He gazed down at Charles. "It seems the farmhouse was out of range, so they were spared." Pete sank back into his chair and swallowed hard. "Rick killed all those people, simply to eliminate me and the children – the bastard!"

Charles felt the blood drain from his face. He had never thought of that. Until now he believed it was he, who Rick had wanted to eliminate from office. But thinking back to what his daughter had said, Pete could be right.

"When Sarah arrived here, she explained how she should have been away that day. But she stayed home, because Josie was feeling unwell when she awoke." Staring into space, Charles spoke mechanically. "Apparently she phoned Laura to say she wouldn't be leaving the children with her after all. That evening she saw the light in the sky, and then the cloud of gas. As you said, the farmhouse was unaffected." Charles hung his head. "I thank God they were spared."

He looked up at Pete before continuing. "If everything had gone according to plan and you had collected the children, you would all have been safe. However, if the children had still been with Laura in the valley..." He paused unable to finish. He took a deep breath. "I gather the next morning Sarah went out to find you, but came across Dave lying in the lane." Again he hesitated and shook his head. "It must have been horrible for her. The poor man was still alive. Can you understand that? Despite the flesh dripping from his bones, the poor, wretched man was still alive. From what Sarah said, I believe he was desperate to pass on the information of what had happened. He told her about a whirring sound and the light that followed. He begged her not to touch him, but to get away from the valley. He believed you were both dead."

Charles covered his face with his hands. "I knew Rick was headstrong, impatient, even, but I never dreamed he was capable of anything like this. He must be insane. It seems he'll stop at nothing to get what he wants and what he wants is Sarah. Even now he's trying to worm his way back into her affections."

"I agree it all fits, but there's one flaw," said Josh. "How could Rick have known that Sarah was going to be away on that particular evening?" He looked at the others. But no one had the answer. "In that case, I think we should go down to the laboratory. We might find something to implicate Rick."

"You're right." Charles rose to his feet. "I should have made a more thorough search a few days ago. But perhaps you, Pete, would rather wait here for Sarah?"

"Yes, I am desperate to see her." He took a deep breath. "But I really need to find out if Rick did this. At least I now know for certain that she and the children arrived here safely. I owe the policeman a great debt." He looked down at his filthy shirt and trousers. "However I think Josh and I should change our clothes first, we can't walk into a government laboratory looking like this; we'd never get past the reception desk. You must have something that will fit us." He nodded towards the window. "And then there's your tail outside. We'll need to do something about them."

CHAPTER TWENTY-TWO

Outside the house, Grant and Jack looked on as Charles made a big show of seeing his friends off. "Take good care of my car," he shouted. He wanted to make sure the security men believed he was staying at home. "I'll see you tomorrow."

Once Pete had backed out of the drive, Charles returned to the house and stood by the window until the car turned the corner at the bottom of the road. Before moving away, he smiled and waved at the two men in the parked car.

Proceeding quickly through the house, he crept out of the back door, carefully locking it behind him. A narrow lane was situated beyond the garden and already he could see Pete and Josh waiting in the car.

"Well that was easy enough," he said, climbing into the back seat. "But to be on the safe side, I'll keep my head down until we're well away from here."

The laboratory was surprisingly quiet when the three men arrived. Both Pete and Josh were astonished at the huge amount of equipment installed. Several large machines displayed numerous dials and levers, while a complex of computer screens flashed out facts and figures.

Charles headed straight for the office, which until a few days ago had been his. "Rick has moved his things in here now, so this should be the best place to start."

"What exactly are we looking for?" Josh was bending over the desk.

"I'm not sure, which means we'll need to check everything." Charles opened a drawer and found the note he had supposedly written.

He was surprised it was still in Rick's possession. Surely the Prime Minister or MI5 would have asked for it. Obviously Rick was keeping it as his get-out clause. Charles marvelled again at how impressive the forgery was. Someone had gone to a great deal of trouble; it really looked like his handwriting.

"Yet I know I didn't write this," he said, slamming his fist down on the desk. "I definitely did not write this note!"

"Alright! But keep your voice down." Pete nodded towards the laboratory. "We don't want to arouse anyone's suspicions. I'm surprised we weren't stopped on our way in here."

"I still have my passcodes and I've made a few friends along the way; Rick was never the most likable person in the lab." Charles thought for a moment. "But then, I suppose he didn't set out to be popular."

"For goodness sake, let's get on with it." Josh glanced through the small glass panel in the office door. "The last thing we want, is to be caught rummaging around this office."

At first he had been keen to check out the laboratory, as it seemed the most logical thing to do. But now he wasn't quite so sure. They would be in no end of trouble if someone decided to call security. Leaning over the desk, he yanked at one of the drawers.

"Josh is right." Charles sighed, as he put down the note and pulled open a drawer on the other side of the desk. "We should stick to the matter at hand." However, after fumbling around in the drawer, he was disappointed. There were a few documents, but nothing of any importance.

Josh was already heaving open another. "I've checked a couple of the others, but there isn't much in any of them." Smiling, he looked up at Pete and Charles. "However this one is more hopeful; it's locked."

Pete looked around the room. "Is there something here we can use to force it?" He picked up a letter opener. "What about this?"

"There's no need." Charles held up a key. "You're forgetting this used to be my office. I kept duplicate keys to everything."

"What did Rick say about that?" Josh raised his eyebrows.

Charles shrugged. "I didn't tell him."

Turning the key, the drawer sprang open and the three men gazed down at the contents. This was their last hope. Would they find something to incriminate Rick? At first sight the top layer looked innocent enough, a few loose papers and a couple of pens. It didn't look good.

Glancing at Pete, Charles began to feel around the drawer. "This is Rick's diary." He held up a thick black book.

Flicking through the pages, he found much was written in some kind of shorthand. There were lots of abbreviations and initials.

"I'll flip back a few weeks, there might be something I recognise. There was a time when Rick and I worked very closely together."

While Charles scanned the diary, Pete continued to rummage around the drawer. Pulling out a small notebook, he found it contained similar abbreviations to those in the diary. It was obvious they would need to work out what these initials meant if they were going to get anywhere.

"Surely there must be something you recognise. You worked with the man!" Pete was beginning to get impatient. He couldn't bear to think they had come this far, only to end up with nothing.

"Yes," said Charles slowly. "A few things are starting to make sense." He pointed to a note made a few weeks ago. "I remember him talking about that. He wanted to test out some theory he had. I told him it was too risky at this stage and there was no telling of the knock-on effect it would have. I tried to explain it to him, but we had an argument and he stormed out. I recall we were at my house at the time."

"Does he mention it again further on?" said Josh, excitedly. "He might have gone on to test his theory, despite your reluctance."

"It's hard to tell. Again he's used abbreviations. It seems he's invented his own kind of shorthand." Charles poured over the diary. "Besides, if he did go ahead with some tests of his own and happened to discover something new, then he's more than likely given it a new name."

"What about the notebook?" Pete thrust the book at Charles. He had hoped they would have found something incriminating by now. "Does anything in there make sense to you?"

Taking the notebook, Charles ran his finger down the first page. He paused on one set of initials. "Yes, here! Take a look, he mentions B.D and there's also a small – v. I feel sure that when he mentions B.D, he's referring to the machine over there."

Looking through the glass panel in the office door, he pointed to the largest machine in the laboratory. "That little beauty," he explained. "Is the main link to the site in Northumberland. I'm certain I've heard Rick laughingly call it Big Daddy." He hesitated as he reflected on that fateful night when all hell had broken loose. "And it was the valves on that machine that had been tampered with."

Pete looked puzzled. "What I don't understand is, how does it work?" He shook his head. "What I'm trying to say is, if the machine is here in London, how can it trigger off something over three hundred miles away?"

"Through the cables." Charles replied.

"But what cables? If any new cables had been laid in the north, we would have all heard about it. It would have been the talk of the valley. I'm sure Josh can vouch for that."

"But they weren't new cables," Charles explained. "We used existing cables – telephone cables. It's all done by computers."

246

Seeing that the two men still didn't understand, he pointed to the computer connected to the large machine. "That computer is linked to another in the old power station. In turn it is connected to a machine alongside it. The computer in the north will do whatever this one tells it to do."

Pete couldn't believe it. "But aren't there any men up there in the power station? When this thing started to go wrong, wasn't there someone on the site who could have shut the whole thing down?"

Charles felt uncomfortable. Though he had insisted on safety guards being installed here at the source, it was obvious they hadn't been enough. With a separate safety mechanism in the north, things might have been very different.

"Yes, there's a small staff up there," he said, quietly. "But they're mainly for security purposes. Only two or three technicians are employed to keep a check on the machines. All instructions are fed from here in London. Once something is programmed at this end, it's impossible for anyone to alter the machines in the power station."

Quickly turning his attention back to the diary, he looked at the next page and compared it with the notebook. "Now look at this. He doesn't mention B.D any more. Here he's written the letters S and G before going on to mention C; T; R; Z.H dash 6D. They could mean anything." Charles turned the pages. "The letters Z.H remain the same, though the numbers seem to change daily."

"The day of the disaster! What's has he written in the diary about that?" Pete was becoming anxious. It seemed Rick had covered his tracks well.

Charles turned the pages of the diary. "V; R and Z.H," said Charles. "He's written the initials in big bold letters with a large exclamation mark and then there's a large letter B inside a circle." Charles looked up. "There is no number this time. That could mean something." He stared down at the diary again. "There are some other letters here, but they've been crossed out. It looks like there's a P; B; and ... I can't make out the last one."

"Z.H, Z.H. Let's start with Z.H." Pete repeated the letters over to himself, but couldn't come up with anything. "For goodness sake think! There aren't too many words beginning with z." He paused. "zap, zep, zam, zip, zero... zero... Is that it? Could the Z mean zero?"

"Yes, yes. It could be some sort of countdown to Zero." Josh clapped his hands together. "We have him!"

"No we don't." Charles interrupted. "It doesn't prove anything. We need a lot more than two initials to go on!"

"But..." Josh began.

"No, Charles is right." Pete slammed his hand down on the desk. "We must find something that tells us what he did and how he did it. Something, which proves, without a shadow of doubt, that Rick was responsible for the whole disaster."

Annoyed that they still couldn't pin Rick down, Josh ambled across the office. "What's this?" he asked, picking up a small metal box.

"Be careful with that!" snapped Charles, recognising the box. "If I'm not very much mistaken it contains ten phials of melted flesh taken from..." Feeling awkward, he broke off. Those phials very likely contained samples from the remains of Pete and Josh's friends. Lowering his voice, he continued. "I hoped I might find an antidote from those."

Josh carefully replaced the box on the shelf. Though nervous, he was curious, so when Pete and Charles had turned their attention back to the diary and notebook, he carefully lifted the lid.

"There's got to be something in one of these books that will nail the bastard once and for all." Pete couldn't believe Rick was going to get away with it.

Charles flicked through the pages of the diary until he found the day after the catastrophe. "Here's something. It seems Rick has got a little over confident and is writing in more detail."

Pete leant forward. "What does he say?"

Charles laid the diary on the table and began to read the pages out loud. "This is it! T sent for C – days numbered."

Charles looked up. He was angry. "It still doesn't prove anything, but my guess is T stands for Turner, the Prime Minister and C is me. Yet as you can see, he still doesn't admit to having set the thing off in the first place."

"Look at the next page, or even the one after." Pete urged. "What else does he have to say? There's got to be something to incriminate him."

Charles looked back at the diary. "S dash OK. CH dash peaky," he read out. "There are two large exclamation marks after the word peaky." Flicking back through the pages to the day of the disaster, he came to the letters Z.H. As Pete had said, Z probably meant zero, but what could the H mean? They would need much more than Zero to go on. H... what could it mean.

"Hour... Zero Hour!" Charles cried excitedly. "The initials might mean Zero Hour!" He stabbed his finger on the first number. "See, he's been counting down the days; Z.H dash 6D could mean Zero Hour in 6 Days, because after that, each day in the diary the number is shown as one less." Hurriedly thumbing forwards through the pages, Charles pointed to another date. "Look, here he says Z.H dash 3D. But if we turn to the day of the explosion, he just writes Z.H and then the letter B in a circle. That could be Blast or Bang or Boom! Oh my God, yes! It could mean any of those, but anyone of them means the same."

Charles looked back at the diary. Underneath the letter B were some other letters, which Rick had scored through. "Wait! Look there's a P. a B and... J. Yes the third one is J, I'm sure of it. Weren't they the same letters mentioned earlier?" Charles hurriedly flicked back through the pages.

"P.B.J" Pete repeated the letters over a couple of times. "Pete, Becky and Josie! Don't you see? That's the kids and me. He crossed us out. He thinks we're dead. Didn't you say that somewhere he says S is well? He means Sarah. She's okay, but we three are dead along with the rest of people in the valley."

"How many samples did you say there should be in here?" Josh's voice came from the back of the office.

Charles swung around. "For goodness sake, be careful with those!" he yelled. "One drop and there's nothing anyone could do to help you." He shook his head. Perhaps he had been wrong to bring these men here; they had no idea of the dangers in such a laboratory. "There's ten phials in there, now shut the lid."

"There are only nine here." Josh looked across at Charles.

"That's impossible." Charles ran across the office to see for himself. "I gave General Lewis ten phials and I know there were ten samples sent back because Rick told me so."

"Well I'm telling you, there are only nine here now."

"Couldn't Rick have started working on the antidote?" asked Pete. It seemed a logical explanation.

"No! That's the problem. Rick told me they wouldn't be starting any experiments on the antidote for another week or two. Naturally they'll be working it out in theory, but not using the contents of the phials. They are too precious to waste. I'm surprised Rick left them in his office for anyone to find. They're far too dangerous and should be under lock and key."

"Incidentally, where is Rick?" Pete looked out through the window in the office door. "Shouldn't he be here?" There were a number of men checking the dials on the machines, but there was no sign of Rick. "I'm surprised no one's come to see what we're up to."

"Rick went with Andy and the children." Charles replied, thinking back to the note Irene had left. "I believe they were going to the park. However, I do know they're coming here later. Rick was keen to show them around the laboratory."

"I bet he was!" Pete yelled. He couldn't believe his ears. "Charles, are you telling me that Rick is with my children at this very moment?" Unable to wait for a reply, he looked across at Josh. "I've got to find them. I'm sure he's going to do something..." He paused. Both men were staring at him. "Oh my God, don't you see? Rick wanted to kill my kids, but it didn't work. Now a phial of melted flesh is missing and at this very moment he's with my children." He glanced at his watch. "When did they leave the house? Where exactly did they go?"

Charles turned pale. "Surely... No! He wouldn't dare...! Andy's with them. He would stop him."

"Andy doesn't know what we know!" Pete screamed. By now he was almost hysterical. A maniac was with his lovely children; he could be killing them at this very moment. "Andy won't be watching the children all the time. As far as he's concerned this guy is their Uncle Rick taking them out for the afternoon in the park. Charles! For God's sake, which park did he take them to?"

Pulling himself together, Charles tried to think. "I don't know, the note didn't say..." He shook his head. "But it was hours ago..." He paused, desperately trying to remember. His grandchildren were in danger, he must remember.

"After that I think they were going to a café for ice cream... Again I don't know which one, the note didn't say." Charles hesitated again, still trying to think. "But afterwards they were coming here. Rick was going to show them all around the laboratory. I can't imagine why Sarah went along with it, but Rick probably persuaded her. She would never have thought... Even I never thought... I'd have rushed out to find them if I'd realised they were in danger."

Pete didn't have time to waste listening to what Charles would or wouldn't have done. All he wanted to do was to find his two beautiful children before it was too late. His heart was pounding. Where would he start? They must have left the park by now. They could be at some café or another, but there was no telling which one.

Pete swallowed hard to shift the lump in his throat. On the other hand, they could be on their way to the laboratory at this very moment. Perhaps he should wait here and see if they turn up. But what if Rick was planning to use the phial somewhere else?

He tried to think it through rationally. If Rick really wanted to use the phial on the children, this was probably the best place to do it. It would be so easy for him to say the children had come across the samples, while he wasn't looking. He wouldn't be blamed; it was simply one of those things.

"I'm going to wait here," Pete said at last. He wasn't really sure if he was doing the right thing, but he didn't know where else to go. "If Rick said he was bringing them all on a tour of the laboratory, then I feel certain this is where he's planning to make his move."

"You're probably right." Charles said. "I'll leave you both to it."

"Where are you going?" Josh asked, bending down to pick up a slip of paper that had fallen from the notebook.

"I'm going to do something I should have done a week ago. I'm going to go public with the whole business." Charles was determined that no one should get away with something like this. From that horrible, little man, Alan Crisp, right up to the Prime Minister himself, they were all going to have to explain to the nation exactly what had happened and how they had tried to cover it up.

"If you go to the Prime Minister, he'll have you arrested before you can utter a word," Josh said, unfolding the paper. "He'll call in MI5 or something like that and say you're a threat to National Security."

Charles smiled. "But I'm not going to the Prime Minister. I'm going straight to the newspapers, or better still the broadcasting companies. The BBC would be my first choice; they have some excellent journalists there. I'm sure they'll be more than delighted to hear about something on this scale."

Pete grabbed Charles's arm. "But without proof, will they listen? And won't that get you into a whole load of trouble."

"Probably, but not quite as much trouble as the Prime Minister is going to find himself in. He has much more to lose." Charles grinned. "I can't see the public being very pleased with him or his government when they hear what's been going on. He'll be voted out of office." He sighed. "Well this is it. I'd better be off."

"Wait a minute!" Josh cried out. "You'd better take a look at this." He held out the paper. "It fell out of the notebook."

Charles took the paper from Josh and read it through. "This is it!" he slapped the sheet with the back of his hand. "This says it all."

"What is it?" asked Pete. "What does it say?"

"It says... wait a minute." Charles was so excited he could hardly speak.

"Let me see!" Pete snatched the sheet from Charles's hand. It was a hastily written note in Rick's handwriting. "Sarah's name is near the top of the page and in large bold numerals is the date of the disaster." Pete read aloud. "Alongside the date he's written, 'Sarah away for the night'. Then there're a few squiggles – doodles" He paused as he scanned the page. "But further down, and in a different pen, he's added something else. Listen to this, it couldn't be a better time to test both my theory and Trojan. CH will take the flack. He should have listened to me." Pete looked up. "That's it! You bastard! We've got you." He couldn't believe Rick had been so stupid as to leave something like that for anyone to find. Why on earth would he have written such a note in the first place?

"Perhaps I should go with Sir Charles?" Josh was speaking to Pete. "Two might be better than one." He looked at Charles. "That is, if you want me to come."

"Yes, it might be best. We'll take the diary, the notebook and this note." Charles peered again at the note. "I don't believe it! This is my stationery. Here, look at the heading. Rick actually wrote this at my home – in my study." Taking a closer look, Charles sank into a chair. "Rick's put another date on this note; most likely the day he wrote it." He pointed it out to Pete. "Thinking back, I believe it was the day we argued about his theory. I thought it was too early to test it out and told him so." He paused. "You might recall Sarah was spending that week with us. She and Rick were chatting together for a while before he came into my study. It's quite possible that she told him about her trip to the theatre. That's how he knew she'd be away from the farm. While I was out of the study for a moment, he must have written it down. It's all falling into place." He held up the letter. "This will make a sound case for some investigative journalist."

Ashen faced, Charles stood up and walked across to the door. Resting his hand on the handle, he turned to Josh. "Well, what are we waiting for?"

****

Alan Crisp was about to enter the staff restaurant at the laboratory, when he caught a glimpse of Charles Hammond. Slipping behind one of the large display boards, he watched Charles striding towards Rick's office.

What could Charles be doing here? But more importantly, who were the two men with him? As soon as the office door closed, Crisp crept outside to the car park intending to speak to the men who were keeping Charles under surveillance. But though Sir Charles's car was parked close to the building, there was no sign of the men from MI5.

He rushed back into the laboratory. This didn't look good. What was Charles up to? How did he have the nerve to return to the building after allowing Trojan to escape into the atmosphere? The man should have been locked up. And where were the men who were supposed to be watching him? Fumbling in his pocket he produced a list of telephone numbers and quickly phoned the mobile of one of the men assigned to tail Charles.

"Where the hell are you?" He yelled into the phone.

Grant's reply was sarcastic. "We're outside the Hammond home. Where else would you expect us to be?" Putting his hand over the mouthpiece, he spoke to his colleague. "It's Crisp! Bloody idiot! These pen pushers are all the same."

Alan seethed, having overheard the remarks. "Well for a start, I'd have thought you'd be here at the laboratory, because this is where Sir Charles Hammond is right now. How did he get past you without being seen? What were you doing? Filing your nails? I should also like to add that he has two other men with him."

Crisp chuckled to himself. It was good to get one over on MI5. They thought they knew it all. Pen pusher indeed! Just wait until he got his promotion, he would show them all. "I don't think your superior will be very pleased when he hears about this," he continued. "Now might I suggest that you get yourselves over here. In the meantime, I'll do your job for you and keep an eye on them."

He put down the receiver and made his way across to Rick's office. The door was still closed, but he decided to make sure they were still inside. He would look rather stupid when the men arrived, if he had to tell them the birds had flown. Was that the jargon they used nowadays?

Very carefully, he crept nearer to the office door, using some of the smaller machines as cover. If Charles were to see him now, all would be lost. He noticed a couple of technicians gazing at him in a curious manner. Smiling, he pretended to check the dials on the equipment, but it was obvious they were unconvinced.

He knew the staff didn't like him. Still, what did he care? If he played his cards right, Rick would be pleased with him. And that meant a great deal to him.

Reaching the office door, he glanced swiftly through the window. Satisfied that all three men were still there, he squeezed into the small space behind a large filing cabinet outside the office and crouched down. At least the men in the laboratory couldn't see him now. They would assume he had gone.

Pressing his ear against the door, he tried to make out what was being said. But he was only able to hear the occasional word when the men raised their voices. Lifting his head slightly, he tried to see if there was any sign of the MI5 men. He wished they would hurry up; it was extremely uncomfortable squatting in this position. If they didn't come soon he would have to do something as his legs were beginning to ache.

Another five minutes dragged by. The pain in his legs was now unbearable. Suddenly the door handle began to turn. They were coming out! Not wanting to be seen, he began to manoeuvre himself around the cabinet. However he had been in a cramped position for too long, and a searing pain shot down both limbs. He screwed his eyes and clenched his teeth to stop himself from screaming out, before falling to the floor.

CHAPTER TWENTY-THREE

"We each have a mobile phone, so we'll be able to keep in touch should we run into trouble." Charles's voice rang out as the office door swung open.

Still crouched awkwardly on the floor, Alan Crisp only managed to drag himself around to the other side of the cabinet in time. He rubbed his painful legs. Where were those wretched surveillance men? Probably stopped off for coffee on the way!

From his position, Crisp saw Charles and another man emerge from the office. His beady eyes followed the two men, as they strode across the laboratory. Charles paused briefly to speak to one of the scientists before heading towards the glass doors.

Blast those two MI5 men! What were they playing at? They were going to lose Charles yet again if they didn't hurry up. It looked as though he was going to have to tail them himself. At least his legs were beginning to recover.

Crisp kept Charles in view until the last possible moment. He couldn't risk losing sight of him. His eyes narrowed, as they fell on something Charles was carrying. What was that? Was it something he had taken from Rick's office?

Holding on to the filing cabinet for support, Crisp heaved himself to his feet and glanced into the office. The third man was still in there. Well he could wait; at least he knew where he was. For the moment, he was more interested in what Charles was up to. He was desperate to learn what was going on.

While squatting there on the floor, it had occurred to him that it wouldn't do his career any harm if he was able to pass on vital information about Charles to his boss, Brian Tate. And once the Prime Minister heard it was he, Crisp, who had discovered Charles snooping around the laboratory, he would be rewarded. Turner was known to be very generous to those who served him well.

The thought of such glory allowed him to forget his aching legs and he hobbled out into the car park, just in time to see Charles's car turning into the main road beyond the gates. Damn blast! His aspirations were disappearing before his eyes.

Hurrying across to his car, he was about to clamber in when he saw the MI5 men speeding through the gates.

"Where've you been?" he screamed, his face turning red. He stabbed his finger towards the gate. "They've gone. Charles and another man, they turned right."

"The traffic was bad, we..." one of the men began.

"Never mind about the bloody traffic, get after them!" Crisp roared.

He pulled a handkerchief from his pocket and wiped his face. It was all becoming too much. He watched the men speed out of the gates. Car horns blared, as they bulldozed their way into the traffic.

"Bloody idiots!" Crisp mumbled. "And they call themselves the Secret Service." As far he was concerned, there was nothing secret about them. They made their presence known wherever they went.

Making his way back to Rick's office he found the third man had disappeared. For one brief moment he was alarmed. Who was he? But more crucially, why hadn't he gone off with the others? And where was he now?

But then he dismissed his concerns. Here in the laboratory a stranger wouldn't get very far without being seen. Once he informed the security men they would soon pick him up. A few questions and he would quickly find out what was going on. His spirits soared. All was not lost.

For a moment, he deliberated over whether he should ring Brian Tate and let him know what he had discovered. But thinking it through, he decided to wait until he had more information. It would be better for him if he were in a position to tell his boss the full story. In the meantime, once he had alerted the security staff, he would take a peek in Rick's office. What could be so important that Charles would risk bringing two strangers here?

****

Charles and Josh were stuck in the London traffic. Despite the introduction of congestion charges, the roads were still busy.

"And they try to tell us the scheme is working! No matter what they do, the roads here in London will always be blocked." Charles thumped on the horn. "For goodness sake, get out of the way!" he roared.

"Take it easy," said Josh, looking around uncomfortably. He smiled nervously at one of the other drivers. "We can't afford to draw too much attention to ourselves. It wouldn't do to be stopped by the police."

He was unused to heavy traffic. Wooler or Alnwick on Market Day he could cope with, but this was something else.

"Yes, you're right." Charles slowed down. "But now I've decided to inform the media about the Trojan Project, I want to get on with it before anyone can stop us."

Josh looked behind. "Does that mean you think we're being followed?" He shuddered, as the memory of his previous encounter with the military flashed through his mind.

"I can't say for certain." Charles glanced in his mirror. "But there was a screeching of brakes as we left the laboratory. I have a sneaking suspicion the men guarding my house might have discovered I'd disappeared."

"But how would they know where to look for you? You could have gone anywhere!"

"Who knows? Perhaps they were tipped off." Charles suddenly turned the car down a narrow street. "There's been a black car behind us for a while, let's see if it follows us down here."

Josh turned around. "There's no black car. A few other colours, but nothing black. I think you're getting jumpy." He was just about to face the front, when he saw a car turning the corner. "Oh-oh! I spoke too soon. Take a look. There's a large black car behind. Is it the same one?"

Charles peered through his reversing mirror. "Yes, and I should know. That same car has been parked outside my house for the last two days. We're going to have to lose them, at least until we get into the BBC. Hang on!" he yelled. "I'm going to double back."

"What the hell are you talking about? You can't double back. We're in a one-way street for God's sake! You'll get us arrested." Josh grasped the door handle tightly. If he got out of this alive, he was never going to come to London again. From what he had seen so far, Colin the lorry driver was right, the place was full of madmen.

But Charles wasn't about to be put off. "We need to do something! We can't let them catch us now."

He proceeded to do a three-point turn, causing the vehicles behind to pull up sharply. Heading back up the street, car horns hooted wildly as he wove in and out of the oncoming traffic, even mounting the pavement on several occasions.

Josh held onto the door handle; fearing for his life. "I want to get out!" he yelled.

"Sit still, man! We're almost there." Charles called out, narrowly missing another of the oncoming cars. "A few more yards and we'll have escaped."

Josh could see the look of sheer horror on the faces of the other drivers as he and Charles headed towards them. He understood how they felt.

Finally Charles pulled out onto the main road. "Hopefully they won't be able to catch up with us. I noticed they didn't follow us back up the road."

"I wonder why!" muttered Josh, wiping his hand across his forehead.

Charles glanced at his passenger. "You weren't really nervous were you?"

"Of course I was bloody nervous!" Josh uttered. "That was stupid, you could have killed us both."

"I'm sorry, but it was the only way to get away from them. It's vital we inform the public of what has been going on." Charles slowed down slightly.

Loosening his grip on the door handle, Josh looked at Charles and grinned nervously. Until now his eyes had been fixed on the road ahead, but for the moment the danger was over. "Okay, but please – don't try that again."

Charles turned the car down a road leading to White City. "We're almost there. When we get there, let me do the talking."

****

Meanwhile Grant, who was driving the surveillance car, pulled over to the side of the road. He smacked the steering wheel with the palm of his hand. "Damn these one way streets! Damn and blast the man!"

"Aren't we going to follow them?" Jack yelled. "He's getting away!"

"Are you crazy? I'm not going to get killed chasing him." Grant laughed and picked up his radiophone. "Anyway, there's no need, I've suddenly had an idea where they might be heading."

He spoke sharply into the mouthpiece. "Sam, are you there?" There was no reply. "Sam, get your butt over to the radio. This is important."

The radio crackled and Sam's voice could be heard. "Yeah, yeah, what is it this time?"

"Hammond's cut free," replied Grant. "But..."

"You idiots. The pair of you are useless." Sam interrupted.

"Hold your horses and let me finish. I think I know where he's going. It's possible he's making for the BBC. If I'm right, we need to head him off. There must be someone in the vicinity. Get them over to White City as soon as possible. We'll catch up once we get out of this traffic. Hammond has a passenger. A youngish man, well tanned, thick set." He thrust the receiver back into its holder.

"Idiots! Useless!" Grant grumbled. "And there speaks a man who's never done anything but sit on his backside in the radio room at HQ. I'd like to see him out here in the field." He started the car. "Come on, let's get over to the BBC."

"I hope you're right about this. What makes you think he's gone there anyway?" said Jack.

Grant pulled out into the traffic. "Simply because the road he took leads to Shepherd's Bush. Why else would anyone who lives in the most exclusive part of London be going in that direction?"

Jack raised his eyebrows and shrugged. "I have absolutely no idea."

****

Sarah pushed open the front door. "The children will love the new clothes I've bought for them. I wonder if they're back yet."

Stepping into the hall she called out for the two girls. "Josie, Becky. Mummy's home."

A loud bark came from the kitchen.

"Betts." Sarah laughed as she threw open the kitchen door. "Well at least you're here to greet me. But I though they were taking you..."

She broke off when she saw that it wasn't Betts at all, but Lad. Standing behind him was Bob.

Speechless, she stared down at the two dogs. Pete! Oh my God! Her heart began to race. Pete must be here!

"Mum! Mum! Come quickly!" She called out at last. "Pete's alive! Thank God! Pete's alive."

"What are you talking about darling?" Irene appeared in the doorway.

Half crying, half laughing, Sarah pointed to the dogs. "It's Lad and Bob. They're Pete's dogs. Don't you see? Pete took them up to Top Meadow with him. If they're here, then he must be with them. He's alive, Mum. He came here to find me. My darling husband is alive."

259

Tears rolled down Irene's cheeks as she took her daughter in her arms. "I'm so happy for you Sarah. I've got to admit, I never thought it possible."

"I want to see him. Where can they have gone?" Sarah pulled away from her mother. "If the dogs are in the house then Dad must have been here to open the door when Pete arrived. They must have all gone somewhere together."

"I don't know." Irene was puzzled. Then she had a sudden thought. "Unless they've gone to the laboratory. I left a note for your father telling him where everyone would be in case he was worried when he came back and found the house empty."

"Yes of course! They'll have gone to meet up with the children. Pete would be anxious to see them and Dad had no way of knowing what time you and I would be back from our shopping trip."

Irene nodded. "They probably thought they would all be back here before you and I got home."

"That's it, Mum," said Sarah, excitedly. "I've got to go to the laboratory. I want to see Pete as soon as possible."

"Yes, of course you do, dear," said Irene, quietly.

She was pleased Pete had lived through the ordeal. Yet she knew Rick was going to be very disappointed. She hadn't failed to notice how much time he had spent at the house since Sarah had come home. Even today, he had gone to the park in an effort to befriend the children.

Noticing the change in her mother's tone, Sarah placed an arm around her shoulder. "Surely you're pleased Pete survived the disaster."

"Yes, of course I am. He's a good man." Irene hesitated. "It's just I think Rick believed..." She smiled. "But he'll get over it."

"Rick!" Sarah was appalled. "No Mum, you've got it all wrong. Rick means nothing to me – certainly not in that way. He's been kind to me and the children. But that's all. He was simply helping me to get through this terrible ordeal. Surely you didn't think..." She stopped abruptly. The look on her mother's face said it all.

"You're not telling me Rick really believed he and I could get together again."

Irene nodded. "Yes. I..."

"Oh my God." Sarah was astounded. "No way. Once I met Pete there was never anyone else. There never could be. If over the last few days I've led Rick to believe..." She shook her head. "I've got to get to the laboratory.

I must explain." Sighing heavily, Sarah continued. "Mum, please stay here in case someone comes back. I'll take a taxi. It'll be much quicker."

Irene stood in the hall and watched as her daughter rang for a cab. She desperately hoped everything was going to work out alright. Why hadn't she voiced her thoughts earlier? She should have warned Sarah about Rick's feelings. But she knew the reason behind her silence. She hadn't wanted Sarah to go back to find Pete; it was too dangerous, and if Rick could keep her here, so much the better. Besides, until now she had honestly believed Pete was dead.

"The taxi won't be long, Mum. The guy said there were several in the area and he would radio one immediately." Her eyes shone. "I always knew Pete wasn't dead. I knew he would survive this terrible thing, just as I did." She hugged her mother. "I'll go outside and wait in the street, I'm so excited I can't stand still."

Standing at the kerbside, Sarah tapped her fingers impatiently against the side of her leg. She wished the taxi would hurry up. Her prayers had been answered. Pete was alive and she was anxious to get to the laboratory to see him. She peered up and down the road. What was keeping the taxi? Why was it taking so long? Just then, the familiar shape of a black cab rounded the corner. She raised her hand. Thank goodness! It was here at last.

****

Charles and Josh were almost at the main gates of the BBC Television Centre. "We've made it!" Josh looked up at the large building. He had seen pictures of it on the television, never dreaming he would ever be here in person. "What do we do now?"

"We go up to the gate and persuade them to let us through." Though Charles tried to sound positive, he was unsure. In recent weeks, security had been tightened. "But don't speak too soon; we've not made it yet. I can't imagine MI5 have given up already."

Driving up to the gate, Charles stepped out of the car and held up his identity card. "I would like to talk to someone working on the news. I have some rather interesting information to pass on."

The two security men took the card from Charles and examined it. They couldn't be too careful. They had come across this kind of thing before; Identity Cards that looked genuine, but on closer scrutiny turned out to be clever forgeries. Only last week, two men on the opposite shift had been hauled over the coals for a similar incident.

"For goodness sake." By now Josh had joined Charles. He looked over his shoulder. According to Charles, MI5 could appear at any moment and here they were, being held up by a couple of guys who wouldn't know a forged ID if they saw one. "This is Sir Charles Hammond, Head of Scientific Affairs to the government and I'm his aide. We have news of the utmost importance. If you don't let us through we'll be forced to go to the other news channel. And let me tell you, if that were to happen, whoever is in charge here will make sure you never work for the BBC ever again."

The two men looked at each other, neither wanted to be out of a job. "Okay, okay, go through," said one, pressing a button to raise the barrier. "They look harmless enough," he said to his companion, as Josh and Charles drove past.

"But how are we to know the difference?" The other man sniffed. "They all look like the good guys these days."

"What would you have done if he'd asked to see your ID?" asked Charles as they approached the main entrance.

"I'd have gone into the booth and smacked him in the mouth." Josh grinned. "I haven't lived through the nightmare of the last few days, plus a hair-raising drive around London, only to be stopped by a couple of men patrolling the damn gates."

Charles jumped out of the car. "I'll leave the keys in the ignition, someone will move it. We haven't got time to find a space."

Both men turned and looked back, as a car screeched to a halt at the gates.

"Come on!" yelled Charles. "They've got to be MI5. The other guys must have guessed where we were heading and radioed in."

Josh glanced towards the gates, before catching up with Charles. The men in the car were arguing with one of the security staff. It appeared the men at the gates weren't keen on letting anyone else in so easily.

Once through the glass doors, Charles hurried across the large foyer to the desk.

"How can I help you?" The receptionist smiled broadly. A small badge pinned to her jacket told him her name was Janet.

Charles explained who he was and how it was imperative that he and Josh spoke to the news editor. "We have information of the utmost urgency."

"I see," she said. Her smile didn't waver. She had heard all this before. "If you would like to take a seat, I'll ring upstairs, I'm sure it won't take too long."

Josh was still watching the main gate. One of the men in the car had jumped out and was pushing his way into the gatehouse. "Charles." He pointed towards the gates. "It won't be long before they're up here."

Charles looked back at the receptionist. She had already picked up the phone. "I'm sorry, Janet, but we haven't time to wait. We need to speak to the editor urgently; we'll go up ourselves. I know the way."

"But... You can't..." Janet dropped the phone and hurried from behind the desk, her high heels clicking on the tiled floor. "If you attempt to leave the reception area without permission, I'll be forced to call security!"

"Do what you must," Charles called out, as he and Josh made their way across to the lift. Pushing the button, he looked back at Janet. "But this is of National importance." He glanced towards the gates. By now the MI5 men were driving towards the entrance. "Janet, if you really want to do something for your country, then for goodness sake stall those men."

Janet glanced towards the glass doors. There was a car speeding up the drive. She clasped her hands together. "How do I know that...?"

"Trust me," pleaded Charles. When the lift doors opened, he gave her one final glance before he and Josh disappeared inside.

Janet was thoughtful as she slowly walked back to the desk. What should she do? She wasn't employed to make such decisions. She heard the car screech to a halt, before two men rushed inside.

"Where are they?" one of them yelled.

"Who?" She tried desperately to look innocent, still unsure as to what to do. "We've had so many people in here this morning."

"Two men, they came in here a few minutes ago. Where are they?" The other man looked towards the lift as he spoke. "Come on you stupid girl, you must have seen them. A grey haired bloke, he had another man with him: young, tall with a suntan. Where did they go?"

Janet didn't like their tone. She wasn't used to being spoken to in this manner. After all, this was the BBC. She made a decision.

"Oh those two?" She smiled. "Yes I thought the young one was rather attractive. He had the most lovely eyes and..."

"Never mind all that, lady! Where did they go?"

"Well, let me see." She ran her finger down the long list of names.

"Hurry up! They were only here a minute ago, you can't have forgotten already."

She looked up. "You have no idea the number of people I've had in here today. I can't be expected to remember them all. That's why we have this list. It tells me where everyone went." She held up the book. "See, all these people have come through..."

"For goodness sake, just tell us where they went!" One of the men broke in.

Tapping her pencil on the desk, Janet glanced at the book again. "Ah yes! Here it is. They went to studio two."

Pointing the way, she laughed to herself as the men ran off down the corridor. In studio two, the rather camp comedian, Geoffrey Hughes, was waiting for his audience to arrive before rehearsing for his show. No doubt he would make them very welcome.

A few moments later, the doors to the reception swung open again and Janet found herself confronted by the two original MI5 men.

"Charles Hammond, where is he?" asked Grant, brusquely. They had hoped to be here before the reinforcements arrived. But the sight of their car outside told them they were too late.

"Studio two." She pointed towards the corridor. "Two other men have already gone down there looking for Mr. Hammond." At least that much was true.

As the men rushed after their colleagues, Janet glanced at her watch. She was due to go off in ten minutes. With a bit of luck she would be long gone before the men escaped from the comedian.

****

The lift seemed painfully slow, but at last Charles and Josh reached the sixth floor.

"Now to find our way to the newsroom." Charles stepped out of the lift and glanced up and down the corridors.

264

"I thought you said you knew the way." Josh listened to the soft hum of machinery as the lift zoomed off to another floor. Someone must have summoned it. He hoped it wasn't the men from MI5.

"Yes, I do. But it's been quite a while since I was up here. I need to get my bearings." Charles didn't sound too reassuring.

"Well don't take too long about it. I'm not sure the receptionist was very sympathetic to our cause."

Charles looked at each of the three corridors leading off from where they stood. He tried to remember which one led to the newsroom. "This way," he said at last. "And don't worry about Janet, I'm sure she believed I was telling the truth."

Josh wasn't convinced. When MI5 burst into reception with their story, Janet may have had serious doubts about Charles's integrity, especially when they flashed their official card.

The corridor seemed to go on forever, leading Josh to doubt if it was the right one. True, there was the occasional sign pointing the way to the newsroom, but for all he knew, the sign could be taking them around in circles.

At last the newsroom loomed before them. "Almost there," breathed Charles. "Whatever happens now, keep going."

****

The first two MI5 men reached studio two. This was it. They would need to tread carefully from now on. The BBC would know a good story when they heard one. They needed to act calmly and convince the editor that Sir Charles Hammond had been working too hard and didn't know what he was saying, which, as far as they knew, was the truth.

One of them opened the door slowly. Going in with all guns blazing, would only confirm whatever Charles was telling them. They would need to be tactful and...

"Come in! Come in! I'm so pleased to see you. You're the first to arrive." Geoffrey gushed. "You lovely people have first choice of the seats." Leaping to his feet he ran across to the men, his eyes sparkling almost as brightly as his silver sequined jacket. He pointed to the front row. "If you sit there you'll be able to see everything. You won't miss a thing."

"What the bloody...?" one of the men said, eyeing the comedian up and down.

"Now now, gentlemen don't be shy. You don't have to do anything. All I want from you guys is for you to sit there and listen to me going through my routine and laugh in the right places. I'm sure you can do that." Grabbing the men's arms, Geoffrey led them across the studio. He grinned. "I say, I can feel quite a lot of muscle there. Big boys, aren't you?"

"Get off!" One of the men yanked his arm away. "What are you talking about? We've come here to..."

"I know what you're here for. You've come to see my show." The comedian sounded huffed. "But there's no need to be like that. As you were first, I thought we could have a few laughs before I went through my routine."

"We're not here to watch some jerk acting the fool, we're here to... What do you mean – the first? Where are the other guys?" The MI5 men looked at each other. Something was wrong here.

"What other guys? I told you, you're the first to arrive." Geoffrey paused. "Wait! I hear footsteps; perhaps these are the others now. Why don't you sit down and relax?" He gestured towards the front row. "I'll check it out."

"Oh no you won't!" The two men pushed the comedian to one side and rushed over to the door. "If there's any checking out to be done, we'll do it."

"Suit yourself," sniffed Geoffrey.

The men stood poised by the door. "Got you, you cunning bastard!" said one, pouncing on the newcomer. "Thought you'd got away didn't you?"

"What the hell are you talking about? It's us you fool – Grant and Jack. We're the guys that called in for back-up." He pointed towards the silver clad figure behind them. "And who the hell is he?"

All four MI5 men turned and gazed at the comedian.

Geoffrey shrugged. "I'm a comedian and I'm waiting for the audience to turn up for my rehearsal for tonight's show. It's my first time at the BBC." He gazed at the expression on the men's faces. "But it's my guess you didn't come here for the show." He smiled. "However, now you guys are here, why don't you stay? You might enjoy it."

"Get out of the way, you idiot. We're MI5 on official business."
Pushing him aside, Grant yanked open the door. "Those bastards have given
us the slip again. My guess is they've gone to the newsroom."

"Where's that?" yelled Jack.

"Sixth floor, I think. It's somewhere upstairs, anyway." Grant was
angry. He didn't like being made a fool of. "Damn receptionist. If I see her
again I'll..."

"We haven't got time to waste on some damn, fool receptionist!" Jack
pushed his way past Geoffrey, almost knocking him over. "We've wasted
enough time on this clown as it is."

"Charming!" The comedian sat down and wiped his forehead as the
four men hurried past him and out into the corridor. He hoped the rest of
the audience wouldn't be the same. Already he could see his act falling flat.

"It was never like this at ITV," he muttered to himself.

Hearing footsteps coming down the corridor, he shrank down in his
chair. This time he wasn't going to move an inch until he saw who it was.

When the door opened, a round-faced lady peeped inside the studio.

"Ooh Alf, he's here," she said. Pushing the door open wider, she strode
across the floor to the comedian. Her husband followed some distance
behind. "I did so want to catch you before everyone arrived. Could I have
your autograph? My name's Barbara." She pushed two small books into his
hand. "The other one is for my daughter. She couldn't make it tonight, but
she watches all your shows. Her name is Susan."

"I'd be delighted." Geoffrey leapt to his feet. "Anything to oblige a
lady." Suddenly he felt a lot better. Perhaps the BBC wasn't going to be so
bad after all.

CHAPTER TWENTY-FOUR

Once Charles and Josh left the office, Pete wondered where Rick might take Andy and the children when they arrived at the laboratory. One thing was certain; Rick wouldn't do anything here in his office. The laboratory technicians were only a few yards away; someone could come in at any moment.

If he was planning to use the missing sample of flesh to kill them, then he will have chosen a place where no one could hear their screams of agony. And this place, wherever it was, would also have to contain something where the remains could be hidden without fear of them being found. But where would that be?

He glanced at his watch. Time was running out. Rick, Andy and the children could be back any minute and here he was, standing around wondering what to do. Come on – think! Pete slapped his forehead. Where would the wretched man take them? This was a large building. Was there a room tucked away somewhere – a long forgotten storeroom in the cellar, perhaps?

Frustrated, Pete slammed his fist down hard onto the desk. Rick knew this place inside out. Already he could be leading his children to their deaths, while he was dithering about not knowing where to go. He was angry with himself. Why hadn't he asked Charles about the layout before he and Josh left.

It was then that Pete caught sight of someone limping after Charles and Josh. He thought about calling out to warn them, but decided against it. It would only draw attention to himself. Hopefully the two men would get safely away.

Once the limping man was out of sight, Pete crept out of the office. Strangely, though one or two of the scientists peered at him, no one seemed to be too upset by his presence and he wondered why. Surely with all that had happened over the last week, security would be tight. But as no one moved to question him, he shrugged it off. Why should he worry, he wasn't a threat to the place. All he wanted to do was find his family. Yet none of these people knew that. He could be here to sabotage the building.

Out in the corridor, he found a small diagram of the building fastened to the wall. Pinpointing Rick's office, he was able to locate his current position. Still scanning the diagram, he saw there were flights of stairs at each end of the corridor. It appeared they eventually led up to the roof. Could Rick be planning to take the children up there?

He recalled the building was very tall. There would be a good view of the London skyline from the top. Rick could be depending on that to get them up there. Pete remembered Andy was with them. If he was a stranger to London, a rooftop view of the City might appeal to him.

Checking the diagram again, Pete swept his hand across his forehead. Could there be anywhere else in the building that Rick might dispose of the bodies? Pete knew the lives of his children depended on him making the right decision. Running his finger around the diagram, it appeared most of the corridors led to offices or small laboratories. Judging from the scale of the plan, none of the laboratories were as large as the one he had left. If one of those was unmanned, might Rick take the children there? He looked up and down the long corridor in dismay. Which way should he go first? But it didn't really matter; he would need to check each direction in turn.

However, after peeping into each of the offices and laboratories, he found most were occupied. Rick would be foolish to try to dispose of the children in any of these. It was becoming increasingly obvious to him that his first instincts were probably correct. The roof seemed the most likely place for Rick to kill the children. Yet, if he were wrong, he would be too far away to do anything to stop him.

Pete pushed that terrifying thought from his mind. If he was going to save his children, he would need to be more positive, and right now the roof seemed his best option. Though for the life of him, he still couldn't imagine what Rick was planning to do with the remains of his victims once he had unleashed the sample of melted flesh.

****

Charles and Josh hurried down the corridor towards the BBC newsroom. Ahead a large sign indicated it was only a few yards away. Charles sighed with relief. They were a mere hair's breadth away from the door that would take them into the news studio. Once there, they would be at liberty to relay their story.

However, looking up, Charles saw a red light above the door. The news was on air. No one was allowed to enter until the light changed to green. He couldn't believe it. They had come this far, only to be stopped by a bloody red light!

The two men hovered impatiently outside the door; both knowing the MI5 men could appear at any moment. Pacing up and down, Charles slammed his fist into his hand. "This is ridiculous," he grumbled. "Whatever they're broadcasting can't be as important as the information we have to offer."

"Stay where you are!" A voice roared from some way down the corridor.

Josh made as if to move towards the door. But Grant swiftly pulled out a gun. "I'd think again, if I were you."

"Oh no! Here we go again," muttered Josh. "I'm getting very tired of people pointing guns at me."

Charles glanced towards the door, wondering if he had time to rush inside. But what if it was locked? He couldn't remember whether they locked the door when the news was on air. But if so, why the hell did they need to bother with the damn red light?

"I don't think so!" The men came closer.

"What do you think?" Charles whispered. "Do you want to risk it?"

Josh didn't want to risk anything. All he wanted to do was get as far away from here as possible. Yet if they were to surrender, would anyone ever hear of them again? As far as the authorities were concerned, they knew too much. "Okay," he replied. "You say when."

"When!" yelled Charles, and just as the men were almost upon them, he grabbed the handle of the door and wrenched it open.

"What the...!" The man directing the news leapt to his feet. "For God's sake! Can't you see the red light is on? No one comes in here while we're on the air!" He turned to one of his assistants. "Get security up here right now." He caught sight of the other four men. "And who the hell are you? What do you all want anyway? We're in the middle of the early evening news bulletin and don't need all this. Get out, all of you. Get out of my studio or... " He stopped abruptly. One of the men was wielding a gun.

"Let's all take it easy, shall we." Grant stepped forward. He was still pointing his gun at Charles. "Both of these men are under arrest." He licked his lips and made a circle with his head. It was something he had seen done in a movie a few years ago and it had impressed him. "We'll escort them from the building and you people can carry on with your news bulletin. You'll be fine and we'll be fine. No one will be any the wiser."

"No!" yelled Charles. "It's not like that at all. Josh and I came here to..." He buckled, as Jack punched him in the stomach.

"It's alright." Jack smiled towards the director. "This guy has nothing of any importance to say to you. In fact neither of them has anything to tell you. They were under arrest, but escaped custody and somehow managed to find their way here. We'll take it from..."

"Charles! It is Charles Hammond isn't it?"

A voice came from the doorway. Everyone turned to see who it was.

"Phil! Philip Fairlamb..." Charles croaked. He was still recovering from the blow to his stomach. "Thank God!"

"It's good to see you again, Charles. But what are you doing coming here and upsetting my programme?"

"I have some vital information and I thought the best place to come was the BBC." Charles' voice was coming back. "You have no idea what's been going on." He pointed at Josh. "What we have to tell you will make your hair stand on end."

By now several of the BBC security staff had reached the scene. "I don't think you have any need for that here, sir." One of them pointed at the gun. "If you would like to hand it over..."

"No way, sunshine." Grant pointed the gun at the security team.

"Put it away!" Jack said, glaring at Grant. "Put the damn gun away. You're not going to use it anyway."

"Okay, okay. I'll holster the gun. Will that suit you?" Grant stuffed the gun inside his jacket.

"For the moment, sir," said the one of the guards, receiving a nod from the news editor.

Phil slung his arm around Charles's shoulders. "What is it you have to tell me?"

"I don't think..." began Jack.

Ignoring him, Phil continued to speak to Charles. "Why don't you and..."

"Josh," said Charles "This is Josh Davies."

Phil smiled at Josh.

Turning back to Charles, he continued. "Why don't you and Josh come to my office? You can both enlighten me on what is so important that you felt compelled to wreck my programme." He glanced towards Grant, who was reaching inside his jacket. There was no doubt in his mind that he was feeling for his gun. "I think it best you leave the gun where it is. Perhaps that way we can all hear what Sir Charles has to say." Though Phil's voice was soft, it held an air of authority and Grant instinctively removed his hand from inside his jacket.

Once inside Phil's office, everyone looked on as Charles told his story.

Phil took a deep breath. "I can't believe it. What you are telling us is absolutely... well – unbelievable. There's no other word for it. Robert Turner's government is totally against chemical weapons. Yet you're saying a secret weapon, orchestrated by the Prime Minister, has been let loose on purpose by some..." Lost for words Phil shook his head. "And you say the government has been trying to hide it from the nation."

"Not the whole government," said Charles, quickly. "Only a selected few; Robert Turner's cronies, so to speak. At least they're the only people I saw when I was summoned to Downing Street on that dreadful night only a short while ago."

There was a long silence.

Josh glanced at everyone in turn. Like Phil, they were unable to take in what Charles had told them. Down here in London everyone was going about their daily business, quite oblivious to what was happening in the north.

"You'd better believe it," said Josh, leaping to his feet. These guys had to be convinced. "I'm here to tell you that I saw the bodies with my own eyes. I've never seen anything like it before and I hope I never do again."

He felt sick when the picture of his friend Dave flooded his memory and for a moment he held his hand over his mouth. Even thinking about it was too much. Taking a deep breath, he carried on.

"It was awful. I agree the government didn't want this to happen. It was Rick who used the weapon for his own ends." He looked at Charles. "Rick forged Charles's handwriting simply to implicate him. Nevertheless, no matter which way you look at it, Robert Turner and his yes-men are to blame. It was the Prime Minister who asked for the making of such a weapon in the first place and now they're covering their backs."

Josh looked around the room. Still no one spoke. They simply stared at him. He shook his head. "For God's sake, you must see that a weapon of this calibre had to be approved by the Prime Minister himself."

It was Phil who spoke first. "This whole business is appalling." He turned to the MI5 men. "Did you know about any of this? Did you know why you were being asked to follow Sir Charles?"

Grant was among those who shook their heads. For a moment he remained silent, deep in thought. "How far did the devastation reach?" he asked at last.

Charles nodded to Josh to answer. At least Josh had been up there and knew more about it than he did.

"As far as I know it covered the Cheviot Hills and a few miles all round, probably across the border into Scotland. Why do you ask?"

"In Wooler..." Grant swallowed hard. "In Wooler there's a police sergeant. Do you know him?"

"Sergeant Gilmore?"

Grant nodded. "So you know him?"

"No. Not personally." Josh took a deep breath. "But I think the sergeant is dead. Pete and I came across a police car and there were two bodies inside." He paused, as he recalled the scene. "We had no real way of telling who they were; only their bones and melted flesh remained. But because we now know one of the constables from Wooler is alive and in London, we can only assume that the remains were of the sergeant and the other young constable." He hesitated. "Was the sergeant related to you in some way?"

Grant looked away. "No. But he was a friend. We met at..." Upset, he broke off. True, he and Ray Gilmore hadn't seen as much of each other as they might have liked, work commitments had a habit of getting in the way. However, they often exchanged letters and had been due to meet up in a few weeks.

He raised his head to find everyone looking at him. "We met several years ago," he continued. "We kept in touch. He was a good man and a good policeman. He didn't deserve to die like that."

"No one deserved to die like that." Josh spoke quietly. He was thinking of how Dave and his pretty young wife had been planning a family. It was so terribly unfair.

He looked at Phil. "Well, are you going to broadcast this news or not?"

"You're darned right I am," Phil replied. "I'm not going to let a story like this slip through my fingers. I'll get straight onto our northern studio, they can send out a reporter and a cameraman; we'll see what they come up with." He barked out some instructions to his assistant, who had been listening to the conversation. "Get onto the Newcastle studio and tell them what's happened. I want someone out there immediately! But warn them tread carefully: make it clear they're not to touch anything and to stay away from the army!"

The man made as if to move away, but Phil wasn't finished. "Find out who we have near the government laboratory here in London, tell them to drop whatever they're doing and get over there." He paused. "And get someone to Downing Street, let's see what the Prime Minister and his Defence Secretary have to say about this."

As his assistant sprung into action, Phil turned back to face Charles. "In the meantime, you and Josh can talk to our news anchorman. Between you, you can work out exactly how to break all this onto the unsuspecting public." He rubbed his hands together. "Believe it or not, I thought today was going to be dull."

CHAPTER TWENTY-FIVE

Pete paced up and down the laboratory roof; all this hanging around was making him nervous. He glanced at his watch, but only a few minutes had passed since he had last checked the time. It was getting late, what if Rick wasn't coming here after all? That bastard could be taking his children anywhere. Pete pushed the thought from his mind. It had to be here otherwise he couldn't help them.

He reflected on how there had been times over the last few days, when he thought he would never see his family again. Yet thankfully, because of a young policeman, his wife and children had escaped the military blockade. Very soon, if luck was still on his side, they would all be reunited. But first he had to deal with Rick, and when he got his hands on him...

A car driving into the car park caught his attention. Watching carefully, he saw it pull into the space reserved for the head of the laboratory. Pete heaved a sigh of relief. It must be Rick. No one would dare to ignore the large sign with its bold lettering. He had been right to wait here.

Looking down, Pete was angry when he saw Rick helping Josie from the car. It was a charade. He wanted to scream out – tell the wretched man to take his hands off his daughter. Instead, he took a deep breath. He must remain calm. It would be a mistake to alert Rick of his presence at this stage. He could so easily react like the madman he was, and push them back into the car before driving off somewhere else. No. For the time being it was important he should stay silent and keep watch. At least he knew where Rick was and he would be ready for him.

In the car park, Rick pointed towards a door at the side of the building. "We'll use the senior staff entrance," he told Andy, holding up a large key. "Very few people are allowed to use that door. But as my guests no one will say anything. Come along then, quick march, there's so much I want to show you and we have so little time." He coughed. "Yes, well – I'm sure you'll enjoy seeing the laboratory. Not everyone gets this treatment, you know." He laughed awkwardly. He was being pushy and needed to slow down.

"Thank you." Andy felt uneasy. He was still unsure about Rick's on – off friendship. He smiled weakly and looked at the building. Suddenly, his eyes were drawn to the roof. He could have sworn he saw someone up there, but checking again, there was no one. Had it been a trick of the light? "I should think you would get a good view of London from up there," he murmured.

Rick followed Andy's gaze. "Yes, indeed you do. I was planning to take you and the children up there. I thought it might amuse you."

He ran his tongue around his lips. This was working out even better than he had hoped. The roof was where he planned to kill Andy and the children. His first thought had been to push them off the top and proclaim there had been a terrible accident. But apart from it being difficult to push all three at once, he realised there would be an investigation into how it had happened. Worse still, one of the children might even survive the fall. Though it was doubtful, it wasn't entirely impossible. And if that were to happen, how would Sarah have time for him if she was constantly caring for Pete's badly maimed brat?

It was then that the samples of flesh had arrived on his desk and a delicious new idea formed in his mind. Using one of the phials to kill them, there would be no survivors. And once he had disposed of the remains, he would simply tell Sarah how Andy and the children had come across the sample and removed the lid before he could stop them. There was nothing she could do without declaring the existence of Trojan and he had already told her what such a thing would do to her father. With her silenced there would be no police, no funeral. It would be as though Andy and the children had never existed.

His thoughts drifted to the stout, concrete container that stood in one corner of the roof. At one time it had been used to store volitile chemicals. But since a more suitable method of storage had been found, the container was empty. Nowadays it was kept locked and he held all the keys. It was where he would hide the remains of his victims.

Over the last two days, he had taken several items up onto the roof and hidden them in the concrete bunker. Shovels, a helmet, a mask, thick overalls and gloves – two pairs of each. It was a very dangerous game he played, but the prize was worth the risks involved.

His final problem had been how to get the children up there, but unwittingly, Andy was helping him out. He had to stop himself from rubbing his hands together and laughing out loud.

"In fact, why don't we go up there first? You might as well see the view before the light fades." Rick almost shook with excitement. At last he was going to be rid of everything that stood between Sarah and him. "Come along, this way." He ushered everyone towards the side door. "We'll be up on the roof in no time at all."

He looked at his watch. The early evening shift would be coming on about now. There was always a great deal of chatter during the changeover, which often meant the staff wasn't quite so intent on watching the monitors. It was all going according to plan. His only concern was how to remove the incriminating video from the surveillance camera without being seen. But he would cross that bridge when he came to it.

"This way, Josie. Hurry along!" Rick urged the child through the door. "Here let me help you." He lifted Josie into his arms and rushed along the corridor. Having got this far without being seen, it would be very bad luck indeed if someone were to come along now.

"Steady on." Andy called out. "You're going too fast! You'll lose Becky and me at this rate. What's the hurry anyway?"

"Sorry, I was forgetting you didn't know the way."

Trying to contain his excitement, Rick slowed down a little. But the prospect of seeing Trojan in action, not only on one subject, but three, made it difficult for him to keep his pace slow. Until now, he could only imagine what happened to those caught up with the deadly weapon. He hadn't yet had the opportunity to speak to Alan Crisp about a possible survivor in the Cheviots. Nevertheless, very soon he would see it for real and had even included a video camera in his preparations. Planning to film the sequence of events, he could watch it over and over again.

Rick looked down the corridor. Luck was still on his side; there was no one in sight. He couldn't believe he had got this far without being seen. Once this was over, he would take a look into the laboratory security, it was too lax by far.

"This way, it won't be long now."

"Do you really think we should bother?" asked Andy. They had reached the stairs and it looked a long way up. "The girls are beginning to tire. Surely it would be better if we went back home. Sarah will worry if we aren't back when she finishes her shopping."

"Sarah will be ages yet!" Rick snapped.

He was almost there. Nothing on earth would make him turn back now. Besides, he didn't like the way Andy used the word 'home'. He was becoming a little too familiar.

Realising the sting in his voice, he forced a smile. "You know what women are like when they go shopping. Or perhaps you don't, you're not married, are you?"

"No." Andy's tone was noncommittal. But alarm bells were ringing at Rick's brusqueness. "I've never found the right girl."

"Well take my word for it. Sarah always shops like there's no tomorrow. We'll be home long before she is." Rick was relieved. It seemed Andy hadn't noticed the impatience in his voice. But he really needed to watch his tongue for a little while longer. He turned towards the stairs.

"Isn't there a lift?" Andy was concerned that the long climb would be too much for the children.

"Yes, there is, but it's been giving some trouble. We don't want to get stuck in there, do we?"

There were several lifts, but Rick didn't want to use any of them. At this time of the day they were usually very busy. Having got this far without being seen, it would be disastrous to be caught with Andy and the children now. Should some prying member of staff ever find the skeletons, he wanted to be in a position to plead ignorance.

"It won't take us long. I'll carry Josie up the stairs and I'm sure a strapping, young fellow like you can manage Becky."

"I still think we should come back another time." Andy felt even more uneasy about Rick's manner. He was beginning to wish they hadn't come here. "The children are going to be staying in London for some time."

"No!" Rick snapped. What was that fool Andy playing at? "What's the point of leaving and coming back another time when we're already here in the building?" Picking up Josie, he began to run up the stairs. "Last one to the top is a Silly-Billy, isn't that right, Josie?"

Josie looked down at her sister and squealed with laughter. "Silly-Billy. You're a Silly-Billy"

Still feeling uncomfortable, Andy followed Rick up the first flight of stairs. Something didn't ring true. If he met a member of staff on the way, he would leave Becky with them and go after Rick and Josie.

And that was another thing. Why hadn't they met anyone? This was a government laboratory, crammed full of State secrets and God knows what else. Surely the place should be full of security staff, especially after the recent crisis. How had he and the children got this far without being asked to produce some sort of ID? But he reminded himself that Rick had brought them in through the senior staff entrance. Nevertheless, someone should have been there to check for intruders.

"Come along you two down there." Rick's voice echoed down the stairwell. "We're nearly at the top."

"We're going to win." Josie called out, excitedly. "We're going to win."

Andy climbed the stairs a little faster. He might be worrying for nothing, yet he still felt he shouldn't let Rick and Josie get too far ahead.

"We're coming, Josie!" Andy called out. He tried not to sound too anxious, for fear of alarming the children. "We're getting closer. We'll soon catch you up."

At last they were at the top. As he looked down on the City below, Andy had to admit the view was quite spectacular. It was everything Rick had said it would be.

"Isn't it superb?" Rick gestured across the City skyline. "Over there is the London Eye. One of the finest pieces of modern engineering of our time, while over on this side is the dome of St. Paul's Cathedral." He took a deep breath. "Superb, there's no other word for it."

"Yes I have to agree, the City looks wonderful from up here." Andy spoke quietly. He was looking for New Scotland Yard. He had hoped to be moved there after finishing his training at the police college. Instead he had been stationed at Wooler under the watchful eye of Sergeant Gilmore. "Can you point out New Scotland Yard?" he asked.

"Oh yes, I'd forgotten you were a policeman." Rick scanned the buildings as he spoke. "I can't see it. Hang on, wait a minute. Yes there it is." He pointed across the rooftops. "It's there, near St. James's Park."

Andy looked to where Rick was pointing. He sighed, wondering if he would ever step inside that illustrious building. "Yes, I see it," he said wistfully.

"Now if you would like to come this way, I'll show you a few other important landmarks." Picking up Josie, Rick began to walk across the roof.

He knew Andy would follow and then he would have them all exactly where he wanted them; alongside the concrete bunker.

"Now let me see. What shall I point out first?"

Rick lowered Josie to the ground and waited for Andy and Becky to come closer before reaching into his jacket pocket. He felt a glow of satisfaction as his fingers curled around the small leather tube containing the glass phial.

Keeping the phial so very close to his body had been the downside of his plan. Only knowing what he would achieve had made the risk worthwhile. However, to be on the safe side, he had tested the stout leather casing using a similar glass phial filled with water – the conclusion being, it would need to be struck very hard before the phial broke. Not wanting to arouse Andy's curiosity in the slightest, he had even practised handling the phial with one hand. Nevertheless, today was the real thing and he needed to be very cautious. If the slightest drop was to touch his skin...

"Look over there," Rick pointed towards a famous landmark. "It's Buckingham Palace." Moving nearer to Andy, he traced his finger across the skyline and paused when Nelson's Column came into line. "And down The Mall, is Trafalgar Square. See, there's Lord Nelson."

Their attention drawn, Rick very gently flicked open the strap of the leather tube. So far, so good, from now on he would need to be very careful indeed. Swallowing hard, he slowly removed the glass phial from the tube.

"Do you see where I mean?" Rick asked, moving even closer to Andy. It was imperative that Andy's attention should be caught up with the view long enough for him to remove the phial from his pocket and snap off the lid. His intention was to drop some of the contents onto Andy first. After that, the children would be easy.

Rick began to breathe more easily. He was almost there; any second now and it would be over. Slowly he lifted his arm. "Of course Nelson looks..."

"Andy!" Pete's voice screamed out across the rooftop. From his hiding place, he had seen Rick fumbling in his jacket pocket and guessed he was about to make his move. "For God's sake, get my children away from him."

Andy didn't need to be told twice. He scooped up the children, one under each arm and ran several yards from Rick.

"Daddy! Daddy!" Josie squealed with excitement at seeing her father. She wriggled frantically in Andy's arms, forcing him to lower her to the ground. "I want my daddy!" she cried out, trying to pull away. But Andy had a firm grip on her arm.

By now Becky had seen her father and she too wanted to go to him. Though she couldn't struggle as fiercely as Josie, she held out her arms towards Pete.

"No!" Rick screamed out when he saw Pete. "No! No! You're dead. I killed you. You should be dead." Slipping the phial into his trouser pocket, a small object fell unnoticed to the ground. "Damn you to hell! You should have died with the rest of them, you and your brats." Turning quickly, he ran back towards the stairs.

"Take the children down!" Pete yelled out to Andy, as he chased after Rick.

Andy nodded, still trying to hold onto the two wriggling toddlers. "We're going to follow your daddy now, Josie. But you must help me with Becky, she wants to see him as well."

Josie stopped tugging at Andy. She wanted to see her daddy, but Becky was her sister and Mummy said she should always wait for her.

As Andy began to lead them across to the stairs, he noticed something lying on the ground. Looking more closely, he saw it was a small leather tube, rather like something that might hold a single cigar.

Rick swiftly ran down the stairs and along the corridor that led to his office. He was surprised to find Sarah waiting for him. He smiled broadly.

"Hello, Sarah. What are you...?"

"Rick!" Sarah interrupted. Her eyes shone with happiness. "I have the most wonderful news! It's Pete, he's alive."

Rick's smile disappeared in an instant. For a moment, he had believed she was there to see him.

"Didn't you hear me?" Sarah grabbed out at Rick's arm. "Don't you understand? It's Pete, he's alive."

Rick's eyes narrowed, and his lip curled into a sneer making his whole face contort into an expression of sheer hatred. Suddenly feeling frightened, Sarah loosened her grip on his arm and took a step backwards. "Aren't you pleased?"

"Pleased! Why should I be pleased?" He looked towards the door as Pete burst in.

"Pete!" Sarah cried out in delight at seeing her husband again.

She moved towards him, but Rick caught her arm. "You don't need him." His voice was thick and menacing. She tried to pull away, but his grip tightened. "You never wanted Pete. You were meant for me; together we would have been happy. But it's not too late." He looked at Pete. "Divorce her. Give Sarah her freedom." He was becoming hysterical. "She has always wanted me. She only married you out of pity. Since coming back to London, she's never left my side. Ask her! Take your kids and go. She'll thank you for it."

"No!" Sarah screamed out. "I want to be with Pete and our children. I love him, I always did. You were a friend, nothing more. I never loved you. I would never have married you."

She struggled to free herself from Rick's grip. But he was holding her too tightly and his fingers dug deep into her arm.

"When you thought he was dead, you were happy to be with me." Rick yelled at her. "You wanted me. I could tell." Stroking her face, his voice suddenly softened and became almost childlike. "Sarah, you'll always be mine. I've always loved you. Don't you see; you and I are one. Together we could have lots of children – our children. You don't need his kids." His grip on her arm loosened slightly. "I did it for you, Sarah. You made a mistake when you married Pete, but you realised it too late. I wanted to help you. My plan was to kill them all so we could be together. I knew you would be away in Alnwick that night, you told me." He looked at Pete. "He and his bastards should have died."

"No! Let me go!" Sarah shrieked. "You're insane!" She tried to pull away from him, but his fingers tightened around her arm.

"Divorce her." Rick hissed at Pete. "That's all I want. Divorce her and you can all go. No one need know."

"But they do know." Slowly Pete edged closer. "Charles has gone to the media. Very soon every home in the country will be aware of what has happened; of what you did."

"No!" Rick raged. "He wouldn't do that." He laughed hysterically. "He has no proof. I'll deny everything."

Pete continued to move closer.

"Stay back!" Rick screamed out. "If I can't have her then no one will. Sarah was meant for me. She knows it." He looked at her. "Why won't you admit it? Tell him! Tell him it's me you want!"

"I can't. I'd rather die." Tears streamed down Sarah's face. "I don't want you. I never loved you."

Rick slapped her face hard. "Liar! Liar! Tell him the truth."

"I am telling the truth." She rubbed her cheek.

"I don't believe you!" Rick screeched.

Pete knew he needed to do something, but he must be careful. Rick still had the phial in his pocket. If he were to rush at him, he could smash it. One drop on Sarah and she would be beyond all help.

"Daddy! Daddy!" Josie's voice rang out from the doorway. Andy and the children had reached the office. Behind them were two men.

"I'm Harry Andrews, BBC News." Pushing his way through, he gestured to his cameraman. "This is George Worth. We were told there's a story here."

"What the bloody hell's going on? How did you lot get in here." By now the laboratory security men, alerted by Alan Crisp, had arrived on the scene.

The sudden sound of so many voices startled Rick and caused him to momentarily loosen his grip on Sarah. Seizing the opportunity, she broke free and ran towards Pete. Rick quickly stepped forward and reached out to grab her, but he tripped and fell to the floor. Though his fall wasn't heavy, it was enough to crush the glass phial in his pocket.

Feeling the broken glass cutting into the flesh on his leg, Rick cried out in horror. He thrashed around wildly on the floor, as the deadly contents of the phial oozed out onto his flesh. The others looked on in amazement, unaware of why he was acting like a child in a tantrum.

Only Pete realised what had happened. "Get the children out of here!" he yelled to Sarah.

The urgency in Pete's tone brought Sarah to her senses. Running across to the children, she hurried them out of the office.

"He was carrying a phial of melted flesh taken from the remains of the people in the north," Pete explained to Andy. "It was one of ten samples brought back to help the laboratory find an antidote. Rick planned to use it on you and the children up there on the roof."

"Isn't there anything we can do?" Andy uttered. He moved towards Rick who was rubbing at his legs, desperately trying to scrub away the sticky contents of the broken phial as it ate into his flesh.

"No!" Pete pulled Andy back sharply. "There's nothing you can do. Stay away from him." He glanced at the others. "That goes for all of you. Stay away! For God's sake, whatever you do, don't touch him!"

Andy placed his hand over his mouth and swallowed hard, when he saw the flesh on Rick's hand begin to melt and hang like treacle falling from a spoon. Running across to the window, he gulped fresh air into his lungs, hoping to quell the sickness he felt rising in his stomach. How could the Prime Minister have asked Sir Charles to make something so vile?

Turning back, he saw Rick was crouched on his knees and still screaming out, either in horror or pain, perhaps both. One of his hands was over his face and now his cheeks and lips were beginning to melt. The security men, stunned into silence, drew back into the corridor.

"Help... me." Rick was finding it difficult to move his lips. "Please... help... me."

Harry, the BBC reporter, took a handkerchief from his pocket and wiped his face and mouth. He was a hardened journalist and had witnessed some terrible sights in war torn zones, yet he had never seen anything like this.

"Please tell me you're getting all this," he muttered to the cameraman.

"You bet I am!" The camera was perched on George Worth's shoulder and had been running from the moment Rick stumbled and fell to the floor. George had smiled at that. If nothing else, a piece of film showing a grown man acting the fool because he had fallen over, would make a good out-take for a Christmas programme. But this! Oh my God, this was something any news cameraman would die for and he wasn't about to miss one second of it. It could win him a trophy at the next Cameraman of the year Awards Ceremony.

"There's nothing we can do for you, Rick," said Pete. "You of all people should know that." Nudging the reporter, he pointed to the microphone. "Is that thing on?" he whispered.

Harry nodded. Yes! His mike and recorder were always running. He was a reporter and a damn good one. He would never leave the scene of any good story, even if it meant throwing up in front of everyone.

Pete turned back to Rick. "But isn't this what you did to all those innocent people up there in Northumberland? Didn't you let Trojan loose on them?"

"What the hell is Trojan?" interrupted the reporter.

"Shut up!" hissed Pete. He turned back to Rick. "Well, wasn't it?" he yelled. "Didn't you kill all those people simply to get rid of me and the children?"

"Yesss... I... did... it..." Hardly able to speak, Rick forced himself to look up at Pete. Even with half his face lying in a pool of slime on the floor, the defiant expression of hatred was still evident. "You... should... be... dead... not... me! You...!" He broke off, unable to say anymore.

284

A choking sound came from somewhere deep in his throat. It was followed by a thud, as his head crashed to the floor.

"Oh my God!" Andy rushed to the door. He had never seen anything so grotesque.

"Will someone please tell me? What the hell is Trojan?" The reporter thrust the mike at Pete. "And how does it fit into all of this?" He pointed towards Rick. "I can't believe what we've just witnessed. Oh my God, his flesh is still melting. When will it stop?"

"I'm not the person to answer your questions," said Pete. "Sir Charles Hammond is at your studio. He'll explain it all. In the meantime, I think we should all get out of this office and lock the door."

Harry nodded. Moving towards the door, he took out his mobile phone. "I'll get onto the studio and ask what they want us to do now."

"You can't use that!" A voice in the doorway screamed out.

Everyone turned to see Alan Crisp. He had been watching everything. Though surprised to learn it was Rick who had caused the disaster, he still wasn't going to let it affect his promotion in the government. With or without Rick, he was going places.

"Who are you? And what the hell are you talking about?" Harry yelled. "Are you saying I can't use my phone in here?"

"I'm Alan Crisp, assistant to Defence Secretary Brian Tate." He gasped, his face turning fiery red. "I'm saying you can't use the phone, the recording or the film. Give them to me!" He held out his hand. "This is official government business!"

"Get out of my way!" Harry pushed his way past Crisp. This was the scoop of a lifetime. He wasn't going to let some jumped up little man from the Cabinet stop him from phoning the news studio. "This story is of national interest. If the government has overstepped the line, they should be prepared to take the consequences and if it includes you – tough."

"Give it to me." Alan wiped his face with a handkerchief, as he chased after the reporter and the cameraman.

"What about him?" asked one of the security men. He pointed at Rick's remains. "Who's going to shift that lot?"

"I've no idea," said Pete. He glanced at Alan Crisp, who was still ordering the reporter to hand over the recordings. "Why not ask him? More importantly, did you see where my wife went?"

285

"She's in a room down the corridor. The children are with her." He laughed. "The other guy is still in the gents. He couldn't take it."

"I didn't see any of you hanging around once things began to happen." Pete snapped, before running off down the hall to find his family.

"You'll never guess what we've got." The reporter yelled into the phone, pushing Alan Crisp to one side. He was talking to Phil Fairlamb. "Oh boy, are you going to be pleased at this." He reeled off what they had seen. "What was that? Say it again, some jerk here is trying to take my phone!" After hearing what Phil had to say, he called out to the security men. "Have you got a computer we can use? They want our pictures right now! And is there a TV? Sir Charles will be on in a minute, we can watch for ourselves."

****

"Sarah! Josie! Becky! There were times when I wondered if I'd ever see any of you again." Pete threw his arms around his family. He didn't know whether to laugh or cry.

"Pete! I never really believed you were dead. I wanted to go back to find you, but..." Sarah sighed. "How did you manage to escape...?"

Pete put a finger to her lips. "It's a long story, I'll tell you about it one day." Holding Sarah in his arms, his mind drifted back to when the nightmare began and he and Josh were trapped in the cave. "Let's just enjoy this special moment."

But the special moment had to wait, as the BBC reporter and several laboratory staff burst into the room. "The TV! Switch on the TV!" one of them yelled.

"Today we have Sir Charles Hammond and Josh Davies in the studio, and what they have to say is of the utmost importance," said the newsreader. "Sir Charles, perhaps I can call upon you to tell us what has been going on."

Briefly, Charles explained how he had been asked to devise a chemical weapon for the government. He ended by saying he had learned of Trojan's escape over the Cheviot Hills from the Prime Minister himself. He left nothing out, even mentioning the cover-up ordered by Robert Turner.

"And just exactly what did happen up there in Northumberland?" The newscaster turned his attention to Josh.

Josh explained how he and Pete Maine, son-in-law to Sir Charles, had only avoided the deadly chemical because they had been trapped in a cave. He went on to describe what they had found on their escape. "But that isn't all. As Sir Charles has just said, the military was brought in to cover up the disaster. Their orders were to kill all survivors before they could inform the public about what had happened. Pete and I have been running for our lives ever since. Even now, Pete is at the laboratory trying to stop his family from being murdered by the man who released Trojan and framed Sir Charles."

While the two men were narrating their stories, carefully edited pictures of Rick's demise were being shown on screen.

Once the interview was over, the newscaster introduced John Beecham, the reporter in Downing Street and asked him if the Prime Minister had made a statement.

"So far, Robert Turner has declined to comment, though the Defence Secretary and a few other members of the Cabinet arrived at Number Ten a few moments ago." Beecham paused. "However I have to say, since this news bulletin began, people have been gathering at the gates of Downing Street. From their tone it would appear they are very angry with the government and with Robert Turner in particular. No doubt the Prime Minister and his colleagues will be aware of this."

Having no further news at this time, John Beecham handed the story back to the studio.

Pete lowered the sound on the TV. "Well it looks as though Robert Turner is in for a rough ride in Parliament."

"I agree." Harry held out his hand. "I take it you're Pete Maine. You must have a story of your own. We'll be doing a follow-up. This story will run right up to the election and beyond."

Pete shook the reporter's hand. "Yes, I could tell you plenty, but not now." He glanced at his wife and children. "I have other things on my mind."

"I understand." However, Harry didn't understand at all. Hard-nosed reporters only understood what made a good story. But on the other hand, he knew there was no point in badgering Pete today. "I'll be in touch. You'll be staying with Sir Charles?"

****

Over the following days, scenes of the devastation in the north, together with a more detailed version of the film shot in Rick's office were broadcast around the globe, causing wide condemnation of the British Government.

In an emergency sitting in the House of Commons, the nation looked on, as the Prime Minister slowly rose to his feet to explain his actions. Oozing with wit and charm, Robert Turner gave the performance of his life in a desperate effort to win round his opponents and save himself and his government. But it was lost on them. Even his own backbenchers were unimpressed. After receiving a vote of no confidence, the Prime Minister was left with no alternative but to tender his government's resignation to the Queen and ask Her Majesty to dissolve Parliament.

While this was going on, Charles and Irene insisted everyone should stay with them until they decided what they wanted to do.

"Do you think you'll ever find an antidote?" Pete asked Charles.

They had all finished dinner and were relaxing in the sitting room.

"I'm not sure." Charles was thoughtful. He had been reinstated as head of the laboratory and charged with dismantling Trojan, as well as finding an antidote to clean up the land in Northumberland. "We have the samples, if only we knew where to start. We can't afford to waste any of them."

"There must be something," said Josh. "Pete, wasn't there a notebook in the police car? Perhaps the policemen saw something we missed."

Pete went upstairs to find the book. He had carried it around since that first day. Surely he hadn't lost it now.

"Here it is." He handed the book to Charles.

Flicking through the notebook, Charles read the last entry. "I wonder," he muttered, thoughtfully.

"What is it?" Pete asked. "Have you found something?"

"I'm not sure." Charles spoke slowly, still looking at the book. "The policeman mentions finding Dave's remains..." He skimmed through a few lines. "He says all the flesh had melted, yet Dave's eyes were lying on top of a pool of the thick slime."

"So?" asked Josh. "Where does that get us?"

Charles looked up from the notebook. "You and Pete said you found Dave's body lying in the lane. Did either of you see his eyes? Think hard. It could be important."

After some thought, Josh shook his head. "I think I saw them, but I can't be certain."

"Yes!" Pete replayed the dreadful scene in his mind. "Yes, I saw them. They were lying there in the road. I remember thinking they were smaller than I thought eyeballs should be. That was shortly before we came across the police car further up the road. They had crashed into a tree. The notebook was on the dashboard. Why? Does it mean something?"

"I'm not sure." Charles looked back at the notebook. "Think back to when Rick was... dying? You said he rubbed his hands on his face and it, too began to..."

"Dad, I don't think..." Sarah interrupted, but her father wasn't about to be cut short.

"Sarah, my dear," Charles spoke quietly. "This is really very important." He looked back at Pete and Andy. "Both of you were there, can you tell me what happened to his eyes?"

"I think I left the room before anything happened to his eyes," Andy confessed. "I really felt ill. But as far as I can remember, they were still in his head at that point. I'm sorry. I'm not much help, am I?"

Pete smiled. "Andy, if it wasn't for you, Sarah and our children would have been murdered. You're the only reason they're still alive. No one could have been more help, than you." He looked back at Charles. "I was one of the last to leave the room and I seem to think Rick's eyes had fallen from his head onto the floor. But I'm sure they were still whole. You could check out the film at the BBC. The cameraman was filming right up until the door was locked and sealed. But why is this so important?"

"Because the cornea of the eye has five layers," said Charles thoughtfully. "I'm not very well up on this, but basically these layers protect the eye. One of them, the Epithelium, is there to block out foreign materials, another, the Descemet's membrane, protects the eye from infection and can regenerate after injury. Then there are the Endothelium cells, they pump fluid..."

"Slow down," cried Pete. "None of this means anything to me."

"What I'm saying is that one or all of these layers may have a resistance to Trojan," said Charles. Now very excited, he leaned forward in his chair. "As I understand it, it normally takes several hours for the regeneration system to heal an injury to the eye. However, it's possible that Trojan's chemicals might have triggered something in the make up of these layers, particularly the Descemet's membrane, which caused them to speed up the healing process."

Sitting back, he gazed around the group. "If that's the case, and if we are able to reproduce them synthetically on a large scale, we may have found an antidote." He looked at Pete. "It might even clean your land. I must say it was a very good thing you retrieved the notebook and even more of a blessing the policeman made a note of his findings." He looked up at Andy. "Do you know the man's name? If so, any antidote found should be named after him."

"Sergeant Gilmore would have made the notes," replied Andy. "He was a good policeman and made notes about everything. If only he or Manners hadn't touched..." He broke off.

"I know, son." Charles decided to change the subject "Have you decided what you want to do now? Do you want to go back to Wooler?"

"I'm not sure. I've always wanted to be a policeman. But Wooler..."

Charles leaned forward in his chair. "Sarah told me of your ambitions, so I've taken the liberty of speaking to a friend of mine on your behalf. He's stretching the rules somewhat, but he's agreed to give you an interview tomorrow morning at Scotland Yard – 11am sharp. I'm sure it's only a formality, Special Branch needs young men who can think for themselves."

Unable to speak, Andy could only nod his thanks.

"What are you going to do?" Charles was now speaking to Pete. "With the farm gone, have you decided where you will go?"

"It wasn't all ruined," Pete replied. "Only the hills and the valley on one side of the farmhouse were lost. I'll need to go back and take a look at what's left. If I know Daisy and Belle, my two favourite sheep, I'll still have a flock of sheep up there. Besides didn't you just say your antidote will clean up my land?" He grinned at Sarah. "And don't forget, my old car is still at York. I want it back. Without that old girl, Josh and I would never have got away from the farm."

"I'll go with him!" There was no doubt in Josh's mind that London was not the place for him.

"Daddy!" Josie ran into the room. Suddenly finding her drawings, she realised her father still hadn't seen them. "Daddy, you haven't seen my pictures!"

****

Meanwhile a few days earlier, somewhere on the road between Peterborough and the north of England, a certain lorry driver was watching the television in Miss Annie's Pit-Stop when the programme was interrupted to inform the public of some breaking news. The newsreader told the viewers how a chemical weapon had been released in northeast England.

"The public only came to hear about it through the bravery of two men, Pete Maine and Josh Davies, who managed to escape from the military and reach London."

Colin's jaw dropped in amazement, as Sir Charles and Josh gave an account of what had happened, highlighted by George Worth's gruesome pictures. The men had told him it was big, but he had never dreamed it would be something on this scale.

"Finally," added the newsreader at the end of the bulletin. "Josh has informed me that both he and Pete would like the BBC to convey their sincere gratitude to a certain lorry driver, known only to them as Colin. They firmly believe that without his help, they would never have survived to report the news. We will bring you further updates as soon as possible. For the moment we'll return you to our normal programme."

"That's you, isn't it, Colin?" Annie turned to the other drivers. "That's our Colin they're talking about. It was him who helped those two men."

By now the drivers had gathered around Colin to congratulate him.

"Well, aren't you going to say something," Annie asked.

But for the first time in his life, Colin was speechless.